# Love and Lovecraft

### K. Bannerman

© 2018 K. Bannerman. All rights reserved.

ISBN (print) 978-0-9864701-9-6
ISBN (ebook) 978-1-9994156-0-0
No part of this book may be reproduced or transmitted in any form or by any means, electronically or mechanical, including photocopying, recording, or by any information storage and retrieval system, without permission in writing from the copyright owner.
This is a work of fiction. All names, characters, places and incidents either are the product of the author's imagination or are used fictitiously, and any resemblance to any actual person, living or dead, is entirely coincidental.

This book was created in Canada.

For more information, contact kim@kbannerman.com.

To my brave, book-loving beta readers:

Jennye Holm, Jeff Holm, Tracy Jenneson, Kate Blood, Jen Thorndale, and Claire Guiot. They have generously given their time and expertise to many of my hare-brained projects.

Thank you all.

# One

The family of Lovecraft had long been settled in Dunham County. Their property was modest, and their residence was known about the region as Lovecraft Cottage, nestled against Mill Road and at the site of the Huntsman's Oak where, for many generations, they had lived in so respectable a manner as to engage the general good opinion of their surrounding acquaintance. The property abutted the sprawling parkland of Northwich Hall to the west, and to the north stretched a deep, primal coniferous forest that carpeted the wild foothills where few men had cause to go, so by its placement, Lovecraft Cottage was quiet and secluded, which suited the family quite amicably. Mr. Henry Phineas Lovecraft, the legal inheritor of the cottage, had spent his younger years as a professor of history in London's Chambers College, but a series of successful business ventures had left him with wealth to spare, so he retired to write memoirs and raise a family in his ancestral home, and his retreat to Dunham County had proven to be comfortably spent. He married a young Dunham woman of the Bierce lineage, and their relationship proceeded not merely from interest, but from goodness of heart, and she gave him every degree of solid comfort which his age could receive. Together they brought forth four daughters into the world, and the cheerfulness of his children added a relish to his existence.

I, as the eldest of his daughters, had cherished his company and wisdom for all my twenty-six years, and the love I felt for both my parents was not only of obedience and respect, but also of good-humor and friendship. They strived to keep a pleasing home full of good books and lively music, a convivial fortress from which we could glean strength. Of course, the events which were to transpire in fair pastoral Dunham were of such a gruesome nature that, after their conclusion and upon reflection, my dear father felt fortunate to have built this serene oasis. Truly, he must possess a remarkable foresight to have sensed such dark times were coming; after all, queer talents ran in the Lovecraft line, and if he possessed the gift of precognition, it would come of no great surprise to anyone. Long afterwards, and as an elderly man, he often reminisced that, without this refuge, he might have despaired at the future of humanity and lost all hope completely.

Lovecraft Cottage is a small, two-story building of white plaster and grey stone, surrounded by abundant vegetable gardens, four large bee hives, and an unassuming frog pond. While it provided for all our earthly needs, and would be judged a respectable domicile by most standards, the cottage paled in comparison to its neighbor to the west, Northwich Hall. Throughout the entire county, Northwich Hall was considered to be the most glorious example of architecture, and a house fit for a gentleman of only the finest breeding. Therefore, while Lovecraft Cottage was in actuality quite comfortable and spacious, it had the misfortune of appearing homely and cramped by virtue of its location. My father did not let this dampen his enthusiasm, but he often peeked over the ancient stone wall that divided the land to gaze across the mile of open parkland at the great estate. Whenever I witnessed Papa in his solitude, staring across the fields to that enchanting prospect long lain empty, I could almost read his thoughts upon his face: he marveled that the Hall was lonesome and dreary, when only a scant distance away, his own home bustled with the chatter and laughter of young women. How could one small house be so spirited, when its regal neighbor remained so derelict and sad?

Therefore, when I heard a rumor from the elder Mrs. Runkle that Northwich Hall had been sold, I hurried immediately home from the village to inform my father that there were soon to be people living in the mansion. I hoped that the news might bring him good cheer. Northwich Hall had sat empty for nearly a generation, and the prospect of a new family—lighting candles in the dark and moody windows, hosting dances and parties for the ladies of the county, perhaps a wife or daughter seeking the companionship of new friends—filled my heart with giddy anticipation. For almost the entirety of my life, I had gazed out my bedroom window at the solemn, cold and closed building, at the rolling lawns peppered with cherry trees, and wondered if anyone would ever be brave enough to adopt such a magnificent project as reviving the neglected house, thereby transforming it from a Gothic ruin into a majestic palace.

The manor's turrets and facade were somewhat Georgian at first glance, but grew ever more exotic the longer one studied its ornaments. The stones had been hewn of a granite so dark, it appeared to my eyes as a mottled black in foul weather and a stern grey in summer, yet the great estate was happily situated amongst rolling woody hills, and contained a natural stream made beautiful without manufactured adornments, fringed with abundant herbage. This jubilant brook circled the western perimeter of the property and terminated in a large, circular pond well-stocked with trout. In my earliest childhood memories, I recalled that the pond had been garnished by a pair of black swans, but when the previous inhabitants had left their great residence, so too had the waterfowl. Its expanse of open parkland was roughly square, and from the south, a gravel drive connected the house with the Green Track, and from thence to Dunham Village. This lane, bounded by parallel lines of swaying elms, skirted the edge of the trout pond and continued past the sprawling gardens, then ducked under a stone palisade that sheltered the main entrance. Here, broad steps lead up to double oak doors that had been locked and bolted for decades.

While the grounds and house were not as large as Delphne Manor in Upper Whatley, it was also not as garish or bold, and retained an august distinction that Delphne Manor had lost when its occupants—the Wendsley-Waughs, a frivolous and inbred lineage of questionable sensibilities—had strung filament bulbs hither and yon. In my opinion, Northwich Hall enjoyed a classic, restrained beauty that hinted at secrets and intrigues, and that suited my tastes much better.

My father, when I found him in the garden and told him the news, cocked one hoary eyebrow in tempered interest. "As wonderful as that might be, I shall not get my hopes up, and nor should you, Harry," he warned, "It's my understanding that Northwich Hall is never to be inhabited again."

I laughed, thinking this to be bit of hyperbole. "And what a waste of a perfectly good house that would be!" I replied, continuing inside to inform my mother. I found her sitting in the front parlor, mending stockings, as our housemaid Beatrice bustled about the kitchen, preparing tea. A small fire crackled in the hearth. The windows were tightly sealed against the spring damp. The parlor possessed a stuffy air that made one's nose itch.

Mama showed none of the hopefulness nor fascination that I had felt when confronted with such gladsome news. As I have previously mentioned, she is of the Bierce lineage; they are a stubborn bloodline, if occasionally given to bouts of obsession and, when matters do not conform to their desires, downright curmudgeonliness.

"Oh, posh, Mrs. Runkle said so!" she teased, and pinched my ear in a method that, while fond, left a sting. My mother never intends to be cruel, but she can be enthusiastic to the point of belligerence, and often assumes all people must feel as she does on a subject. As a younger woman, she had been described as headstrong and determined, but in her middle years, those same qualities could be interpreted as bullish, and when my mother got an idea in her head, she became an unstoppable force. Woe be to anyone who stood in her way!

"Why would the postmistress lie about such a thing?" I said.

Mama set her mending down in a huff. "You mustn't believe a word of it, Harriet!" she scolded, "I heard tell from Mrs. Poole that Mrs. Runkle has grown dotty over the course of the last six months, and we must take everything she claims with a generous heap of salt!" She picked up the stockings, shaking her head in dismissal so violently that her grey curls and frilly lace mob-cap danced. "I sincerely doubt anyone would purchase Northwich. It's far too much work for the investment. No, my sweet, Mrs. Runkle can't tell her elbow from her knee! I suspect she's remembering the last family to inhabit Northwich Hall, and thinking herself back twenty years or more."

I settled in the opposite chair. "You mean, the Poseys."

Mama looked over her demi-glasses. Her mood curdled.

"That is a name we dare not speak, my sweet."

I let the statement hang in the air between us, and as Mama reclined and settled back to her mending, I selected my next words with great care. "I know we must not mention them, but …"

"Tsk!" She jabbed one finger into the air. "Not a word!"

We sat in uncomfortable silence as the fire popped and crackled. At last I could bear it no longer. I stood and began to climb the stairs, but Mama would not let it go.

"Not a word, Harriet!" she called up after me. "Not one single word!"

I plodded up the steps and made her no promise. On sunnier days, my three sisters preferred reading in the garden, but with a damp spring drizzle covering the land, I knew I'd find them in the library at the top of the stairs. It had a large window overlooking the Mill Road that, in the afternoon, provided a good, strong light. As predicted, Jane sat at the drawing table with paper and pencils, Mary rested on the couch where she was stitching together a quilt, while Emma's nose was firmly planted in an old volume of plates, which from a glance at its illustrations, explored the idiosyncrasies of light and lenses.

I'd recently passed my threshold for a marriageable age, but Jane was two years younger, and so Mama still held hope of finding her a decent husband. Jane was a sweet, steady, ever-hopeful girl, and possessed an elegant bearing and respectable manner. Her face was heart-shaped with delicate cheekbones that supported a pair of lively, wide grey eyes, and her hair was the color of autumn leaves—a vibrant gold shot through with red—that looked especially striking against her flawless complexion. As a result of these natural endowments, Jane enjoyed the gaze of many young men, but most were too flummoxed by her beauty to engage her in deep conversations, and this was a pity, for she had a quick mind to match her fair face.

All was not perfection, of course. Like any young woman, Jane could be swept away by her fancies, but in my sister's case, that was doubly dangerous, for she had an unusual talent for manipulations. If Jane had been smitten by any fellow in Dunham, he'd quickly find himself ensnared in her charms like a fly in a spider's web. So far, none of the villagers had lost their capabilities for rational thought or for free will; I'm sure this was due, not to Jane's benevolence, but to her finding the neighboring boys too dull to suit her tastes.

As if created to balance Jane's delicate sentimentalism, my next youngest sister, Mary, was a rational creature, forever inclined to logical thinking. She was a scientist in all things, and she carefully considered the natural philosophies and their influences on her work. Her choices were measured. She found comfort in order and facts. Her appearance reflected her meticulous character: every black hair was carefully pinned in place, every braid tightly woven, every pleat of her dress straight as an arrow. Even now, sewing her quilt, she worked with boundless care and attention to detail, with each stitch wrought the same length and distance as its fellows. She had no great passion for quilting, but it was the only way she could create a blanket that was long enough to cover her from head to toe, and she took pride in her work, even if there was no love to fuel it.

Just as her external form was deliberately crafted, so too must be her internal processes, for Mary's memory was legendary; it did little good to argue with her, for if she'd read a snippet of trivia once, it never left her.

And she was generous with her gifts. Mary spent her days teaching singing to the village children, leading the village choir, composing music on piano or violin, and collecting a compendium of folk tunes. Her singing was legendary. Such was the power and beauty of her voice that, when Mary sang, the whole world bent its ear to listen. Her notes carried pure and clear with perfect pitch and a powerful volume, and this was unsurprising, for she must have possessed extremely large lungs. After all, Mary was over six-and-a-half feet tall, larger than Papa by a head, with broad plough-board hands and oxen shoulders.

I glanced over her arm to examine her work.

"Very pretty," I said.

Mary barely broke her concentration long enough to say thank you.

"She's going to go blind, sewing such tiny stitches," Emma warned. "Mary, rest your eyes, or you'll give yourself a headache by suppertime!"

Oh, Emma! As the youngest of the Lovecraft girls at eighteen years of age, she could be timid and prone to distraction, but there contained a kindness and archness to her bearing that made it difficult for any person to think poorly of her, and by her character, Emma was the most fun, given to spritely flights of play. She was neither a beauty, like Jane, nor highly intelligent, like Mary, and her lack of confidence in both of these extremes had made her unsure of her place in the world. To make matters worse, all three of her older sisters were unmarried, and that left her to be a very poor prospect, with little hope of securing a good match. Because of our failures to enter into matrimony, she could see only a future like my own, as an impoverished spinster with no romance to sweeten her days.

Emma, small and bird-boned, possessed an unruly mop of curly red hair and an aspect of the fairy folk about her appearance. She could be dreamy and imaginative—sometimes too much so—and she could be lost for days in her tinkering and her inventions, yet for any of her detriments, I loved Emma with all my heart. Her eyes sparkled, her manners were honest, her heart bent towards the fabulous. She endeavored to follow the latest fashions, but it was difficult in our secluded hamlet to know the trends, so her frocks were often an artistic interpretation that reflected her love of color and whimsy and ruffles. Emma and I had bound ourselves together as we watched Jane and Mary accomplish so much with ease, and we supported each other as we struggled to hone the same attractive qualities that they came by naturally.

Of course, Emma had her own supernatural talents that set her apart from the rabble, and I think in many ways, she was the most affected by the series of events that were to happen in Dunham County. She was very nurturing, very caring, and she took deeply to heart the struggles and pains of another; the root of Emma's Quirk lay in her empathy and deep compassion. Our Quirks remained ephemeral to the discerning eye, but hers produced measurable results, for the sting of a cut or a bruise would soften under the touch of Emma's healing fingers. While Mama remained uncertain of the morality of our abilities, she encouraged Emma to exercise her talents whenever possible, and even congratulated my youngest sister on her fine work. None of the rest of us were ever so openly celebrated.

Emma set her book in her lap. "How was the library today?" she said.

"Only one visitor," I replied, "Jerold Chowder brought a donation of novels, most in poor condition. He didn't stay long."

"I think he's still fond of you," said Jane.

Inwardly, I cringed, for I knew the reverse to be true, but outwardly I smiled. "Oh, I think not."

Mary looked up from her sewing. "Is there any news from the village?"

I took a seat on the couch by the far window and gazed out towards the road. Feigning a bored voice, I said, "No, not really ... Mr. Rabbit has caught a cold. Mrs. Winterbottom and old Mrs. Tippler are hosting a tea on Friday. Oh, yes, and one more thing ... someone had bought Northwich Hall."

To my satisfaction, all three of my sisters perked up, and like a triad of owls, they all asked, "Who?"

"Who?!"

"Who?!?"

I laughed. "Mrs. Runkle didn't provide any names," I replied.

"They must have great ambitions," Emma said in a reverent hush.

"Or great fortunes," said Jane. "Can you imagine the income it will require to restore the place? Just taming the gardens will take a small army!"

Mary set aside her needles and thread. "It may have been purchased, but that doesn't mean it will be inhabited. It could simply be an investment."

"Wouldn't it be wonderful for it to be a home again?" I said. "I've always loved Northwich Hall. It has such a mysterious aura!"

"There's no mystery," said Mary, ever rational, "It's only old, ruined, and dirty."

"I think it's positively spooky!" said Emma.

I liked how my youngest sister's eyes gleamed. "Precisely!" I dropped my voice to a whisper. "And with the fate of the poor Posey family, to cast such a dreadful pall over its history ..."

Jane scoffed at us both. "Be quiet, both of you."

"You mustn't speak of it," said Mary.

And of course, that's all that was required for Emma to lean in close, eyes afire. "Why? What? What mustn't we speak about?"

Mary glowered at me, for letting loose the tantalizing hint of a rumor in front of our most-curious sister. "The Poseys, the last family to live in Northwich Hall. You've heard their name, no doubt."

"Only in passing," Emma said, "No one ever tells me anything!"

"Well, it was a long time ago and best forgotten," Mary decreed, but I did not concur.

"The incident happened before you were born," I said, "I was only five, and Jane was three, and Mary was not yet here at all."

"Mama has said we're not to gossip," Mary warned, "Foolish superstitious nonsense!"

But Jane, suitably inspired by Emma's infectious interest, chose to ignore Mary and turned to me. "I do remember bits, but like a dream," she said as she sat beside me on the couch, smoothing down her skirts. "I don't know if I can trust my recollections."

"See?" Mary continued, returning to her stitches, "All of it, nonsense."

"You're no fun," I said, "Go on, Jane. What do you remember?"

Jane closed her eyes. "Well, the Posey family lived in Northwich Hall then, and Mr. Posey was said to be related to royalty, although I'm not sure on the lineage. He was a crabby old fellow, and Mrs. Posey was of middling age and in good health, but frightfully ugly, with great ungainly mule teeth and wild, scrubby black hair. I don't think they had much fondness for each other; he liked her only for her ability to give him three sons, and she liked him solely for his fortune."

"You can't possibly know that," Mary said, "You were only three!"

"I know this from later conversations with Papa," Jane replied. "He's not so afraid to speak of the incident, if you catch him in the right mood."

I took up the tale. "It was summer, I remember, because the Huntsman's Oak was in full leaf, and so was the elm in the garden, and the view from my room was partially obscured. The hour was very late, with only a half-moon to light the meadows, when a ferocious knocking came upon the kitchen door. Papa opened it to find Mr. Posey. His trousers were torn to shreds and his hair was uncombed, mud caked his face and hands. He claimed that the Devil had come to Dunham County, and eaten his children up, and whisked his wife away on the back of a fearsome black billy-goat."

Emma's blue eyes were as wide as coins.

Mary took her opportunity, and reached over to pinch Emma's ear, and our youngest sister yelped in terror.

As we laughed, Emma thumped Mary on the shoulder, as effective as a kitten swatting a lion.

I took up the tale. "Papa and some of the men from the village went up to the house. They found the whole place in disarray, but no sign of Mrs. Posey or her sons. All four had vanished from the face of the earth and were never seen from again."

"What about Mr. Posey?"

"Bundled off to Broadsmoor Asylum, I'm afraid, ranting about the Devil all the way," said Jane. "Poor fellow. I heard he hung himself."

"I heard he poisoned himself," said Mary.

"No, no," I replied, "He sliced off his own head with a carving knife."

Emma gave a little squeak of horror. "I don't care how he died, it's all positively ghoulish!"

"Well, it's certainly not a topic for polite conversation," said Mary. "I'd rather not dwell on the particulars."

"It's terribly sad, perhaps it's best not to talk about it." Emma agreed.

Jane lifted her pencil again. "Then I, for one, shall respect Mama's wishes fully," she said as she returned to her drawing. She could be frightfully sanctimonious, that one.

But I reclined against the arm of the couch and glanced out the window. "I can think of nothing more interesting to talk about," I admitted, "I'd like to know what happened to Mrs. Posey and her boys. Surely there must be some hint or clue—"

"Finally," said Mary, "A lick of sense amongst the three of you."

"—some clue if the Devil whisks you off to Hell. You'd leave fingernail scratches in the floor, at the very least."

Mary sighed, rolled her eyes, and under her breath, muttered, "Codswallop."

"Maybe it is codswallop," said Jane, "I mean, how could one even slice off their own head? I don't think that's possible, is it?"

Emma lowered her book. "I'm happy I never knew that story before now. Is that why no one but us ever visits the grounds of Northwich Hall on their rambles? I don't think I would've enjoyed our visits half as much if I'd known the house has such an awful legacy." She glanced at me. "Now that you've told me, it feels less spooky, and more sad. What a horrible history … perhaps Mrs. Posey still haunts the place."

"Honestly," said Mary, putting her quilt aside. "The three of you would scare yourselves silly, given half a chance! No better than a bunch of schoolgirls!" She affixed us with a stern glare. "There's no phantoms in Northwich Hall. It's only a dilapidated building with a tragic history, nothing more. And I applaud whomever has purchased the place! They'll give it a new story, and inject a bit of life into your haunted ruins."

"Our walks won't be the same, knowing someone is living on the grounds," I said. "The new owners will arrive and change the whole place to suit themselves, and it'll lose all its enchantment. They could even withdraw access rights and keep the public from roaming on their land, if it suits them."

"They wouldn't dare!" said Emma, scandalized.

"They might," Jane replied. "It would be highly unusual, but not impossible."

"We ought to visit this afternoon, before they come and change it all," I said.

Outside the window, the drizzle had stopped. The clouds parted, and the sun shone a little brighter. "There, see?" Emma said with an eager grin, "The weather clears just for us!"

Mary grumbled, setting her sewing basket aside. "Fine, let's go, if only to stop you three from spinning mad tales and giving each other nightmares."

Thus, we found ourselves taking our afternoon stroll eastward, across the rolling greens and towards the imposing mansion, with its Gothic facade that grew only more grey and gloomy as we drew near. This was a walk we often took, through the overgrown gardens and along the weedy paths that circled the murky, slimy trout pond, but normally we gave the main house with its black windows a generous berth. Today, however, we wandered into its shadow, emboldened by the idea that this now all belonged to a stranger. The house looked the same—dour, silent and brooding—yet it would soon be bright and gay with occupation, and this abstract potential imbued it with a spirit that was slightly more convivial than in days past. It was no longer dejected and forgotten, but poised on the exciting edge of a unknown future. I was seized by a fierce curiosity, and my heart bursting with sudden courage, I sprinted up the wide stone steps to peer with cupped hands through the leaded glass on either side of the main doors.

"Harry," Emma scolded, "Get back here!"

"What do you see?"

"It's very dark inside," I said to Jane, "I can't see much at all."

Emma looked around and said, "Can't you feel that?"

And yes, I could: the cool sensation of eyes upon us, a trembling sense of anticipation that started in the pelvis and skittered up the spine.

"It's nothing," Mary dismissed very quickly, which only served to show that she could feel it, too. "We ought to go."

Jane, standing farthest back in the driveway, gave a small gasp. "A curtain moved," she said, and pointed to the second story windows. "Someone is already here!"

And as she said these very words, the latch on the double doors clacked, and one swung open on squealing hinges.

All four of us snapped our attention towards the yawning entrance.

Yet no one stood inside.

The maw of the dim, unlit hall stretched before me, beckoning me. My pulse quickened and I took a single step back, suddenly afraid. A glance over my shoulder to my sisters proved that they were just as hesitant as me. Emma had sought shelter behind Mary, and Jane had retreated almost as far as the trout pond. I took a deep breath and called inside,

"Hello?"

The sound of my voice echoed back from the cavernous beyond.

"Come, Harry," said Emma, fretful, "We mustn't trespass in the house!"

"We can't leave the door open, either," I said, "That would invite all manner of creatures inside! The new owner would be very displeased to find a family of hedgehogs nesting in the cupboard, don't you think?"

I pushed it open and peeked inside, taking a step across the threshold.

"Then you ought to CLOSE the door instead of wandering inside, don't you think?" Mary insisted.

"Harry, this is very poor form," hissed Jane from around Mary's elbow. "Close the door and come along."

"Hello?" I said again to the empty lobby.

As my eyes adjusted to the gloom, I began to see shapes and colors of opulence: carved furniture from an older age, with wooden faces carved into the backs of chairs and braided ivy adorning the table legs. There were matching alabaster end tables, and on the walls hung colorful tapestries depicting Greek reveries. I spied paintings, too, of Arthurian kings dressed in golden finery holding court. Directly in front of the main door, the grand central staircase ascended to a landing against the west wall, then divided into two sweeping circular stairs that curved around to the north and south, with balustrades gilded in a soft, lustrous gold. Above the landing hung a portrait of a beautiful woman wearing a shepherd's chiton, surrounded by frolicking lambs in an idyllic Arcadian meadow. A massive chandelier of gilded branches hung from the vaulted ceiling, but its countless white candles were unlit, and the shadows that pooled around the furniture were inky and fathomless. Only the light from the door and the leaded windows percolated inside, bouncing off the white marble floor and glinting from gold and crystal.

Goodness! I'd expected the house to be empty of furniture and the floor covered with a carpet of dust, but instead I found Aladdin's cave! Every item was decadent and marvelous, breathtaking and expensive, of a quality befitting a fairy-tale castle. I drank in my surroundings, my breath in my throat, my mouth slack with wonder. Imagine a vast museum of priceless treasures appearing next door, inviting you to explore its secrets!

How could I resist? I took another step inside.

Directly to my right, a granite arch led into a high-ceiling hall suitable for entertaining, with couches along the edges and an ornate parquet floor for dancing. Gauzy linen curtains covered the south-facing windows, and their diffused light illuminated the space in cool colors, an array of silvers and creams; a few of the chairs were still covered in white sheets, which gave the impression of a circle of tired ghosts gathering together to rest and convene. A piano sat in the far corner next to the swoop of a gilded harp. There were more paintings on the walls, but these were not as grand and eloquent as those hanging in the main vestibule. Only one painting appeared to be of outstanding quality: a gentleman's portrait hung above the huge slate fireplace. He wore a tall black hat and held a cane with a silver head in the shape of a fish, and his aristocratic expression was bold but not ungainly. In fact, the more I looked upon his picture, I found his melancholy face and mournful eyes to be quite bewitching. He was not a handsome man, but nor was he ugly: his expression contained enough of the restless, romantic, untameable poet to offset any unbalance in his features, which on a barrister or bookkeeper might seem pedantic and bland.

"Harry!" came Jane's frenzied whisper from the front door. "Get back here!"

"Just a moment!" I hissed back.

From the quality of the furniture in the ballroom, I suspected that a gentleman of wealth and breeding—but possessing an inclination towards an older style of fashion—had moved into Northwich Hall. The legs of the chairs were carved in a curled style that my grandmother enjoyed, and the artwork slanted heavily towards neoclassicism. I decided he must not want for money, either, for there was an abundance in all things, save for the whisper and warmth of human company.

As my gaze circled the huge assembly room, it fell upon a small archway on the opposite corner of the vast space, leading to an unlit corridor, which was undoubtedly a servant's passage. The feeble squares of sunlight cast from the curtained windows could not reach quite so far, and the light of the ballroom provided only a murky glow, but as my eyes adjusted, I saw deeper into the recess.

There, half-obscured in shadow, stood a monstrous, teratological figure of immense bulk and size, lurking in the darkness. It hunched against the wall, and every muscle remained as still as stone. The hairless, naked skin glowed with a sickly pale pallor, but it was streaked with sinewy black lines like the stripes of a tiger. The face was grotesque, misshapen and deformed, and its hands were clasped at its waist, too large and cumbersome to be human. Set deeply in that disfigured face of ink and ice, glittering like orbs of polished amber, were two ferocious, living eyes.

I shrieked.

My shoes slipped on the tiled floor and I collapsed on my hip, dropping my brown shawl, but then I was sliding backwards, pushing myself into a sprint towards the front door, and I snatched up Mary's hand and ran, and my frantic, sudden action cascaded through my sisters until all four of us were sprinting down the driveway and across the parkland, haring for home.

# Two

This singular experience peppered our conversations for the next two days, popping up at random intervals whenever Mama's back was turned. Emma was fascinated, Mary was skeptical, but Jane remained openly hostile towards me for my indiscretion. She didn't bother to hide her disapproval. My actions had been very rude, and she clearly thought me to be only a step or two above a common thief.

Her frustration culminated into a sole comment, given with cutting disapproval one afternoon as we read our books under the Huntsman's Oak. Mary sat on a patch of lawn nearby, and Emma wandered through the flowers with her most recent invention, a small leather box cradled in two hands, the purpose of which she had not yet shared. Jane was reading a thin volume of Gothic fiction, recently unearthed in our grandmother's hope chest, and some plot device within it spurred a memory of our recent exploit, and she set the book down upon her lap with a disapproving shake of her head.

"You deserved a good scare for trespassing," she scolded.

I, engrossed in my own reading, looked up with confusion. "Pardon?"

"What sort of lady wanders about a stranger's home?" Jane continued, having secured my attention. "Where were your manners, Harry? Mama would be horrified!"

"I must've left my manners at home, right next to your sense of adventure."

Mary laughed, Emma snorted, and thus prompted, Jane's expression of insult melted into a sigh of surrender: I refused to show any remorse for my actions.

"You can't tell me you weren't curious, too, about what was inside," I continued, "To find Northwich suddenly inhabited? Fascinating!"

"But the look on your face when you came racing out!" said Emma, "Goodness, Harry, I thought you'd seen a ghost!"

"I can't even say for sure what I saw," I admitted. I leaned my shoulder against the trunk of that ancient tree, our sentinel of twisting roots and spreading canopy that guarded the head of the driveway to Lovecraft Cottage. Many decades past, for an unknown reason, the tree's growth had prompted one branch to sprout low to the ground; now stout and strong, it was the perfect height for us to sit. As wee children, my sisters and I had claimed this spot to gather and converse when out-of-doors, for it afforded a modicum of privacy which could not be found on the bench by the kitchen door. On pleasing days, we naturally retreated here, and the Huntsman's Oak held us close in its leafy embrace, keeping us secure.

"But was it a person?" Emma pressed as she returned to us, lowering the little box in her hands.

"I don't know," I admitted.

"A statue?" said Mary.

"I don't think so. The face was lopsided and disfigured, hardly artistic. And the eyes were very bright! And it wasn't made of marble—it looked like skin covered with dirt."

Jane seized on this. "Like a golem, perhaps? A giant made of clay?"

"That's more commonly called a statue," said Mary.

"You're not being helpful," Jane snipped.

"I was admiring the furniture, and it was lurking in the far doorway of the great hall, watching me. I wish I could describe it better," I admitted, "I only saw it for a fraction of a second."

Emma's eyes twinkled. "What if I could freeze that second, for us to examine at length and at leisure?" she asked. She sat next to me on the branch, and held up the little, caramel-colored box; its only marking was a tiny hole on one side, and I caught the wink of sunlight on a recessed lens. "I think I've devised a way to capture light and hold it fast."

This proposition spurred Mary to look up from her book. "You've modified your camera obscura? What are you supposed to use when painting, now?"

"Mama will be most upset, if you've ruined another one," Jane replied.

Emma scowled at both of them. "A good number of things have been ruined in the pursuit of new inventions, and we're all the richer for it," she replied. "One shouldn't be afraid of ruining things if one hopes to create an object with the power to change the world."

Jane remained unimpressed. It was not uncommon for Emma to tear a perfectly good item to pieces and leave a trail of broken springs and gears in her wake. If we did not react with amazed delight to her invention, it was because we'd lived so long with so many of them, cluttering up our cottage. Returning to a topic more to her taste, Jane ignored our youngest sister and said to me, "The art and furniture must've be fine pieces, to tempt you inside."

"Oh! Such beautiful items, Jane! And portraits, newly hung! And tapestries—I've never seen anything of such quality."

Mary raised her book to read again. "It sounds to me like the new owner of Northwich Hall appreciates art," she said, "A statue is the most likely explanation."

Jane scoffed. "You're just in a sour mood because you were as frightened as the rest of us."

Mary scowled but didn't disagree.

"But when did the new master arrive?" said Emma. "I've seen no lights or chimney smoke. He must've come in the dead of night! Have you seen any carriages or wagons? Or servants? Or activity at all?"

"No, but—"

I wished to describe again what I'd seen, but Fate provided no opportunity. As if summoned by Emma's comment, we heard the patter of little hooves upon the packed earth of Mill Road, and over the crest in the hill came a light phaeton with two sprightly white ponies. It rolled passed us, never pausing, and continued down the drive to the courtyard on the far side of our house, where the coachman drew rein and parked. We caught the lilting call of our mother's voice upon the cool air, and saw Mama standing on the paving stones before the front door, waving one hand over her head towards us and gesturing to the carriage with shivering enthusiasm. "Hurry, girls! Oh! Come, come! Hurry now! We have visitors!"

The reason for her clucking and fussing was soon made abundantly clear: two young men in fine suits stepped from the carriage, followed immediately by a matronly woman in bonnet and fur cape, her silver hair in ringlets and blue bows. I recognized her at once.

"Mrs. Darling," I said, forcing a smile. "How very delightful to see you."

But Mrs. Cassilda Darling looked right passed me, for she had eyes only for Jane. A woman of lesser rank might be more subtle in her appreciations, but Mrs. Darling lacked delicacy in all things, from the heavy set of her features, to the width of her hips, to the manner of her conversation. She wore layers upon layers of fine silk skirts and cashmere shawls, which were meant to impart an aura of decadence, but really only added to her bulk. "What a beauty you've become, Miss Jane! Isn't she quite lovely, boys?" she crooned. Mrs. Darling possessed a particular drawl, steady and stately, that gave the impression of wealth and breeding, but also hid her constant judgment, endless scheming, and slow wit. She gestured to the young men. "Please, let me introduce you to my nephews, Frederick and George. They have come up from Bath to stay with us. Freddie, George, these are the

Lovecraft girls—Jane, Mary, Emma, and Harriet."

Most certainly, my name was said with just a hint of vinegar.

Frederick Darling stepped forward and pressed a kiss to the top of Jane's hand. He was very tall and very confident, with perfectly coiffed black muttonchops that framed his face. He had a narrow nose that spoke of regal heritage, and when he smiled, he showed two long rows of straight, gleaming teeth. This was a young man who had been assured on many occasions of his comeliness and desirability, and he dared not deny any young woman the enviable pleasure of his company. To do so would be cruel.

The second man, George Darling, was not as graceful or elegant, and fumbled as he bowed to my mother. He was shorter by a head, with a thick build, soft belly, curly chestnut hair, and nimble, lady-like hands; clearly, he was unaccustomed to country living. I don't think he'd ever picked up an ax or drawn water from a well, and he'd certainly never weeded a garden.

"How lovely to make your acquaintance," Frederick said to Jane in a voice that was low and dusky and, frankly, a little overdramatic.

Mama ushered us into the afternoon parlor, where the warm light would be most pleasing on Jane's features, and we each took our seats around the room. Mrs. Darling claimed pride of place on the couch.

Jane, ever polite, waited until they were settled to ask, "What brings you to Dunham, gentlemen?"

"Our uncle has need of help with the business," said Frederick, "Our aunt has made us welcome."

"Isn't that lovely," said Mama, "If you're assisting your uncle, you'll wish to introduce yourselves to the people of the village, most certainly! Mr. Darling has been a pillar of the church and is a wealth of knowledge in all matters of accounting, and I'm sure he'll enjoy showing you all facets of his trade."

Her meaning was clear: as the Darlings had no children of their own, the business would fall to the nephew who could best integrate himself into the political workings of Dunham County. Frederick and George had entered themselves into a contest, with the winner gleaning a very comfortable inheritance and a prosperous business, to boot.

And, if Mrs. Darling's intentions were to be deciphered, they would also win themselves an ideal bride in the form of Miss Jane Lovecraft, who was recognized throughout the countryside as the beauty of the village.

I watched them converse with an analytical eye. Frederick, the older of the two, was certainly more self-satisfied. He possessed a clever, quick watchfulness that leaned towards shrewdness, but if he had any inclination towards criminal behavior, he covered it with a refined smile. His black hair showed hints of silver, and crows feet had appeared in the corners of his dark eyes, but by his vitality and mannerisms, I guessed his age at no more than twenty-five. His clothes were of the finest quality, and he wore a ring of Blue John on one finger, and a gold fob inset with slivers of jet on his pocket; clearly, he appreciated fine items. He kept his eyes riveted on Jane like a hound sighting a bird.

George was, in comparison to his older brother, more gregarious. He smiled easily, laughed often, and he did not stare so baldly at Jane. Instead, he made it a habit to transfer his gaze from girl to girl, addressing each of us in turn with silly, frivolous questions about dresses and lace, gushing about his most recent tour to the north country, and casting a few barbed remarks in the direction of his sibling. It was clear to me that social interaction was a great effort for him; he kept one eye on Frederick, and if the elder boasted about one accomplishment, the younger made sure to boast about another, of equal or greater value. I liked George more than Frederick, but that didn't necessarily mean I liked him.

Mrs. Darling leaned close to Mama, and my focus swiveled from George and his inconsequential prattling to the older ladies. In a low voice, she said, "Have you heard about the new owner of Northwich?"

"I've heard there is a new owner, but nothing more," said Mama, "Have you any particulars, Cassilda?"

With that simple question, the whole conversation pivoted to one of great interest to all parties.

Mrs. Darling settled into her preferred place at the center of the discussion. She nodded, clearly savoring this knowledge before sharing it. "I have heard the new owner has recently returned from the west of the Americas, and is in possession of a great fortune built on the trade of furs and pelts."

This caused a stutter in the conversation.

"A fur trader?!" said Mary. "Surely you're joking!"

"I am most certainly not," said Mrs. Darling, scandalized that the quality of her information would be called into question. "Miss Mary, a lady does not waste her breath with jests and riddles!"

If anyone knew this to be true, it was Mary. I'd never heard her share a joke in all her life. Any humor she injected into a conversation was strictly accidental.

"How horrendous!" said Mama with bewilderment. "Who could've predicted such a thing! A wild-man in our midst!"

Emma let out a little squeak of fear, but Jane sparkled with excitement.

"Goodness, Mama, not all of the Americas are uncivilized. From where does he hail, Mrs. Darling?" she asked, "Upper or Lower?"

If I had asked the question, I would surely have received a crisp reply, but Mrs. Darling was fond of Jane, and wouldn't dare wish to sour any hope of possible nuptials. "I do not know, my dear," she answered mildly. "My husband says the fur trade is liveliest in the north, so I suppose this stranger must hail from Upper America."

"What would possess a fur trader to purchase Northwich Hall?" Emma said with no small measure of anticipation.

"Who can say?" Mrs. Darling whispered mysteriously, most likely because she did not know the answer. "I suppose even a savage wants a bit of comfort when he grows old. His name, so I've heard, is Mr. Aloysius Blackwood. I do not know if he is titled."

"If he had a title, I'm sure you would have heard it first," said Mama.

"Quite right, my dear," said Mrs. Darling. "I doubt he has any connections."

"But he must be immensely wealthy," said Emma.

Mary leaned forward. "Have you seen him?"

"No," said Mrs. Darling, "But Mrs. Runkle has provided a description. She claims he looks quite banal, all things considered, and even a bit on the ugly side. Skinny as a lamp post, I think she said, with a face like a haddock."

"Oh, that Mrs. Runkle! What a terrible thing to say!" laughed Mama, clapping her hands together. "She is perfectly awful!"

"Well, she has gone quite senile, you know," Mrs. Darling continued, "We can no longer trust her to deliver the correct mail to the right person! Why, only last week, she gave a parcel meant for Mrs. Rabbit to young Miss Eleanor Cripplegate! Can you imagine, making such an error! Those two are on opposite ends of the spectrum, and I dare say, Miss Cripplegate was quite distressed at the implication that she is no better than a baker's wife! No, no, if Mrs. Runkle keeps muddling names, I predict we'll need a new postmistress by next year, but I don't know who!"

"Miss Chowder?" said Mama, but this earned a vigorous snort.

"I should think not! Miss Chowder is engaged to Mr. Peel of Upper Whatley and she will be married by then, and quite unavailable for the position. I've heard Miss Winterbottom may soon be engaged, as well, to Mr. Crumpsall, but that is not yet common knowledge, so one must be careful, to whom one tells it. There are so few unwed young women in the county, and as we all know, a wedded woman is much too busy with the running of her household to work outside the home." She arched one plucked brow in my direction. "Perhaps you would be interested, Miss Harriet? You have no greater responsibilities."

"I have the village library," I replied, aghast.

Mrs. Darling was unimpressed. "No one would miss it, I'm sure." To her nephews, she said, "A woman should not waste her time in reading fictions and phantasies. It only excites the blood. No good comes of it." Returning to me, she added, "At least, as postmistress, you'd have a useful function, rather than continue to be a burden on your poor aging parents." She turned to my mother. "There is no more pathetic tragedy than a lingering child, my dear Mrs. Lovecraft. You have my sympathies. Spinsterhood is such a disagreeable situation for all concerned."

At that moment, it was certainly not reading that excited my blood. "I must say, Mrs. Darling, that if you think such a state is disagreeable, then you may take that assumption and put it up—"

"No one will ever pry our lovely Harry from her books," Emma shouted over me.

Mary added, "She is very devoted to education in all its forms."

I opened my mouth to continue my regrettable sentiments, but Jane leapt in to join the conversation.

"Our father has instilled in us all a fondness for literature, but Harry's love is deepest. Simply put, no mortal man can compete with all the authors of the past for her affections." She cast a pretty smile to both of the Darling men. "I'm sure Mrs. Runkle can continue in her position until one of the younger girls is ready. I should love dearly to ask her directly about this strange Mr. Blackwood."

"I'm sure he is not very entertaining company for a young lady," said Mrs. Darling, and to Mama, she added, "I assume a fur trader from the snow-bound wilderness would not be accustomed to the busy life of a village. Even sleepy little Dunham must seem hectic for him."

I stole a glance at Jane. She looked positively gleeful.

"We ought to call upon him and welcome him to the village, just as we are welcoming Frederick and George," said Mary in all innocence. "That would only be polite."

Mama patted Mary's knee. "We shall, we shall, my little duckling. But let us give him time to adjust. We have Frederick and George here now to amuse us with conversation. Let us ensure that we give them our full attention!"

That night, as we readied for sleep, Emma perched at the end of Jane's bed and said with a cheeky grin, "Which one of the Darling boys catches your fancy, Jane?"

And Jane, who was brushing her hair by the mirror, scoffed. "Neither, thank you very much," she replied. "I shall never be a Darling!"

Jane and I shared a room on one side of the hall, and Mary and Emma shared a room on the other. Their window overlooked the road and the Huntsman's Oak, while our room had a wide view of the back garden, the stone wall, the park lands, and the distant hulk of Northwich Hall. I sat by the window and stared across the moon-lit lawns to the mansion. Silver light glittered on the trout pond and the dewy grass. The constellations danced above in a cloudless sky. All the scene was painted in blues, blacks, and starlight.

"Oh, that woman!" I snarled. "Spiteful, wizened, manipulative shrew!"

"Don't let her trouble you," Mary replied. "She isn't worth the effort."

"She didn't insult you so baldly," I said. "I'm sure, if she called you a burden and a tragedy, you'd have had a few choice words to say."

"I'd have kept my mouth shut and excused myself from the room like a lady," said Mary, "Then I'd have retired outside, found a garter snake, and hid it in the cushions of the phaeton, and laughed at the sound of her screams."

"Oh, the poor snake!" said Emma, "If it was up to me, I'd select the juiciest cat turd from garden."

Jane laughed. "Only the best for Mrs. Cassilda Darling!"

Mary reached over and patted her hand again my cheek. "You're no burden, Harry." Her touch imparted a deep, calming sense of affection.

"I do wish you'd managed a shake of their hands, Harry," said Emma. "Your Quirk could tell us the fullness of their intentions."

"It's rude to pry in another's heart," I replied, "And besides, I don't need a touch of their skin to see, neither Darling gentleman had any interest in me. Their shared goal is written all over their faces." I caught the reflection of Jane, rolling her eyes, in the mirror.

"Who else could Jane pursue that would be half as eligible?" said Mary. Her question was tinged with a measure of hopelessness. "Especially now, with Teddy Crumpsall otherwise engaged to Cecilia Winterbottom?"

"But that is not common knowledge, and could still be dissolved before announcements," said Emma, but her hope was misplaced.

"I'd rather take a Darling than a Crumpsall, thank you very much," Jane replied.

"I heard that Dr. Gelder lost his wife last year, and he'll soon be in want of another," I said. "Or maybe Jane would prefer Lester Glumm from Upper Whatley?"

"Oh, glory, no!" Emma said, unable to repress a shudder, "Have you spent any time down-wind from him?! Lester has the funk of rancid cheese!"

"You are much too kind, Emma," Jane corrected, "No, Mr. Glumm possesses a fragrance more in keeping with a dead rat."

Mary rarely laughed, but she did then, big and boisterous. "Well, you could do far worse, Jane. At least a Darling boy will be able to keep you in style."

But Jane refused to hear more of our suggestions. She waved her long fingers as if shooing a fly. "I have no intention of being kept, Mary. I am not a prize to be won."

Emma reclined across the end of the bed, folding her hands under her head. "But Harriet is already too old, and if you don't marry, then Mary can't marry, then I can't marry, either. And we'll all be spinsters, forced to live off the charity of others once Papa dies!"

"Mercy, Emma!" Mary scolded, "Our father is a long way off from dying!"

"But she's right," I said absently, still watching the distant hall, "When Papa dies, the cottage goes to cousin William, and he has no great fondness for any of us. He'd rather rent the cottage and make it an investment than let us live here further. It's in Jane's best interest to find a match with the successful Darling, whichever one that happens to be … For your sake, I hope it's George. He, at least, has a bit of warmth about him."

"Certainly there are better prospects," Jane replied.

"Like who?" I challenged.

Her expression grew crafty, flinty, and determined. "Perhaps I should pursue Mr. Blackwood of Northwich Hall?"

Mary and Emma both laughed at that.

"I'm quite serious," Jane replied. "We only know what Mrs. Runkle said of him, and she's not exactly reliable."

"Harry thinks she saw him," Mary said.

"What I saw, and the man that Mrs. Runkle described, are diametrically opposed," I said, "Bland and skinny? No. That's not what I saw."

Mary wrapped a blanket over her shoulders and sat in the wicker chair in the corner, tucking her huge feet under her knees. The chair creaked in protest. "I still believe it was a mere statue, Harry, given the spark of life with the power of your imagination," she said.

I closed my eyes and summoned up that blink of an image, seen in a heartbeat and fixed in my mind with the shock. "The figure was huge and bulky, with pale skin covered in a lattice of black lines. Its gold eyes gleamed and shone like amber beads, like the summer sun glinting over honey, like the unblinking stare of a lion." Then I shook my head, casting off the vision. "I can't say any more. I only saw him for an instant, but I know he was watching me. I would admit that it could've been a statue,

Mary, except for the vibrancy of those eyes."

"Well, I still think you were foolish to skulk around in another person's house," said Jane as she climbed under her quilt.

"You're a little too curious for your own good, Harry," Emma agreed.

"And you three are too timid for my liking," I replied, returning my gaze once more to the distant manor.

And before my very eyes, I saw a singular point of light flash to life in the uppermost tower, like the dawning of Venus before the start of day.

# Three

I woke early and dressed quickly, descended to the kitchen before Beatrice had lit the fires, and I was out the door with the rising of the sun, striding towards Northwich with a basket of gifts hung over the crook of my arm: a loaf of hearty rye bread, a small wheel of sharp cheese, a bottle of Papa's own wine from the cellar, and a well-thumbed copy of "The Fair and Magisterial History of Dunham County", that wondrous volume complied by the late Mr. Bugwell so very long ago. More that food or wine, I was eager to share the book, most of all. It did us no honor to ignore our new neighbor, nor did it do me any good to lie awake in bed, speculating about the stranger who'd lit a lamp and spent the entire night in the tower.

In the east, the cheerful pink light tinged the clouds. The clear sky to the west promised a pleasant day. One might expect a chorus of songbirds to greet the new day, but all I heard were the raucous crows as I crossed the grass. They followed me as I turned between the lines of swaying elms and walked towards the grand house. My bravery, which had seemed ironclad upon leaving home, began to flag around the last pair of trees. The shadows cast by Northwich Hall appeared a little deeper and more menacing than elsewhere, and the overgrown hedges and garden weeds crowded together, as if the plants were whispering one-to-another about my uninvited appearance. They found my dew-damp skirt and wet boots sadly lacking in quality.

The gravel drive curled around the edge of the trout pond before reaching the portcullis, and I paused at the water's edge. An observer might think I was admiring the great stone facade of the building, but in truth, I was mustering my courage.

"Good morning, Mr. Blackwood," I muttered to myself, practicing.

The spiteful birds cawed and laughed from the ridge of the roof.

I pulled myself up and stood a little straighter. "Good morning, sir," I said again, louder and with more conviction. I would not be chased away by my imagination or the teasing of crows.

Because I was looking straight ahead at the building, I saw only a rapid motion on the surface of the trout pond through my peripheral vision, but I heard the splash and felt a few drops hit my dress.

With a gasp, I skittered back from the rippling water.

The surface was black and murky, covered by a shimmering green scum. Whatever manner of creature lurked below the waters was hidden by that mysterious verdant film, but for a fraction of a second, I saw the wake that its passage had created, and instinct told me that the fish must be enormous. I supposed, after the Poseys left and the grounds were given to the village council for safe-keeping, no one had cleaned out the pool, and over the years of abandonment, a trout had been left to grow to colossal proportions.

Good Lord, I thought, here was the reason the black swans were gone: it had devoured them!

I hurried away from the edge, climbed the steps to the main doors, and rapped on the wood. The hollow sound echoed and faded.

I rapped again.

This time, I detected the scurry of distant footsteps. The curtains moved in a first floor room, up and to my right. The reflection of the rising sun did not allow me to pluck any features from the person inside, but I knew they were there, so I raised my hand and gave a merry wave. "Hello!" I said, "Good morning!"

The curtain promptly shut.

I waited with patience—what if they were descending to the entrance hall?—but after a length of time that would've allowed any passage from cellar to turret, I realized they were not coming to greet me. I can't say I was disappointed; I knew now that someone was home, and my curiosity was piqued while my fear had vanished, but they were in no mood to welcome visitors and I was in no mood to be insulted.

I left the basket on the doorstep. It was a gift, freely given.

"Welcome to Dunham, Mr. Blackwood!" I yelled up towards the windows, and gave another merry wave. If he was peevish, then I shall combat his peevishness with abundant good cheer, and assure him that I would not trespass against his private nature.

Given the cool spring morning and the pleasing temperature, I strolled around the overgrown gardens for a while, enjoying the hidden statuary that peeked from under brambles and ferns. A faun here, a nymph there—from their presence, one could assume Mr. Posey had been fascinated by ancient mythology. Moss choked the narrow cobble paths and the flowerbeds had long been run over by wild blooms, but the gardens possessed a beautiful abundance that spoke of independence and self-gratification: they grew because they wished to grow, not because a gardener tended them. If Mr. Blackwood was watching me from his upper windows, I did not feel it, and I took great delight in cataloguing the plants. Hollyhock sprouts, henbane, clusters of petunias in the corners, tulip shoots stabbing out of the black earth; as always, when given the opportunity for solitude, I was in no hurry to return home.

Perhaps I should explain why.

In our little cottage, it was almost impossible to find any peace or tranquility, and whenever I brushed up against another person, I was bound to feel a little wave of their innermost turmoil. Just as Jane could turn a man's thoughts, or Emma could prompt a body to heal a little faster, or Mary could sing butterflies down from the trees, I was haunted by the emotions of those around me. With a touch of my hand, I could read an intention as clearly as if it had been spoke aloud. I could never escape these sensations, not fully. The constant distraction of human companionship was exhausting, and so I cherished my time in isolation, when I could hear my own thoughts easily. I have never claimed my Quirk is mind-reading, though to a person unfamiliar with my abilities, it might appear so. Queer talents run through the Lovecraft line, as I've said before, and I had been blessed with a distracting sensitivity to the people around me.

Nor was it only human companions that broadcast their feelings so openly. Horses and alder trees could be particularly excitable, creating a riotous cacophony in my head should I brush passed them. On days of particular sensitivity, and with a little concentration, I could sweep my fingertips over the soil and detect ripples from the past, dancing like faint, fairy whispers across the landscape.

Mary once asked what the voices said, but I struggled to answer. I feel them, rather than hear them, and that makes it impossible to pluck a clear word from the murmur. I do not perceive history as a story, but as a sensation. Because she is the most rational and well-read of all my sisters, I hoped Mary could suggest the best explanation for my perceptions—perhaps she knew a better phrase to define the persistent whispers that hounded me—but as I tried to explain the nature of my distractions, my younger sister became increasingly wary. When I was done, she warned me to say nothing to anyone about the depths of my affliction.

I protested; it was no affliction! All of us Lovecraft girls possessed a unique trait, a Quirk, and this was mine! But Mary reminded me that Mr. Posey had gone mad and been locked away in Broadmoor Asylum for quizzical behavior, and if my imagination ran towards hearing whispers, then I ought to be careful with whom I shared such information. She gave me a fond hug and told me not to worry; she refused to believe for a single second that I'd lost my wits, and in that moment of contact, I'd felt her love and concern for me, radiating off her skin like afternoon sunshine. Mary's hugs were huge, consuming things. She was my little sister, but she was the largest little sister in the whole village.

Honestly, I don't wish to make my Quirk sound miraculous. It has left the pursuit of a relationship impossible. Friendships are troublesome. Romance is futile. People are duplicitous in their nature and, even in the bloom of love, a mood can be changeable and fragile. When I was younger, I'd been courted by some of the men from the village but they'd found my Quirk to be bothersome, at best, and terrifying, at worst. Jerold Chowder had been so frightened by my knowledge of his lying, fickle ways that he'd accused me of trickery, and once our engagement was formally dissolved, he'd given me a very wide berth. Papa said not to let the matter trouble me—after all, Jerold was a turnip-headed ninny with no great prospects and any nuptials would only result in ugly, ugly children—but I decided then to abandon all hope for a happy marriage. It was too easy for my heart to break. A talent for reading a person's most hidden feelings did not lend itself well to social situations, and consequently, I enjoyed the company of children and dogs and books, for they were transparent and loyal with their emotions. I found adults and cats to be tiring, for they often professed one thing and felt quite another.

After leaving the basket at the door, I spent an hour or so in the gardens, finding blessed felicity in the delicate sentiments of the growing flowers, cherishing my solitary explorations. When I returned home across the pastures, my three sisters were sitting in the breakfast-room, finishing their meal. Mama had already gone to town to run errands, Papa had sequestered himself in his study to work on his memoirs, and Beatrice was clearing dishes.

Jane smiled as I entered. "Where have you been so early in the day, Harry?" she asked as I removed my bonnet.

"I took a gift to Mr. Blackwood," I said.

They all looked to me eagerly. Emma audibly gasped.

"I have nothing to tell you," I said, waving away their interest. "He wouldn't see me. He was home but didn't come to the door, so I left the food on the doorstep."

"How crude!" said Emma. "Don't you think? Terribly boorish behavior in a gentleman?"

"We know nothing about him," said Jane mildly, "Perhaps he's shy. Or terribly disfigured. Maybe he doesn't wish to terrify the country girls."

"Or maybe he's only tired," I replied as I sat at the table and took a triangle of toast from Emma's plate, "The man was awake all last night. A lantern burned in the tower until dawn."

Mary set aside her tea cup. "Which means you were up all night, watching him?"

"Mostly," I said. "Aren't you just the smallest bit interested?"

Mary and Emma scoffed, but Jane gave a coy smile.

"Of course, Harry," she replied, "No one has seen him, gossip is rampant, and the man spends all his hours locked up in the house. How could one not be intrigued?"

The brass bell at the front door rang. Beatrice went to greet whomever had arrived, and she came back to the table with a spindly boy at her heels, all elbows and knees and crooked teeth: the baker's son, Earl Rabbit. His age sat squarely in the awkward years between child and man, and his gaunt face was speckled with dots and bristles, poorly shaved. He held his cap to his chest and seemed unsure what to say to the gaggle of women, watching him from around the breakfast table.

"Look what the hedgehog dropped on the doorstep," Beatrice teased. "Go on, lad. Don't stand there like a lump! Deliver your envelope and I'll find you a coin for your trouble."

"Good morning, Earl," said Jane.

"M-m-m-morning, miss," he stammered, his cheeks turning crimson.

"Isn't this a fair distance out of town for you to come?" said Emma, and she was not so distractingly pretty as Jane, so he turned to her with a sense of relief.

"I don't mind doing the deliveries for Mrs. Runkle," he replied. "She got her hands full with Marvin today." And he stood a little straighter, to show he was more mature than his friend, even though they were the same age. He shook his head sadly, ruefully. "I just don't know what's gotten into the boy!"

But under his feigned concern, his expression was smug and self-satisfied. There had always been a current of competition between the two, and if Earl had been given a chore—and payment—meant for Mrs. Runkle's nephew, then I imagine he felt quite proud of himself.

Jane tipped her chin towards his hand. "What have you got there?"

The crimson patches on his cheeks returned. "Oh! Yes! F-f-for you, miss," he said. "It's a l-l-letter."

Jane took it as Beatrice gave the baker's boy his pay. "Thank you, Earl," said my sister, opening the envelope as the housemaid scooted him away, and once he was gone, Jane gave a little laugh of surprise. She began to read:

Dear Miss Jane,

I hope this invitation finds you in fine health and vigor. It was our great honor to make your acquaintance yesterday afternoon, and I am of the belief that your spirited conversation and generous hospitality has, so far, been the high point of our visit to Dunham County.

George and I wish to invite you and your elder sister Harriet for luncheon this afternoon at the house of our uncle. Sandwiches and tea to be served promptly at 1 p.m. We eagerly anticipate your conversation and company.

Regards,
Frederick Darling

Mary groaned. "You'll have a lovely time with the Darling brothers, no doubt. Long, tedious discussions of economics and accounting, punctuated with little bursts of egotistical self-aggrandizing."

If she heard the sarcasm, Emma didn't respond. Instead, with genuine desire, she said, "I can't come? Why is Harry invited, and not me? That's hardly fair! I'm far more engaging company!"

"Consider yourself lucky, Em," said Mary.

I admit, my stomach had started to sink. More of Cassilda Darling's biting compliments? I shuddered at the thought. "Do I have to accompany you? Take Emma in my place."

"No, you must come," said Jane, "You were specifically invited! What if one of the Darlings has his designs on you? How disappointed he'd be, if Emma was to take your seat at the table." She regarded the letter like one would examine a used tissue. "They haven't left us much time to make other arrangements."

"I'm sure that was done on purpose," said Mary with disapproval.

"Crafty Cassilda and her schemes," I replied. "That woman will do whatever she must to entrap you, Jane. I wouldn't be surprised if there's a leg-hold hidden under the mat on their doorstep."

Jane laughed at that. "Then you must come, Harry. I'll need you to help pry it open."

"Beg your pardon at my intrusion, miss, but your mother might have had something to do with this," Beatrice replied as she gathered up the used plates. "I heard her tell Mrs. Darling that you had no plans for the week, and would be eager for a diversion, and would never refuse an invitation to lunch."

"Pah," said Jane, "Meddlesome hags!"

"That is our mother you're talking about," Emma said.

"Does the title not fit?"

We all gave little shrugs and nods of agreement, Beatrice included.

"Fine, we'll go, and we'll have a lovely time," I said with determination, "And we shall see which Darling fits you best, Jane. Perhaps, if you're lucky, you can use your Quirk to bend him into a decent human being."

# FOUR

Eons ago, long before ancient man first stepped upon this landscape and endeavored to tame it and shape it to fit his desires, a clear cold trickle of melted glacier water dribbled from the distant molar-shaped peaks of the Barnacle Mountains. As the ice fields vanished, the trickle became a gushing stream, and with its persistent motion had carved a broad, fertile valley between a series of rolling hills, very pleasing and sensible in composition. The river, which was broad but not deep and swift but not dangerous, was known to the cartographers of the nation as Dunham River, but for those who lived in the valley, it was simply called the Waters, for no other freshet, creek, or tributary in the vicinity matched its importance. The Waters traveled generally in an east-west direction, cutting the county in two equal halves, with Upper Dunham to the north and Lower Dunham to the south. Lovecraft Cottage, Northwich Hall, and a cluster of farms were located in the more fertile soils of Upper Dunham, while the Darlings, as well as the majority of the village and businesses, were situated in Lower Dunham.

There were four main methods of crossing the Waters. These included a wooden footbridge to the west which was too small to warrant a name; the Village Bridge, a wide, arched stone construction which crossed in the center of the town; narrow Church Bridge; and the rickety East Bridge. East Bridge would have been a very long way to go, as it was on the farthest edge of Dunham County at the opposite end of the valley, almost into the neighboring county of Hornwoode. The Village Bridge was the most centrally located and therefore the busiest crossing, often clogged with wagons and barrows during the week and, on holidays, by carriages or pedestrians. Church Bridge, however, lay more accommodatingly in the direction of the Darling home, so that was the route which Jane and I chose.

We walked down Mill Road to the crossroads, then headed west as far as the Church of St. Dismas. Generations past, it had been built as a place of sanctuary and reflection, but time had worn heavily upon it, and as churches go, it was no longer a friendly building. Instead, the weathered granite edifice appeared heavily battered as if recently in a brawl, and the arched door looked less like a welcoming entrance and more like a hungry scowl. On either side of the door were two squinting stained-glass windows; they watched people pass over the bridge and promised eternal hellfire and damnation to those they found lacking in piety. The square-sided steeple had sunk on its foundation and listed slightly to one side, tilting at a just enough of a degree for one to doubt one's senses. All around the building, the churchyard was humpy and bumpy, speckled with crooked stone crosses and long tufts of lush green grass, and like a crouched gargoyle, the church perched on a rise in the land to guard the bridge.

We hurried past. Father Noonan stood in the door, looking lonely and staunch in his black robes, and he waved as we scurried by. As children, we had avoided the church, for there were too many tales of ghostly dogs haunting the grounds for us to find comfort or succor in this holy place. One particular folktale, The Grim of St. Dismas, was enough to cause Emma to squeal in fright whenever she spotted a black mutt, even if the poor thing had a lolling tongue and a wagging tail.

Of course, our family rarely attended on Sundays, for like many of the Bierce lineage, my mother was staunchly agnostic. My father had once been a religious man, but he claimed he'd seen too much of the world to accept the priest's stories without a generous measure of salt, and my mother approved of him spending his Sunday with his bees, rather than with a congregation. However, as I had grown, I'd found Father Noonan's stories to be quite engaging. He was a mild, even-tempered man, passionate about history and full of wonder, originally hailing from Hornwoode. I waved back and bid him a good day. When time allowed, I always enjoyed a good conversation with the clergyman, but today our schedule did not permit such distractions.

Once across Church Bridge, the twin-rutted road led into a deep, uncultivated wood. This lush forest of yews, cedars, hemlocks and maples was friendly and soothing to the eye, and like a pretty watercolor painting, the wagon-track curved and meandered amongst the copses, carefree and capricious. Most of the woodland road was flat and easy, very suitable to walking, but in the south, it sharply rose, climbing in steady paces towards the high flat plateau of Dreadmoor Heath.

While the forest was inviting, the grim heath was not. There, the soil was a noxious mix of greasy black sand and gummy peat, and a wide swath of heather and gorse covered the entire south-western quarter of Dunham County. There were no creeks nor hills to soften the heath's appearance, nor farms to cultivate corn, nor bowers of green trees. The heath was as welcoming as the moon, and the wind whipped wickedly over it, whistling through granite boulders that stuck like rotten teeth from sockets of viscous mud.

It was here, between desolate heath and comely forest in the sheltering lee side of the hill, that Mr. Reginald Darling owned a sprawling county home, surrounded by a wooden fence and set next to a bubbling spring. In summer, their house and outbuildings floated on a froth of honeysuckles, dahlias and hellebores, but in late spring, the yard was covered with a low velvet of green and a scattering of daffodils, and one had a clear view of the path, fences, and plaster walls. The house was painted a butter yellow, and so was the chicken coop and the pig shed behind, and this color matched well with the thatch of the beehives and the wicker of the fencing. If one admired the Darling property in isolation, it appeared quite lovely and civilized.

However, if one stepped back to look at the wider vista of hill slope and valley, the little homestead took on a different, darker character. One noticed the nearness of the high barren heath, all covered with stunted brambles and rocky outcroppings. Such feral, unpredictable elements gave the impression of circling tigers, lurking around the house and preparing to spring, and transformed the cheerful home into a rabbit cowering in the curve of the hill.

Jane and I walked arm-in-arm through the woods and up the road towards the Darling House. She kept her rose-pink parasol firmly closed, and I held my straw bonnet to my crown to keep the wind from whisking it away. We knocked upon the door. An elderly housemaid opened it and invited us in, and guided us into the parlor where Mrs. Darling was already waiting.

"Thank you, Eunice," she said, and the old woman silently slipped away to the kitchen. "Girls, look at the two of you, how lovely to see you! Have a seat, please. The men have gone onto open land to hunt for grouse, but they'll return within the half-hour, I'm sure."

"Thank you, ma'am," said Jane, sitting alongside the fireplace. "It's very kind of Frederick to invite us for lunch."

"Oh, my dears, I am happy for it! The boys are eager to strengthen your acquaintance!"

Eunice brought a folded wooden table, and then tea and cups, and then plates of ham and leek sandwiches. Mrs. Darling poured out a cup for each of us.

"Now," she said with great pomp, and I had the sudden suspicion that this luncheon had not be George or Fredrick's idea, and they may not even be aware of our attendance, "Do tell me: how is your mother?"

"Very well this morning," said Jane.

"And your father?"

"Also well," I replied, "And our other sisters, too."

"And the man of Northwich Hall, have you had occasion to meet him yet?"

Ah, here is the true reason for our invitation, I thought to myself, but replied, "No, he has been very reclusive. I went earlier today to greet him, but he was unavailable to come to the door."

"I've heard further rumors from our precious Mrs. Runkle," she began, licking her thin lips. "He's quite repulsive, I've been told, and very persnickety."

"She has seen him again?" said Jane.

"Oh, yes, early in the morning, before the shops are open. Apparently, Mr. Blackwood is a regular visitor to the postal counter, but he only comes in the hour before dawn to gather his parcels and mail away his packages. He is in daily correspondence with a university in California, she says, and very secretive about the nature of his work." She dropped her voice. "He does not like the heat of the sun, she claims, and avoids all human interaction, if it can be helped."

"Mrs. Runkle is a busy body," I said, and Jane looked scandalized by my opinion, but Mrs. Darling giggled and clapped her hands.

"Oh, she is! And we are richer for it!" the woman squealed, "She is a font of information! She tells me that Mr. Blackwood is a fussy fellow of a private disposition, so reclusive that he keeps no staff to attend him. Doesn't that make him all the more interesting to the rest of us!"

A thump and bump at the rear of the home caught our attention, and soon enough, three men entered into the parlor, showing great surprise at our presence. Elder Mr. Darling, the uncle, had an athletic, spry form for his fifty-years, and his chestnut-colored hair curled around the tops of his ears and the nape of his neck with only a sparse sprinkle of grey. Upon seeing visitors in his parlor, he gave us a merry, toothy smile and removed his tweed cap to bow low in Jane's direction.

"Good afternoon, Miss Lovecraft," he said, "Very pleased to see you again! And you," he said to me, doffing his hat in my direction, "Miss Lovecraft, it has been a long time since we've crossed paths. The Easter Egg Hunt in late March, no? When you were reading fairy stories to the children at the library?"

"Sir," I replied, holding out my hand and shaking his palm firmly. "A pleasure to see you again." His emotions erupted through me like a jolly song in a silent room: he felt tired and elated from a pleasant morning spent in the open air of the heath, and he was famished from all his hiking.

Frederick and George came in, one after another, and both took seats on the sofa. Made brutish with hunger, George grabbed a sandwich and began to devour it in a series of huge bites, but Frederick kept his manners about him. He resisted the sandwiches' allure and folded his hands on his lap, and said, "Ladies! What a delight!"

"How was your hunt?" Jane asked, "A success, I hope!"

"Not at all," George said around a mouthful of chewed leek and bread, "There's nothing alive on that barren plain, I swear!"

"It's most strange," said the elder Mr. Darling to his wife, "Not a bird nor beast upon it. I've never seen the place more quiet."

Mrs. Darling cared not a whit for the animals upon the heath or their absence, but I was intrigued. "Nothing?" I said, "How curious! Thinking back now, I heard no songbirds this morning, either, which struck me as odd at the time."

"It is quite odd," Mr. Darling agreed, "No tracks, no scat, no hint of movement. I've never seen the place so desolate! It's almost as if every scrap of life has been removed, and all traces of them scrubbed clean."

"Is that not unnatural?" said Jane, "The heath is normally such a lively place this time of year, with all the hawks and sparrows returning after winter."

"I'd hoped to bag a grouse for dinner," Frederick replied, "I am sorry, auntie. I've brought nothing home for Eunice to prepare." He turned his attention to Jane. "I am an accomplished hunter, you know. I took down a twelve-point stag last year while traveling in the highlands; what a magnificent creature, it was! A most impressive, sweeping rack of antlers! The mounted head decorates my office in town—I have a very large office, you see, with a central location, and a staff of three, and many good clients, and they find the stag's head makes a wonderful conversation piece."

"How lovely," said Jane, overwhelmed by this volley of information.

"And you, George?" I said, hoping to steer the conversation away from Frederick's blustering, "What do you do to amuse yourself?"

He had already finished his second sandwich and was reaching for a third. "I'm not an accomplished sportsman, that's certain," he laughed, "But I enjoy a night on the town, from time to time, and a spot of gambling to make the heart flutter. Do you play cards, Miss Lovecraft?"

"I do!" I said, "I particularly enjoy cinch and jubilee. We should play a match."

This perked him up.

But instantly, Mrs. Darling squashed that idea flat. "We are here to enjoy a civilized luncheon, not gamble away our savings with childish vices, Georgie. Come, girls, eat up before my famished nephew devours it all." She plucked one sandwich from the plate and, before taking a delicate bite, said, "Tell me, Jane, has your father laid eyes upon this Mr. Blackwood?"

"No, ma'am," she said, "The gentleman has eluded us all completely."

"Hardly surprising. I should think the new owner of Northwich Hall will have a difficult task ahead of him, and very little free time to do as he wishes, given the dilapidated state of the place," said Frederick, "It must be a frightful mess! Can you imagine the interior? Given the decades that it's lain empty, most of the cellar will need to be drained and the roofs will be full of holes."

"And the chimneys full of bats," George added. "A total infestation!"

Mrs. Darling gave a visible shudder.

"The property can't be much of an investment," said Frederick.

Said the elder Mr. Darling, more to himself than the rest of the party, "It's a wonder the whole place hadn't collapsed in on itself years ago."

Mrs. Darling waggled one sandwich at her husband. "Oh, a ruin! Wouldn't that have been lovely! It would've made a better ruin than that lump of stones in Upper Whatley." She turned to Jane. "Can you imagine, having such an inspirational vista from your own backyard? Dunham would have been the envy of artists and poets everywhere!"

"There's no hope of that now," said Frederick sadly, "I was told on good authority that Mr. Blackwood could not be dissuaded from buying the mansion to restore it. I myself inquired with the intention of purchase, but the price was simply too steep for the worth of the property."

I didn't believe an accountant of Frederick's limited quality could afford a place as grand as Northwich Hall—not for a single second!—but I laid my hand upon his wrist as an appeal to pass the plate of sandwiches, and his intentions flared over his skin as bright as sunlight on snow: this was a ruse on his part, a means of impressing Jane with both his supposed wealth and his good sense in refraining from idle spending. He had boundless ambitions to impress his uncle and a consuming desire to possess a wife, and Jane seemed the easiest route to achieve both. To that end, he wished to be seen as sensible and dependable by her, for he knew these to be traits he possessed that his younger brother lacked.

I took the sandwiches from him with thanks. My head swam. I didn't usually target my Quirk so purposefully. The effort left me befuddled.

"Yet Mr. Blackwood purchased it?" Jane continued, oblivious to my queasiness.

The elder Mr. Darling arched his brows. "The Village Council set upon it a very high price without option for negotiation, but Mr. Blackwood could not be dissuaded, no matter how inflated the cost. I spoke on the matter with Mr. Chowder yesterday, and he suspects the council could have asked any amount, and the gentleman would have been happy to give it." He waggled a sandwich at his wife. "The council is, of course, quite divided on the sale—some are pleased with the outcome, and scrambling to find a good use for all the money. Others are not so pleased, now that a stranger is lord of the manor, and all of us are to live in his shadow." Mr. Darling took a sandwich from the plate, but before taking a bite, added, "We shall see how it all turns out, but the future of Dunham doubtlessly hinges on the quality and intentions of the man who now rules Northwich Hall."

"But why he would want it so badly, to take such a large loss on its acquisition?" I said.

Mrs. Darling dropped her voice to a hush. "No one in their right mind would buy the place, not after what happened to poor Mr. Posey and his family," she whispered. "Your mother has told you the story, yes?"

Both Jane and I nodded, but George leaned forward. "I do not know it."

"Mrs. Posey and their sons all disappeared, and Mr. Posey went mad with grief," I replied.

Mrs. Darling shook her head. "But that is not the whole of it," she said.

"It isn't?" said Jane. "That's all we've been told."

"Oh, goodness," said Mrs. Darling, "Mrs. Posey and the sons went missing, that's true." She leaned forward, her smile glittering with devilish delight. "But my dear, one of the sons came back."

Jane gasped.

"Yes, yes," Mrs. Darling continued, "He came back, but he was not right in the head! So the story goes, Mr. Posey dug a well in the cellar, but he uncovered something sinister: glowing eyes in the darkness, you know, and distant howls of tortured souls. The boys were compelled by sinister forces to climb down into the well and investigate, but they did not come back up, and Mrs. Posey was so heartbroken, she threw herself down the well, too, and dashed herself to pieces on the stones. Mr. Posey had lost his entire family, all in one foul swoop." She took her cup, savored a sip of tea and provided a dramatic pause. Then, upon swallowing, she said, "A few months later, once the funerals were long-since finished and the village had moved on, the eldest son crawled back up from the depths of Hell. One might think Mr. Posey would be happy to be reunited, but this was no loving occasion, girls! The son was depraved and warped and ghastly to behold—so I've heard, his body had been mangled into a terrible abomination! Three eyes, abscesses over the entirety of his body, and an unquenchable thirst for human blood! Only the Lord knows what terrible tortures happened to him down in the unholy abyss." Her eyes grew as wide as marbles, and her fingers played over her lace cuffs like a priest manipulates a rosary. "I heard that Mr. Posey, terrified of this demonic figure confronting him, shot his son in the chest and killed him dead, then tossed the body down the abyss and covered it all over with paving stones. Then he locked the well and the stones and the gates to Hell behind an oak door banded with iron, and flooded the cellar of the house."

"Of course, after that, he was never the same," Mr. Darling continued, "How could he be? Mr. Posey had looked upon his son's face and seen true evil, and in destroying it, he destroyed himself, too."

A stillness fell over the sitting room.

Then George whispered, "Blimey!"

"The village council has held possession of Northwich Hall ever since, but they priced it very high to keep safe an unwitting buyer," the elder Mr. Darling added.

Mrs. Darling gave a gruff snort, and said, "Yet Mr. Blackwood owns it now, and he could not be dissuaded, even with the stories or the expense."

Jane glanced at me. "That does make one wonder what he's up to."

"It does," I agreed.

···—o○o—···

Further conversations revolved around dull topics, and we left the Darlings in mid-afternoon as a gentle rain began to fall, giving our thanks and making light-hearted promises to visit again. But, as soon as we were around the corner and hurrying down the hill into the wood, our voices pitched low. "Do you believe it?" said Jane.

"Of course not!" I replied as we walked down the steep track. "Wouldn't you think, if a doorway to Hell had opened so close to our house, we'd have noticed something? Surely the relentless screeches of yowling demons would have kept us up at night."

She chuckled. "But don't you think it interesting that Mr. Blackwood is so driven to own the place!" she said, "I wouldn't pay any amount of money for a house with such a frightful reputation."

"Maybe he's unaware of the history."

"Maybe he's very aware," she replied.

The rain increased, and we took shelter under her rose-pink parasol as the road carried us down from the plateau of Dreadmoor Heath and into the verdant embrace of the forest vale. The leaves tinged the sunlight with a fresh green hue, and the air filled with the smell of growing things. Drops pattered on the leaves.

"We should ask Papa for the truth of it. He'll tell us, if we ask directly."

"He'll say we're being silly, Harry," Jane replied. "But we should tell Emma and Mary. They'll be fascinated."

"To think, we've lived so close to such a tragic story for so many years, yet we've remained blissfully ignorant!"

"I wonder what else we've missed, simply because we've been too close to the source," Jane replied. "What else have we not questioned because we've always accepted it as fact?"

"We do not know what we do not know, and know not even to know of its absence," I replied.

"Goodness, I feel the very fabric of my reality unraveling," Jane laughed.

After a few quiet steps, I said, "Honestly, it does make me wonder what really happened to poor Mr. Posey."

"Such a terrible story to tell over lunch," she said as we crossed a large puddle in the path, inching around the edge where the ferns and bushes grew.

I waited until she was across before saying, "You know as well as I, Cassilda Darling wouldn't let the loss of a guest's appetite get in the way of a good yarn."

"Of course not," Jane agreed, "And Frederick, thinking to boast about buying Northwich Hall. Never in a million years would I believe it!"

"Oh, but he didn't buy it! Not because he isn't rich, but because he's in possession of so much good sense!" I laughed. "Wealthy and frugal! And he's the best hunter in all the land, even if he didn't find a grouse. He said so!"

"We shouldn't tease him; he's well-established and a fine prospect, all things considered," Jane giggled, "But I can't stand a braggart, especially if he shows no skill to back it up."

"He's quite determined to win your affection," I said. "He wants to possess you fully, Jane, and will go to any length to demonstrate how sensible he is, compared to George's gambling and carousing."

She looked surprised, then waggled her finger at me. "Did you use your Quirk? You ought not to peer in someone else's thoughts, Harry! That's an invasion of their privacy!"

"Pah!" I laughed. "It doesn't take any great army to invade Frederick's thoughts, that's for sure. I'm sure you could turn him to your will with very little effort." I snapped my fingers. "George is impulsive and without as much self-control, but I wager, in Fredrick, you have yourself the ingredients for a willing and devoted slave."

Jane laughed. "Oh God! How awful!" She hooked her arm over the crook of my elbow. "I don't want a husband to control, Harry! How dull that would be!"

I opened my mouth to agree when a sound caught my ear, and I paused. It was difficult to hear over the patter of rain drops on the leaves and umbrella, but the faint, moist, suckling sound seemed so out-of-place that I was certain I'd heard it. There was a small squeak to it, like the gentle slap of slick flesh.

Jane stopped at my side, perplexed.

"What's that?" I said.

Jane listened. "I don't hear anything."

I strained to hear above the rain, and caught it again. The sound was accompanied with a breath, a huff of sorts, but moist and bubbling. "There. Hear it? From the trees?"

Jane leaned forward.

"I do …" She peered through the fresh spring leaves. "Is there something up in the canopy?"

The sound abruptly ceased, as if it was suddenly aware of our interest.

We walked on a few steps but now in silence, both of us listening intently, and after a few minutes we were rewarded with another breath, behind us and above in the leaves.

"I think we're being followed," Jane whispered.

"By what?" I replied.

Another quiet slap, moist and damp.

"A squirrel with consumption?" she replied, and I chuckled. It was such a small sound, and I did not yet know the magnitude of the creature following us.

We walked on through the tunnel of branches and leaves, and we saw the distant opening that led into wide fields towards the Church Bridge. The forest was thickest here, but the track was straight, and there was only two or three hundred feet until we were out from under the canopy. Jane appeared outwardly calm, but her pace had quickened, and when she grabbed my hand, I felt the anticipation wicking off her skin. I didn't mean to intrude on her heart, but her fear was rising.

"Hurry," she urged.

I heard the sound again, closer now, but I could not tell if it came from the right or the left.

We no longer worried about avoiding the puddles. She held the parasol above us like a shield.

"Hurry," she pressed again.

The breaths were close, very close, almost directly above us. I heard the rustle of wind in foliage, the patter of rain on parasol, and the rough exhalation of something very large, but I saw nothing, except for shivering green leaves and diamond-drops of water.

Then, the sound stopped.

And directly before us and over the path, the thick limb of an ancient maple tree creaked. We both saw it dip down as if carrying a great weight, and Jane pulled up short with a gasp.

"Up there," she said, pointing to a leafy bower.

"Where?" I asked, my eyes seeking any hint of an animal.

"On the branch," she replied.

Standing in the middle of the track, we peered into the tangle of buds and leaves, the shimmering twigs made resplendent with rain water, and it was only very slowly that I realized my mistake: what had appeared as the rough, textured bark of an empty branch was, in fact, drawing in and out like the rolling sea, as if the tree itself had grown lungs and the ability to breath. No tree moved like that. My fingers crept down Jane's forearm to clamp my grip around her wrist, and she telegraphed through her touch the terror that coursed in her blood.

Something had engulfed the trunk of the tree, perfectly camouflaged to appear as if made of wood. It was colossal, but so fully disguised that we could not measure it.

I glanced at her, she glanced at me.

I gave a small nod.

Together, we burst into a sprint, hand-in-hand under the branch and towards the tunnel exit as fast as our boots would take us, with the parasol abandoned in the middle of the track. My own fear and adrenaline was magnified by the fear coming from Jane's hand. We heard the beast crashing through the canopy above, moving with simian grace from branch to branch, yet whenever I stole a glimpse back, I saw no clear indication of the body that followed us. It blended seamlessly into the background—first greens, then browns, then back to greens—but the noise of its movement and the thrashing branches revealed it to be massive, larger than a man and as unstoppable as a rhino.

We burst out onto open land with our breath heaving thick and fast in our throats. Never had I been so happy to see the Church Bridge, miserable St. Dismas, the cock-eyed steeple and humpy graveyard, and a little farther down the river valley, the little stone shops and streets and post office of sleepy Dunham! When we reached the apex of the bridge, Jane and I turned with our arms locked together and looked back to the forest, which now seemed pleasant and unassuming in the cool spring drizzle.

Jane pointed. "There!"

I followed her finger, and I was almost certain I saw something ripple amongst the tree branches, like the glistening green body of a gigantic serpent, slithering amongst the leaves.

# FIVE

The nearest building was the rectory of the Church of St. Dismas, and in a little niche beside the dwelling's entrance, a small brass lamp burned a tiny flame, all day and night. We fled over the bridge and towards this flicker of warmth and civilization, hurdling the graves in our hurry to the rectory door and the succor we might find within.

Traditions can be such ridiculous things. Those of sentimental disposition may defend them, but I suspect the main function of a tradition is to promote thoughtless action, and more often than not, they provide us with the excuse of mindlessly plodding through our day without regard. I'm sure, if I were to ask every single inhabitant in Dunham County why the Church of St. Dismas kept an oil lamp burning next to the rear door, none would be able to provide me with an honest answer. Surely there would be a great deal of speculation and conjecture, but before the conversation concluded, they'd fall back to the excuse of tradition. It has always been done thusly, and so we will continue to do so, until the stars burn out and the universe goes dark.

Certainly I'd never questioned the tradition of the oil lamp before we found ourselves dashing headlong towards the rectory door, our hands clasped tightly. The low clouds and cool rain had darkened the day, but that tiny speck of light became a beacon of encouragement in a time of distress, and we hurried towards it, and pounded heavily upon the wooden door. Never had I been so happy for such a cheerful spark to guide us.

The door creaked open. There stood Father Noonan. He was a educated man of thirty or thirty-five, with a graceful disposition and an aristocratic air that had been somewhat stifled by the restrictions placed upon him by his profession. I think, given leave to follow a secular path, Noonan might have been a rascal and an explorer, but the steady nature of his career had given him an uncontestable path to follow, and that left him with a charitable character, unfettered by the weight of uncertainty or the hunger of ambitions. Years ago, during one of our conversations, I had brushed my hand against his wrist and caught a snippet of his inner state, and I'd found him to be a complex yet deeply contented individual who consciously and willingly poured his considerable intelligence into his faith. Father Noonan was a very stable, very thoughtful person, and I liked him a great deal, even if we did not always agree on matters of religion. He had cropped dark hair, expressive brown eyes, and a full set of straight, even teeth that produced a memorable smile. My mother often lamented at the cruelty of fate, that the most handsome man in all the county should be bound to a life of servitude and unwavering abstinence.

"Good evening, ladies, what can I—" He noticed our pallid faces, and his expression shifted from one of politeness to genuine concern and astonishment. "Goodness, what is the matter?"

"In the woods," Jane panted, pointing back across the field.

"Come in, come in," he urged, and stepped back to give us entrance. Wet and bedraggled, Jane and I stumbled into the rectory of St. Dismas, and my heart only began to slow when I heard the bolt slide shut with a bang.

He ushered us into the kitchen and invited us to sit at the small table, where a single setting of potatoes and lamb hash had been set. Father Noonan poured out three small cups of red wine and set one each before Jane and me before taking his own.

"Now, take ease, ladies, and catch your breath," he said kindly, "And when you are ready, tell me what's happened!"

Jane took up the tale; I was still too winded. "There was a creature in the woods! A snake, I think! As big as a dragon!"

To his credit, Father Noonan did not tell us we were wrong, but he certainly balked at telling us we were right.

"A snake! Are you certain?"

"Something … very large …" I panted.

"How large?"

Jane held out her hands, as far as they could spread. "As big as a tiger!"

"Good Lord!" he exclaimed.

"We saw it quite clearly," Jane assured him. "I know what I saw!"

"Are there snakes of such size on Dreadmoor Heath?" he inquired, "It would need plenty of food, which of course the heath could provide, but I can't see how it would have escaped anyone's notice long enough to reach such proportions."

I finally wrestled my breath into a manageable rhythm. "Mr. Darling said no animals are left on Dreadmoor," I said, "Perhaps the snake has eaten up every scrap of life."

Father Noonan furrowed his brow at this piece of information. "So a wyrm of monstrous size has infested our safe haven—if true, you're fortunate to have escaped it!" He stood quickly and grabbed for his cloak, which hung on a hook by the door. "I'll head directly to the mayor, and put forth a warning, and send out men to capture it and kill it immediately."

Jane seized upon this idea. "You must! No one is safe with it lurking in the trees!"

"Please, stay here, ladies," he invited, "Once the village has been warned, I'll accompany you home myself."

Father Noonan, abandoning his dinner, rushed out into the spring rain, leaving Jane and I alone in the drab, antiquated kitchen. We heard him in the yard, harnessing his spotted pony to the little trap, then the vehicle rattled out to the road at top speed.

Once he was gone, Jane said, "How lucky we are, that Father Noonan was here!"

But I, with my breath now easy in my chest and the wine warming my belly, had begun to suffer second thoughts. "They'll never believe us," I said, "There's no wild creature larger than a badger in all of Dunham County."

"That was no badger!" she replied.

My hands had turned quite cold, so I stood and stoked the fire in the kitchen until it roared. "But what could it have been?"

"An anaconda!" she replied. "Isn't that the fabled serpent of Amazonia? What if we are being overrun with anacondas?"

"Jane, that's ridiculous," I said.

"You saw it, just as I did! Green and brown! Isn't that the color of an anaconda? Or is it a boa? I get them mixed up."

My sister had settled her opinion and would not let it go.

"Be reasonable," I urged as I returned to the table, and a fresh burst of rain splattered across the window. "I can't explain what we saw, but that doesn't give me liberty to leap to conclusions!"

She took a sip of tea. "But you agree, it was a snake."

"I do, but one snake does not make an infestation, and there's no evidence that it has come from far overseas. I'd say it's more likely to be a fat garter snake of our boring garden variety than some far-flung dragon."

Jane held out her hands, encircling her fingers. "That was the circumference of the beast I saw, Harry. Huge!"

"Oh, the poor thing is just pudgy," I replied over the rim of my glass.

Between the good wine, the warm fire, and my conjecture, her terror was melting into good humor. "Do snakes even get fat?" she asked.

"Apparently so," I replied. "That one in the vale is positively tubby."

"Oh, Harry," she said with a laugh, "You're being ridiculous."

I was, but it was worth it, to see her relax.

"Don't worry, Jane. The vale isn't large, and I'm sure the mayor will be happy enough for an excuse to go hunting," I replied. "They'll have found the poor thing and dispatched it by the end of the day, and then they'll parade it around town, and we'll be absolutely embarrassed by how small it is, because our fear has made it three times larger than it is in reality." I took another sip of wine. "Out of all of this, we get to enjoy a ride home with Father Noonan, so that's a pleasant end to the afternoon, plus we'll have a good story to share with Mary and Emma."

"And won't they be envious, that we were invited to the Darling's house, and enjoyed such an adventure," she replied with a chuckle.

·· —o-o-o— ··

Halfway between the village and home, the squall broke and the clouds began to clear, and when the pony and trap clattered down our driveway, Mama hurried out in a flap of skirts and shawls to see what was the matter. When Father Noonan disembarked and held out one hand to assist Jane, Mama launched into scolding us for bothering the priest. "You have good strong legs!" she snapped at us, slapping my thigh, "Could you not walk? Did you have to pester the Father until he'd give you a ride home? He must, you know! He must be charitable! It is his duty! He can't say no if you ask!"

"I was not harangued," he laughed, "The ladies encountered a creature in the woods and were pursued by it to the Church Bridge, so they came to my door seeking help. I would never turn away someone in peril! Why, for that very reason, the lamp of St. Dismas is always lit."

"Pursued? Pursued? Goodness, by what? A badger? Oh, dear girls! Oh, come in, come in!" my mother fawned, "Oh, you kind and sweet man, how good it was that you were there to lend a hand! Do stay for dinner, we would be happy to have you join us at the table. Beatrice! Beatrice! Set another place for the Father!" She ushered him in the front hall. "Mr. Lovecraft will be ever-so-happy to have you join us. He enjoys your conversations. He tries to engage me in spiritual topics, but I tell him that religious nonsense only clutters up one's thoughts, and he does not listen to my good sense, Father, but insists on discussing such fanciful things with the girls. Doesn't he, Harry?"

"From time to time, yes," I said.

We'd come through the hall and into the afternoon parlor, and she offered Father Noonan a seat by the hearth. "I'm happy to take the burden of such a conversation from you, madam," he replied with a charming smile.

"I have other, more pressing concerns," she replied. "Running a house takes all my mental faculties, you understand. A woman in my position simply has no time for philosophies and spirits—Beatrice! Have you set a place for the Father? Did you hear me from the yard?" Then, back to the Father, she said, "Very good of you, to bring Jane and Harriet home."

"As I said, the ladies were chased," he replied. "They were in a sorry state when I opened the door."

"Oh, girls," said my mother with disapproval, "What has taken your fancy now?" Then, back to Father Noonan, she said, "Harry reads too much. Her imagination is too lively and it has no outlet."

"We saw something in the trees, Mama," Jane began, and as Papa arrived from his study, she turned to him, "It was a serpent of gigantic proportions. Father Noonan has informed the mayor."

"And he's sent his sons into the vale to look for any trace," the priest said, "I'm sure it will be dispatched by morning."

Papa, who rarely rose to any emotional pitch, gave a sedate nod. "That is very good to hear," he replied, "I see no need to worry, then, if the Chowder boys are on the trail. I was about to make my rounds of the apiaries, which I do every night before dinner. Would you like to join me, Father?"

So the men went into the garden, and Mama rounded on us.

"Well?"

"We think it was a snake—" I began, but found myself cut off abruptly.

"Not your wee beastie in the woods, Harry!" she dismissed, "I want to know about the Darlings!"

Mama yearned for every particular about our visit, and she would not let us go until she'd wrung each nuance and innuendo out of us. How were the brothers dressed? Did they incline their heads when Jane spoke? What topics did we discuss? Did they eat heartily, or sparingly? On and on came her questions, as unrelenting as the river current. Jane would commit her allegiance to neither gentleman, yet she remained polite and pleasant, and when at last she was able to slip from Mama's grasp to head out the Huntsman's Oak, she did so with a palpable air of relief.

Once my younger sister had fled for the freedom of the outdoors, the full force of my mother's interrogation fell upon me.

"Well?" said Mama, "Well?"

"It was a fine luncheon," I said, "Conversation was pleasant enough."

She reached out to pinch my cheek. "I'm very happy you accompanied her, Harriet," Mama said, "With such an important choice laid out before

Jane, I take comfort that you're on hand to talk sense into her. She looks up to you and values your opinion very highly." She paused, obviously waiting for some tidbit of information, and when it was not forthcoming, she prompted me with a flutter of hands. "Well, what do you think, between the two of them?"

"Which would I prefer?"

"No, silly duck!" she replied with a trill of a laugh, "Which man is better suited to Jane?" Then, waggling her fingers, she said, "There's no hope of marriage for you, I'm afraid, so we must do everything we can to support Jane in her search for a match."

I glanced out the window to my three sisters, strolling through the gardens towards the driveway and the Huntsman's Oak, and beyond them, my father and the Father examining the beehives. "Well, I suppose I like George best," I said. "He seemed more humble, though he does not suffer from an excess of wit. Certainly, he is more generous in sharing his opinions, and he does not allow a lack of education on a subject to silence him."

"Oh, Harry," Mama sighed, and when I turned from the window to look at her, I noticed tears glimmering in her eyes.

"What's wrong?"

She dabbed at her face with her handkerchief. "Oh, my steadfast Harry, I just ... ever since Cassilda's visit ... oh, I feel as though I have failed you."

"Failed me?" I said as she took her seat by the fireplace. "In what way?"

Mama took another deep sigh. "I've always known you are the plainest of our children, and I should have helped you more. Jane is a beauty, and Mary is robust. Even Emma, with her delicate features, will find it easy to attract a gentleman to care for her and protect her. All three have something to set them apart. But you, I'm afraid ... you have no discerning characteristics to attract a man, and thus will be left alone in your twilight years."

One might think I'd be insulted by such a blunt assessment of my mousy brown hair, grey eyes, unremarkable features and solitary nature, but I've known my mother my whole life. She means well.

"It's not all bad, Mama," I replied. "I have my novels to keep me company. I may yet find someone who shares my love of reading."

"But would they want you at your advanced age?" she said, "And, would you want them, if no one has yet claimed them? What if they are working class? Or worse yet, an actor? Oh, oh ..." She pressed the kerchief to her mouth to suppress a sob, and once she'd dabbed the fresh tears leaking from her eyes, she added, "I should have tried harder to find you a suitable fellow. I should have petitioned more on your behalf, or told a few fibs to increase your talents. Maybe if I'd said you were a better beekeeper, or that you make the best cakes in all the county ..." With that, she began to cry.

"There's no need to resort to lies, Mama," I said. "You've not wronged me in any way!"

"You aren't angry?"

Honestly, my mother.

I pressed a quick kiss to the crown of her grey head and felt the sting of her grief and disappointment through my lips. "Not in the least. I may be unremarkable in all aspects, Mama, but I like who I am. And I'd rather be pleased with myself and live alone, than have all the men in the world chase after me while my heart is full of self-loathing."

A clatter of dishes in the kitchen caught her ear and distracted her. "Oh, goodness ... Beatrice! Beatrice, have you set another plate! Did you hear me before?"

I'm sure, if there is a God, even He flinched at the shrill tone of my mother's demands. The glass vase on the mantle shivered, the wires of the piano hummed, the cat in the corner fled for the door. If Beatrice hadn't heard, it's because my mother's voice had already rendered her deaf.

But with the force of her emotions now focused on poor Beatrice, I was satisfied that she'd collected herself. I joined the other three at the Huntsman's Oak, rolling my eyes as I reached them.

Mary was the first to speak. "Mama is in a bit of a state? We heard the wailing."

"You know how emotional she can be, especially in matters of matrimony," I replied. "But honestly, the topic of which Darling makes a better husband is the least of my concerns at the moment. Did Jane tell you of our chase through the woods?"

Emma nodded rapidly, like a bird. "And Jane says it was an anaconda?"

I took a breath to speak, but Mary spoke before I could agree. "That's ridiculous," she determined. "We're half-a-world from Amazonia."

Jane looked at me. "They don't believe me. They think I've gone mad."

"No, I don't think you're mad," Mary replied with a measure of frustration, "I only think you're mistaken. You might have seen ... I don't know ... a hedgehog."

"It was no hedgehog, slithering through the trees and painted to look like tree bark," I said, and when she began to protest, I added, "Or, if it was? Then I deem it to be the most remarkable hedgehog to ever live, and well worth studying further." I took a seat on the low branch and said, more to myself than to my sisters, "I think we should go into the vale ourselves, to the very spot we saw it, and pick up its trail."

This earned a stern refusal from both Emma and Mary, and a gasp from Jane.

"No, Harry! I will not go back into those woods! Not before the men have rooted it out!"

"We'd be perfectly safe, as long as we're together," I insisted, "Nothing would dare attack us."

"The Chowder boys have probably found it already," Mary assured.

"And even if they haven't," Jane continued. "The rain will have washed away any tracks, and the sun is going down. Maybe in the full light of morning we could hope to be successful, but at this hour? We'd be courting danger! We could easily trip and fall in the dark woods, and leave one of us nursing a broken leg!"

Emma shook her head. "And that would be far beyond my Quirk to remedy."

Jane took my hand in hers. "Tomorrow, Harry. We'll all go tomorrow, once the sun is up and the forest is safe."

The terror she'd felt had mellowed into a nervous ache, all bound together with anxiety and timidity. I felt my resolve faltering. Then, startled, I slipped my hand out of hers.

"Jane!"

"I'm sorry," she said, and she looked remorseful but resigned, as if to say the use of her Quirk couldn't be helped. "I know it's rude to influence another, but you've got that stubborn look in your eye, and when you get like this, nothing dissuades you! And you can't think it's a good idea to put yourself in danger again! I only wanted you to come to the decision on your own."

I was frustrated, but of course she was right. Maybe it was the lingering sensation of her touch, or maybe I was coming to my senses of my own accord, but the light was failing, and night was coming, and I'd be an idiot to think we could find any track in the darkness.

"In the morning, then," I said as Beatrice appeared in the yard to call us to dinner.

··—o-o-o—··

But in the morning, instead of waking by the crowing of the rooster or the calling of the crows, I was wrenched from my dreams by the piercing tea-kettle squeal of my mother, coming from the direction of the back door. The windows trembled as the door slammed. I hurried downstairs in my nightgown, expecting bedlam, with Emma close at my heels.

Mama met me at the bottom of the stairwell.

"Do you know anything about this, Harriet?" she said sharply, and brandished a basket in my direction. Inside was my brown shawl, neatly folded.

I blinked twice. Sleep muddled my thoughts. It took a moment for my addled brain to recognize it.

"Mr. Blackwood has returned the basket?" I said.

She did not look pleased. "Well, I certainly don't know who has returned it, child! I found it by the frog pond, along with this!"

Tucked under the shawl was a letter in an envelope, addressed to 'The Brown-Haired One'.

"That must be you," Mama said, "No one else in this house lays claim to such a plain and forgettable identity!"

I took the envelope and flipped it over in my hands. Emma was at my elbow in a thrall. The envelope had been folded from simple cream-colored paper, hot-pressed and elegant, and when I opened the flap, I found the letter written on the same stock. In an artistic hand, it read,

Thank you.

"So? So? Is it from Mr. Blackwood?" said my mother, hungry for information.

"It must be," I replied, "Although why he'd choose to communicate through the written word, and not stay to knock on the door and speak directly with me, is a mystery."

"Perhaps you intimidate him," Emma said.

At that, my mother erupted in gales of laughter.

I took the letter and went out to the garden, and Emma followed me. Both of us stood there in our nightgowns, surrounded by the blush of fresh lavender bushes, and she watched as I ran my fingertips over its surface, eyes closed, to listen to the faint impressions upon it.

"What does it tell you, Harry?"

"It's been out of door for a few hours, I can feel there is … there is …" I closed my eyes. "Well, there's a sense of gratitude, but we don't need my Quirk to know that. Only the ability to read!" I smiled. "But there is hesitation, too. Uncertainty."

"I was right. He must be shy."

"Yes, I think so." I opened my eyes and she took the letter to examine it herself. "And there's a sense of urgency … of gobbling."

"Like a turkey?"

"No, like a wolf," I laughed. "I guess he must be very hungry, for I left him enough cheese and bread to last the week, but I think he may have devoured it in one sitting."

She peeked at me over the edge of the letter. "You can tell that from one little slip of paper?"

"The impressions are fading from the item, but yes."

Emma gave a little grunt. "Well! I wish I had such a useful Quirk. All I can do is make people feel a little better when they're ill."

"What do you think I should do?"

"Why do anything?" Emma answered, "You've reached out to him, and he has been polite in returning the basket and acknowledging your generosity. The poor man wants nothing to do with us, so I say we oblige him."

I took the letter back. "He's shy, but that doesn't mean he wants to be alone," I said.

Mary and Jane hurried out of the house, both neatly dressed; I suppose, in an emergency, they wished to look presentable. When I displayed the letter, Mary scowled and took it in hand. "I've been awake and sewing since sun-up," she said in her gruff manner. "No one came by way of the road, or I would've seen them."

"He might have come across the fields," Emma pointed out. "Or maybe he visited under the cover of night."

"You think he might have snooped around the house in the night?" said Jane, scandalized. After our encounter with the serpent, she seemed particularly on edge, and she took the letter from Mary to examine it more closely. "I don't like the thought of some strange man skulking through in our yard."

Emma leaned forwards. "Do you think, instead of a snake, it was Mr. Blackwood following you in the woods?"

"I'm certain it was not," I said, and Jane laughed.

"Not unless he was swinging through the trees like an ape."

"We haven't seen the man yet," Mary pointed out, "Maybe he is an ape?"

"I suspect he may be invisible," Jane replied.

"He's an invisible ape," I added.

"With fine handwriting, if this is to be judged," said Mary.

Jane held the letter at arms length to admire it. "To be sure, a very talented and artistic invisible ape. I like this Mr. Blackwood more and more!"

Emma frowned. "Are you teasing me?" she said. "You're all being silly now."

"Oh, Emma, I'm sure Mr. Blackwood means us no harm," Jane began with a laugh, "But we shall all go this morning, the four of us, to see if we can spot the beast in the trees." She pinched Emma's cheek. "And you must bring your little camera obscura with you, and show us all how it works."

But a movement on the road caught Mary's eye, and she said, "Look, here comes Mrs. Runkle!"

"In a great hurry," Emma said.

"Maybe the Chowder boys found our tubby garter snake," I said to Jane, and she laughed.

We four, two in dress and two in nightgowns, headed to the front of the house to greet her, and by the time we reached our front door, she was hustling down our drive past the Huntsman's Oak. Her hat was askew and her shawl fluttered after her like the wings of a chicken. Her knees wobbled, her frail hands trembled, and her glasses had slid to the bottom of her button nose. It was rare to see Mrs. Runkle away from her beloved postal counter, and even rarer still to see her so far removed from the center of the village, for Lovecraft Cottage was no small distance to cover and she was hardly athletic, but still, there must have been a font of strength in her core. After all, she was grandmother and guardian to Marvin Runkle, a young man of questionable character and intellect, and how such a fragile woman managed to wrangle that spirited half-wit, I'll never know.

I raised my hand to greet her, but my smile vanished when I saw her distress.

"Girls, girls," she said, "Where is your father?"

We ushered her into the house and set her in the morning parlor, on the couch in a window square of sunshine. Emma fetched her a drink of lemonade, and Mama bustled in from the kitchen, alerted by our voices. "What is it, Mrs. Runkle?" she said as she came through the hall, "Goodness, Edith! You look stricken!"

"Did they find the snake?" asked Mary, but the old woman shook her head.

"The Rabbit child, the troublesome one, you know," said Mrs. Runkle, still panting. She took the lemonade from Emma and swallowed it down in three desperate gulps. Her hands quivered, her lungs heaved.

Jane looked to me quickly, then sat alongside Mrs. Runkle and took her hand. "Be calm," she said, stroking the gnarled fingers, "All will be well. Be calm, Mrs. Runkle."

A drowsy look dropped over the woman's face and her breath slowed.

Mama was not pleased by such a blatant use of a Quirk, but instead of chastising Jane, she sat in her chair across from Mrs. Runkle and said, "Do you mean Earl Rabbit, Edith?"

"Yes, yes, that's the one," Mrs. Runkle said softly, "When his mother rose to build the fires in the bakery ovens, he was missing from his bed, and the lad is no where to be found. His shoes are in the corridor, his coat is on the hook, but Earl is vanished completely! Worst of all, the latch has been snapped from the window, as if a great force pulled it open! Of course, Mrs. Rabbit is in a state, as you can imagine." Old Mrs. Runkle's voice adopted a little more fire, as if she was waking from a stupor. "She's certain that Earl has been ripped from his bed against his will, and Mr. Rabbit is assembling a search party, and has asked Mayor Chowder to put out a formal request for assistance. I was asked to fetch Mr. Lovecraft and ask if he will join the search."

"We all know Earl is troublesome," I said, "Is it not more likely that he crept out his window in the night to get into mischief, and broke the latch in his hurry? He's fourteen years old, is he not? About the right age to look for trouble, or worse, have a schoolboy crush." I sat beside her. "That must be it. He's mooning over a girl. He'll come wandering home once he realizes the hour."

"But no one in the village has seen him," said Mrs. Runkle. "I have asked, up and down the Waters …"

"And what girl in Dunham would admit to Earl as a suitor?" Mary scoffed.

Jane released Mrs. Runkle's hand and smiled pleasantly. "I'm sure we'll find him on the road between here and Upper Whatley, where some milkmaid has caught his fancy. He went to visit her and misjudged the time. Has anyone asked your Marvin?"

Mrs. Runkle shook her head. "Marvin and Earl have not seen one another for almost a week—some misunderstanding between them. I don't know the nature of their quarrel, but Marvin will be of no help in this matter. Oh, Earl's mother will give her son such a thrashing, if you're right! There's a party heading up onto Dreadmoor Heath, and another searching the fields and canyon west of Dunham. I do not know more—I left in such a hurry for your home as the men were organizing their searches."

"Can we help in any way?" said Mary.

"We can make sandwiches," said Mama, and Mrs. Runkle seized upon this offer.

"Yes, yes! Gather supplies to feed the men as they come back! That would be much appreciated."

"Of course," said Mama, flapping her hands to scoot us towards the kitchen, "Go on, ducklings, make provisions and take them to the village. Be as useful as you can. Harry, go and fetch your father, and tell him he's been summoned."

By this hour, Papa was in the garden with his bees, and I found him repairing one of the skeps by the stone wall. He had a tuft of golden straw in one hand, and an awl in the other, and the bees danced about his head with a merry buzzing. They never stung him, nor any of us; I thought very little about it, for I'd accepted that he was a kind beekeeper and his wards treated him with fondness, but I suppose, in a way, his close friendship with the inhabitants of his apiary was a kind of Quirk, too.

When he saw me coming, he held up one hand and hailed me. I returned his greeting, then said, "Earl Rabbit is missing, and you've been asked by the mayor to join the search party."

My father is a kindly man, but Earl's reputation proceeded him, and Papa hunched his shoulders and set aside his tools with resignation. "Oh, goodness. Wild creatures yesterday, wayward youths today, what will happen tomorrow? Dunham can not handle so much excitement."

"Earl has only slipped his mother's apron strings, I'm sure," I replied. "He probably thought he could find the snake himself."

"A quest for glory, hey?" My father shook his head. "And his mother's in a state, no doubt. There'll be no bread for any of us until he's found, I suppose."

My experience of the day before still played in my mind. "You don't think he could be in any true danger, do you?"

"Earl is not a very hearty lad, but I doubt he could be overtaken by a garter snake." Papa looked at me with a grin. "You don't believe Jane's nonsense that this serpent is an anaconda, too, do you?"

I considered my words. Any description of the massive slithering beast in the forest would sound utterly ridiculous, and I regarded my father too highly to play the fool. He spoke to me as an equal, not a child, and I wouldn't want him to think I was letting my imagination get the best of me. He might treat Jane's assumptions or Emma's dreamy phantasies with fawning affection, but he'd always been plain-spoken with Mary and me, and I wouldn't wish to jeopardize his good opinion, so instead, I replied, "No, that seems outlandish. But there was a large animal in the trees, and the latch was broken on Earl's window. Mrs. Rabbit is sure he's been abducted, yet I can't think of anyone who would have an interest in the boy."

"And I've never heard of any reptiles that open locked windows to eat up young men." Papa chuckled at the thought. "Nothing of great interest ever happens in Dunham County, Harry, and I'm sure today will not change that. Earl has gone a-wandering. This is nothing more than an excuse for the village to come together, hike through the fields, and enjoy a communal dinner afterwards. As we are all aware, Mayor Chowder loves an assembly."

When Papa left for the village, I joined my sisters in the kitchen. However, the whole time we prepared food, Jane shot glances in my direction, and it wasn't until we were walking down the road with baskets of sandwiches, halfway to the village and flanked on both sides by long pastures, that Jane was brave enough to speak. "You think this must have something to do with yesterday's encounter. I can see it written plain on your face."

"I'm wondering if we were incredibly fortunate," I replied. "It didn't grab us, so it took Earl, instead."

"But Harry, you said he'd gone on a jaunt to see a milkmaid—"

"I did say that, yes," I replied to Emma, "But I don't necessarily believe it."

At that moment, a voice hailed us. We turned to see Frederick Darling galloping across the pastures on a fine grey steed. He wore a dark suit and mustard-colored tie, and when he doffed his top hat to Jane, I noticed it had a yellow band to match. There was a radiance to him that matched the freshness of the morning sun, as if he were constructed specifically for the purpose of riding through dew-drenched meadows in the virginal light of day, and I found his perfection and precision distasteful, wondering to myself if his purity and excellent bearing had not been devised as a mockery of all natural processes. His chin was clean shaven, not a single speck of mud marred his shoes, and such unearthly impeccability from head to toe rankled me like the dragging of fingernails over a chalk slate. "Ladies, good afternoon," he said, then startled at his own greeting. "Or, as it would seem, not good in the least! Auntie told me you had an unfortunate encounter in the forest yesterday, and I feel personally responsible that I did not accompany you home, and left you in such danger!"

"No one could have predicted it," said Jane. "Don't concern yourself further, Mr. Darling. Dunham is a safe and quiet place, and there's never been any cause for worry."

"Please, call me Frederick," he said, "I offer you profuse apologies and assure you, I'm happy you are well." With his gallant amends now made to Jane, he sat back and addressed us all. "You're on your way to help, I assume?"

"We are," I said, "Where are the men searching?"

"Every track and trail," came his reply, "George and Uncle have headed up to the heath, and I have taken the low lands."

"What about the vale below your uncle's house?" I said.

"It has been thoroughly examined, Miss Harriet! Between last night and today, I don't think there's a single stone left unturned. A number of local boys searched the bushes last night, they've grown up here and know the hidden spots better than I ever could. I decided to stick to the open land, where I'd have a good view from the back of Uncle's horse." His mount sidestepped and tossed its grey head, straining to run. Jane reached out with one hand to stoke the animal's velvet nose, and it calmed under her touch.

"Have you noticed anything strange?"

"No," he said to me, "Nothing out of the ordinary! Dunham is as perfect as a postcard."

"Today, I fear that perfection is only a veneer," Emma said, "This place is too quiet, too calm. There's not even the twittering of birds."

Frederick nodded gravely. "Perhaps you're right, Miss Emma. As I told your sisters only yesterday, the heath was as quiet as the grave, and now it seems the rest of the countryside has fallen still, too," he replied. "As for the character of the boy, did you know him well?"

"No more or less than anyone," Emma said.

"He could be a bit of trouble, especially with a slingshot in hand, but he rarely came as far as our cottage. He certainly never visited the library, nor sang in Mary's choir; there was little chance to cross paths, except for visits to the bakery." I added, "If his absence is voluntary, I'm afraid we have no idea where he might have gone."

"I doubt he left of his own volition," Frederick said, "Without coat or shoes? On a cool spring evening? No, he'd have to be a fool to leave those behind."

It's true, Earl was no great philosopher, but even he would've seen the benefits of a jacket and boots on a damp night.

"Then let us not keep you," said Jane, releasing the horse's head, "The boy is out there, waiting for you to rescue him."

Frederick cast her a sunny smile and put heels to flank, and the stallion shot off like a cannon ball over the fields. We watched him disappear over a rise in the land.

"Well," said Mary, "He's very earnest. He may be a bit of a blowhard, but he seems to have a good heart. It's a rare gentleman who would give of his time to search for a boy he does not know."

"You're too kind, Mary," replied Jane.

"Mr. Darling wishes to make a good impression on the village, and he could not do that by staying home, or even focusing his attention on the heath. Here, in the low lands, is where he's most likely to encounter those whose good opinion he seeks," I said, crossing my arms. "No, Freddie is the more cunning brother, and knows a good opportunity to win favor when he sees it."

"Perhaps you are too harsh on Mr. Darling," said Mary with disapproval.

"Perhaps," I agreed, but I did not alter my sentiment.

Our route took us passed the school house and the mill yard and down to the Waters, where the bridge arches over the steel-blue river like a lazy grey cat. Up the other side, the road took us into the heart of town and straight to the village hall. Here, women gathered with their gifts of sustenance, brought in trade for gossip and news. Mrs. Cripplegate was there, and our cousin's new wife, Mrs. Beirce. In the corner stood Eunice, the Darling's housemaid. Shock and horror suffused the very essence of the room. Sweet little Earl, they all said. At the far end of the hall sat Mrs. Rabbit, silent as stone.

"Mrs. Rabbit, I'm sorry," said Jane, "Please, if there's anything we can do …"

But the poor woman, fidgeting with the hem of her flour-dusted apron, was too melancholy to speak. She was a sparse and skinny thing, and her misery added a greyness to her face that gave her the bearing of a wraith.

The rotund Mrs. Chowder swanned from the crowd to shoo us away, leaving a fug of pungent perfume in her wake. As the mayor's wife, she'd adopted the role of commander amongst the ladies, and they were happy to defer to her authority in times of trouble; let Matilda Chowder take responsibility for all decisions, if she relished the task. There was no detail too trifling to escape Mrs. Chowder's appraisal, and no item too grand that could not be improved by her opinion. "Give her air, ladies," she said, wafting her hands about as if we were a cloud of flies, "Can you not see, the poor woman is a fugue of despair?" Our baskets caught her attention. "Ah, more victuals for the men! Come, bring them over here, set them out in a line, just so!"

She gestured towards a long table, already groaning under the weight of casseroles and salads.

Emma, Mary and Jane followed Mrs. Chowder obediently, but I lingered behind, and when I returned to Mrs. Rabbit to sit next her, I took her hand in mine.

"Mrs. Rabbit?" I said softly.

Her brown doe eyes rolled in their sockets to meet mine.

"Can you tell me what happened?"

She said nothing to me, yet through the warmth of her skin I perceived the rapid anxiety and drowning loss in her heart, and it prickled through my capillaries like ice water. She was beyond all verbalization. Her eyes filled with tears until her sorrow tumbled down her cheeks, and I felt in my soul the panic she'd experienced upon finding Earl's bed empty, and the window opened wide, the lock broken, and the bracing air wafting in from a world abnormally still. There'd been no hint of steps upon the dewy lawn, no broken twigs in the hedge, no footsteps to mar the dust of the road. No, Earl had been swooped away so fully, so completely, that the only trace of the boy to remain was the impression of his head upon his empty pillow.

Then, for a singular heartbeat, I felt a flash of memories in her: a bright salvo of emotions flaring and dying in an instant. I bolted upright, eyes wide. The memories had been hidden as if behind a stone wall, but the wall fractured, and I experienced a sudden slash across my vision as bright and red as blood. As always, I felt as she felt, but suddenly I saw as she saw, too, and the visions overwhelmed me: clawing fingertips, a gust of wind amongst grey curtains, and most arresting of all, two fiery scarlet eyes surrounded by billowing black smoke.

I dropped her hand in shock.

She'd witnessed something, but the memory was gone.

No, not just gone. Ripped out.

"What did you see, Mrs. Rabbit?" I asked.

The tear-streaked woman with an empty mind turned her face to stare at the wall.

"Miss Lovecraft, dear, leave her to her grief," Mrs. Chowder insisted, "She's been struck dumb with emotion. It does no good for you to pester her!"

Mrs. Chowder grabbed me by the hand to pull me away from Mrs. Rabbit; I felt a sudden gush of sopping haughtiness, of pretensions, of looking down one's nose at all the lesser folk. The strength of it made me gag. I snatched back my hand. "Has she said anything?" I pressed. Could she, even? I wondered. The missing memory was a raw, oozing wound across the center of her soul, leaving her psyche in shreds.

"The poor dear has said not a peep," was Mrs. Chowder's curt reply. "And I doubt she will! That little rascal may have been a nuisance for most of us, but Earl was her oldest son, and dearest to her." The mayor's wife clucked in her throat. "Doctor Gelder has been summoned from Lower Whatley. He'll be here by the turn of the hour."

"Was there blood in Earl's room?"

"What? Oh, glory no! There was nothing of the sort!" Mrs. Chowder hushed, and dropped her voice to hiss in my ear, "Don't start a panic, Harriet! I've had enough trouble from you, squashing rumors of a giant serpent hanging in the trees! There's been no violence done!"

But that merciless injury across Mrs. Rabbit's mind stabbed at me. There had been violence done, but of an invisible nature, and it had left Mrs. Rabbit with the will and intellect of a cabbage. I felt sick to my stomach, looking at her piteous figure, slowly rocking back and forth in her chair. The horrible discovery of her wound filled me with revulsion: how could anyone regard that slash of bright red, the splash of gore, the punch of emotional pain, and not come away reeling?

I couldn't stay here a moment longer. The people, the sensations, the clamor: I needed quiet and solitude, I needed to hear myself think. Without bidding Mrs. Chowder good-bye, I hurried from the hall and went out into the world like a possessed hound, straight to the woods below Dreadmoor Heath.

A moment's hesitation overtook me as I drew into the forest, but I was too focused on my goal to feel much fear, and I entered that tunnel of verdant green with the sharp stab of Mrs. Rabbit's memory fresh in my mind. It drowned out any good sense or lingering doubts. The day was sunny and bright, very different from the moody gloom of yesterday's rainstorm, and the forest seemed much more friendly and welcoming. The puddles had evaporated into little circles of mud, and I strode along the track without impediment, heading directly for the overhanging branch where Jane and I had first caught sight of the serpent. Of course, the beast was long gone, but I hoped the trees might share their information with me. It was as I stood there, looking up into the branches, that I heard my name cried out in the distance, and I turned to see Emma hurrying along the path, her basket swinging from the crook of her arm.

"I saw you leave in a hurry," she said.

"That Chowder woman," I muttered, and she nodded in understanding.

"And here is the spot where you and Jane were so frightened?" she said, looking up and one hand rooted in her basket. "There is nothing so dreadful today." She withdrew her camera obscura, that little caramel square with an unblinking eye, and held it gently in her two palms.

"You've come to capture an image?"

"What good are my inventions if they can't help, in some way?" she replied, her eyes still roving over the leaves and branches. "I shall fix this spot and time, and give us opportunity to return to it, again and again, for further study."

I did not fully understand how Emma's camera obscura worked, but nor did I understand any of her curious inventions or their intended functions; she was prolific, but not precisely accomplished, and a machine was just as likely to provide an unforeseen function as the proposed one. For example, her attempt to create a miniature smelter had instead resulted in a lovely contraption for making toast.

So I left her to her experimentation, and I veered to the right to explore the underbrush. Twigs caught at my stockings, ferns clutched at my shawl. I pushed through the greenery as one might wade through the shallows at the beach, with my eyes gazing upwards to the bowers, seeking any hint of the serpent that had dogged us.

Moving from tree to tree, I touched each as I passed. Most of them kept their secrets, but my fingers grazed one alder and perceived a hint of life within, but also the trace of life without: a creature of immense vitality had lain in wait in the alder's branches. The sensation was old, easily overpowered by the exuberance of the tree's vital force. Whether the animal had been a cat or a squirrel or a creature of more mysterious origins,

I couldn't tell.

I examined the soft earth at the base of the tree, but there were no footprints, no scraps of hair, no spoor.

Nothing.

The forest lacked any trace of an animal's passage. The wind whispered through the upper canopy, but no mice scurried in the leaves nor birds sang on the branches. The woods were utterly devoid of life, the air was still and deathly quiet.

To my left, halfway up a small slope leading to the heath, I heard a flap.

A flash of color moved amongst the green. I peered closer. Amongst the green and brown bracken, a scrap of pink waved lazily in the breeze.

My blood chilled. I was in no way prepared to find Earl's remains, and the adrenaline that flooded my veins turned my skin clammy.

"Emma!" I called out.

She hurried up the slope, and I heard her gasp as she spotted the misplaced color through the leaves.

"Do you think—"

I swallowed my apprehension and pushed through the bushes with my heart in my throat. Reluctant yet unable to turn away, I swept my hands over the ferns and pushed them aside for a clear view.

We both let out a rushing sigh of relief. Jane's umbrella, caught up in the brambles, had suffered a rip across the side, but such a tear could be easily mended.

I plucked it up and closed it, and handed it to Emma. "Take it back to Jane, and tell her that we've seen no evidence of anything in the trees. Whatever followed us is no long here."

"There's nothing here, Harry," she said, "Is it not strangely quiet? Where have all the birds gone?"

She set a kiss on my cheek before heading off in the direction of town, and I watched her go, back down the road through the grove of maples. They bowed and swayed in the wind. I wondered for a moment if there might not be another movement there, too, of a body swinging high in the boughs. I listened for the moist squeak, that rustle of a reptilian body pushing through young leaves, but as the twigs shivered and rattled, I heard only the click of bare branches, high above my head.

Was it lurking in the canopy, perfectly still? Was it watching me, even now?

"Miss Lovecraft!"

I half jumped out of my skin as a voice cried out from the top of the hill.

Looking up the slope through the tangle of branches, I saw the elder Mr. Darling along with a small retinue of young men, all dressed in hunting clothes and holding rifles at their hips. "Halloo!" he said, waving over his head.

I waved in reply. They waited as I climbed out of the steep ravine to meet them at the edge of open land.

The heath of Dreadmoor spread out to the south. The humpy ground of gorse brush and heather tussocks looked brown and grey against the wide blue sky. Up here, on the high plateau, the wind galloped unfettered for miles and miles, and it pulled at my skirts and threatened to rip the bonnet from my crown. If I looked behind me, I could see the valley and forest, the silvery ribbon of river weaving through it all, the steeple of St. Dismas, and the squat buildings of Dunham Village clustered together at the narrowest point of the Waters. Past them were pastures, the road leading to the north, and in the far distance, the hollow where my own cottage nestled. But looking southward, I saw nothing but a fierce and feral landscape, punctured here and there with ancient outcroppings of lichen-speckled boulders.

"Good day, gentlemen," I said, then felt guilty for saying it, for as Frederick had recently pointed out, it was certainly no such thing. "Have you had any success?"

"Nothing at all, miss," Mr. Darling replied, taking my hand to help me up the last few feet of the rocky incline. His touch ached with dismay and fatigue. "We've walked most of the trails across Dreadmoor Heath and, as I mentioned to you only yesterday, we've found them vacant of life."

It had been the same in the vale. No whispers of rabbits in the grass. No squawks of magpies in the branches.

"Not even a lizard?" I said.

"Not a one."

"That's odd, is it not?"

"Everything has fled," he said as our group rambled along the edge of the heath in the direction of the Dreadmoor Road, which cut across from the south. It was the only wagon track that crossed the heath to link our village to Upper Whatley. A figure was striding along the track towards us, and as Mr. Darling hailed him, I recognized the weathered face and battered derby hat of Mr. Tippler, the tin smith. "Have you spotted any remains, Mitchell?" he called out.

"Not a whit, neither man nor beastie," the man replied around his black pipe stem.

"Where the dickens can they all have gone?" Mr. Darling replied.

"I don't think the beasties have died," Mr. Tippler continued, "I can find nary a trace of any flesh—oh, mercy, I'm meaning the animals, not poor Earl! Nothing so gruesome as that!"

"We've found naught as well," Mr. Darling replied.

"No life at all, either on the heath or in the woods? This is wicked, indeed," said Mr. Tippler with another puff on his pipe.

But I'd felt the tingle of a creature's passage in the woods, so I knew the land could not be completely empty. "Something must be out there," I mused, half to myself.

"I heard about your snake, Miss Lovecraft," said Mr. Tippler, "I'm afraid I've seen no hint of it, either."

I heard gruff coughs from the men, and looked to a few faces. The expressions were kind, but clear: they had already dismissed our sighting as the fanciful visions of frightened women.

"I did see something, gentlemen."

"I believe you think you did," Mr. Darling replied. "But even a serpent leaves a trail."

Mr. Tippler took a puff of his pipe and said in a cloud of smoke, "A snake's track looks like a rope dragged in the dust." Then he motioned towards the village. "But there weren't no tracks around the Rabbit home, so unless a great eagle flew out of the sky to snatch Earl from his bed, I don't think this is the work of a humble beastie." He waggled his pipe to Mr. Darling. "The boy has run away, I tell you. He won't be back. The whole town will want to give him a pummeling for all the trouble he's caused."

Some of the men grumbled. A day away from work could hardly be spared, especially for a scoundrel like Earl.

"Could a large animal be hiding in the forest on the top part of the river valley, to the west of the county?" I held fast to my hat as a fresh gust roared passed. "There's the canyons, and plenty of caverns along the upper reaches of the river, and no one living up there for miles."

"I doubt it," Mr. Tippler said with finality. He tipped his old hat back on his bald head and used his pipe stem to point across the heath. "There's no forest for the beastie to hide in, or gardens to browse, or chickens to steal. Only bare rock, miss, and I can't think of any creature that would want to spend its time there."

Mr. Darling nodded in agreement. "The lads and I have been all the way along the top of the cliffs. If a creature was hiding in the woods, we'd have spotted broken vegetation on the boundaries, I'm certain.'

One of the younger men, Mr. Rufus Cripplegate, crossed his arms and shook his head in dismissal. With the sharpness of anger, he said, "I have a cow ready to drop her calf any moment now, and I can't be gallivanting all over the county, looking for the lad. Damn foolish waste of time."

"Has anyone checked the grounds of Northwich Hall?" I asked.

A grumble of discontent rumbled through the men.

"Bill Crumpsall and his son Teddy went out that way this morning," said Mr. Tippler, "But I don't know what good it will do. The new owner has no fondness for meeting with the public."

"Has anyone seen him yet?"

"Not that I know," said Mr. Darling.

"Perhaps Mr. Blackwood has seen something from his high tower, and does not even know the significance of it," I said.

"Well," Mr. Tippler replied, "If he has, I doubt he'll own to it. Not very talkative."

"A stranger in our midst and a young boy missing? He'd best say something, if he knows what's good for him," said a wiry fellow by the name of Gully, who was a year or two younger than Emma. There were nods of agreement and frustration.

"Calm down, lads," said Mr. Darling, then to me, said, "Hurry on back to the village, Miss Lovecraft, and tell the ladies we'll return for lunch after we've walked the south bank of river as far as the caverns. Go on now." As Mr. Tippler and the rest of the men filed away along the trail, Mr. Darling leaned close and added, "The boys are whipping themselves into a frenzy. It's better to keep them moving than to start speculating."

I understood completely.

But instead of heading back to the village, I turned my nose, not north towards my home or east to the village, but northwest, through the copses of saplings that grew along the southern riverbank, in the direction of the footbridge and the rambling woodlands and sprawling gardens of Northwich Hall.

I crossed paths with squat, red-headed Bill Crumpsall and barrel-bodied, bandy-legged Teddy at the river crossing, upstream from the village by a mile or so. Years ago, a massive fir tree had been planed and set out from bank to bank, and the log made a serviceable bridge for walkers, but it was certainly not designed for the use of horse or carriage. By the time I reached the footbridge, Bill was halfway across, hand outstretched to steady himself; he was the butcher, and his arms were heavily-muscled from years of carving meat and hacking bones, so much so that he appeared top-heavy as he stumbled across to shore. Teddy waited impatiently for his turn to cross. When I emerged from the copse of slender elms, Bill seemed surprised to see a woman strolling along the narrow path.

"You shouldn't be out here!" he warned from the far side of the river, "Tis no safe place for a lady!"

"Nor for you, neither," I replied, "Who knows what dastardly creature has stolen poor Earl away! It may hunger for grown men next!"

"I'll be just fine, Miss Lovecraft," he said sharply. He didn't like the slur against his strength and independence; a fellow takes great pride in his ability to conduct himself, and rarely thinks about his own safety, preferring instead to remind women of their delicacy and peril.

"Hullo, Miss Harriet," said Teddy from the far side. "You look well today!"

"Thank you, Teddy," I replied, "Were you able to speak with Mr. Blackwood?"

"We knocked but he wouldn't answer."

Bill hopped to my shore and added, "The fellow ain't friendly to visitors."

"True," I replied as Teddy began crossing, and I waited until he'd joined us on the south shore to say, "I'm on my way home, Mr. Crumpsall, but I'll take a slight detour and drop by Northwich Hall. Perhaps my charm will work where yours has failed."

Teddy gave a great, galumphing laugh. "Will you say hullo to Jane for me?" he asked. He'd always had a fondness for Jane, and tried very hard to attract her eye, but without much success.

"I'll be happy to," I replied. "She's with my sisters at the village hall, though, and you can say 'hello' yourself if you're quick back to town." If I'm not mistaken, a pink tinge crossed his freckled, nut-brown cheeks. Let Jane deal with Teddy at her heels, and give the young man a bit of hope.

I continued on my way, and the grove of saplings yielded to a series of stone walls and muddy cow fields, eventually crossing a road and becoming Northwich land. I cut across the pastures to the driveway, up the gravel track between its flanking trees, and as I drew closer to the mansion, I was hardly surprised to see the cold chimneys and closed curtains. The upper windows were dark mirrors reflecting the brightly-lit garden, and today, the pond was perfectly placid, without even a giant trout to mar the surface.

I stepped boldly up the door (had I not been here many times before? It had become perfectly normal, it seemed to me!) and I rapped upon the wood. My boldness stemmed from the understanding that my earlier visits would be repeated, my knock would be ignored, and my presence rebuffed. Nothing had come from my previous call, and nothing would come from this one, either.

Oh, how wrong I was!

# SIX

The door flew open to reveal a horsey face atop a bony body, dressed in an expensive black suit and crisp white cravat. The man's eyes were goggled and his high cheekbones were sharply arched, giving him the appearance of a deep-water eel brought rapidly to the ocean surface. This impression was only enhanced by the pale, fishy pallor of his skin; his greasy hair, slicked with Macassar oil and neatly parted in the middle; and his aura of haughty disinterest. On his narrow nose, he wore a most curious set of eye-glasses. They were comprised of three lenses, one layered upon the other, and held in place by silvered filigree work and brass hinges; two of the lenses had been flipped up, so that he stared at me through a single pair, tinted blue. By my quick estimate, he was a year or two older than me, approaching thirty. He looked up, down, behind me, directly to me, his expression darting from interest to snooty disdain to disgust with the speed of a flittering sardine.

"What do you want?" he said. His voice pitched low with revulsion.

"Mr. Blackwood?" I said in surprise.

"Yes. Yes, it is. Yes, I am. What do you want?"

I held out my hand and tried not to cringe when he took it in his own clammy grip. "I wish to make your acquaintance, sir, as we are neighbors. My name is Harriet Lovecraft."

His touch felt reluctant and squeamish. It brimmed with revulsion.

"Miss Lovecraft, is it?" he said, withdrawing his hand and wiping it on his jacket. He flipped another pair of lenses down, red ones, so that he examined me through two lenses instead of one. "Look at you."

"Me?"

"Yes. Who else?" He flipped down the third, these ones silvery-green, and nodded. "Your mission is accomplished, Miss Lovecraft, we've been acquainted. Now go away." He began to close the door.

"Have you heard about the missing boy?" I asked.

That gave him pause. He stared at me hard with those oversized peepers, then flipped all three sets of lenses up to better regard me without impediment.

"What boy?"

"Earl Rabbit," I said. "The baker's son. One of the youths from the village. He has disappeared."

One lip curled up. "How dreadful."

I narrowed my gaze. "You don't sound very concerned."

He caught himself, and purposefully increased his measure of emotion. "Of course it's a tragedy, but I've never met the lad. If you're looking for him, I haven't seen him. I haven't even left the grounds today. I know nothing about this affair at all."

He started to close the door again so I set my boot against the frame. I was not done with him yet, not after so many days of being denied the answers to my curiosity.

"If I may be so bold," I said, "It would be in your best interests to visit the village and introduce yourself to the good people of Dunham. They've started to suspect you of being anti-social, and a quick 'hello' might assuage their fears and keep them from bringing torches and pitchforks to your yard." I gave him a pleasing smile. "A precautionary measure, you understand."

"If you may be so bold? I've seen no indication that you are anything else," he replied. His goggle eyes narrowed, his fishy lips pulled down in a persnickety scowl. "Why ask my permission? Your boldness, your audacity, seems to exist without boundaries and under no man's authority. But … " His expression mellowed. "But your suggestion is not without merit. It's very kind of you to be concerned for my reputation."

"You're my neighbor, sir. If you're innocent of any wrong-doing, I should want you to be well-regarded." I looked at him askance. "Have you seen anything strange around Northwich Hall?"

"No."

"Nothing? No hint of the boy in your garden?"

"None."

After a moment's consideration, I added, "No large beasts lurking in your wood?"

He paused at that, and narrowed his eyes even more. "What kind of beast?"

"I'm not certain," I replied. "A snake, perhaps. I was only afforded a glimpse, but it was huge and multi-colored, and it moved through the trees without effort."

"How precise a description," he said with deep suspicion. "Tell me, Miss Lovecraft, does hysteria run in your family?"

I scowled. "Quite assuredly, no."

"Any weakness of the mind? Are you prone to fits or fainting spells?"

"Of course not," I replied, "You think I hallucinated?"

He scowled back. "I suspect it was nothing more than a trick of the light, don't you? I certainly would exercise caution in sharing my experiences, lest someone mistake my stories for lunacy."

We stared at one another for a heartbeat: he examined me for any hint of rising insult, and I returned the examination to judge if he was baiting me.

"Well," at last I said firmly, "Thank you for returning my basket and shawl. I hope you enjoyed the bread and cheese, and found the book of interest. The wine was my father's vintage, from the grapes on the south side of our cottage."

He blinked twice.

"Cheese? Wine? What the devil are you talking about?"

I furrowed my brow. "The gift I left on your doorstep? You brought back the basket with the note of thanks, and left it by our frog pond."

"I did no such thing—" he began, then stopped abruptly. "Oh, yes. Eating food." His eyes grew mean and cold. "And reading material, too. How very lucky I am, to have such a generous neighbor who knows the worth of a good book. I must go, Miss Lovecraft. Do not come back."

He shunted my boot from the threshold and slammed the heavy door. I heard the chunky, decisive clunk of a lock.

I stood long enough at the door that I saw the curtains move in the upper window, and Mr. Blackwood stared out to see if I remained, and when he saw me, he flapped his hand to urge me to leave.

What a wretched cur! I didn't think he had anything to do with Earl's disappearance, but that didn't keep me from the impression that he was sparse, spiteful, and secretive, and I didn't like him much. I turned on one heel and began to walk across the lawns, homeward, my head held high.

But to my immense surprise, a few minutes later, I was hailed by that same gentleman, and when I turned my head toward Northwich Hall, Mr. Blackwood was hurrying to catch me across the broad open land and wild grasses, a tall hat on his head and a black jacket flapping over his shoulders. He'd removed his glasses and now carried a fancy ebony walking stick.

When he pull a-pace, he was panting heavily from exertion, and two rosy spots had risen to his cheeks. His beaver hat was of the finest quality I had ever seen, and his long black coat was trimmed with a luxurious silver-tipped fur collar. The head of his cane was a silver fish with emerald eyes, identical to the one held by the man in the portrait in Northwich Hall's ballroom. Once he'd caught his breath, he said, "I've suffered a change of heart. Let me accompany you."

"Thank you, that's very kind, sir."

"Upon reflection, I think you may be right, Miss Lovecraft. I've been reclusive, and that will not serve me best in the community. Perhaps you would be generous enough to introduce me to your father and mother?"

"It would be my pleasure," I said. "The village is very small; a visit won't take much time away from your more-important pursuits. I've heard you have a plethora of packages that come and go from Northwich Hall?"

He gave a pinched, pained smile. "It seems the villagers already know a few facts about me."

"Mrs. Runkle, the post mistress, keeps a close watch on the public."

"And what is it that you do, Miss Lovecraft?" he asked as we fell into step with each other. "Can I expect this conversation to be broadcast so widely?"

"I try to restrain myself from idle gossip, sir," I said, "My sisters and I help keep the house and gardens. I also look after the town library, Jane teaches piano to the younger girls, and Mary leads the village choir. Emma does not do much at all, given the choice."

"Ah, yes, there are four of you," he said, "I was in the upper window when you first dropped by." He gave a chuckle at remembering. "You left in quite a hurry."

I slowed my step, forming my next question with deliberation. "Your front door was open, sir, and I was afraid that vermin would come inside, so I made to close it; I took a moment to admire your furnishings, for the Hall has been vacant so long, and I caught sight of something curious in the shadows." I stole a glimpse at his face. "It gave me a fright."

He appeared stern and unmoved. "One of the statues."

"I'm certain it was not."

"Well, I live alone," he replied.

"No staff to assist you?"

"None."

"I'm quite sure I saw someone."

"Perhaps it was a ghost."

I raised one eyebrow in his direction. "Do you know the history of Northwich Hall?"

The eyes glanced quickly at me. A curious curl appeared over his mouth, the faintest hint of a mocking smile. "Do you?"

We walked five or six steps before I said, "I thought I did, but I've been informed that there is more to the story, so I'm not sure if I can honestly answer your question. I thought I knew, but now I suspect I do not."

"It's healthy to question the limits of your own knowledge, from time to time," he said. "You speak of the Posey family, I assume? It's a curious history, but I'm unconcerned by hearsay and old wives' tales."

"I can assure you, it's not hearsay. A very real tragedy happened to the Poseys."

"Terrible things have happened over every square inch of this Earth, Miss Lovecraft. We'd have no choice but to cower in our bed if we wished to avoid all hauntings and spooks." He waved one hand in the direction of the northern forests. "I bet there was some great battle waged on that hillside in long-ago times, or a tragic murder in those dreadful woods, or a highwayman that stalked his victims on the Mill Road … the list of sad events goes on and on. Given enough time, every place becomes stained."

His philosophic rationalization did not fool me. "While that's quite true, I don't think this is an instance of a mere coincidence, sir. I was told you were willing to pay any price for the property."

"Good Lord, you are very well informed, Miss Lovecraft," he said. "Northwich Hall is a fine house. I've seen only a few that are finer, and none of them were for sale." He waved the cane about his head. "Long, lush pastures? A deep forest and a river? Gardens and cellars and towers? I'd be a fool not to purchase it."

We crossed the open lawn and entered into the small path that linked Northwich Hall with my own small cottage, up a weedy incline and through the green wooden gate of the stone fence. "I also heard you were a fur trader?"

"Not me, but my father," he replied, "He amassed a great fortune off the land and rose through the ranks to become a man of learning, but I am not designed for such a rustic life, and doubt very much that I'd succeed on the same path that he took. I am a scholar, Miss Lovecraft, and not particularly suited for the bitter cold or hard labor of living rough. I wished to pursue my interest in science, but I soon exhausted all libraries and resources, from Alaska to Mexico, and when my father left me in possession of a comfortable future, I decided to re-locate to Dunham. It may be small, but at least it's better connected to the universities of London and Berlin."

"You're a man of science? I should introduce you to my sister Mary," I replied, "She's a natural philosopher at heart."

We'd reached the back door of my cottage. I gave a polite knock before opening it. My mother, summoned from the breakfast-room by the sound of my tapping, was very surprised to lay her sight upon the man behind me.

"Good afternoon, sir," she said, questioning.

"Mama, may I present Mr. Aloysius Blackwood."

She gave a squawk like a chicken, as if a jolt of electricity had run through her. "How wonderful to meet you!" she said, taking his hand in hers and pumping madly. "Do come in! Tea? Scones? Beatrice, put the kettle on and gather a nice selection of nibbles for our guest! Come in, come in! We are very delighted to make your acquaintance!" Mr. Blackwood found himself dragged into the parlor. "Harry, where are your sisters? Go and fetch them, tell them we have an honored guest, be quick about it, girl!"

"I think they may still be in the village," I said, "I left them with Mrs. Chowder."

"Then run! Go now! 'Tis only two miles! I shall keep Mr. Blackwood entertained until you return. Sir, will you dine with us this evening? How lovely it is to make your acquaintance!"

Did the gentleman give me a pleading glance for help? I think he may.

But before he could be fully exposed to my mother's marital manipulations, and introduced to all of her daughters of suitable age, I heard my father shouting from the roadway. We rushed out to the yard, all of us: Mama, me, Beatrice, and Mr. Blackwood together.

Papa jogged up the road, waving his hands over his head. "The boy has been found!" he yelled, straining to catch his breath. From his sickly complexion and his stricken expression, the news could not be good.

"Where?" I asked.

But Papa had run too far. He leaned against the Huntsman's Oak, chest heaving, trying to form words.

"The upper footbridge," he gasped.

"I was just there, not half-an-hour ago!" I said.

But my father, long acquainted with his daughters' Quirks, grabbed my wrist. He could not tell me with words, but Papa knew me and my talent: he could impart with touch the full spectrum of emotions that he felt, and that would work to his satisfaction.

Icy dread flowed up from his strong fingers, a horror beyond words. My father, normally a bastion of sedate logic and placid clemency, was utterly terrified.

No further explanation was required. I gathered up my skirts and sprinted as fast as my boots would carry me, back through the garden and over the Northwich pastures, towards the river valley and the footbridge.

··—o○o—··

When I arrived at the north shore of the Dunham River, a clutch of men were disassembling the walking bridge with axes and iron bars. At first, I misread their actions, and thought them to be pulling Earl from under the water, but then I noticed that they were hacking chunks of wood from the planed fir, and extracting him from the very heart of the tree.

Mr. Tippler watched from the shore, puffing on his pipe.

"What are they doing?" I asked.

A section of bridge fractured and splintered. The men strained and tugged, and levered open the tree along its grain.

"Well, he's all caught up now, ain't he," said Mr. Tippler.

The men, some of them turning green, began extracting strips of flesh from the wood.

"He is imbedded in the underside of the walking bridge?" I said with an extraordinary measure of confusion.

Tippler breathed out a puff of smoke. "Aye, that's what it looks like." He waggled his fingers. "I heard that Teddy Crumpsall came back this way after meeting with you, and he noticed that the old bridge had sprouted a few fresh leaves. Thinking that to be mighty queer, he bent over the side to examine it, and spotted a bare foot sticking out of the bridge on the far side, as if the old tree had come to life and grown around the body." He shook his head slowly and drew on his pipe once more, then said in a low and grave voice, "The work of the devil, I say. This is wicked magic."

I fumbled for words. The bridge was made of a single solid tree, without boards or nails. How could such a thing be possible?

I watched as the men used fingers and ax blades to pry strips of human flesh from the inner core of the trunk. Red blood ran like fresh sap.

"How … how can this be?"

The old tinker just looked at me, shrugged, and puffed on his pipe.

There was a cry and shouts of exclamation as more of the body was revealed; the clamor frightened a scattering of starlings silently roosting in a nearby tree. The men rushed to carve more of the timeworn trunk away, revealing a face lodged in the heartwood. The young nose was smashed, the dull eyes were open but spiny with splinters, and the rough texture of the wood had scraped most of the skin into raw meat. Had he been alive when entombed in the tree? Good Lord, there were scratches and blood: signs that he'd fought against his imprisonment, howsoever such a thing was achieved.

A terrible thought occurred to me.

I'd crossed the bridge on my way to Northwich Hall and chatted cheerfully with the Crumpsalls, and at that very moment, I'd walked directly over the body of poor tortured Earl Rabbit, his trapped face only inches from the soles of my feet.

# SEVEN

Mayor Chowder could let no such tragedy befall our little village without alerting the greater authorities. By the following afternoon, a company of the regiment arrived from Hornwoode and set up camp in the pastures across from St. Dismas. Like the sprouting of mushrooms in a single night, neat lines of white canvas tents appeared in an instant, and just like that! the village doubled in size. The narrow streets grew crowded with 100 new men and an equal amount of horses, and every businessman, from the grocer to the blacksmith, rubbed his hands together with anticipation and looked upon the hungry men with a greedy eye.

In any similar situation, such an influx would produce bedlam, but the soldiers were disciplined and highly focused on their task at hand: to seek out any hint that could explain the bizarre nature of Earl's fate. Those in positions of authority were unwilling to call it a murder, but in pubs and alehouses, the consensus was that a foul deed had been performed, and it remained in general agreement that the event was the most uncanny to ever occur in quiet Dunham, and thus demanded answers. How could the boy have been so fully encased in the body of a long-dead tree? What sort of logic could explain such strangeness? While the excitable Mr. Poole devised conspiracies involving fairies and the man in the moon, and Father Noonan chalked it up to the omnipotent will of God, no one could provide a decent solution to the fundamental nature and very foundation of the death.

How could we expect to know more of the who or why, if we could not even explain the simplest aspect of how it had transpired?

In the days following Earl's discovery, soldiers went forth in shifts to look for clues to the itinerary of the boy's abduction. How had he gone from bed to tree? At first, ladies did not venture out at night, and small children were kept close to home. Fear gripped our hearts, but the constant sight of red jackets and black horses eased our minds that we were protected, and slowly the town returned to its old patterns. Gossip remained lively and brimmed with conjecture. The bakery, of course, remained closed. Dr. Gelder diagnosed Mrs. Rabbit as fallen into a catatonic state after suffering a terrible shock. There was no medicine that could revive her, and Mr. Rabbit had worn himself into a stupor with restlessly pacing the countryside, having lost—for all intents and purposes—both his son and his wife.

Mary took it upon herself to experiment. She spent every leisure hour in the garden trying to understand Earl's fate. If only she could conform the laws of physics to recreate the manner of his demise, using logs and bits of cooked chicken left over from dinner, she might be satisfied. She scooped cavities in the wood with the head of an ax, or pounded the chicken into a pulp with the sledgehammer, but each attempt was futile. Dear stubborn Mary found herself unable to engineer the murder scene. Her experiments were, ultimately, of no consequence but her actions brought her a small comfort.

Jane and I sought comfort in our own ways. I searched through Papa's books for similar circumstances, but past historians proved reluctant to share any gruesome mysteries, opting instead to speak of Dunham's farming practices and family lineages, and I could locate no such evidence that such a baffling manner of death had ever transpired; his death was unhelpfully unique. Jane drew pastoral images of rivers and bridges, as she often did under stress, and her landscapes were beautiful, tranquil things, reminding us of quieter days.

Emma locked herself in Papa's tool shed and busied herself with her inventions. We knew not what she was up to until one afternoon, when a great shout erupted from the yard.

"Harry! Harry! You must come!"

And so I did, along with Jane and Mama in tow, hurrying out of the kitchen with skirt hems held aloft. By the time we reached the tool shed, my youngest sister had rushed to the yard to meet us, brandishing one of Mama's small silver bread plates above her head. It was smeared and streaked with black ink, and the finely decorated edges had been bent into warbled lines.

Mama shrieked upon sight of the plate.

"I've done it, Mama!" Emma said in triumph.

"And so you admit it!" came the horrified reply, "Oh, my good silver! Ruined! Mercy, child, you will be the death of me!"

Emma ignored our mother's final throes, and turning to me, said, "Look!"

There, scorched into the reflective surface, was an image of trees and path. I recognized it instantly as the vale below the heath, where we had found Jane's parasol.

I gave a gasp. "This is the result of your camera obscura?" I said in wonder, "Goodness, Emma! I can't believe it!"

Can you imagine such a marvel? To see a singular point in time solidified in light and shade, the full host of blacks and greys, with each line frozen like a spider in amber. I took the plate in hand, agog with wonder.

"And look!" she pressed further, pointing to a section of the image.

There were the trees as I remembered them, and the grassy verge, and the underbrush, and amongst all the greenery I saw a figure, blurry with motion, that must have been myself wandering through the ferns like a wayward phantom. Emma's finger led my eyes up to the branches, where the pointed tip of a large intrusion hung down from the leaves. The edges were crisp, for it had been as still as a statue, but in form it did not possess the lacy delicacies of vegetation. It was thick and stout, sharply tapered, like the rounded conclusion of a massive fang.

"Is that—"

Jane screamed. "There it is! The snake's tail!"

"We didn't see it because it must've been garbed in the same pattern as the trees," explained Emma, "But without colour, there's only form, and it's so different from the shape of the branches that it's easier to see in black and silver—"

My mother would hear no more.

"You have ruined my grandmother's silver!" she wailed, "Ruined it! What am I to do with you? And today of all days, when we have the Cripplegates for dinner! How am I to entertain them with soot all over the bread plates? Oh, by all that is good in the world! First my daughters are chased by a dragon, and then poor Earl is murdered, and now my plates are ruined! I feel faint!"

"Mama, surely you must be amazed—"

"I am only amazed by your sister's foolish nature!" she wailed in my direction, "Oh, mercy! Mercy! Does no one care for my delicate constitution? Do you not see how much you wear upon me, Emma!"

Jane and I traded glances of utmost disbelief, but Emma seemed genuinely wounded by Mama's fit. "You have so many silver plates, and I didn't think you'd mind if I used—"

"You didn't think. A more true statement has never been uttered!" Mama continued, winding herself up. "Give it here, my daughter, and we shall never speak of this again. Come along! Hand me the plate, and we shall clean it off as best we can before Beatrice sets the table."

"Mama," I protested, "Surely even you can see the importance of what

Emma has created!"

"A few squiggles of ink? A smudge of a person? And this snake of yours, which to me looks more like a vine? Oh, I see what Emma has done: she has ruined a perfectly good platter," came the reply, "What does this show that a fine painting could not? And without benefit of color, and all black and silver ... if Emma wishes to capture pictures, then Jane must teach her the art of watercolor. That skill will provide her with more opportunities than this nonsense!" My mother took back the bread plate and rubbed one finger over the finish. "Ah, see? It comes off with no trouble. No lasting harm has been done."

"Mama!" I said in horror, but too late.

"Harriet, you will not encourage such ridiculous, ruinous behavior in your sister," Mama replied firmly.

But Emma had endured enough, and she fled from the yard with tears on her face, turning down Mill Road and running towards town.

"Oh, Mama!" I spat, exasperated, and took off after Emma to comfort her.

My youngest sister was very fleet of foot, and I only managed to catch her when she stopped to rest against the stone rails of the Village Bridge, half way across the span. A more pathetic vision would be difficult to conjure: Emma's face was blotchy and puffy from crying, her skirts were covered in dust and soot, and her hands were spattered with black ink. A smudge of charcoal ink marred her chin. The trickle of villagers crossing the bridge paid her very little attention, and some of the younger women gave Emma a side-long look, but no one wished to embarrass her by mentioning her frightful condition.

"Hateful old shrew!" she sputtered as I reached her.

I embraced her without care or regard for the state of my own clothes. "You have devised a wonder, Emma. Our mother is simply too small-minded to recognize it. But you must show me how you accomplished such magic—every step! Use up all the silver plates in the dining room, I insist! I want you to cover them with pictures! Honestly, they'll come to me upon Mama's death, and I'll be most upset if they're clean and shiny when I inherit them."

This coaxed a faint smile from her.

"I haven't yet figured the best way to fix the image to the plate," she replied. "There are still a few problems to solve with the process."

"And you are the best qualified to discover them, you clever girl," I replied.

Mary and Jane were hurrying along the road towards us, and I hailed them. "Oh, you poor duck!" Mary said as she enfolded Emma in her arms.

Jane, shaking her head slowing in wonder, said, "Oh, Mary, I wish you'd seen it! Emma caught the vision of the creature in the woods, and it was just as I remembered it!"

"If only we still had the plate, we could show the regiment," I said, "But I suppose there's no hope of that now. It'll be cleaned and buffed to a high shine, and covered in biscuits, and Mama will have warned Beatrice against leaving any silverware within Emma's reach."

Our spot on the bridge offered an unobstructed view up the river to the pastures where the army tents had been pitched, providing a fine vista of men riding forth in groups of four. A few of the younger boys were fishing on the north bank, and among them sat Marvin Runkle, the short, tow-headed, freckled boy who had been Earl's constant friend. The others had moved past the loss of their schoolmate with the capriciousness of youth, but Marvin stared into the glittering waters, forlorn. He toyed with an empty slingshot, but ignored the smooth stones along the shore.

"I've heard he's not recovered," said Mary, seeing the direction of my gaze.

"He's lost his only friend," Jane replied. "And no one can give him the pale comfort of knowing how or why."

Mary sighed. "I have no idea how it was done. I've tried with hammers and stones and brute strength, but … are you quite sure, Harry, that you saw them carving the body out of the tree?"

"It was as if Earl and the tree were one, grown together, with the ancient and long-dead tree sprouting a few little leaves," I replied.

We fell into an uneasy silence, each tending to our own thoughts.

The cluster of men trotted up to the bridge on their groomed black steeds, their crimson uniforms bright and merry, their brass buttons sparkling. They were led by a middle-aged officer with a broad face and clean-shaven jaw, sitting erect in his saddle, and as the horses reached the apex of the bridge, the officer lifted his hand and hailed us. He had eyes of the palest ice-blue, and his curled moustache was a fiery ginger red, but his most arresting feature was the puckered white scar that bisected his chin and right cheek, doubtlessly attained in a long-past skirmish.

"Ladies, good afternoon," he greeted in a melodic baritone.

Jane replied, "Good afternoon, sir."

"My name is Captain James Crankshaw. This is Mr. Richard Marsh, Mr. Daniel Keel, and Mr. Elijah Frame."

We each introduced ourselves, and there was a great flurry of doffed hats, tipped chins, and flourished hands. The captain smiled to us each in turn, only giving a little pause at Mary; with her mammoth frame, she could be quite arresting to those who assume all girls are petite and small. To his credit, he covered his awe by feigning a cough and he tipped his hat and smiled at her. "Very lovely to meet you all. Could you point us in the direction of the undertaker's home?"

"Mr. Winterbottom lives on the far slope of the river, in that direction," said Jane, pointing downstream towards the beige, two-story house on the eastern edge of town. "You may find him there, or you may find him in the pub yonder, The Shuttered Door. On many afternoons after tea, he meets with Mr. Poole to play at darts."

"Oh, no, Jane, if he is not at home, he will certainly be at the bakery," said Emma, turning back to the captain, "Earl was the baker's son, you know. The funeral is scheduled for tomorrow, and if there are further arrangements, he'll be with the grieving family."

Captain Crankshaw nodded in thanks and nudged his horse to a trot. The soldiers began to follow obediently, save for one, the fellow introduced to us as Mr. Marsh, who paused his horse and looked with great concern at Emma. "Excuse me, miss, but are you well? You look stricken."

She blushed. "Thank you, yes, I'll be fine," she assured. "T'was a difficult afternoon, but my sisters have endeavored to make all right."

"You have a smudge of soot on your chin," he noted, and fumbled in his sleeve to withdraw a plain handkerchief. "Please, take this with my best wishes. Once you've dried your tears, I hope you have no further occasions to use it." Mr. Marsh passed it to her and carried on, but not before he gave one more tip of his hat to Emma.

"What a generous fellow," said Mary as he trotted away.

But I was barely listening, as I was wrapped tightly in my own thoughts. "Highly unnatural, all of it," I muttered to myself, watching the curve of the Waters and the froth upon the current.

"When you talk in all seriousness of Earl embedded in a solid tree," Jane began, "I start to think the laws of science no longer apply to our current situation."

Mary gave a snort of derision. "You can't simply abandon the laws of science, Jane. They don't turn off or on like the flick of a switch."

Rolling her eyes, Jane leaned against the bridge rail and said, "But consider the facts, Mary. Don't you think we invalidate the laws of science with our Quirks? Every time we use them, we make a mockery of what science knows! Emma shouldn't be able to ease pain with a touch of her hand, yet she does. I shouldn't be able to sway one's opinion, but I can. And Harry shouldn't be able to read minds, but—"

"I don't exactly read minds," I corrected, and Jane cast me a withering glance.

"Close enough, Harry," she replied. "We've never questioned our Quirks because they're all we've known, but don't you think it's a little strange?"

"So, do you think your ability to play the piano has some mystic quality?

Or Emma's inventions spring from some occult source? Or that my singing voice is phantasmagorical, too?" Mary challenged, "Of course not! We simply have talents like anyone else."

"No one else in Dunham has talents like ours," I pointed out.

"Not that we're aware, no," said Mary, "But maybe they keep them close to their hearts, too. Or maybe all of our Quirks can be attributed to the Lovecraft line—maybe strangeness is in the blood."

A shout echoed over the Waters. Upstream, the boys had caught a trout and were congratulating each other.

"I won't give up on the laws of science," she continued, "It's the foundation upon which all knowledge is built. If the laws appear wrong, it's only because we've not yet discovered what influences them."

Her devotion to the natural philosophies remained unshakable.

"Fine," I said at last, "Science has not abandoned us, but you have to admit, it's taken an unexpected turn."

At my comment, Mary relented. "I will admit, none of our Quirks and talents are as drastic as embedding a living man in solid wood." She gazed off into the distance. "I don't pretend to understand how you can do the things you can do, but nor am I willing to give up and proclaim science worthless, simply because one or two things have yet to be explained."

"But we agree that something strange is going on," I replied, and I turned to recline against the bridge side, "And Earl didn't end up in the bridge of his own choice or volition. Someone must know what's happened, and I am not content to stand by and tremble in terror." I turned to my sisters. "Come with me to the footbridge. Maybe we'll see some small detail that the men missed."

"I have choir to attend in the hall," said Mary.

"And the Cripplegates are coming for dinner," said Emma.

"And I've promised Charlotte a piano lesson after we are finished dining, and I dare not wish to disappoint her, not when so many other things are in turmoil," said Jane.

I scowled at them all for being so d-—responsible.

"Besides, Harry, what do you hope to find?" Emma asked, "There isn't a square inch of Dunham County that hasn't been searched."

Yet the situation gnawed at me. Perhaps I'd spent too long alone with my moth-eaten books; I felt there might be purpose here, and a puzzle to solve.

Jane lay her fingers upon my wrist with the light touch of a feather. "Listen to reason, Harry. You don't wish to look further. You'd rather let the men, who are trained in combat, deal with this dangerous situation," she said. I knew, a half-second after she touched me, what she intended to do, but by then, it was too late. Jane felt that my intention was too much beyond our scope or accomplishments, and my younger sister used her considerable charms to turn my opinion, so that we instead returned home to help care for the younger children. As always with Jane's Quirk, I knew my pliancy to be her doing, but I was compelled to feel good-natured about it. A bout of Jane's hocus-pocus makes one cheerful, even if they find themselves suddenly going against their original intentions.

··—ooo—··

By the evening, my autonomy had returned. I was frustrated by Jane's trespass against my free will, but I was grateful, too, for the way it soothed my mind: I'd been in a fretful state since witnessing Earl's mangled remains, and I'd slept poorly for days. Her touch could calm the most troubled constitution. Still, she knew she had trespassed against me, and as we prepared for bed, she apologized.

"I really don't like doing that to you," she admitted as she slipped under her quilt and blew out the candle.

Jane was, at the very core of her being, a caring girl and full of sympathy for those around her. This was lucky for us, I suppose, given her ability to bend one's will to her own needs. A streak of cruelty through someone with Jane's talent would be the making of a tyrant.

"Give me your hand," I said, holding my palm out towards her bed. In the darkness, she slipped her fingers into mine.

Her apology felt deep and genuine. She had acted out of love, not malice. There was a tone of self-loathing in her, too, which surprised and humbled me. She looked up to me, and it had torn at her, to bewitch me against my wishes.

"Do you believe me now?"

I let her go. "Yes, I do. You feel badly about it."

"Very!"

"I forgive you," I said, "But only with the promise that you'll never do it again."

"I promise," she said, "But you can be rather stubborn, Harry. It's your worst trait."

Yes, I suppose I could be a bit of a mule when I have a notion in my head. Even now, as Jane rolled over and her breathing slowed, I was in no mood for rest. My thoughts tumbled over and over like stones under a waterfall: the serpent in the woods, Earl's raw face, the peevish Mr. Blackwood, the stalwart Captain Crankshaw. So many elements that did not yet fit together! In frustration and grief, I wept quietly, hiding my face in my hands; after all, Earl had been a bully and a pest, it's true, but that didn't mean he deserved the end he'd been wrought, torn to pieces to free his corpse from its bizarre tomb. Eventually I calmed, and by then, Mary and Emma were snoring from the other side of the hall.

Lying there, unable to sleep, staring at the ceiling in confused sorrow, I finally gave up trying. It was no use staying in bed.

What was it that Jane had said on our walk home from the Darlings' luncheon? Oh, yes.

'I feel as though the very fabric of my reality is unraveling.'

Down the stairs I went in my nightgown and bare feet, out the kitchen door into the courtyard. The garden was moonlit and drowsy, the air heavy with mist and pleasantly cool. I strolled to the Huntsman's Oak and sat on the low branch for a little while, watching the moths flitter from daffodil to crocus. The Mill Road was empty. To my right, it stretched away towards town, and to my left, it climbed up towards the wild hinterland. Directly across the roadway lay rolling cow fields as far as the distant farmhouse of the Cripplegate family.

Despite our encounter with the snake in the woods, I didn't believe Earl's death was the result of a mere beast. Why would it stalk him in his bed? Why would it drag him to the footbridge? And most tellingly, why would it leave him stuffed in the middle of a tree, rather than devouring him? Animals have simple motives, and none of them fit.

People are more complex, but I couldn't think of any reason why a person would wish Earl harm, either. Dunham was tiny, with a population of less than 300. Everyone knew each other. I wasn't certain that a villager could have dispatched Earl in such an brutal manner, but nor could I think of an individual who would want to. What would motivate a person to target poor Earl? He was annoying, yes, but of no great threat to anyone. He scribbled in books and he chased chickens and he threw rocks at pigs, but none of these are a capital offense in Dunham County! To go to the trouble of snatching him from his house, leaving behind no trace of their passage? And then somehow to interweave his living skin and struggling bones amongst the fibers of the time-worn bridge? Who, how, and why?

As I sat there, wrapped in widening spirals of perplexing thoughts, I grew more and more aware of a faint rustling sound, emanating from across the yard, amongst the lavender bushes.

I sat upright.

It was the same noise I'd heard with Jane in the woods: a hushing breath and a soft swish, like the passage of a rat in the long weeds.

Fear sparked in my chest.

I squashed down my impulse to run. I knew I must not react immediately, but stay calm and still, and train every sense towards it. Some living thing was here, only a few feet away from me, yet I saw no hint of it. The peaceful garden remained as still as a pastoral painting. I saw nothing, and yet …

Four or five paces from my bare feet, a patch of mist swirled as if recently disturbed.

I drew up my naked legs. The sound had come from one far corner of the garden, and the hint of motion from another. My heart thumped in my ears. If this was the snake, then it must possess the ability to move very quickly, to have gone from one side to the other in the blink of an eye.

I searched the grass for many long minutes, finding nothing.

Then, a twitch caught my eye.

The snake lay directly across the path to the door. Its colors were a perfect mimicry of the moonlit lawn. If it had only lain still, I would never have spotted it, but the serpent's thick body slithered across the path, disturbing the mist and the dewy grass.

Good Lord! It was as big as a tree branch, its girth as thick around as my bicep!

I climbed a little higher into the oak to watch the creature move in slow and patient undulations through the plants. The skin was the same color and pattern as the lawn and the leaves. It matched the environment so perfectly that I had to stare hard at its passage, just to keep track of it.

Then, tearing my eyes from it for a second, I glimpsed across the yard and saw a coil of rope by the front door of the house, only a few paces from the stone well in the middle of the yard. An idea occurred: if I grabbed the serpent and wrapped a loop of cord around its neck, I might be able to pull it to the well and shove it down into the inky depths, trapping it. Mary was the fastest runner; she could fetch the regiment, and they could eradicate the monstrosity, and together we'd return Dunham County to its quaint and unremarkable habits.

This plan rang clear in my mind. I focused all my attention on that invisible motion, the slithering wyrm slipping through the trembling grass. I took a deep breath.

I sprang.

Both hands seized up the body, squeezing tightly around it, and I pulled back with all my strength, heels digging into the soft dirt. There was a yowl not unlike the high-pitched cry of a startled cat. The snake thrashed. It jerked at my shoulders. I pulled, teeth gritted, to drag it out of the flowerbed.

Then, under the pressure of my grip, the cool, silky flesh yielded. Instead of recoiling, it whipped itself three times around my arm and jerked me towards it, much stronger than anticipated. I realized in horror that the beast hadn't made sounds of passage on either side of the garden because it was quick.

No, I'd seen it move in two places at once because it was immense, and I'd sadly misjudged its size and shape and identity.

This was no snake.

The color of the skin, which had so perfectly matched the grass, now flickered and changed like the sky at dawn. Shifting veils of blue and turquoise overtook the greens and blacks. The changing hues leaked along the tendril and up to the Huntsman's Oak, twisted around the tree, across the yard, between the stone paths. Tendrils slithered between the flower beds, reaching almost as far as the house. Even if I had Mary's strength to lash a rope around it, this monster would never fit down our well! It had been flattened against the ground, but now it reared up in surprise: the body was as big as a bull, with massive tentacles spreading across the entire front yard and its limbs wrapped around the trunk of the oak. Two eyes flashed open at the base of the low branch, the pupils a warm gold flecked with dark chocolate brown.

Like the devil fish of the Pacific or the octopods of the Mediterranean, this beast was a master of camouflage, able to transform its shape to hide against any background. The seething tentacles moved with remarkable power and dexterity, and my eyes swam as I tried to focus on the ever-changing skin: its limbs had been green as grass, its shoulders had taken the shape of a root boll, its body had been rippled like bark against which it had pressed itself, but with my interjection, all of that changed. Now, at the point where I grasped the tentacle, shimmering tones of blue-grey and silver poured out in waves, the hues of molten lead and candlewax.

It wrapped another tendril around my arms and pressed lines of suction cups to my skin.

And then, flowing from its touch, I felt its soul.

Such all consuming loneliness, such despair, such terrible disgust that eclipsed any meager sorrow that I'd ever before experienced! The beast's loathsome melancholy filled me up like brackish water. I struggled to escape, I fought to breath, but the tentacle only clenched tighter as I felt myself dragged deeper and deeper into its heart.

It released me suddenly and I pitched backwards to the earth, stunned. The amber eyes blinked twice. Seeing that it had winded me, it turned and fled in the direction of our back garden.

Without thought for my own safety, I dashed after it. The creature slipped around the frog pond and over the stone wall, and I heard the moist slap of its tentacles on the rocks, but I lost sight of it in the pastures.

The sea of long grass moved and swayed with its passage but it had once more changed its color to match the landscape, and it plunged headlong towards the driveway of Northwich Hall and, beyond the road, the copse of swaying alder saplings. If it was heading for Dreadmoor Heath, it would pass over the river and through the woods, and once it met the trees, it would winnow into the branches and disappear, and I would lose it completely.

So I ran full tilt after it, nightgown flying. It didn't pause; the devil was as fast as a galloping horse. I knew I couldn't catch it, but I wanted one clear view of it—the gigantic churning knot of tendrils and golden eyes—just to assure myself that I wasn't completely insane.

I saw the wake of grasses part at the roadside, and the dark form roiled over the dusty track, then down the opposite verge. The surface of the river erupted in a series of splashes, then it crawled over the cobbled rocks on the far shore, fully exposed to the night air and the silver moon. My breath caught in my throat.

It looked back at me, of that fact I am most certain. Those round, amber eyes met my own gaze, and for a moment, we stared transfixed, openly appraising each other. Then, reluctantly, the curling, coiling tentacles slithered up the shore and into the trees, and it crawled as smooth as quicksilver up the trunks of the willows, until its skin had turned the same pallid color and it vanished fully.

Maybe it watched me from the safety of the trees. Maybe it fled for the heath. I don't know. I stood in the middle of the wide park land, trembling, flexing my hands open and closed. At the point where I had seized its tentacle, I could still feel the phantom sensations of its colossal despair, as keen and persistent as a paper cut.

I knew, without hesitation, that it had no intention of hurting anyone. Not me, not my sisters, not Earl. It was freakish and repulsive, true, but this creature was not responsible for the death of the baker's son, and I would stake my life that it had never laid one harmless tendril on the poor boy. No, the beast was sad and lonely, but one emotion thrummed even more powerfully than its grief.

It was utterly terrified.

# EIGHT

I bolted inside and ran directly to Papa's study, straight to a singular volume that I had loved as a child. I grabbed it off the shelf and tucked it under my arm. Then I flew upstairs, bare feet thumping on the steps, and rushed into the bedroom, where I seized Jane's shoulders and shook her awake without a scrap of mercy. She groaned and pushed me away.

"I saw it!" I hissed.

Her eyes flashed open, her chin dropped. "The snake?"

I opened the book and set it between us, flipping through pages like a woman possessed. "As big as a horse! Fast, too!"

She tried to shake the sleep from her head, still woozy and dazed. "In the woods?"

"No! In our garden! It raced across the fields towards the heath!"

My hurried explanation had woken Mary. She appeared in the doorway, squinting and disheveled. "You're dreaming, Harry."

"It wasn't a dream!" I insisted. I pushed up my sleeve to show them the circular marks of suction cups, still red against my pale flesh, then I returned to the book, and when I found the page I'd wanted, I turned it to show them. "This! It looked like this!"

The finely-wrought illustration had given me terrors as a child, and the memory of it had sprung to my mind as soon as I'd witnessed the fullness of the wriggling, struggling, thrashing form. This volume had been one of our favorite books as children, a wonderful compendium of monsters and myths, and the lithograph I displayed to Jane and Mary showed a gigantic squid with moon-shaped eyes and a gleaming, ebony beak. The mess of wicked tentacles had wrapped themselves around a huge sailing ship, cracking it in two, dragging it down into the depths.

Jane's face turned ashen.

"Good Lord!" she whispered.

"Just like this!" I said, staring with disbelief at the picture. The body was stout and strong, heavily muscled, with a hint of spots across its broad back. Years ago, Emma had drawn a smattering of screaming stick figures in the surrounding sea; tonight, I felt a curious kinship with them. Very carefully, very cautiously, and fully aware of the magnitude of my statement, I said, "There was a Kraken in our yard."

Jane shook her head. "Impossible! Such a thing does not exist!"

"What we saw—"

"No! We can't possibly have seen a squid in the vale, giant or otherwise!"

Mary examined the lithograph with a serious scowl. "Some scholars postulate that the Kraken may exist in the deepest oceans."

Jane rounded on her with a snarl. "But we're miles from the sea! And a squid doesn't live on land!" she insisted, "I don't even think it could!"

"I don't see why not," said Mary, "The class Cephalopoda aren't quite like a fish in the traditional sense. They don't have gills, they absorb oxygen through their skin. A determined specimen might be capable of enduring short bouts out of water."

"You're not helping!" Jane cried.

"My intention is not to help or hinder," Mary replied in her droll voice, "I'm only providing the facts."

From across the hall, Emma gave a mewl of frustration. "Go to sleep, all of you!"

"Harry saw the monster," Jane replied.

At that small comment, Emma snapped awake and dashed into our room, her hair in a wild tangle. "What?!"

"It isn't the monster! It's no more monstrous than Mary!" This earned me a sour look from my sister. "I only mean, you're large and strong, but kind-hearted, too. And very clever. And handsome."

She dismissed my fawning compliments with a wave of a hand, then asked, "Are you certain it didn't take Earl?"

"Absolutely," I replied.

"But you can't KNOW that, Harry," Jane replied.

I scowled. "I can know that, Jane, in the same way you bent me to your will when you thought it best." I showed her the suction marks once more, and she gasped.

"It grabbed you!"

"I grabbed it first," I admitted, "These are marks of defense, not an attack."

"But, Harry, what if—"

"It could have torn me in half, Jane, but it did not," I replied. "It holds no ill will against us, and the poor thing is as confused by Earl's death as you or me."

But as much as I tried to soothe her fears, the situation had flooded her with emotions that almost crackled in the night air. She was very afraid, not only for me, but for all of us.

A gruff harrumph caught our attention.

My father stood in the hall, dressed in striped nightshirt and tattered night cap. "What's all this?" he said, his face crinkling into a smile, "A meeting of the minds in the middle of the night? In my own home? And I, not invited?"

Emma threw her arms around him and pressed a kiss to his cheek. "Sorry to wake you, Papa."

"Oh, it wasn't you, hedgehog. Your mother woke me up, informed me that we are under attack, and told me to confront the intruders; she, of course, is still a-bed, certain that the sky is falling. Shall I assure her that all is well?" His expression took a impish spark. "Or should we all start screaming at the top of our lungs? That'll whip her into a real free-for-all!"

My sisters all looked to me.

I hesitated. Only a moment ago, I was determined to tell everyone about the creature, yet now, with my father, I faltered. I could still feel its sense of cold desolation, the sweeping agony of forlorn alienation. My heart melted, just a little.

"No, Papa," I said, "I suffered a bad dream, that's all."

He looked disappointed. "Ah, well, then go back to sleep, all of you," he said, straightening his cap. "We're safe in our beds and the window is locked, and I am quite certain that nothing can harm you as long as you four are together."

---

But there was no more sleep for us, not after my encounter, and in the morning, when my sisters and I walked together into Dunham to speak with the captain, we discovered that a soupy fog had rolled in during the night, and the weather had turned cool, moist and uncomfortable.

We detected the noise of a commotion before we even reached the slope down to the river, and as we crested the hill, it sounded as if the entire village of Dunham was in an uproar. Bodies moved through the fog like wraiths. Once across the bridge, we found the streets bustling with people, and as they coalesced out of the murk, we saw stricken faces; Miss Cripplegate looked as though she had been crying, and Mr. Poole held his shoulders up and his hands tight into fists. Soldiers mustered along the streets; they lit torches to push back the gloom. We quickened our pace, and soon spotted Mrs. Runkle outside the post office with her knitting in hand. The old woman looked flustered by the waves of people and horses. We went straight to her.

"What's happened?" Emma asked.

Mrs. Runkle shook her head. A few stray curls of grey hair slipped loose from under her mob cap. "Oh, lambs, it is wicked!" she cried. Her thin voice crackled with fear. "The youngest Darling fellow is gone and no one knows where!"

Emma covered her mouth with her hands to hide her shock. "George Darling!"

"The very one!" Mrs. Runkle said, "Mr. Darling came rushing into town shortly after dawn, looking for his nephew. And now Mr. Chowder has been woken from his bed, and the regiment has been called, and goodness! Has he been taken? Has he gone for a stroll on the heath and been turned about in the weather? Lord only knows, my lambs, but there's no clue of his fate!"

"He's lost on the heath, surely," Jane replied.

"George is strong and sensible," Mary added, "He's in no danger."

"But ... but ... but Mr. Darling said! There's not a single footprint leading away from the house!" Mrs. Runkle continued, voice wobbling, "His shoes are all accounted! And his coat left by the door! And now Frederick Darling has gone a-searching for his brother, and what if he is turned around, too?"

The old woman was frantic with worry, and I could only imagine how concerned Frederick must have been, waking to find his brother vanished. We left the post mistress and hurried to the Darling house to give our condolences, and there we found Mrs. Cassilda Darling, left alone and in a state of panic. She was still dressed in a green silk dressing gown with her hair unbound and unbrushed. I suppose Frederick and his uncle had departed immediately upon finding George missing from his bed, and they had abandoned her in their haste.

"Oh, mercy! Sit down, madam," said Jane. She guided the woman into their parlor to place her on the couch. When she wrapped one caring arm around the woman's shoulders, Mrs. Darling clapped her hands over her face and dissolved into tears.

"Goodness, Mrs. Darling, all will be resolved!" said Emma, "George will return."

But she shook her head, mouthing words but too frantic to speak.

Mary hurried to the kitchen. Eunice had not yet arrived and the kitchen fires were cold. I heard my sister building a fire in the oven, then put water on to boil. "George is a healthy and active fellow. He'll be fine, I'm sure," she said over the rattle of cups and teapot.

"He'll come rambling back through that front door, none the wiser, and laugh at us all for making a fuss," Emma chirped as she sat next to Mrs. Darling. "And then we can play a game of cards and put this all behind us. With time, Mrs. Darling, I'm sure all will be resolved."

"No, it will not," she whispered.

I leaned forward. "I beg your pardon?"

Mrs. Darling wiped her tears from her face with the cuff of her sleeve. "Surely you must see, Harriet, that this is the same as with poor Earl, and he was not returned in one piece." Her eyes were huge, owlish things, staring into the middle-distance like an oracle. "George has not left this place of his own accord. He would not! He's no Frederick; he has not a single adventurous bone in his body."

Mary returned and pressed a cup of tea into the woman's hands. Mrs. Darling drank deeply. I saw that Jane had laid a hand upon her wrist to calm her, and Mrs. Darling was responding in kind, with the color returning to her cheeks and her breathing slow.

"Alright, then," I said, for we would get no further with platitudes and comfort, "Tell us what you found."

"Oh, girls, it was horrible," she said, "The room was locked from the inside. Reginald was forced to take the ax to the door. When he pushed it open, he found the chamber in ruins and the window thrown wide open and our beloved George no where to been seen. He has been abducted! And what are we to do? How can I tell Reginald's sister that we have lost her youngest son? How will I ever look upon her again knowing that I have failed her?" Mrs. Darling began to cry afresh. "Oh, Regina will despise me! We have been tested and found wanting!"

"You're over-reacting," said Mary. "At most, George has only been gone a few hours! Even if he has no sense of adventure, perhaps he went for a walk to the village, and was simply lost in the woods. The fog is growing thicker, and you know how easy it can be to find yourself muddled up in this weather."

Mrs. Darling shook her head. "He would do no such thing! What does it matter, heath or forest or village? George would not venture out in the middle of the night, not once the fire is roaring and the sherry is poured! There's no man less suited to tramping through the wilds! I could imagine Frederick attempting some sort of daring trek by starlight, but not our stable, responsible, bookish, prudish George!" She shook her head again. "No, this has the wicked stench of Earl's disappearance about it. A young man, in the bloom of youth, ripped from the sanctity of his home? A great evil has come to Dunham, girls!"

Mary took my arm and pulled me aside, leaving Jane and Emma to attend to the crying woman. "Does this not seem eerie to you?" she said, "Why should Mrs. Darling be so frantic? Women are in constant peril from the evils of the world, not men."

"The culprit doesn't seem to care a whit for gender."

"Thank goodness the regiment is here," she said, crossing her arms. "We can count on them to protect us."

I scowled in thought. "Can we?" I asked, "If this creature prefers young men as its prey, then the soldiers are in more danger than you or me."

Mary looked down at me. "Has your Kraken whisked him away?"

The sensations of its emotions on my skin percolated through my memory.

"No," I said, "Absolutely not. It had no intention of hurting anyone. I think it prefers to avoid any human contact; it couldn't get away from me fast enough! If something has taken George, then it's a creature we have not yet encountered, and perhaps," I added, more to myself than Mary, "Perhaps we're not its intended target."

Mary thought on this for a moment.

"So," she began, "The groups of young men now searching for George have put themselves in a most terrible and precarious position. It should be you and I looking for him, don't you think?"

I agreed heartily.

Mary and I left Jane and Emma to care for Mrs. Darling, and we circled the house and the pig shed, but found no trace of George's trail from the upper window of his room. I reached between the fence and laid my hand upon the back of a mud-speckled sow, and found the animal to be in a state of distress, but its emotions were easy to decipher: pigs are blunt and sensible, without any of the delicacy or subtlety found in human creatures. The poor thing had been startled in the night and woken from a dead sleep, but it had avoided the yard and cowered in the shed until danger had passed.

We could either descend into the forested vale, or ascend to the heath, and we debated the merits of each route until we decided that the heath made the most sense. If George had been abducted, his kidnapper would most likely wish to take him far from the village, rather than head down into the forest and towards a settlement. Dreadmoor Heath was more secluded, wide and empty, and most likely the place where a foul-minded predator would feel most comfortable.

Mary and I climbed the track, arm-in-arm, up onto the barren, misty wastes. I paused at the edge of the Darling property and looked out across the landscape, the heather and gorse now painted in muted greys and purples, and I spotted the ghostly grey pillars of venerable stones, moss-covered and cockeyed, laid out in circles and spirals by long-lost fairy kin. Every feature was shrouded in so many veils of fog that they became blurred and smeared together; I could see no solid lines in any direction. From far above the cloud bank, the weak, watery sunlight cast a lambent glow across the rubble, but it came in all directions rather than from overhead, so our shadows were transient patches that shifted and danced as the breeze shunted the clouds across the sky.

Mary cupped her hands to her mouth. In her immense voice, she called "George!"

The name only echoed back, faint and forlorn.

"There's no evidence he came this way," she pointed out. "There's not a single track in the soft earth."

It was true, the road leading into the heath was unblemished. The mud was smooth as silk.

"There were no tracks with Earl, either," I said as I tied my brown shawl more tightly around my shoulders. "Let's go out and see what we can find."

Into the nothingness went Mary and I, my shoulder touching her arm. The heavy air beaded into drops on the wool of our shawls and in the curls of our hair. Down in the vale and the river valley, the temperature had felt cool, but up on the heath the breeze grew bitterly cold, and the water clung to our skin and made our muscles shiver. We agreed to only walk an hour along the path before coming straight back, and I was happy with the arrangement: a cup of hot tea would be welcome after such an expedition.

Mary and I spoke very little to each other. The weather was restless, the wind relentless. It cared little for our desire to peer into the distance, and the thick fog prowled in tightly around us like a closing fist. She reached out to take my hand in her own.

"I can't identify anything," she said. Her apprehension grew in paces like a dull ache at the back of my skull. "Those are the fay stones, are they not?" Mary dipped her chin in one direction. The largest of the hulking, lichen-spotted rocks, placed in a circle on the highest point of the heath, loomed to our right.

"I think so."

"Then we've come farther than I thought."

"It's difficult to tell direction and distance," I replied, "George doesn't know the shape of the hills like we do; it would be easy for him to lose his bearings." Then I cupped my hands and yelled out, "George!"

Again, only silence answered.

"It makes no sense," Mary said, "Why would he venture out here alone?"

I crouched down and touched my hand to the ground. It felt still. Then, a little tremor skirted over the dirt, a flash of sensation, though I could not tell which one.

I replied quietly, "He wasn't alone."

"You feel something?"

"I don't know," I replied, bewildered, "Trees hold onto the impression of an animal's passage, but the rocks aren't as efficient. I don't feel much of anything here … and yet …"

There it was again. An imprint of human emotion, but warped, as though I was looking at a face in carnival glass. I furrowed my brow but couldn't translate it.

Frustrated, I stood and clapped the dirt from my fingers. "I don't know, Mary. I can't read it. It's obfuscated."

"Well, the weather is straining to turn stormy," she replied, looking to the sky and the thickening clouds, "We ought to head home or we'll be caught in a squall."

I was about to agree when, behind Mary's shoulder, I saw one of the faerie stones shift in its socket.

I gripped her forearm, spun her around, and pointed towards the rise in the land. "Look!"

She cast about for a hint of what I had seen.

"What is it? I don't—"

Mary had no opportunity to finish her question. The mist turned each boulder greasy and grey, but the top surface of one seemed to rise up like a vulture spreading a pair of drooping wings. I heard the moist suckling of flesh pulled from smooth rock.

She grabbed my hand. "Come on!" she said, pulling me after her in retreat.

We raced along the track in the direction of the Darling house, and I glanced over my shoulder but saw nothing. If it was the same tentacled beast I'd met the night before, it had blended itself perfectly with the landscape. It could be hidden in the mist, or behind the gorse, invisible to my searching eyes. I heard nothing except our breath as we ran full speed along the track, and somehow, the silence made our flight a million times worse.

Then Mary screamed and stopped suddenly. I slammed into her, slid on the slick mud, and down I fell. A sharp ice pick of pain stabbed through the middle of my ankle.

How can I describe the thing in our path? How can mere words and the limitations of a human tongue encapsulate the full horror of its monstrous deformations? Never had I witnessed something so alien and foul, so out-of-place in a familiar environment. Directly before us lurked a behemoth of immense size, stooped over like the body of an old man, but muscular and sinewy, and wholly lacking the fragility of age. The figure was pale grey from the top of its antlers to the bottoms of its two spindly legs, with unruly ropes of bristly black hair surrounding a round moon face painted in an alabaster white. Wreathed in fog, the giant appeared as a dark smudge against a cloudy background, but I could identify enough of its components to know it was not the beast of last night. No, this body was tattered like an immense bundle of buried rags, with mossy edges that hung down around its thighs, the filthy threads waving in the breeze, and when the wind caught the rotted fabric, it billowed and flapped like vast bat wings. In the center of that white circular face, a pair of tiny eyes sat in black hollows and glowed red like pipe embers. The ghastly creature possessed long, spidery fingers that reached out like roots towards us, each one tipped with a bony claw. The black-lipped mouth cracked its face in two, revealing row upon row of glittering glassy needles. Lines of silver spittle hung from its jaws.

The eyes! The eyes were like nothing I'd seen before! Hypnotic, deeply-set, the pupils tiny pinpricks of black swimming in a sea of molten scarlet. They filled me with terror and froze my bones.

The wide mouth peeled opened with a ravenous smile.

And, to my surprise, it began to sing.

In equal measure to the strangeness of its visage, the melody rang out pure and sweet, providing a swell of enchanting notes that floated like moths upon the air. The pain in my ankle melted away. My blood grew honey-warm, and began to radiate waves of pleasure through my cold limbs. Those red eyes held me frozen in place as the song wound its way through my ribs. I sighed, and felt myself falling into the notes like a tired body tumbling into a clean bed.

Mary screamed.

Her voice dashed me out of my stupor. I scrambled back. She looked behind us, towards the fairy stones, and with the spell broken, I wrenched my eyes away from the moon-faced, antlered titan. To our left and behind, the hump of the heath rose up like a tidal wave, then dove forward, and with a slick snap, long tendrils wrapped around the titan's bulky neck, dragging it down like a rip tide. The devil thrashed and fought, bit and scratched, tossed its stag antlers back and forth, as the kraken jerked it, wrestled it, wrangled it to the dirt. As they tussled, locked in combat, Mary picked me up under the shoulders and dragged me after her. I stumbled as pain flared again in my leg, and it wasn't until we were on the track heading down towards the vale that I wrenched my arm from hers.

"I need to go back!" I said, and she looked at me with wide, incredulous eyes.

"Don't be a fool, Harry!" she roared.

But I could still hear the howling and yowling in the fog.

"Go get the regiment," I demanded, then left Mary and returned the way we'd come.

Their clamor drew me like a beacon. Half-dragging my injured leg, I grabbed a stick from the ground and brandished it like a club, and as I waded towards the noise, the two creatures appeared out of the fog, churning the ground into a mire of sludge and broken gorse. I still could not fully comprehend the scene which unfurled before me, so exotic and bizarre it appeared to my mortal eyes: two giant abominations grappled for superiority, as outlandish and terrible as a nightmare, yet they were as real and solid as the club in my hand. The ground quaked with every step, my ears ached with the commotion, and the vanilla scent of crushed gorse filled the air. The antlered figure was quick of foot, but it struggled to extract itself from the kraken's unyielding limbs, which seemed almost countless in number and endlessly nimble. One, two, five, seven—just as the antlers swept down, tentacles would wrap around them and render them useless, like garlands on tree branches or vines in the jungle.

The glassy teeth clacked at empty air. Bits of moss and dirt scattered through the air. Tentacles wrenched the gigantic head down. The devil struggled against the kraken's strength, and at first I thought the kraken would win, but then the tentacles began to flag. In the midst of that marble-white face, the hypnotic eyes grew focused, and I saw the cephalopod falter in exhaustion.

The corpse-white giant recognized an opening. Its opponent tired. One spider hand, not so entangled as the antlers or legs, reached out towards the kraken's bulging eyes, with every intention of ripping them from its unprotected head.

But neither of them had noticed my return, and that was my advantage.

Teeth gritted, I lurched into the fight and swung the stick hard against the devil's jaw. Engrossed in battle, the antlered titan hadn't heard my approach, and the needle teeth clattered and shattered, sending shards of silvery-white in all directions. It collapsed to its knees, stunned and confused. The tentacles withdrew as well, shocked at its foe's sudden collapse. The giant turned its moon-face to me and howled in fury and confusion.

Then it gathered itself up and sprang to the north, limping and clutching at gorse bushes, one skinny hand cradling its chin. It hopped, hobbled, ragged wings a-flutter, leaving no footprints, and vanished into the mist.

An ugly stillness fell over the heath. I stood, huffing and catching my breath, slowly growing more aware of the throbbing ache in my ankle. I'd twisted it when I fell, and I sank to the ground as the pain suddenly blasted up my leg and into my thigh. My breath came out as a sob. I began to cry.

A soft and gentle touch wiped the tear that trickled down my cheek.

One tentacle slipped around my swelling ankle. I dared not look at the eyes; they were too full of intelligence, and I was very afraid of what I'd find if I searched out its feelings. But as I studied its curves and swirling colors, I noticed that it had suffered injuries, too. A deep gash crossed its brow where the skeletal fingers had attempted to find purchase and tear its eyes from its body.

"Oh, you're hurt," I said, my own injury momentarily forgotten.

The kraken brushed aside my hands. It would not allow any pity from me. Instead, it drew its body up from the ground and swept two tentacles around my waist, and clutched me close to its side. I know nothing about sea creatures, it's true, but I always assumed an octopus would feel squishy out-of-water. This beast, however, was not squishy at all: I felt sinewy muscles rippling under the surface of its dewy skin, propelling us forward over the heath in a series of waves. It carried me close in an tight embrace and I pressed my face into its flesh, feeling the rhythm of its movement over the uneven landscape like sailing in a ship, up and down, a gentle undulation that curled and rolled like ocean waves along the shore.

I probed its emotions and found a wellspring of concern. The monster was worried for me. It was afraid of what we'd chased away, but it was grateful, too.

Over Dreadmoor Heath we flew, plunging down into the trees of the valley, through the alder copses and westward along the river shore. The swaying gait lulled me. I thought of Mary, and I worried for her safety, but I knew we'd chased off the antlered fiend in the opposite direction of the Darling house, and with Jane and Emma to help her, she'd be able to make her way back to the regiment and safety.

Upstream from the village, the river valley rose high on both sides into chalk cliffs that forced the waters into churning rapids. The kraken clung to the sides of the canyon, moving ever closer to the Barnacle Mountains, and it pressed me so close to its body that I was almost swallowed up by its torso. Soon the river valley dimpled into a series of limestone caves along the northern shore, and we plunged from the canyon heights to splash across the rapids. I gave a little squeak, surprised by the pressure of its grip, as we squeezed together through a fissure, then slid down a subterranean waterfall. Two tentacles held me close and secure, and a third caressed the back of my head, and all the rest propelled us forward. Our journey took us through dripping caverns far underground, and sometimes we traveled on a clear path, and sometimes we clung to stalactites from the ceiling, but the pace never slowed. On and on in the lightless murk we galloped forward, and I pressed my face against the damp skin, terrified of our destination; I'd never been fond of close spaces, and claustrophobia rose in my chest, stabbing at my heart like a spear. I perceived very little in the dark, but the beast exhibited no hesitation nor fear of falling; clearly, it had no need for sight when a phalanx of perceptive suckers could feel out every inch of the trail.

Then, in the distance, I spied the faint glow of a distant light.

We turned a curve in the tunnel and the cave's limestone floor became tiles of slate, hand-crafted, while the cavern walls became plastered stone. Little alcoves held lanterns, which by their fragrance were burning coal oil, and I could see that we were in a corridor of fine quality and solid construction. This was no natural cave, but a cellar. There were doors and passageways, and thick stone columns along with arched ceilings and wooden benches. I could scarcely believe my eyes as we passed a rack of wine bottles.

"You collect wine?" I said to the monster, incredulous.

But it didn't pause. Instead, it hurried down the corridor, suckers slapping on the smooth tiles. Other hallways opened up, linking little rooms and cells to the main passage. Some of the rooms contained shelves of cheese wheels, others were a place to store coal. It was all very efficient and open to my examination, except for one chamber, which had been sealed shut behind a heavy oak door reinforced with bands of battered iron.

The monster carried me into one chamber and set me gently upon a cot covered with a green wool blanket. I imagined it could've been a monk's cell, it was so neat and sparse and precise, with nothing hanging from the cream-colored walls and no windows to distract from one's meditation. The amber eyes ranged up and down, making sure I was still in one piece, and then, with a little grunt, the creature backed out and disappeared down the corridor, leaving me in the gloom of the corridor lamps.

My ankle had swollen to the size of an apple. It throbbed and pulsed. I laid down upon the cot, marveling at my present situation, and after a half-an-hour, I became aware of a distant voice approaching down the corridor. Soon enough, I recognized it.

"I am very sorry, Miss Lovecraft," said Mr. Blackwood as he appeared in the door of the cell, "I never thought he'd fetch you and bring you home."

I saw a tentacle lying along the corridor, with the bulk of the creature out of sight behind the door frame.

"He's a he, is he?" I said.

"Pretty girls are his weakness," Mr. Blackwood sneered. "Or, in the present case, a serviceable one. Your sister Jane is far prettier, to be honest."

"She was not involved in the fray and did not require rescuing," I replied tartly.

"Either way," said Mr. Blackwood, kicking viciously at the tentacle on the floor, "He should not have brought you here, to the cellars of Northwich." With one fierce stomp, Mr. Blackwood's boot came down on the tentacle. It recoiled in agony.

I gasped in horror at such cruelty. "How dare you!" I snapped.

Mr. Blackwood curled his lip. "He's loathsome and impulsive, Miss Lovecraft. You must agree, something so revolting does not deserve any kindness."

"I do not agree in the slightest!" I said. "He's been chivalrous! He saved me from a terrible fate!"

The peevish, horse-faced man turned to the bulk of the beast, still out of my line of sight. "Is that true? Did you find it?" He shook his head in wonder. "Well, well. The day is not a complete travesty, after all." Then, noticing my raised foot and misinterpreting it as comfort, he said, "You must go home immediately. I have no use for you here."

One tentacle reappeared and tugged at the bottom of Mr. Blackwood's grey trousers.

"Absolutely not! She can not stay!" he spat at the monster, "I do not want her in our home."

"My ankle is swollen," I replied evenly, "I don't know how far I can walk."

Mr. Blackwood looked as if he'd swallowed a bitter bolus of earwax. "Oh, for the love of all things holy …" He strode away and back, his heels clicking on the tiles. I heard the slap of a hand against flesh, and I could only assume that he'd struck the poor thing for its kindness. When he reappeared, he said, "You will stay in this chamber. Do not go wandering around the cellar, understood? I'll fetch a length of cotton to bind your leg, and then I'll hire a horse from the village to carry you." To the beast, he said, "Make sure she doesn't go poking around. If she finds herself in further trouble, I place all the blame on you."

He turned to go, but I was too full of questions to be silenced.

"What was it that attacked your friend?" I asked after him. "Is that the creature that took Earl, and now has taken George? Where has it come from?"

My comments dragged him back to the door.

"There's another imbecile gone?"

"Yes," I replied.

The hermit and the octopus exchanged a dark glance.

"Not good. It's hungrier than I thought," said Mr. Blackwood.

"Hungry? What's hungry?" I pressed.

But he strode away, and I heard him growl in reply, "This is none of your concern, you meddlesome old bat."

# NINE

I wept a little then, more from the mix of discomfort and adrenaline than from any real sorrow, but I was afraid that Mr. Blackwood might not return as promised, and leave to me to rot in the cellars of Northwich Hall. He was such a disagreeable man! Prideful, pompous, wicked to the marrow of his bones! There was not an ounce of charity in his wizened heart.

The cephalopod, on the other hand, lingered outside the door like a beaten dog, afraid of incurring its master's wrath upon Blackwood's return. I felt horrible for it. I imagine it spent its days alone in this dark, damp basement, tucked out of sight like a prisoner in an oubliette. One tentacle had curled itself around the door frame, as if it did not wish to be ogled or struck, yet still craved the warmth of human kindness.

Eventually, I pulled myself together and, sniffling, I dried my face upon the edge of my shawl.

"Shouldn't you be near the sea?" I asked the tentacle.

The tip, which had been flickering like the tail of a cat, ceased to move. One great yellow eye peered around the doorway.

I sat up on the bed and swallowed my sorrow, tried to steel my voice so that I wouldn't sound weak or vulnerable. "I only thought that something like yourself would be more comfortable in the wide expanse of the ocean, not trapped underground like a rat. This can't be your natural environment. No loving God would create an animal like you to live in a cave."

The body slipped into the room, shy but curious. Now that I had a clear view of it, I saw that it was not quite like the kraken: one might mistake it to be an octopus the size of a mule, but its athletic legs had the ability to be strong and stout. It was capable of holding itself up in a terrestrial environment and it needed no water to support its weight. The skin changed hue from dappled orange to rich purple, with the nearest tentacles deepening into an indigo blue. There may have been a beak underneath the mess of constantly-shifting tendrils, but I couldn't see it.

"And I suppose, I can infer from Blackwood's discussion with you, that you were looking for whatever has stolen away Earl and George. And that you are of equal intelligence to Blackwood, and perhaps even a greater intelligence, for while he may show disgust to you, he doesn't talk down to you as one might to a pet." I toyed with the swollen bulge of my ankle. "He is a terrible person, I think. Very proud."

The beast poured itself over the floor to pool at my feet and wrap its tentacles around my leg, and it poked and prodded as if wishing to know the full extent of my injury.

"I'll be fine, I only twisted it when I fell. I don't think it's sprained."

The suction cups made little kisses along my calf.

"Well, that's not very proper," I scolded it, but with a smile to soften my disapproval, "I don't even know your name."

I placed my hand over the space between its eyes, examining the gash as I probed its aura for a hint of its intentions. It—he, I suppose, Blackwood had given it a pronoun—he leaned into my palm. He was terribly lonely. His despair was like a gulf of black ink, seeping around the edges of his emotions, polluting every impulse with depression. He'd been alone and cut off from his own kind for a very long time.

"You have no way of communicating with Blackwood, do you," I said. "And he's the only other living creature you see."

The great beast flattened himself and oozed under the cot with one tentacle curling itself around my leg and another around my wrist, a comforting gesture that I found amiable and caring. He would not abandon me to the forgotten corners of Northwich's basement. He would stay and ensure my comfort, even if he could not vocalize his intentions.

"Thank you for your kindness," I said.

The tentacle radiated a spark of happiness that cut through his loneliness like the light of a candle.

"Well," I said, reclining on the cot, "If it's conversation you crave, then you must come and visit me every night in my garden. The invitation is formal, sir, and I will accept no excuse."

The spark blossomed into an electric sensation of happy surprise. The color of his skin shifted from oranges and blues to a brilliant joyful yellow, and the sudden change made me laugh, in spite of the circumstances.

When Blackwood returned, holding up a lantern in one hand and a strip of cotton cloth in the other, I'd been dozing in comfort, and wondering at the nature of his strange relationship with the cephalopod under my bed. But Blackwood answered none of my questions. He waited in silence as I wrapped my ankle tightly, his mouth clamped closed. When I was done, he held out his arm and helped me to my feet, and said, "I've hired you a horse. I expect your father to reimburse the expense."

I turned to the amber eyes peeking from under the cot.

"Thank you for your help," I said.

One tentacle slipped out and a sucker kissed the back of my hand.

Blackwood gave a disgusted groan at this show of gentlemanly behavior.

With difficulty, I hobbled up the circular stone stairs to the main floor of the mansion, then through the maze of halls and rooms to the front entrance. The horse was a dappled nag, all knobby knees and scruffy hide. I'd been thoroughly turned about in the lightless cellars, and I was pleasantly surprised to see that it was not night, as I'd assumed. Instead, the mists of morning had transformed into a clement afternoon, and the late-hour sun painted the yard in gold and orange. I'd been in the basement of Northwich Hall for most of the day. I climbed astride the old horse, as graceful as a sack of oats, and Blackwood gave a slap across its rump to send it away, with no word of goodbye to me. The horse plodded across the pastures towards home, tearing mouthfuls of grass.

My mother was a-flutter with concern, my sisters full of questions, and Jane the worst of them. She had worked herself into a dreadful anxiety, and when she saw me, she threw her arms around me and pressed a kiss to my cheek. "I was certain you were dead!"

"Oh, Jane, did I not assure you? Our Harry is the resourceful one," said Papa over his newspaper, sitting by the fire. "Only a bit turned about in the fog. How lucky for you to have stumbled across Mr. Blackwood!"

"He is your savior, my duckling!" said Mama, "We must send him a gift. What would he like? I shall make him cake. Do you think that will be sufficient?"

My father shook his papers straight and folded them closed. "That depends on the quality of your cake, my dear," he said, "But I'd suggest you ask Beatrice to do the baking, if we do not want to turn the gentleman against us." Then, to me, he said, "Glad you're back, Harry. I shall return the horse to town and inform the Darlings that you're unharmed."

"And Mr. Blackwood has asked for the recompense of the horse," I said, gesturing to the window, where I'd left the nag tied at the fence post. It seemed happy to stand with head slung low, eating the lawn.

Jane helped me upstairs, fussing like an old woman to tuck me into bed with my foot raised on a pillow, and a cup of piping hot tea procured, and a scone with a pat of butter to munch upon. When I was perfectly comfortable, she sat at my bedside and said, "Tell me everything that happened to you!"

So I did, omitting no detail, and when I was done, I bid her to do the same.

"Mary ran headlong to the Darling cottage," she said in a rush, "And we flew outside to find the whole heath alive with the screams and howls of the fight, and we were so terrified, Harry, that we could barely think of anything except to flee, and Mary feels the worst of us, and is very sorry, for she blames herself for abandoning you fully, but none of us were brave enough to come find you!" Jane took a restorative breath. "We ran immediately to town to fetch the regiment, but by the time we returned with as many soldiers as they could spare—which was very few, I must say, it was quite a disappointment—there was nothing to be discovered except ruts in the torn earth, in all directions! You—and the titans between which you had inserted yourself, you foolish goose—had vanished completely!" She clenched my hands tightly, which caused a spray of crumbs to erupt from the scone. "And we suspected you'd been carried off and eaten up! And when we told the captain, he said we had seen nothing more than shapes in the fog, and had we not caused enough trouble with our silly little snake stories?" Her face flushed red with frustration. "The captain said there was an upstanding young man in need of finding, and the regiment had no time for wayward ladies chasing after lizards, and we insisted that you were in grave danger, yet no one believed us!"

Emma and Mary appeared in the door.

"A few of the soldiers took pity on us in our distress, but what could they do?" said my youngest sister, "They had orders to follow, and their numbers were already stretched thin searching for George, and their nerves frayed with the strange circumstances of Earl's demise."

"I should not have left you," said Mary meekly. "I'm a terrible sister."

"All is forgiven," I said firmly.

"Let me at least tend to your ankle," Emma said, and she seated herself at my feet. I consented to let her unwrap the bandage, and Emma ran her fingers over the swollen joint. A pleasant warmth radiated out from her touch, and the pain eased, just a fraction.

"Has George been found?"

"No," said Mary to me. "Not a single hint of where he's gone."

"But a third is missing now, too," said Emma. "This afternoon, when the search parties returned from looking for George, Teddy Crumpsall was not among them."

"Teddy!"

Mary nodded. "No one saw him disappear. One second, he was with the company, and then he was not!"

As her hands continued to massage my injury, Emma said, "Papa has told us we're not to worry, it will turn out as it should in the end—you know how he can be, so frightfully philosophical—but Mama is in absolute fits at the thought of Dunham's most eligible bachelors, disappearing one by one!"

Mary crossed her arms and scowled. "At this rate, we'll be forced into spinsterhood for lack of options." She glanced at me. "No offense, Harry, but it's not my intention to grow old in Lovecraft Cottage, tending to Mama and Papa in their golden years."

Nor had it been my intention. However, I'd long since reconciled myself to my fate, and I waved her comment away.

But Emma seemed particularly horrified by this revelation. "Oh, sweet mercy! We must find George and Teddy!"

"But where should the soldiers look for them?" Jane prompted, "Earl was only discovered because part of his foot stuck from the solid wood of the bridge. What if George and Teddy are fully encased in a rock wall or a giant wych elm? They might never be found."

I leaned back in my pillows. "Mr. Blackwood made a curious comment: he stated that something is hungry," I told them, "And I am quite sure he meant the second creature on the heath." I suppressed a shudder at the memory of those fiery eyes, the frayed and desiccated body, the mossy rot of its ragged clothes, the gleaming crystalline teeth. "I can not hope to understand what I witnessed on Dreadmoor, but if that monstrosity is abducting the young men with the intention of consuming them, there may be very little left for us to find."

We four sat a moment in quiet contemplation.

"How can any of this be possible?" Mary wondered, more to herself than to us.

I crossed my arms. "The rules of nature have abandoned Dunham County of late," I said. "Between the outlandish creatures on the heath and the impossible manner of Earl's death, I don't know how much we can rely on common sense. The answer to our problem lies far outside the boundaries of our rational thinking. We do not even know the words to ask the question, and thus, we can't even start to understand the answer."

"And that's the dickens of it!" Emma replied, "Captain Crankshaw clings to rational thought. Mary tried in vain to describe what she saw, yet he insists there is no such thing as ghouls, and this is nothing more than the work of a rabid wolf!"

"D——arrogance!" I said, causing them all to startle, "That the man could think Mary to be mistaken! That gruesome demon looked nothing like a wolf!"

"No matter what evidence is presented, he refuses to see anything more than a sick animal," she continued, looking very much like she could burst into tears at any moment, "He would not listen to our side of the tale, and said we are all hysterical, and imagining things that are not there."

Jane reached out and grasped my wrist. Her fear and frustration sizzled across my skin and skittered up through my veins.

I gritted my teeth. "We're at war, without the assistance of our friends, and we do not even know the identity or motive of our enemy," I replied.

"What do we do?" Emma said.

"Well, we can't just sit here, can we," I snarled as I struggled to sit.

"You're in no position to go anywhere," Jane scolded, "Emma's done her best, but at least give your ankle a few hours' rest."

"The swelling has already gone down a little—"

But Jane would have none of my bravado. Instead, she brought me a book from Papa's library to read, a great tome on the heroes and gods of old, and told me to remain in bed with my foot raised. She and Emma and Mary would scout the valley and return with information. They would take Mr. Marsh of the regiment with them, for security. I was to stay firmly put.

I read about the kraken, the leviathan, the behemoth. I searched for a hint of the antlered creature, but found nothing to match its appearance. There were stories of the men of Keltica, who wore stag's heads to terrify their opponents, but that didn't match what I'd seen on the foggy heath. No, it had been all rags and bones and skeletal limbs, with fingers like claws and jaws like an angler-fish. I read about the Yellow Emperor of ancient Carcossa, who kept a kennel of dog-beasts in the yard of his castle—great leprous things with matted fur and fangs sheathed in bronze, trained to devour the heads of trespassers—and I read about the ferocious Amarok, who prowled the barren ice fields of the high Arctic, feasting on the souls of greedy hunters. I read of the Waheela of Upper America, and the dog-pigs of Namibia, and the Gbahali of the humid Liberian jungles, more alligator than canine. I read all of these things, yet none of them seemed to fit the beast which I had confronted.

At last, exhausted, I put the book aside. Why would such a creature prey upon the good people of Dunham? What had we done to suffer such an infestation?

It had started with the Poseys, I was certain, and the nucleus of the problem was Northwich Hall. What foul curse had Mr. Blackwood awoken? I curled upon my bed and soon found myself asleep, dreaming of blood-thirsty stags and emotionless, alabaster faces holding haunted, molten eyes.

I woke that night, long after everyone else had gone to bed, and I limped from my room to the kitchen. I'd slept early and fitfully, and that had left me wide awake at the midnight hour.

After replacing the book in Papa's library, I found myself drifting to the garden, although I was not so eager to go as far as the Huntsman's Oak and sit in its branches. There was a small bench by the back door, and I sat there, looking out over our little frog pond. The moon reflected in its waters like a disc of silver dancing on a plate of jet. Past the pond lay the hedge and the stone wall, beyond which stretched fields of green wheat all the way to the Dunham village, which from this great distance looked like a tiny cluster of hunched jurors, deliberating together, in the distant wrinkle of the river valley. Despair began to creep into my thoughts. Poor little Dunham! What terrible beast was stalking the paths around its edges, stealing its citizens one-by-one?

What had all three victims had in common? I could not figure a common thread. They were of differing ages and occupations, taken at different times. What had linked them together, and sealed their fates?

All of them, male. That's a start.

And all of them, in the county of Dunham.

And all of them ... well, was there another trait?

Earl Rabbit, and George Darling, and Teddy Crumpsall. Earl had been the son of the baker, George is an accountant-in-training, and Teddy is the son of the butcher. All three of them, accomplished in their own ways. None of them, poor or destitute. They were young men who had great prospects laid before them, and all in the most robust of health, and vigorous with the competition of bachelorhood.

Could that be the key?

I slowly grew aware of eyes upon me. I smiled and looked up with the intention of greeting my monster, to whom I had given a formal invitation and for whom stealth was second nature.

"Are you there?" I said, "Come and sit with me. There's no need to be shy."

The surface of the frog pond shivered. Two amber eyes popped up from the center, looking back and forth to make sure the yard was empty.

"I'm alone," I said. "They're all asleep."

Water sloshed, waves lapped at the stone edge, and the kraken hauled himself from the black water and dragged himself to the bench, where he curled around the flower pots. One cool, wet tentacle wound itself around my hand, and I was suddenly flooded with the sensations of gratitude and friendliness.

"I'm happy to see you, too!" I assured him, "How long have you been in the frog pond?"

There came an assurance that all waiting was worthwhile; when one lives alone in a dark cellar with no distractions or entertainments, one becomes adept at patience.

"How beastly," I whispered, "Blackwood should not keep you locked up in such a manner."

I was mistaken.

"You're not a prisoner?"

Assuredly not. There was no sense of liberty lost, only of careful consideration.

"Oh," I said as I sorted through the web of feelings, "You are able to come and go as you wish, but you dare not be seen, and that restricts you."

Affirmation. The tentacle slithered a little higher up my arm, and a second embraced my bare leg, leaving little kisses behind my knee. Through this secondary tendril, I felt elation and wonder at my willingness to accept his eldritch appearance.

I smiled kindly. "I don't have many friends," I replied, "Like you, I tend to avoid human contact. Forgive me, I wouldn't presume to place my own loneliness in competition with yours, but I've lived a life apart from others because this sensitivity of mine makes relationships very difficult. I'm happy to make your acquaintance, sir, because you are the first creature I've met who is honest with his feelings, and does not try to hide sadness or forlornness or frustration behind a mask of insincere levity or a litany of empty words."

A pop of surprise, a warmth of shared understanding, followed quickly by a sense of common purpose.

"Yes, I suppose we are very much alike," I replied. "Though I am not nearly as pretty as you, what with your various colors! Goodness! Some of them are so exotic, I don't think they even have a name!" I ran my hand over one tentacle, and from the touch of my fingers spread a flush of green-blues and apricots, speckled like leopard spots. "How will I ever describe you to my sisters?"

He gave a surge of bashfulness at being described as pretty.

"You've been alone too long with no one to pay you compliments," I said, "That must not be left to stand. I think you've shown yourself to be brave and honorable, and those are very attractive traits, and do much to redeem any faults."

Four or five tentacles wobbled in the air.

"No, I hardly think those are faults at all," I assured him. "I'm sure you can do all sorts of marvelous feats!"

He wrapped one into a clever knot, and a burst of humor sparkled across his skin and made me laugh.

For a few minutes we sat in mutual comfort, trading emotions back and forth in a silent conversation. He was of such a good character, full of optimism and openness, that I found my own nature rising to meet him, and all of the dark futility I'd previously harbored at our village's present situation seemed to drip away. His positivity was infectious. We would find the antlered demon, he was certain of it.

I bent close to him and stroked my palm across his multitude of pale suckers. "How can you be so sure?"

One tentacle caressed the side of my neck. Through its light touch, I felt an iron-clad determination. This was his quest. He would not rest until he'd found the devil and destroyed it.

Unbidden, I felt dread for him. Under any other circumstance, I would have kept my foolish heart to myself, fearful that my concerns would be misconstrued as meddlesome if I exposed my opinions so baldly. If our conversation had been comprised of words alone, I would have pushed down my concerns and hid my doubts, for we'd only just met, and who am I, to put such weight on a new acquaintance?

But the tactile nature of our conversation gave no ability to lie, and there was no hiding how I felt. Before I could temper my concerns, he knew that I was worried for him.

"Be careful," I said regardless, "I want more time to get to know you. I'd be terribly disappointed if you were lost, because I've only just found you."

Such a flood of affection crossed his skin, I blushed to feel it. He'd been lonely for so long and in the company of such a churlish gentleman, he hardly knew what to do with my declaration; one sucker set itself upon my cheek and provided me with a kiss of remarkable passion and zeal.

"It's been a very long time since I've enjoyed such attention," I replied, somewhat breathless at the tingle which his kiss left upon my face, and I curled against him, caring not at all for the dampness of the ground or the beads of pond water that had collected between his tentacles. We sat together in joyful silence until the moon fell below the western horizon, and our wordless conversation was so full of warmth and devotion, it chased away the chill of the spring night. At long last, a hint of light in the east meant we needed to say farewell, and as I watched him go, I found myself already eager to see him again.

# TEN

In the morning, just past ten, Mr. Marsh rode to our door.

We were in the garden: Mary and Jane were weeding, Emma tended the beehive, and I sat on the bench by the door, knitting and reflecting on last night's visitor, but I was torn from my introspection by the thunder of hooves. The black stallion galloping up the Mill Road in a flurry of dust made a most thrilling sight, and when I recognized who had spurred it on in such haste? I wasn't surprised.

Emma set down her tools and hurried to the edge of the garden, casting back the veil of her bonnet. "Hello!" she greeted merrily.

Mr. Marsh dismounted with a spring in his step, although he seemed timid, too, and a bit tongue-tied in Emma's presence.

"Good ... good morning ... hello," he stammered, fidgeting with his fingers. He was a tall, slim man with a comely face, and his hesitation only added a charming naivety to an otherwise confident bearing.

The expression was not lost on us. Jane and I traded knowing glances.

"I've come with an invitation," he said, and he withdrew an envelope from his pocket. "The boy in the post office has a great deal to deliver, and I was asked to help."

Asked to help, or volunteered? I thought with a wry smile. Lovecraft Cottage was no small distance from the town, and only the Cripplegates lived nearby.

By this time, Papa had noticed the commotion in the yard from the window of his study, and he and Mama hurried to the front door, looking fretful. Given the nature of recent news, they could be forgiven for jumping to dire conclusions.

"There's no emergency, sir, madam," Mr. Marsh assured, seeing their concern. "Only a harmless delivery."

"Well, that is good news," said my father, who sat beside me on the bench.

"I was worried we'd lost another young fellow. Have there been any leads, sir? Any information that's come to light?"

Mr. Marsh shook his head sadly. "I'm afraid not."

By this time, Emma had opened the letter, and she gave a little laugh before passing it to the rest of us, so that we might read it with our own eyes. I could scarcely believe it at first, the content seemed so ridiculous in light of recent events, but I suppose life must go on, and even in times of despair, one must endeavor to enjoy the fruits which our existence provides us. It does no good to be sad at all times; one must break up the darkness with points of light, so that we might remember the joy of hope. Even the blackest night contains a multitude of stars.

"A dance!" said Jane as she slapped the dirt from her fingers. She took the invitation from Mary and looked it over herself. "Can he be serious?"

"I think it will be lovely," Emma replied, "A happy excuse for us all to gather together and meet the newcomer," and then, almost as an afterthought, and aimed in Mr. Marsh's direction, she said, "And for us to introduce ourselves to the regiment, too, and show them how grateful we are for their assistance in these troubled times!"

Mr. Marsh's cheeks turned almost the same scarlet hue as his coat.

"In point of composition, the letter is in no way defective, but Mr. Blackwood has shown no inclination to sociability before now," said Mary. "It's very out of character."

Mama tut-tutted. "We hardly know the gentleman. Maybe this is how they do things in the West. Mercy, there must be very little to do in that godforsaken wilderness; perhaps they take whatever frivolity they can, regardless of the situation."

"If I was surrounded by wolves and bears at all times, I would find it hard to enjoy myself," said Emma.

"You see? Mr. Blackwood is of a differing constitution," Mama agreed, "We must attend and enjoy his hospitality, if only to show that we are not cowering in our houses like scared mice. No, I think this is a fine turn of events. A good opportunity to show off my girls to the young men, and see if we might secure a husband for Jane, at the very least."

Mary and I traded looks, and she rolled her eyes, but our mother was too preoccupied to notice.

"You shall all wear your finest, of course," Mama continued as Papa and Mr. Marsh fell to easy conversation between them, and we girls were shepherded inside to make arrangements, "And Jane, perhaps you should wear your hair down and in curls? It is the most alluring gold, very fetching, and I'm sure Frederick Darling will be in attendance, and in need of a distraction from his worries."

"Oh, Mama, I'm sure he won't be thinking of procuring a wife at a time like this," she said as we moved into the kitchen.

But Mama was unmoved; once set in motion, my mother's scheming could not be stopped. She was a juggernaut of matchmaking. "Emma, I insist that you wear that mauve dress from last season, the one with the low neck. I've heard on good authority that puffed sleeves are the fashion in town, and I have a length of mauve left over from its constructions, and with only a few alterations, we should be able to add some puffed sleeves to that particular gown. Mr. Blackwood will not have seen it, and in all ways, it flatters your coloring and figure."

"You can't think to match Emma with Blackwood," I snorted.

"Of course I am, Harry! Be sensible! A good fortune cries out for Emma's creative influence," she scoffed, "And can you imagine it? Crossing the lawns of Northwich Hall to visit your little sister, when she is married and becomes the lady of the mansion! How lovely!" She pinched Emma's cheek. "A dream come true!"

"Not my dream, surely!" Emma replied, but her protests only rose a titter from Mama.

"Of course it is," she insisted, "Imagine, my duckling, how many silver plates he must own, and all of them, waiting for you to blacken!" She pinched Emma's cheek again with such ferocity that it raised a scarlet mark, and seemed more like a threat than an observation.

"You're ahead of yourself, Mama," Jane reminded. After all, Jane was still of marriageable age, and if anyone was going to snag a wealthy landowner, it ought to be her.

Personally, I thought the idea of a marriage to Blackwood, no matter how wealthy, was a disgusting and stomach-churning proposition. The man was too arrogant, too irritable, too nasty. How could anyone love a man that would slap an octopus? I said as such, and my mother looked at me as if I had gone loony.

"I'm not familiar with that turn of phrase, Harriet. Is it French?" Then, already onto her next scheme, she waved it away. "But no matter. You will join us, too, I suppose, and do as best you can under the circumstances. Your ankle may not allow for dancing, but it won't keep your tongue from conversation, and perhaps there will be a game of quadrille. I'm terribly disappointed that you missed your window of opportunity, but you still have a fine intellect and your little library to keep you busy. Perhaps a career as a caregiver for your beloved parents will fulfill you in ways that a blessed marriage could not." She clapped her hands. "Alright, girls! Off you go! Upstairs to assemble your outfits. The dance will not be until tomorrow, so there's plenty of time to hem skirts, fix bonnets, and make yourself presentable!"

We retired to our rooms, if only to escape Mama's excitable character. Emma seemed most embarrassed by the suggestion of a match with Blackwood. "He's the last person I would dance with, Harry," she said to me, as if I should care. "I promise, there's nothing about him that I find appealing in the least." She looked out the window to the garden, where Papa and Mr. Marsh were discussing something dreadfully important, waving their hands in the direction of the village. Emma's face took a soft cast. "There are other people to whom I'd like to be better acquainted."

"Mr. Marsh? That twig of a soldier?" scoffed Mary, "I could break him in half!"

"You keep your hands off him!" Emma said. "I will dance with Mr. Marsh, and Harry can dance with Mr. Blackwood, and we'll all be contented."

"Dance with whomever you wish," I encouraged, then aghast, added, "Wait ... me? Dance with Blackwood? You don't think I have some sort of interest in him, do you?"

"Of course you must," said Jane, "You're the only one among us who has spent time with him. You know him better than anyone else in the village."

I gagged. "No, no, a thousand times, no!" I said. "If I have, in any way, given the impression that I am interested in pursuing a courtship with Mr. Blackwood—"

"He has treated you kindly," Mary replied.

"That is not true in the least!" I said, "He has been short-tempered, haughty, boorish—"

"He did hire a horse to carry you home," Jane pointed out.

"And he asked for reimbursement for the gesture," I replied. "He did not hire a horse out of any kindness to me, Jane, but to get me out of his house at the earliest possible convenience!"

"You're prejudiced against him because he is proud," Jane said.

"No," I corrected, "I am prejudiced against him because he is an ass."

"I think Mr. Blackwood may have his sights set on you, Harry," said Mary, "Even if you are too blind to see what blossoms between you."

"Nothing blossoms!" I insisted.

Mary shook her head. "He wrote you a letter of thanks, did he not? He has, in his own curmudgeonly way, shown his affection for you."

I stopped short, brow furrowed.

"The basket of food? You mean, that letter of thanks?" As my sisters turned to me, I said, "I have my doubts that Blackwood wrote it."

"You do?"

I turned to Jane. "He knew nothing of the basket when I brought it up, and he tried to cover with stumbling appreciation, but ... let us see."

I limped down the stairs with all three sisters in a parade behind me, into the kitchen where Mama had left the dance invitation on the table. I snatched it up and headed back to the second floor, where I had squirrelled the thank you note away in my personal stationary. I sat upon my bed and laid them side-by-side, and it became instantly apparent that they had been written by two different hands. The invitation was all elegant loops and swooping flourishes; the thank you was finely-wrought, but straightforward and conservative, as if the act of penmanship took great concentration.

"Mr. Blackwood wrote one, but not the other," I proclaimed.

"So who wrote this?"

I looked at Jane. "Do you think an octopus could write?"

Mary laughed—not a faint chuckle, or a polite giggle, but that big booming laugh that comes after drinking too much cordial. "You think your kraken wrote it?"

"Maybe," I said. "If so, he has remarkable penmanship for a squid." After a moment's consideration, I added, "I suppose the use of ink is not wholly unfamiliar to his kind."

"What about the golem in the hall?"

I turned to Emma. "What if they're one and the same? What if I did not see a man, but a master of mimicry?" I took the thank you note in one hand, caressed the soft texture of the cotton paper. "We already know the monster can hide himself as almost anything, and take the color or shape of any background he wishes. What if he attempted to take a human form, if only to say hello?" I flipped the letter over, trying to pull an impression from its surface, but too much time had passed and the paper felt inert in my fingers. "The poor thing is consumed with a powerful loneliness and despair. I can only imagine that he was eager to meet us, when Blackwood wanted only to push us away."

"And yet, Blackwood has consented to open his house to everyone and host a ball for the entire village," Mary replied, "Like I said before, this is a very strange change in his character."

"What is he up to, I wonder," I said, more to myself than the other three.

·· —o-o-o— ··

The evening of the dance came fine and warm, with a blushing breeze from the south that carried the portents of summer. Mama and Papa hired a carriage, and we drove the short distance between our cottage and the sprawling grounds of Northwich Hall, more circuitous than a walk across the fields but certainly more in keeping with the quality of our costume. Despite Emma's care, my poor ankle was still swollen, and I'd squashed it uncomfortably into a boot; I certainly wouldn't have survived a trek across the park. My inability to walk easy was not the sole reason, though: Emma had adorned her bonnet with a riot of feathers and ferns, and such an installation would have crumbled to pieces by the time we reached the trout pond. Papa had considered a wagon for my comfort, but Mama insisted on a carriage to save Emma's hat.

As it were, the driver drew up before the main doors and revealed a Northwich Hall which none of us had ever before seen, and I'd wager, could never have fully imagined. These were no longer dark, dreary ruins: every casement was ablaze with lights. Happy faces could be spotted through the tall windows of the ballroom, and each one appeared breathless with the splendor of Mr. Blackwood's exceptional home. The sound of merry, sprightly music filled the air. Papa helped us all down from the cab, and with my arm hooked over Jane's, we mounted the same steps from which, not so long ago, we'd fled in terror.

"Goodness!" Jane whispered. Her changeable moods of eager delight and shy apprehension skittered over her skin like water beetles.

"He must have hired a small army of staff," I said as we reached the doors. They swung open to reveal a butler in a pressed suit, a portly, middle-aged man with a neatly-trimmed black moustache and very respectable manners.

"Good evening," he said, holding the door wide and stepping back to announce our arrival. "Welcome, Mr. Henry Lovecraft and family."

In we limped, Jane and I cleaved together, our eyes sweeping over the room with rapt delight. The main foyer glittered under the gilded chandelier, ablaze with a hundred candles. In the ballroom, the portrait of the young man looked down upon dancers and musicians, and a line of electric lights flickered, and the crystals dangling from the chandelier flashed like diamonds, and all was a-swirl with gaiety and color. The fullness of sensations left us in a trance. The dust covers had been removed from the chairs, the gauzy curtains had been thrown back, and the windows opened. A quartet played a buoyant tune, and lines of couples swirled around the center of the floor, creating a sea of familiar faces. There was Miss Poole dancing with Jerold Chowder, and one of the Winterbottom twins dancing with Miss Charlotte Cripplegate. To my delight, I saw Mrs. and Mr. Tippler dancing, too, with the old tin smith kicking out his heels and his wife's face turning ruddy as she gasped for air.

I could scarcely believe it when Mr. Blackwood appeared from the side of the room, his arms outstretched to my father, as if they had been long-time friends.

"Good to see you, Mr. Lovecraft! Welcome, welcome!"

Who was this obliging gentleman that shook my father's hand and kissed the back of my mother's fingers? Certainly, he looked the same as the Blackwood I knew, identical in goggle eyes and horsey chin, but his demeanor was antipodal to all that I had come to expect of him! No persnickety frown, no cantankerous grumbling! He was the model of the perfect host, asking questions of my parents and laughing—good lord, laughing!?—at my mother's jokes.

"Oh, and your girls," he said, aiming his conviviality in our direction. "Miss Mary, you look stunning this evening, and Miss Jane, the rumors are true, you are an angel. And can this be Miss Emma? Goodness, you could have been plucked from any of the finest gatherings in London. Your bonnet is the very pinnacle of artistry." Then, he stopped before me. The facade cracked, just for an instant, as he said, "Hello, Harry."

"Good evening, Mr. Blackwood," I replied. "Hosting such a lavish party is very generous of you."

"We all need our spirits lifted," he said, and his unnaturally chirpy smile returned. "You're looking in fine fettle this evening. Your ankle is giving you no trouble, I hope?"

"I won't be dancing, but I'll be content to sit on a couch and watch the rest of you have fun," I said, "Truly, it warms my heart to see Northwich Hall so full of life. The poor thing has lain abandoned for too long."

Mr. Blackwood held out his arm, and I took his assistance, and from the corner of my vision, I saw my mother's eyebrows rocket into the center of her brow. Blackwood and I began to stroll towards a green velvet couch in the far corner, underneath the window and with a fine view of the portrait, and when my family was far enough behind that they could not join our conversation, he said, "I'm glad you're here."

What warmth was this?!

"Really?" I said, "You couldn't boot me out fast enough, the day before yesterday."

"I had work to do," he replied.

"So I see," I said, gesturing to the refurbished home.

But Blackwood shook his head. "No, no, not this. I hired an outfit from London; they came up and it took them no time at all. When one has money, anything is possible." His expression soured. "Well, almost anything." He helped me sit upon the sofa. "Can I get you an ottoman, to raise your foot? Something to eat or drink, perhaps?"

"Why are you being so kind to me?" I asked directly.

"Because," he said, and his expression soured again, "We have a mutual friend who would be very upset with me if I did not make your comfort my priority."

My heart leapt. "Is he here?"

"Of course not. He's down in the cellar where he belongs. I dare not let him distract you," Blackwood said, "Harry, I have a favor to ask of you."

He hurried away to fetch me a glass of wine and he bid one of the servants to bring a footstool, and when I was very comfortable, he sat next to me. People were staring. The spinster librarian and the eccentric hermit? This would doubtlessly fuel the village gossip for the next six months.

"A favor," I prompted.

"A task so simple, even you can do it. One of people in this room is responsible for the murder of Earl Rabbit," he said, "I need you to sit here with your damaged ankle and examine them for any hint of their motive."

I glanced around, sure that I'd misheard him. "Sir, none of them look at all like the devil on the heath!"

"You call it a devil?" he said, "Well, one of these villagers will know more about your devil, Harry, because one of them summoned it here."

"These are friends and relations, people I have known all my life! Do not be insulted, Mr. Blackwood, but you are the only one I don't know. I assure you, none of them are guilty."

"What about the militia? They've been invited, too."

"But they didn't arrive in Dunham until after Earl's disappearance," I said, "Ergo, they can not be the guilty party."

Blackwood did not look discouraged. "Someone has brought this evil to your precious little county."

"And how can I be sure it's not you?"

When he smiled, he exposed all his teeth like a cornered dog. "You don't like me much, do you, Harry."

"I'm not sure what I think of you," I replied truthfully. "You're very learned, very adventurous. I suspect you know more of science and nature than any other man here, including my father. If you weren't so caustic, I think we could have roaring conversations on a variety of topics."

"But?"

"But you're mean and dreadful and terribly callous. I can not forgive you for how you treat our mutual friend."

He scoffed at that.

I reached out one hand and touched his wrist, but he recoiled quickly.

"You will not touch me, Miss Lovecraft. I will not allow it."

I couldn't hide my surprise. "You know of my Quirk?"

"A quirk? Is that what you call it? Good Lord, doesn't that sound harmless!" He laughed sharply. "You and your sisters all have these Quirks, do you not? They're symptoms of a greater disease, Miss Lovecraft, to which you have been inoculated over the full course of your life. You've grown up in the midst of a plague, and your body has formed defenses to keep you healthy when any other person would crumble."

I shook my head. "I don't understand—"

"Of course you don't," he replied, "A fish only recognizes the presence of water once it's been ripped from the sea. You can't perceive what's happening around you, because it's always been around you, and you've known nothing different with which to compare." He shook his head. "We get ahead of ourselves. Someone in this house has killed Earl, and possibly George, and now that Crumpsall dunce, and he will kill again, given the opportunity. I need you to watch for any deviance, Miss Lovecraft. You say you know these people best, therefore you are the one best equipped to recognize any errant behavior between them." He stood. "Watch, and catalogue what you see. Look for an air of verisimilitude that is too earnest for honesty. I'm entrusting you with a very important duty, Miss Lovecraft, and when I visit you again at the end of the night, I shall expect results."

Mr. Blackwood gave a sharp bow and strode away into the crowd, which closed behind him as a refreshed line of dancers took to the floor and the orchestra struck up a new tune.

# ELEVEN

The musicians played and the evening progressed. I tried to shake off the treacherous feelings which Blackwood's accusations had inspired in my heart, but I could not. How could any of the villagers turn on their own? A Whatley man might pick a fight with a Dunham fellow, but in all my memory, I couldn't think of any instance of such violence done upon a neighbor. I watched as my sisters danced with young men, one after another, and I weighed each fellow for his vices and virtues, but none seemed particularly malevolent. Jane spent her time comforting Frederick; he looked poor and grief-stricken, and after a while he reluctantly danced with her, but I could see that his mind was quite distracted with other tragedies. Mary consented to let Jerold Chowder lead her around the floor, but she was more interested in a spirited conversation with Mr. Tippler regarding the peculiar nature of Earl's entombment, and once she was free of Jerold's attention, my sister and the tin smith eagerly traded theories as the party eddied around them on the dance floor. Emma waltzed with a variety of soldiers, though I'd be lying if I said I didn't notice her return, again and again, to the handsome Mr. Marsh. None seemed more suspicious than another. They were flirtatious and competitive in winning affections, but nobody acted particularly guilty.

To be honest, if anyone felt guilty, it was me. I'd neglected my duties in informing the soldiers of the horror I'd witnessed upon the heath, and because of that, Captain Crankshaw held fast to his theory that the disappearances were the result of a rabid wolf. How outrageous! My gaze sought the captain and located him on the far side of the ballroom, conversing with Mayor Chowder and standing a little detached from the rest. I wondered if I should try to attract his attention, and draw him over to me, so that I might openly confess the scene which I had witnessed up on misty Dreadmoor.

But that would demand I reveal the existence of Blackwood's accomplice, wouldn't it? I wasn't sure if I was prepared to do so.

Why not, I wondered? A spark of jealousy flared in my heart. Upon reflection, I discovered that I wanted no one else to know of him; I desired his company for myself, and no other. Never had I felt such a selfish urge! I wished for no one to intrude upon our friendship, not even my sisters, and I was left bewildered at the strength of my own desires.

Marvin Runkle lurched passed as he asked Charlotte Cripplegate for a dance, wiping his nose on his sleeve, and Mrs. Runkle sat next to me as her grandson took to the floor. "Good evening, Harriet," she said. "You are injured?"

"I'm afraid so," I replied. "I've only strained my ankle. I'll be fine in a day or two."

She pinched her lips and patted my knee. "I suggested to Marvin that he might ask you to dance to one of the country reels, but that wouldn't be a very good idea, would it!"

"He seems to be well-matched to Charlotte," I said. The two of them were of the same height, and they both moved with just enough awkwardness to counteract the other, in the same manner that two waves cancel each other and result in calm water.

The old woman gave an assenting node. "Your sisters are a doing a fine job of entertaining the young men; you just sit and relax." For a while, she regaled me with ripping tales of post office deliveries and her latest knitting project, and I let her carry the conversation as I watched the faces go by.

The Winterbottoms, the Cripplegates, the Bierces. Even Father Noonan was here, although he wasn't ready to commit the sin of a Scotch Reel. I knew these villagers all so well. I'd grown up with every one of them. Save for the soldiers, the only person I did not know was Mr. Aloysius Blackwood, and he had been remarkably judicious in sharing any tidbits of information about his past.

Then, a thought occurred.

"What about Mr. Blackwood?" I asked Mrs. Runkle, "I've heard that he sends and receives a great number of parcels?"

"Oh, yes dear!" she gushed. "He is very industrious!"

"To whom? From whom?"

The old woman blinked her tiny eyes behind her spectacles, thinking hard to remember. "Oh, let me see, universities and colleges in far Cascadia, mostly. One was called … Ravensrodd? That is a town in California, is it not? I don't know it, to be sure, but the man has been most active in sending books and boxes, large and small." Her face squeezed into a map of wrinkles. "When I shake them, they sound like they're filled with rocks and dirt."

"Why would someone send dirt?"

"He must be a geologist, I think," she replied.

"I thought you told Mrs. Darling that he was a fur trader."

"Did I? Perhaps I did. He could be a naturalist, I suppose," she replied. "Whatever his title, he's a busy man."

I nodded towards the portrait. "And who do you think that is?" I asked.

"An ancestor of noble genealogy," Mrs. Runkle replied. "A man of Mr. Blackwood's character would like a reminder of his own royal lineage, should he have one. Now, if I had a spot in my home for a lovely big painting like that, I'd much rather have a landscape, and pretend it's a window, wouldn't you? Then you could think it's summertime in the garden, no matter what the season."

"You enjoy gardening?"

"Oh, goodness, yes! There is no finer pastime!" said Mrs. Runkle, very merry. "Have you walked through the gardens of Northwich Hall? They are the loveliest you'll ever see, I think. Did you know, my husband helped with their construction? My lovely Warren, God rest his soul, he kept the park for Mr. Posey, and trimmed the hedges, and raked the leaves. That was very long ago."

"Then you must know the grounds of Northwich Hall quite well," I replied.

"Once, I did. Mr. Posey was a stuffy fellow, always with his nose in a book, but Mrs. Posey could be kind. She was a fine cook, so I heard."

"And their sons?"

"The boys were troublesome, but then again, what would one expect? Their father did not discipline them, and spirited boys must have a firm hand to control them, or their liveliness and natural competition curdles into wickedness. Too much youthful energy, you know." She giggled and held out her old hands. "If only one could harness all that pluck, and keep it for a rainy day!"

"Do you remember when they went missing?"

"Oh, I have a hard time remembering yesterday, my dear. My head is too full of thoughts, and the memories fall out." Mrs. Runkle's face wrinkled deeply as she considered the past. "Missing boys ... Dunham does seem to suffer from that particular malady. I do recall, though ... one boy came back. The eldest one, I think. Silas? Simon? His name escapes me, but yes, he came back from whence he had been taken."

"But Mrs. Darling says he was not ... well."

She clucked and shook her head. "Such a nasty affair," the old woman replied, "But who knows the truth of it? Certainly not me. My dearest

Warren, he didn't see the eldest boy after his return, but one afternoon he heard a horrible caterwauling from the tallest tower! The most unnatural cries! And until his dying breath, my brave Warren claimed the voice was Mr. Posey's, calling out his son's name at the very moment his mind cracked in two." She gave a little shudder. "And then Mr. Posey went to Broadmoor, and that was that. The village closed up the house and relieved my faithful Warren of his duties, and he never returned to the grounds as long as he lived."

"How dreadful!"

She nodded sadly. "But it was a long time ago. I barely recall it. And still the gardens grow, for they don't care a whit for human drama." Her expression shifted to one of calm and mildness, as if all her troubles had been lifted. "What were we talking about? I've forgotten."

"How Northwich Hall has been revived," I prompted. "I'm happy to see it bursting with life again."

"Oh, as am I, Harry dear!" she replied. "Returned from the dead! Did you know, my sweet Warren was the grounds keeper?" Then she waved across the room. "Oh, look! There's Mrs. Posey! I was quite sure she was dead, too." She tottered to her feet. "I must go and give the hostess my best regards, and apologize for thinking she was rotting in a grave."

The old woman tottered away to join Mrs. Cripplegate by the punch bowl.

None of these people were guilty. I found myself weary of thinking such a terrible thing. The quartet was skilled but their music was lively and boisterous, and as more of the militia arrived, the hall grew very hot and crowded. Every person that brushed against me left an impression of their heart—lusty, jolly, jealous, drunk—and I felt a headache threatening.

Emma was sweeping around the dance floor again with Mr. Marsh, and Jane was sitting on a couch opposite me, deep in conversation with Frederick Darling. Mary was engaged with the Poole sisters in a friendly debate, all of them stating their positions amid complaisant smiles and general encouragement, defending their opinions with good cheer. My sisters were enjoying themselves immensely.

Meanwhile, I was stuck alone on a couch in the corner, searching the multitudes for a troubled conscience. My spirits sagged. Oh, if only I had a book to read!

I rose to my feet and limped out of the room into the empty foyer. The doors had been left open to allow a draught of night air. Quieter, fresher, cooler: in all ways, more agreeable than my previous spot on the sofa. But while there were oil-paintings and carved tables, a plush carpet and a massive glittering chandelier, a multitude of finery to decorate the entrance hall, there were no chairs. The butler stood by the door, and I hobbled to him.

"Could you tell me where I might find a quiet place to sit?"

He looked flustered. "I'm afraid I can't, miss."

"Oh, well, my ankle complains, and I cannot dance, but nor can I stand another moment of that delightful music," I explained. "I understand that Mr. Blackwood may not wish the rabble to scurry through his home, but if you could point me towards a drawing room or parlor—"

The butler shook his head. "No, I'm afraid this is not a matter of choice," he explained. "I can't, because I don't know where such a room could be found." He looked embarrassed. "I've not been given the freedom to visit any more of the house than the foyer, the ballroom and the kitchens."

"Oh!"

His stoic facade softened, and he admitted, "I've not even set foot on the upper floors. So as much as I wish I could take you to a drawing room to rest, miss, I'm afraid I have no liberty to do so."

"What an odd term of employment," I replied.

"Very," he agreed, then looked reluctant to say more. He'd revealed too much.

I thanked him for his honesty, and before I shuffled down a corridor, I assured him that I would take full responsibility for my trespassing if I was discovered; as a butler, he'd receive nothing but praise and recommendations from me. I left the foyer and wandered into the depths of the house, looking for a couch upon which to rest, and soon came to a set of open doors.

I entered, and felt my breath stolen away.

The library was as big as the ballroom, but lined with shelves, adorned with comfortable furniture, and illuminated with candles. The soft light glinted and winked from a countless number of gilded spines, and everything was painted in the soothing shades of wood, gold, and velvet. A lectern, holding a ponderous medieval tome, sat next to a desk that was larger that our kitchen table, and upon the desk sat a globe made of precious stones—jade, lapis lazuli, malachite—cut and set into the shapes of continents. Finely crafted Bakhtiari carpets with dense designs of floral motifs covered the hardwood floors, and a small iron fireplace contained a crackling fire, just large enough to remove the damp chill from the air. A spiral staircase led up to a narrow balcony so that one might reach the highest shelves, and the arched ceiling was painted with a frieze, in which the seven seas were portrayed as lovely young women, dancing with ribbons.

Goodness! I could scarcely comprehend the sheer amount of knowledge bound up in these four walls! Any question could find its answer here! I wandered in, agog, my eyes rising up to the thousands of volumes around me. In all my life, I'd never seen such so many books!

"Hello?" I called out, "Is anyone here?"

Despite the candles and fire, no one answered.

In the far corner, under a triad of arched windows overlooking the night-time garden, a soft chair beckoned. Surely, there could be no sweeter Heaven. I hobbled across the library, sat heavily and gave a rapturous sigh.

On the shelves nearest to the chair, the books offered up their titles in gold and silver. I tipped my head to one side to read them: Folktales of Dunham County, The Medieval Kings of Belgium, Flowers and their Symbolism, The Philosophies of Ibn-Aja'in, Ancient Kingdoms of Carcossa, A History of the Brass City, and many more. I reached over and plucked one from the nearest shelf, entitled A Treatise on the Use and Practice of Building Rites, and opened it. Inside were a number of color plates. To my shock, they showed illustrations of the human body and its most private, internal systems. I'd expected architecture, not dissection.

Were these Blackwood's books? Or his father's? Such a collection would have taken years to acquire, but what use would a fur trader have for such a vast library? And where would he have kept such a thing? I imagined a room in a log cabin in the deep and savage woods, big enough for thousands of volumes and constructed from an entire forest of trees, and thought the idea to be utterly ridiculous. Then I flipped to the front of the book where an old, faded bookplate had been pasted. A name was written there: *John Posey*

Oh! These had belonged to the late Mr. Posey! I had no idea he'd been a collector of books, nor even where his interests lay. It made sense, though, that Mr. Blackwood had purchased the library along with the house, and had simply incorporated them into his own collection. Perhaps the furniture and paintings were not Mr. Blackwood's, either. To think, for all these years, a marvelous library had lain empty and forgotten, and within sight of my home!

As I flipped through the plates, with their gruesome illustrations and a heavy reliance on red ink, I felt a gentle tickling around my ankle, as light as the crawling of a spider. When I looked down, I saw the rust-colored tip of a tentacle sprouting from under the chair.

"You're here!" I whispered joyfully.

I put the book aside, lifted my skirt, and looked between my ankles. The cephalopod was pressed flat against the rug, his body the same intricate pattern as the wool, a very elegant display of blue flowers and green leaves against an orange backdrop. I took the tentacle and pressed a kiss to the top, and for a moment the camouflage flickered into waves of delighted yellows.

"You mustn't be seen," I said, concerned, "Blackwood thinks you're down in the cellar."

If emotions are colors, then his were tinted with mischief and self-determination. Let Blackwood think the monster was cowering in the cellar; the cephalopod would much rather spend his evening relaxing in the library.

As I held one tentacle, another snaked up and snatched the book from my side, and deftly flipped it closed before sliding in back into the bookshelf.

"I was reading that," I said, reaching out to take it back.

But that same tentacle wrapped itself around my wrist and gently pushed my arm away from the books. I felt a sudden flicker of concern.

"You don't want me to read these," I said.

Agreement.

"There's nothing wrong with a woman reading," I insisted, "How else am I to learn anything new about the world?"

But no, the concern remained.

"How positively primitive of you, sir," I replied. "There's no need for alarm. I do not blindly believe everything I read, and my father has been careful to cultivate a critical mind in myself and my sisters. He encourages us to read and discuss every volume we can lay our hands upon."

But when I reached out again for another book, this time Ancient Kingdoms of Carcossa, the grip tightened.

"If you don't release me, I'll be forced to call for help, and I don't think that would fare well for either of us," I replied.

One amber eye peeked around the underside of the sofa, and it contained an unmistakable gleam of pleading. The beast didn't wish me to look further, but for what reason, he could not articulate. The best he could hope to impart was a strong emotion of restraint, concern, and warning.

"If I promise not to read these books, will you let me go?" I asked, and in reply, the tentacles slackened their grip. I sat back on the chair. "Fine, then I shall promise. But be warned, I will ask Mr. Blackwood the meaning of all this. There's no good reason why you should keep a curious person away from literature. It's only through reading that we may expand our mind and experience other times, other places, and other philosophies."

The tentacles (good Lord, how many were there? Eight? Ten?) slithered around my feet and snaked up my calves in a manner most unseemly, but the suckers probed the swelling of my injured ankle with tender concern.

"I'll be fine in a day or two," I said, "I'm not the kind of girl to stay a-bed very long, and Emma's attention has helped speed the healing process. She's exceptionally skilled and caring. And what about you? How is that gash above your eyes mending? It was particularly nasty."

Both eyes appeared, and between the carpet pattern, I could see that the wound had almost closed, leaving only a faint white scar that didn't change colors as fully as the healthy flesh.

"Oh, that's lovely! It makes you look very dashing." I ran my fingers over the top of his ... head? ... And an emotion of warmth and fondness percolated over his skin as he leaned into my touch. "Do you know what creature that was, that we encountered upon the heath?"

If I'd expected an answer, I found only confusion and confliction. Yes, he did but no, he did not. What could that possibly mean? I, too, was growing frustrated by the limitation of my talents—emotions are all well and good to feel out a situation, but they're horribly inefficient when one needs particulars.

"Does Blackwood know? If I ask him, will he be able to explain?"

This met with emotions that ranged from fear to anticipation to outright refusal.

"So you don't wish me to ask Blackwood, and you don't wish me to read, and I'm determined not to return to the ballroom because it's far too noisy for my comfort," I said, "Alright, what do you propose we do to pass the time? Do you play chess?"

One tentacle wrapped itself around my wrist and pulled me gently until I stood. Then it pulled again, come with me, and he let me hobble after him, through a second door and down a maze of corridors and galleries, avoiding all people by the merits of such a vast and labyrinthine building, until we reached an exit. The creature pushed aside the door and suddenly, we were outside in the garden, on the far side of Northwich Hall.

The moon shone full and bright upon us, and the land was silent and still. Any guests were far away at the other end of the building, with the whole expanse of the south wing between us. The beast curled itself down to the shore of the fish pond, surging like a knot of kelp tossed in the waves of a storm, and as he slipped under the water, I sat at the edge of the pond and watched him with rapt delight: he was eerie and moved in a most outlandish way, but he was graceful, too, and there was an alien pulchritude to him that intrigued me. Under the night sky, his skin appeared as sleek as oil, rippling with a thousand colors, all shades of brown, purples and blues. The twilight gloom held just enough flickering starlight to create points of reflection on the gloss of his limbs, so that they appeared bejeweled with diamonds and sapphires.

The tip of one tentacle crawled ashore and inched through the grass towards my foot. It delicately touched the bare skin of my ankle, as if seeking to console me. I was curious to know what activity he had in mind, and I stayed perfectly still as he moved slowly, patiently. One wide eye watched me with rapt fascination.

I reached down and touched the tentacle. Strong, lean muscles moved under the slick, mottled skin. The limb had an intelligence of its own, quite separate from the body of the beast.

But from the direction of his eyes, I felt his intentions as clearly as if he had spoken. He didn't wish to hurt me. Our conversations from the night before last had left him ravenous for communication. For too long, he'd been alone, locked in the prison of his own biology.

I had been focusing on one tentacle, and he had many. I suddenly realized the tendrils were seeking out information from other parts of my body, too: one was stroking the curve of my shoulder, another had plucked at a wisp of my hair. I was surrounded on all sides by a network of limbs, ten at least, and as thick as fence posts at their roots. They arched over my head and blocked out the sight of the far forest, creating a wreath of suckers.

While he meant me no harm, he was also reluctant to let me go.

I leaned in close to the nearest eye. "I'm the first person to understand you in a very long time, and for that reason, you don't wish to release me, yes? But if we're to be friends, you can't hold too tight." I drew my hand over one tentacle, causing a shiver. "Trust me, I won't run away."

The net of tentacles relaxed, recoiled a few inches.

"See?" I said, reclining amongst the suckers, "I'm not going anywhere."

A sense of relief flooded through its body, closely followed by that intense, unmatched curiosity and the longing of desire. The tentacle that had been tickling my ankle moved up to my calf. It stroked the skin of my leg.

"A curious proposition," I said, and laid my hand upon his skin, so that he might feel my consent as strongly as I felt his attraction.

The flicker of the tentacle tickled my skin, moving steadily upwards to my thigh. I could have pushed it away with ease, but I didn't; my own curiosity burned like an ember in my belly. I'd spent years avoiding the touch of another, and with this small approach, I found myself hungering for intimacy. Up, up it crept, slow as treacle, and the higher it reached, the more my breath caught in my throat, and the more anticipation I felt in my chest. The limb, flexible yet firm, was as moist and hot as a tongue, and as it slipped under my petticoats and along the naked cleft between my legs, I gave a little gasp of pleasure. More arms rushed forward to support my shoulders and my spine; they wrapped around my torso and lifted me gently from the earth, holding me aloft as that one persistent, curious, patient tentacle slipped into my body like a thief, wriggling and quivering in a most delicious manner.

Such bliss I'd never felt before. It curled and coiled, pushing itself deeper, insisting that it enter as far as my caverns could allow it. It pulsed, thickened, stretched my flesh, shivered and flickered in the very depths of my frame, so that I could feel its undulating motions through the bones of my hips, vibrating outwards like the ripples on a still pond. The breath in my throat came faster, deeper. For long minutes, it eagerly explored the depths, stroking the velvet flesh as though licking the moisture from my body, with just enough resistance and pressure to illicit heady waves of ecstasy. My blood quickened, my eyes closed. The pleasure moved into realms I'd never before known, overwhelming all my senses fully. I was no longer sure which direction was up or down: what was the night sky? What was the dark waters? The world became a blur of darkness, and as the creature carried me towards the pond in his slippery serpentine embrace, I knew nothing of fear—let him drown me, I didn't care. All I knew was that I had become the vessel of his fiery warmth, full to bursting, and I never wanted him to leave.

When, too quickly, the storm of heaves washed over me and I felt that joy draining away, I realized I was no longer on dry land, but half submerged in the waters of the trout pond. My dress floated around me like a lily pad. While the limbs still held me aloft, the beast himself was fully submerged, and the great golden eyes watched me from under the glassy surface with an unmistakable gleam of anxiety and hesitation.

I ran my hand over his forehead, a foot or so under water. He trembled, shy and sheepish, and perhaps a little dazed by the flood of my emotions resonating through our joined bodies. Yes, that must be it: he'd felt that exhilarating rise to crescendo, too, and the ferocity of my reaction had startled him.

"Oh, that was delightful!" I replied, breathless and awestruck.

One tentacle whipped around my wrist as a suction cup pressed itself to the skin of my forearm, and gave a moist smack of a kiss. The sensation that accompanied the kiss was unmistakable: he'd never felt such riotous pleasure. Plus, he'd managed to coax a frenzy from me and was feeling rather proud of himself.

I wrapped my two arms around his nearest limbs and hugged them close. "And I suppose you do this to all the girls?"

Such a refusal! No no no! I found myself covered in a thousand kisses, from my head to my toes.

Plus, an unmistakable question that could only be deciphered as, where do we go hence?

"Are you proposing that we pursue a courtship?" I whispered, "Because—and please do not be insulted—I suspect that my parents will be aghast with this advancement." I untangled myself from his embrace and struggled out of the pond, all sodden skirts and petticoats, and leaving a trail of water after me. "My mother has reconciled herself to my spinsterhood; not in a million years could she have foreseen me in a relationship with a beast of the abyss."

One tentacle slithered from the pond and wrapped itself around my wrist, and a second rose up to caress my neck. It was tender and sensual, and I kissed the tip of it. I sensed the vulnerability flowing through his skin: a mix of regret, and excitement, and a little bit of mischief. He was concerned that he'd put me in a compromised position, and worried that I would think less of him.

"Your place in my heart has not changed, but no, I shan't tell anyone about you, if that's what you wish," I assured him. I arranged my dripping dress and sat on the wet ground, and let his touch dance across my hands and neck. My body still tingled all over and I hadn't yet caught my breath. I laid down across the cool grass. For long minutes, we engaged in a silent conversation, all touch and caresses, with him resting under the dark water and me reclined under the stars.

"How could I tell anyone?" I said at last. "I don't even know what to call you."

"His name is Nate," came a reply from the door.

I gave a yelp of surprise and propped myself up on my elbows to face the source of the voice.

Mr. Blackwood stood on the step with his hands clasped at his back.

"How long have you been there?" I said, surprised and flustered.

"Just long enough to know that he's finally professed his heart to you," the man said with disdain.

I looked back to the beast in the pond, now slipping under the surface of the water as if hiding in shame from the man in the doorway. I turned back.

"You're mean," I replied. "You take delight in his embarrassment."

"I do," said Mr. Blackwood. Then he strode out across the lawn towards the trout pond. "Miss Lovecraft, you are a very peculiar woman," he said, "Not many would submit themselves to the depraved desires of a monster, yet retain their wit or dignity afterwards. By all accounts, you should be reeling in madness after his touch." He harrumphed. "At the very least, you should be as shamed as he is, don't you think?"

"Of course not," I replied, "I'm not the one skulking in dark doorways, peeping on people in compromising positions, and being—for all intents and purposes—a perverted mockery of a gentleman!"

Blackwood laughed as he sat beside me, and said to the mirrored waters, "Oh, Nate, don't hide away in the pond again. It's pathetic." He turned to face me. "I leave you in the ballroom to find a murderer, Miss Lovecraft, and instead I find you here, taking sinful pleasures under a wild moon like some untamable nymph." His face grew crafty. "I knew there was a reason he likes you, Harry: you're a trollop at heart, and just as wicked as him."

"I am not wicked, you ridiculous man, and you can't bully me into thinking so," I replied. "And you call him Nate?"

"You disapprove?"

"I only thought you might have given him a name that was less … less …"

"Normal?" Blackwood gave a snort that was derisive. "There has never been anything normal about Nate, that's for certain. He was once much more adventurous, but he's grown cautious lately, after a number of unfortunate mishaps have left him with a shaken confidence and an uncertain position in the universe. Still, I shouldn't be surprised that he'd nurture an affection for you. A passion for books? A fascination for the weird? Unrestrained in your habits? Yes, you two have much in common."

The tentacles withdrew into the water. I thought Nate had retreated into the depth of the pool for the rest of the evening, abandoning me to Blackwood's conversations.

But instead, Blackwood looked out across the black surface of the water, and tipped his chin in the direction of the far side of the trout pond. Silent and statuesque, a anthropogenic giant rose out of the water, but he stood awkwardly and stilted, as if he could not balance properly. It was the same hulking figure I'd seen in the shadows, striped white and black, hunched and deformed.

"Oh, well, that's much better," Blackwood called out with no small measure of sarcasm, "Practice makes perfect."

"I did see him!" I exclaimed in the figure's direction, then to Blackwood, I said, "He is a homunculus?"

Blackwood snorted. "Hardly. Homunculi are tiny."

"But then what—?

"Who knows what Nate is? He defies most descriptions," he said, "But yes, you saw him once before, Miss Lovecraft, when you stepped into our house to admire the tapestries in the foyer." Blackwood shuddered. "All covered in slime from the bottom of the pool, of course, but in his mostly-bipedal form. Towel him off and he can take to two legs for a little while. He can't stay that way for long, though; he gets cranky when he dries out. Headaches, muscle cramps, that sort of thing. And anyone with half a brain and an eyeball can tell he's not right, you know. He's got a knack for looking like carpet patterns and tree trunks, but he's terrible at appearing human." Blackwood folded his long hands over his knees. "You saw him in the woods, too. That was how I knew of your … what did you call it? Your quirk? One who is not so tainted would have crumbled into insanity at a glimpse of our mutual friend. Most normal people can not comprehend him, and if they suffer from any weakness of their constitution, they crack."

I had so many questions, I didn't know where to start, but before I could articulate any of them, I heard a commotion at the back door, and turned to see my mother arrive in a fluster of shawls and skirts and scarves. She pulled up quickly in shock at the sight of Mr. Blackwood and I sitting by the pond. Jane and Mary were close behind her, and the three of them stared openly at us. And thank goodness for that, for my mother and sisters were so engrossed with the horror of intruding upon a private scene between the gentleman and the spinster that they missed the monster on the opposite shore, slipping silently back into the murky water.

"Oh! Goodness! My apologies! We have interrupted your private conversation!" Mama gasped.

"Not in the least, madam," Mr. Blackwood replied as he stood and helped me to my feet. "Harriet had fallen into the pond. I was happy to rescue her."

"Harry!" scolded my mother with huge disappointment, "Oh, sir, I am so very sorry to have inconvenienced you with her clumsiness! Harry, whatever possessed you to come outside and visit the garden? Your ankle, my sweet! Do you need reminding that you are injured?" Mama waved to my sisters. "Mary, help your sister, and Jane, go fetch your father, we must head home or Harriet will catch her death of cold in her wet dress! Look, already she has the flush of a chill in her cheeks!" My mother turned to Blackwood with a look of helpless frustration. "My eldest daughter is not always proper, and has a streak of silliness in her, as you might have noticed. Again, Mr. Blackwood, I am so very sorry!"

"There's no need for apologies," he insisted, sounding the very model of kindness. He turned to me and said, "I've enjoyed every minute of your company, Miss Harriet. You are a singular woman with unique tastes, the likes of which I've never before seen."

Mary bundled me up in her arms with no effort. Before she carried me away, I said, "Thank you, Mr. Blackwood, for being so understanding. Please impress upon our mutual friend that I will cherish this evening in my memory, and I look forward to meeting with him again, very soon."

"Oh, I'm sure you do," Blackwood said with a devilish glint.

# TWELVE

The next morning, quite unexpectedly, Mr. Blackwood rapped upon the front door and caused my mother to scurry about like a startled hare, gathering biscuits and cheese and tea and fruit, while I was set across from him in the parlor like a prize pig on display at the fair. I smiled to him, he smiled to me, Mama fluttered and fussed around us, and when she'd assembled a small feast, he bid my mother to leave, for he wished to speak with me in private. Her departure was, to say the least, a curious mix of eagerness and reluctance, with both her hands clasped at her chest like a greedy child about to open an oversized Christmas gift.

When the door closed and the latch clicked, any kindness in his face vanished. Blackwood affixed me with his terrible gaze. "You know why I am here," he said.

"Our conversation of last night was interrupted."

"You were remiss in your duties, Miss Lovecraft, and left your post when I had clearly assigned you a task."

I felt a flush rise to my cheeks, so I lowered my chin to hide my smile. "And how is our mutual friend today?"

Blackwood groaned. "Oh, he pines for you, Harry. It's wretched to watch." His lip curled in disgust. "Once upon a time, he was useful, but now, he lives only to see you again. It's enough to make anyone of sound mind feel nauseous."

"Will you tell him, I feel the same?"

"No," Blackwood grunted, and with cutting sarcasm, added, "I'd lose him completely to your considerable charms. Best to let Nate suffer a little, I think, if it motivates him."

Then he glanced at the teapot, then to me. Then back to the teapot, brows arched.

Oh, bother.

I poured us each a cup.

"You wish to know what I discerned while watching your guests," I said as I handed the tea cup to him.

"And?"

"I neither saw, heard, nor felt anything that would lead me to the identity of our culprit," I replied. "But I can say, in all certainty, that I spotted no terrifying, massive, rag-garbed giants in attendance, not a single one."

"Things are not always as they seem, Harry," he said in a droll tone. "You know that as well as I."

"If you're referring to my Quirk, then yes, looks can be deceiving."

He took up his cup and slurped at the tea, then said, "I was referring to our mutual friend."

I took a bit of cheese and savored it before saying, "You may think of him as a mere beast, Mr. Blackwood, but he has the heart of a poet and the mind of a scholar. It is terribly unfair of you to treat him with so little consideration, when he clearly possesses every faculty afforded by the presence of a human soul. He is kind, generous, brave—why, before we visited the pond last night, Nate and I had a conversation, and he warned me against reading any of the books in the library of Northwich Hall."

At that, Blackwood fully sputtered, and had to put down his cup and dab at his mouth with the sleeve of his coat.

"He told you that? He spoke to you?!"

"He's very clever at communication," I replied, pleased that my comment had flummoxed him, "With a mixture of intentions, actions, and the colors of his skin, he is able to relay quite a bit of information."

"What exactly did he tell you?" he said in a patronizing, saccharine sneer.

"That I mustn't read any of the volumes in your possession. Can you explain to me, sir, why he wouldn't wish me to read Posey's books?"

Blackwood scowled, thinking, weighing out what to tell me. "How well did you know Mr. Posey?"

I shrugged. "I was five when they suffered their unfortunate incident. I only remember Mr. Posey a little; he'd come and share long conversations with my father, and drink bottles of brandy, and leave with his head in the clouds to stumble home across the fields."

"What would they talk about?"

"I don't really know," I replied. "You'll have to ask my father. But Papa was a professor of history, and by looking at the titles of Posey's books, I gather they had that interest in common."

Blackwood weighed this information, and then said, "John Posey was a bibliophile, Miss Lovecraft. A lover of books. And the more strange or obscure, the better. His collection is unparalleled."

"Is that why you bought Northwich Hall? For the books?"

"You have grown up alongside the greatest library in all the Western world," he said, "I would have paid any price to own it. I'll be honest, it took me a very long time to find it because the dolts of Dunham Village council were ignorant of the actual value of the property to which they'd been entrusted. Half the books on those shelves were thought lost to civilization forever."

"I had no idea!" I said.

"Nor did they. And I suspect that our mutual friend does not wish for you to stumble across something abominable," he continued, "New ideas are powerful things, Miss Lovecraft. You must take great care when entering Posey's library, for there are dangers lurking on those shelves that you can not yet comprehend."

I frowned. "I'm no bubble-headed nitwit, easily overtaken by whims and phantasies, " I replied.

"No, I don't believe you are," Blackwood agreed. "But Nate knows, better than most, how dangerous a book can be; those ideas can change everything in a moment of weakness. He is afraid for you. Surely he has told you that, too."

"In a fashion."

"I believe, Miss Lovecraft, that someone in the village has read a book that they ought not to have seen, and on the outside, they appear just as they always have, but on the inside, they have soured into the most foul and contemptible monstrosity. Up on the heath, you saw the creature's true face, but we do not know the man to whom it belongs, and that is what we must decipher if we wish to stop the disappearances."

"But a man can not change his form."

"No?" Blackwood laughed at that. "Nate would certainly argue that point."

I was about to ask questions when the fullness of his statement hit me like an arrow between my eyes. My expression must have been one of utmost shock, for Blackwood grinned in a very satisfied manner.

"Yes, Miss Lovecraft, just as he has a name, he once had a human face, too, and sometimes he tries to come back, but it's always a terrible catastrophe. You saw an attempt, only last night!" Blackwood took a biscuit to dip in his tea. "Dreadful! A glimpse of his horrid, pseudo-human mask gives children nightmares, strikes the elderly with incontinence, and sends cattle into a stampede."

"I thought ... I assumed ..."

"You assumed he was a devil trying to look like a gentleman, rather than a gentleman trapped in the guise of a devil. Really, Miss Lovecraft, what's the difference? We all have demons lurking in our hearts." He continued in a dry and unimpressed manner, as if discussing the weather rather than the transmutation from man to monster. "My half-brother Nathaniel has been trapped in this grotesque state for almost five years now, and I am often amazed that his despair has not completely overwhelmed his reason. If it was me who had undergone such a terrible transformation, I think I would have gone mad with frustration. No, Nate has such an abundance of … of … of sickening cheerfulness …" Blackwood scoffed. "He has always been a frightful optimist, and meeting you has inspired a return of his overbearingly sunny disposition." The gentleman shuddered in revulsion. "Since he first laid eyes upon you in the vale, you have been his constant interest: Harry this, Harry that, blah blah blah. Frankly, I'm sick of hearing about you."

"I beg your pardon," I said, blinking twice, "He possesses the capacity of human speech?"

Blackwood rolled his eyes. "Oh, God, yes, he won't bloody well shut up. It gets tiresome."

The thought of actual, real, honest-to-goodness conversation made me dizzy. My heart soared at the hope of speaking, of sharing conversations, of whispering words to each other. "But … but … when does he talk?"

"When he's not an octopus," Mr. Blackwood sneered, as if it was a stupid question for me to ask. "Rather hard to hit all the v's and p's with a beak instead of a mouth."

My mind reeled. "Please! I wish to talk with him!"

"He finds it tiring to take a human shape. He is a man only rarely, and even then, he spits and slurs a great deal." Blackwood reclined on the couch. "I'll ask, but don't get your hopes up, Harry. He's a disgusting specimen in both of his forms."

I rested back against the couch, looking to the fireplace in a daze. "How is this possible?"

Blackwood finished his biscuit. "You haven't the faintest inkling of what is possible, Harry, and I doubt you have the imagination to understand it if I told you."

I reached out and grabbed his wrist then, and he recoiled but didn't push me away. I burrowed myself down into his emotions like a shipworm, and I found his feelings were brazenly displayed, with nothing hidden from himself or anyone else. Sometimes, people keep the worst parts of themselves locked away, but not Aloysius; he was proud that, at his core, he was an angry, resentful man, driven by a greedy and scientific curiosity. His teasing of Nate seemed to be the only happy respite from a life of churning bitterness and depression. Both boys had grown up with a library of cursed books, and they'd been inured from the ill effects by their consistent exposure to the foul vapors, constantly broadcast day and night. I, too, had shared the same history: a life in the shadow of Northwich Hall had resulted in a vaccination from these insidious emissions, which wafted out of the unholy volumes like a foul stench. That queer malformation had manifested itself differently in all of us, depending upon the cellular fabric of our corporeal frame. For myself, it had heightened my ability to read a person's emotions. For Aloysius Thorne, it had meant an intensified ambition to control the dark mirror energies that leaked into the world, compounded with a clever mind for invention. It had spurred him and inspired him to build tools that would allow him to traverse boundaries not meant for man to cross. For Nate, it meant—

"Wait," I said. "Your name is Aloysius Thorne!"

He startled as if I'd run a current through him. His goggled eyes flashed open.

"Witchcraft!" he hissed.

"And Nate … he is Nathaniel Blackwood. And you have stolen his surname and fortune!"

"How can you know all that?" he said, bewildered. "Is this the nature of your exposure to the books? You've learned to read a man's innermost thoughts?" He recoiled, twisting his wrist out of my grip, and his lip curled up in disdain. "That's how you've communicated with our mutual friend, and given him hope when there is no hope to be had!"

"It was clear as day," I whispered, stunned by the force and power of the impressions. "Your name was there, as if written on a page."

"And all your sisters are as empathic as you?"

I glanced sidelong at him.

"Yes," I lied.

"Then I shall make sure to give each of you a wide berth," he replied, standing and adjusting his jacket. "Let me warn you, Miss Lovecraft: the books are not safe. I encourage you to keep your distance from them. Many of Posey's most unique volumes were not written by human hands, and they emit foul energies that corrupt those who come too close, like the poor Posey family. Madness lies within their pages. Do you understand?"

"I think so."

"Nate read only a few lines in a single book, and his place in this universe was forever altered," said Blackwood—or was it Thorne?—as he walked to the door. "And now, another person has read from an unholy book, and been lost to humanity. One of Dunham's villagers has been transformed into a miscreation for purposes as yet undefined, and we must beware, for he will wear the face of a friend until it's too late. Be on your guard, Miss Lovecraft, and tell me as soon as you can of any deviations you might see."

"I promise," I replied.

And with that, he departed.

# THIRTEEN

My mother had expected a wedding proposal. Instead she found me in tears, hunched over my tepid cup of tea. She rushed to my side and curled her arms around me, and crooned in my ear, "Oh, duckling! Oh, my poor Harry! Never you mind that horrid little man—you will make a fine spinster! You love doggies, do you not? Dogs and books to your heart's content! As your Papa is fond of reminding us, all will be sorted in the end."

I hugged her close and when my sobs eventually mellowed, she pulled a kerchief from her sleeve and gave it to me to wipe away my tears.

"I'm not worried about my status," I replied, "Mr. Blackwood is the least of my concerns! I'm frustrated by this horrible situation, Mama!" I took a deep, shuddering breath. "I fear one of our friends or relations has been co-opted into lunacy, and I am terrified to find out who. No one is quite what they seem."

"What the dickens are you talking about?" she said, concerned.

"Mr. Posey, Mama!" I replied, "What happened to his sons is happening again!"

"Oh, dear," she said, holding her hands to her mouth. "Oh mercy! Not again!"

"What was Mr. Posey like? You knew him before his descent into madness. Was there any hint of his violent character?"

Grief washed over her. "No, dear, not at all. Mr. Posey was the very model of a fine and educated gentleman! He always seemed so rational, so logical, right up until the end. It frightened me when they took him off to Broadmoor, because he and your father were two peas in a pod, they were. Whatever faults Mr. Posey suffered, I was afraid your father might share." She patted my hand. "But we are blessed that your father is of sterner stuff, and did not falter or fall under the influence of his friend's lunacy. If you wish to know the details of Mr. Posey's character, then you must talk with your father. He will be able to give you perspective where I can not." She shook her head sadly. "Of the couple, I knew Mrs. Posey better, but she was a dour woman with very little lightness of spirit. I don't think there was much love between them, and they spent most of their time on opposite ends of Northwich Hall, avoiding the other completely. They would dine with us fortnightly, but the evening was often dull."

"And the sons?"

"Odious, all three of them," she replied. "A noxious combination of their mother's dreary disposition and their father's strict temperament. I'm not surprised that they fell to ruin; they had a weakness of the mind, Harry, that spoke of inbreeding and pollution."

How much had the boys been influenced by the pernicious vapors of their father's evil library? We Lovecraft girls had managed to mold our talents into useful skills, but then again, we enjoyed a bit of distance from the offending books. The Posey boys would have been surrounded by cursed books; the situation would have been inescapable.

"Did they read?"

"The Posey boys?" said my mother, "Oh, good heavens, no! They were not very bright, I'm afraid. I remember once your father saying that the boys had never been taught to read."

"So they didn't share Mr. Posey's love of books."

"The only love they had was for impishness," Mama said. She dropped her voice low. "For the most part, harmless pranks, you know. Dropping pants, or giving each other a fishy." She brought her index fingers and jabbed them forward, as if to stab someone up the backside. "Whenever they visited for dinner, they were always swapping out the sugar for salt when no one was looking."

"A nuisance, then."

"As most boys are, if they are spirited and unsupervised." She waggled her hands to the window overlooking the garden. "But ask your father, Harry. He'll know better than me."

And so I went out to the yard where Papa was tending his beloved bees. He saw the perplexed expression on my face, and ushered me over to the bench by the door, where we could sit together in a shaft of warm sunlight.

"I can infer that Mr. Blackwood's visit did not go as your mother planned."

"I have no interest in marriage, nor does he," I replied.

"Oh, thank goodness for that," Papa said with great relief.

I took my father's hand in mine and felt the rising concern in his affections. "You have always been honest with me, haven't you?" I said.

"You're the most sensible of my daughters, Harriet," he replied with furrowed brow. "I've never felt that there was a topic we should avoid. Why would you ask now?"

I took a deep breath. "Mr. Blackwood told me of Mr. Posey's library, and I've come to ask you about the man you once called your friend."

My father looked to the ground, as he often did when sorting his thoughts.

When he began to speak, his voice was low but clear. He spoke as though he had often wished to talk of Mr. Posey, but had suppressed the impulse for a very long time. The words flowed out like water bursting from a broken dam, a powerful cataract that was, at first, rushed and eager, then measured and paced and confident.

"John was a good man, a very interesting man, who possessed a boundless curiosity for the world. His family had a long and illustrious lineage, and he spent his family wealth in the search for answers to questions that mortal men ought not to ask." My father smiled. "I was a professor of history for many years, but John's knowledge was far superior to mine. My education had come from lectures and essays, but his research had led him to foreign lands and exotic cities, to ruins on the edge of the known world, and his library reflected the treasures he'd found in those far-flung places. Oh, how he loved his books. He hoarded them as a dragon hoards treasure. He knew the place of every single title on the shelf, and it didn't seem to matter how many hundreds of volumes he possessed, he knew the contents and condition of every one, and always wanted more."

"Mr. Blackwood claims the books are dangerous."

"Not all of them," said Papa, "Most are full of wondrous stories, nothing else."

"But ...?"

Papa tipped his head to one side. "There are some that are more than mere books, Harry. I have seen a few of them, but John would not let me touch them, never mind read from them. He claimed that three, in particular, were of a treacherous nature." He laid his elbows on his knees and looked towards the horizon, focusing on some distant point in his memory. "Let me see if I can remember their titles ... ah, yes. The Final Confessions of Bai Xi, Concubine to the Yellow Emperors, that was one of them. There was also The Widow's Rites, which he had uncovered on the slopes of the Himalayas, and purchased from an old yak herder. Oh, and Songs of the Scented Gardens. That was a particularly frightful one, if I remember correctly."

"It sounds lovely," I replied.

He shook his head. "Dangerous, and made more dangerous by its beauty. I remember seeing that one, though I was forbidden to lay a finger upon it; the volume was hypnotic. Edged with gold, bound in albino human skin." He whistled low. "It was as seductive as a siren, calling to Jason and his

Argonauts. It practically hummed with unearthly power."

"And you knew of these books, sitting for years in an abandoned house, yet did nothing?"

"What could I do?" he said with a shrug, "The Village Council locked up the estate, and I figured they were as safe there as anywhere else in the world. At least I knew they hadn't fallen into the hands of a tyrant." He grinned. "As the years passed, I thought less and less about them. I hoped they'd rot, I suppose—I hoped they'd succumb to moisture and mildew, and vanish from the world forever." He shook his head. "But now they are Blackwood's. Do we trust a man like that with such power? Especially if he knows their full value?"

I thought on this question. "Mr. Blackwood has a greedy and self-serving disposition, and a boundless ambition that drives him, but I don't think he's without a conscience. I laid my hand upon him, Papa, and I didn't feel that he was evil, only misguided. Perhaps he was once a good soul, but he's since been spoiled by circumstance." I looked to my father, and noticed for the first time that his face belonged to an old man, and most of his hair had turned white and wispy. His chin was more sharply pointed, his eyes sunken into hollows, his skin as frail and translucent as tissue paper. Through his hand in mine, I felt the soft sensation of relief percolating through his fingers, as well as the happy quietude of nostalgia. I said in a whisper, "Mrs. Darling said that Mr. Posey had been digging a well when he uncovered a portal to Hell, and the Posey boys tumbled down the well into that infernal underworld, only to return as demons, and Mr. Posey was forced to kill them. Is that true?"

The spot between his hoary eyebrows furrowed in thought. "Well, isn't that an interesting interpretation."

"But is it the truth?"

My father shook his head. "No one knows the truth, Harry. Once the Poseys had children, John was so afraid to have such perilous items in his possession that he dug a hole in the cellar to bury the books. He threw them down into the abyss and covered it over with paving stones." He looked out to the fields. "But perhaps the boys were curious, and the books did not wish to remain hidden. Maybe they called out in dreams and visions." His face turned towards that great hulk of a house, poised like a sentinel in the distance. "Maybe the boys climbed down into the pit and read passages from those foul volumes, until the things that crawled back up into the light were no longer the Posey children, but something foul and sinister. Maybe they ate their mother up, and they would've eaten John, too, and escaped into the northern forests if he hadn't destroyed them." He looked back to me. "All of this is fanciful conjecture, Harry. I don't know the truth; no one does. But one night, whatever the circumstance, John bludgeoned his sons to death with a silver mace, pushed their corpses down into the well, and set fire to them, then sealed their unholy remains behind a big oak door bound with iron."

I'd seen the door myself in the cellar of Northwich. A skitter of terror traveled up my spine.

"You believe this?"

Papa gave another shrug. "It was John's final confession to me, before he was bundled off to Broadmoor Asylum. John believed it, and that was good enough for me."

"And the books?"

"I know not what happened to them. I figured John had burned them in the fires or hidden them on the property. He went mad—one could no longer trust his perceptions. When Dr. Gelder committed him, John refused to speak to me again."

I thought for a moment of the titles on the shelf, and none matched the three my father had warned against. But one title sprang to mind.

"I did look at one of Mr. Posey's books," I admitted, "But it was quite strange, and not at all what I expected. I thought it would be architecture, but instead, it was anatomy." I cast my mind back. "It believe it was entitled, A Treatise on the Use and Practice of Building Rites."

My father's eyes widened and he leaned forward.

"Did you read it?"

"I only looked at a few of the plates before I was distracted," I said, "They looked more like a doctor's manual than building plans."

"Building rites," he mused. "Neither architecture, nor anatomy, nor superstition, but a mix of the three. Harry, building rites are ceremonies used to ensure the stability of a foundation. Coin, statues, little slips of paper ... any of these will work. They're set into the cornerstone of a church or pushed into the concrete of a foundation to ensure the building is blessed." He shook his head in wonder. "But given your description, it seems Posey's book was a guide to the most ancient of rites, when a coin or a statue would not do. It is a very old custom, known throughout the world—the Japanese call it hitobashira, the Maori call it raukakai, the Babylonians call it takpertum. The Old Gods demanded blood, my love. They were never content with symbols. They wanted a living creature to be sealed in the foundation, so that the spirit of the dead could guard the building for all time."

"No one ever did such a thing!" I exclaimed.

"No? I'm sure the myth is not without roots," he replied. "So the story goes, our own St. Dismas Church in Dunham had a black terrier pup buried in its cornerstone, and on moonlit nights, you can hear the thing yapping."

"You speak of the Grim!"

"I do."

"I thought it was just a story to scare Emma."

"Stories have their roots in many truths," Papa said. "Was Earl not bound up in the wood of a bridge? Perhaps the Old Gods have returned, and want their share of blood once more." He shook his head. "These are sad and unsettling times, Harry, and we must be open to all manner of strange things, if we hope to survive them." He squeezed my hand and said, "I'm not a religious man, Harry, but even I believe the world is full of miracles and marvels, and hold faith that all will be well in the end."

# FOURTEEN

After speaking with Papa, I retired to the Huntsman's Oak, and found Emma there, fiddling with her camera obscura. Her red hair and elfin features gave her the appearance of a pixie in a child's primer, but the look upon her face was full of more determination than a flighty fairy could display. When she noticed my slight limp, she set aside her device and invited me to sit with her.

"Mama has not diminished your enthusiasm?" I said, dipping my chin towards the little brown box.

"Not in the slightest," she replied, "But I'll need to find a new source of silvered plates. She's instructed Beatrice to count the set at the end of day and lock the cupboard."

"Perhaps Mr. Blackwood has a few spare silver platters in the kitchens of Northwich," I said. "He doesn't strike me as the kind of man to host frequent dinner parties."

She laughed. "I think he did a fine job of hosting a dance, if you ask my opinion."

Her care of my ankle had done much to restore my abilities, and we sat on the branch together as she administered her final treatment, running her fingers lightly over the injured area. The swelling was gone, the pain reduced a dull ache. Truly, as Papa proclaimed, the world is full of marvels; my youngest sister is one of them.

"You spent a great deal of time with Mr. Marsh last night," I said. She glanced up at me with a blush on her cheeks.

"Did I? I suppose I did. Do you think it was improper? I doubt anyone noticed." But her smile was cheeky and she avoided my gaze.

"I'm sure a few of the local men felt their noses to be bent out of joint," I added. "After all, they were waiting for you to notice them, but you spent all your time in the company of one of the soldiers. And an outsider, to boot!"

"No, were they angry? Oh, Harry, you tease me," she laughed. "I ignored no one." Her eyes gleamed. "But isn't he handsome?"

I shrugged. "If a uniform is to your taste."

"Jane was so good, to sit with Frederick Darling and keep him company," she continued, bowing her head once more to her work, circling her fingers over my leg. "It mustn't have been easy for him to socialize, with the fate of his brother still unknown. A very dutiful fellow, don't you think?" Then she paused and looked up at me with an impish grin, and said, "Mary tells me you were discovered by the pond in the company of a certain gentleman, and that same gentleman called upon you this morning, and goodness, won't tongues start waggling!"

"I don't hear any tongues waggling but yours," I replied.

Emma lurched forward. "Well? Has he expressed interest?"

"In me? No. Most certainly not."

She looked disappointed and skeptical.

"You and Mr. Blackwood would make a lovely couple."

"Oh, God! Now you're teasing me," I said, "No, I have no intentions on that man. He's a bully and a selfish curmudgeon, and he assumes the worst of people. I think …" I smiled as I looked off in the direction of the northern forests, "I think my heart belongs to another."

Emma's fingers stopped abruptly.

"What?!" Then, gathering her wits, she said, "Wait a minute, who would be of interest to you?"

But instead of answering, I said, "You've done a wonderful job of my ankle, Emma. You're so gifted; we really are fortunate to have you." I swung my legs down and stood in the driveway, testing my weight upon my foot. Suddenly I thought of last night, with kisses running up and down my naked legs from a thousand suckers, and the pleasure of drowning in those delightful sensations, a mingling of touch and desires shared between two creatures in an endless loop, back and forth, and my pulse quickened just a fraction—

"No, you will not ignore me, Harriet Philomena Lovecraft!" she insisted, batting my shoulder with one small fist and interrupting my train of thought, "Who has your affections? Tell me right now, or I shall scream!"

"You don't know him, Emma," I said.

"I know everyone in Dunham!" she replied with fire.

I chuckled at that. "Please, forget I said anything. I speak out of turn."

"You're blushing! Good lord, you've gone bright red!" She looked to the garden, to where our sisters were tilling the vegetable beds, and yelled, "Mary! Come here! I need you to help me wring a bit of information from our uncooperative sister!"

I scoffed. "I'm being silly," I said, "Never mind."

"You're in love!"

"I am not."

"Oh, I dare say you are," she replied.

"There are more pressing concerns than a foolish school-girl crush," I insisted, squishing down the rising heat in my blood and trying, desperately, to forget last night's encounter, "Mr. Blackwood believes that the murderer lives amongst us, and that we can discover his true face if only we keep our wits about us."

Emma, looking scandalized, swung her legs astride the Huntsman's Oak. "Who would be so diabolical? I mean, Earl Rabbit didn't deserve such an atrocious end. If I was to assign guilt, I might think Mr. Winterbottom to be a possible suspect, for an undertaker would benefit most from Earl's death. But, no, I don't even think that likely!"

I took her hand in mine, studying the long fingers and graceful nails. "Mr. Blackwood said that we've grown up near a font of unearthly power, and it has shaped us in ways we don't even recognize. Our Quirks are the expression of that proximity—perhaps someone else close to the library of Northwich Hall has developed a more malevolent Quirk of their own?"

"Who?" said Emma, "Not Mama and Papa, surely."

"No," I replied, "But the Cripplegate farm is not so far away. What if Charlotte Cripplegate has a Quirk too?"

"Charlotte is kind-hearted! She would never hurt anyone!" Emma replied, coming to the defense of her friend, "In all the years I've known her, she's never exhibited any strangeness! And you know how poorly Charlotte keeps a secret—she would've told me, I'm sure!"

I pondered over this, gazing down the road and across the shorn fields towards the Cripplegate home, with its friendly red door and its welcoming willow tree. "I can think of no one who would make a suitable suspect," I said, more to myself than Emma.

As we chatted, Papa headed towards us along the driveway. He wore his canvas hunting coat and a tweed cap. "Girls, I am heading into town to join the men, and we'll be looking for George and Teddy," he said as he passed, "Mr. Poole informed me last night that a group will search the caves and canyon at the west of the county, and I'll be back before supper."

"Let me come, too," I said, "Emma has restored my ankle; a walk would do me good."

"And me," said my youngest sister, although at her suggestion, my father shook his head.

"Harry, you may come if you think you're up to the challenge, but Emma, your mother would strangle me if I was to put you in harm's way," he said, "She's already informed me that she has high hopes for you, and plans on marrying you off to Mr. Blackwood within the month, if he has no further interest in Harry."

Emma gave a mewl of disappointment, but I ran to the house to grab my boots and my shawl, and met Papa at the road in only a few minutes.

We walked into Dunham and joined a small knot of twenty men at the crossroads by the church. Some were villagers, but most were soldiers. The elder Mr. Darling, Frederick, and Mr. Marsh could be counted among them, as were Mr. Chowder and Mr. Crumpsall, desperate for any news of his son. A sense of anticipation and anxiety ran high, and the emotions felt like the faint tingle of static electricity in the still air, and made the fine hairs of my arms stand on end. After the gaiety of last night, everyone was in a quiet and retrospective mood, and we followed the path along the river towards the east end of the county in contemplative silence.

Well, they were contemplative. The whole way, I schemed and plotted to keep them out of the caves; the last thing I wanted was this cohort of intrepid explorers to descend into the caverns and stumble their way to the Northwich cellars, and disturb Nate in his underground lair. Such a confrontation would go poorly for both parties.

But this was never to be, for we didn't make it so far.

A mile passed the splintered ruins of the footbridge, Mr. Tippler held up a hand to bid us to stop. A light, silvery fog swirled between the alder saplings, pulled by the current of the Waters. It created playful eddies in the air.

"What is it?" said Mr. Darling.

The old tinsmith held his ear high. "Not sure," he said.

I strained to listen, too. I hoped to catch a hint of Nate's passage, but there was nothing.

"Carry on, friends," Mr. Tippler said, and began to walk forward.

I was still listening as the cohort passed by. Mr. Marsh, who was last to pass me, said, "Will you come?"

"In a moment," I replied.

To my disappointment, he lingered. "I hear nothing."

"No, nor I," I said.

"I would be remiss to leave a lady alone in the forest," he said with an air of gallantry.

Mmm. So Mr. Marsh was to be my chaperone, was he?

"You do me honor to extend your assistance, but I'm quite accustomed to this countryside," I replied. "I assure you, sir, there's no need for concern."

He remained unconvinced. I saw at once what Emma found appealing about him: in addition to a comely face, he had an alertness and boldness that did him credit. We began to walk again, and when I stumbled over a small rise in the trail, he took my hand to help me steady myself, and I was afforded a peek at his innermost core. Perhaps it was rude of me to pry, but Emma is my youngest sister, and I'm protective of those I love.

In the barest second of our skin touching, I recognized him to be a very good soul, with honest intentions and a measured ambition. He was young and impulsive, yet intelligent and charitable. There was no sense of lecherousness or greed in his intentions; he was open and confident, full of hope, and had not yet suffered an occasion to doubt himself or fear failure. He seemed utterly devoid of cynicism. Emma had chosen to give her heart to a very fine fellow, and I hoped their friendship could be given time to nurture in a place not darkened by tragedy or death.

"Yes," I said, more to myself than him, "You'll do nicely."

"I beg your pardon?' he said.

"From where do you hail, sir?"

He gave a modest smile, made more attractive by his honest bearing. "Oh, not far away. My family is from Lower Whatley, miss, and I grew up on the southern border of Dreadmoor Heath."

"Goodness, then we are neighbors!" I laughed.

"Miss Emma was pleased to hear that we knew of many similar places," he said, "Is she well today? Did she enjoy the dancing last night?"

Ah, here is the root of his gallantry. I grinned at his attempts to be subtle.

"She had a very good time, indeed," I said, "And spoke excitedly this morning about her spins around the dance floor. She danced with you, did she not? You have made an impression, sir."

He looked bashful and charming.

"Will you extend to her my best wishes?"

"Of course," I said, "Although I can already tell you, she'll be jealous that I have spent a full conversation with you. May I suggest you come and dine with us at Lovecraft Cottage when this whole terrible event is concluded? I'm sure Emma will be thrilled to introduce you to our mother." God have mercy.

He smiled as our paces brought us up to the group again, but his mirth cooled when we noticed that the group was no longer progressing along the trail into the narrowing fissure of the canyon. Instead, the men had stopped, and silently stared up at the rock walls. Some were shielding their eyes from the sun, while others had covered their mouths with their hands. Mayor Chowder had retreated to the bushes and was loudly ejecting his breakfast into the weeds.

"Good Lord, Harriet, do not come any further!" said Papa in a rush, and his face had a green pallor, and his eyes were full of horror.

But I looked past his shoulder to follow their gaze, and saw great slashes of red across the chalky white walls of the canyon.

Common starlings had clustered over the rocks in vast and uncountable numbers—a conservative estimate would say there were thousands of them—and they twitched and flicked their brown wings like an undulating curtain of feathers, but they remained utterly silent, with not a tweet to be heard. They had thronged to the blood that had splattered over the embankment, and they pecked at this nourishment with a starved desperation rarely seen in song birds. I took a step back, overwhelmed by the sight. Mr. Marsh kindly grabbed for my hand with his left, as if to impart strength to me, and pointed with his right.

"Look!"

At the top of the apex of the twin blood spatters, two bodies dangled from bramble vines, their heads almost severed from their spines by the length and violence of the drop. But it was neither George nor Teddy, the objects of our search, who hung like forgotten shanks of beef in the butcher's window, blanketed in songbirds that were voraciously pecking them raw. It took a full minute for me to recognize the sparse, skinny legs and thread-worn aprons, the gaunt and skinless faces now frozen in horrible, unblinking masks of death.

"Good Lord," I whispered, "It's Mr. and Mrs. Rabbit!"

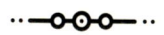

·· —o-o-o— ··

The Rabbits are dead.

The thought circled around and around in my mind as I made my way home, encouraged by the men to leave before the corpses were cut down, and accompanied by Mr. Marsh to ensure my safe arrival. We spoke very little, he and I. When we reached the militia's camp outside Dunham, he procured the use of a horse after relaying the news, and we rode home between the fields with me sitting before him, stunned into uselessness.

"Have you ever seen so many birds all in one location?" he said as we plodded along Mill Road. His voice was thin with wonder.

"No," I replied, "In fact, there's been a distinct lack of birds for the last few weeks; I'm happy to see they've returned."

"But with a hunger for human flesh?" he replied.

We said nothing more until we reached Lovecraft Cottage.

Upon arriving home, I left him to share the news with Mama and Emma.

I ran as fast as my legs would take me towards Northwich Hall, where I pounded upon the doors with such fury that surely I woke Cerberus in distant Hades. It took a very long time to see any hint of life within: the house was extremely spacious, after all. I guessed that the staff from last night had departed back to the city, shooed away by a grumpy employer who would want them around no longer than absolutely necessary.

At last, the latch clicked, the door opened.

But when I stepped inside, I found the foyer empty.

The ballroom was vacant, too. So was the parlor, the sitting room, the library. But someone had unlocked the doors to let me in, so I returned to the main entrance.

"Nate?" I called, "Are you here?"

I didn't mean to sound so stricken, but my words came out in a quaver. At once, I felt a tickle on the nape of my neck. It startled me, and I stepped back with my hands to my throat. One long tendril hung from directly above.

My eyes followed it up to see Nate wrapped around the chandelier. He was a sinuous, seething tangle of constant motion, and colored gold to match the gilded fixture.

When I flinched, he hesitated, so I took the nearest tentacle in hand.

"No, I am not afraid, I simply wasn't expecting you to come from over my head," I explained as he descended silently, and I felt the cool emotion of relief flood through his skin and into my fingers. "But I need to tell Blackwoo—I mean, Thorne. I need to tell Thorne that there have been deaths in the village."

The skin mottled into swirls of bright azure and indigo: a rush of surprise and a question.

"The Rabbits," I answered. "The parents of the first boy."

He dropped with a moist smack to the floor, and I realized there must be no bones in him to break, for his bulk squished flat before rearing back, and he drew himself up onto six of his legs. One tentacle wrapped itself around my wrist and he pulled me up the stairwell.

"Wait, wait," I said, resisting.

He stopped on the landing, and we stood together under the portrait of the woman and lambs. The amber eyes came close until they were on par with my own, showing unmistakable confusion, and surely he had no skull, either, for his brow furrowed deeply and his face contained more expression than any stiff, solid, unyielding bone could allow.

I took a deep breath and said, "I only wanted to say that I'm sorry I left so quickly last night, and it was rude of me to abandon you, especially after your half-brother was so vulgar to intrude upon us during our intimacies, and I wish I could've stayed in your embrace until dawn." I smiled slyly. "All day, I have thought of nothing else but you, Nathaniel Blackwood, you mysterious and marvelous gentleman." Then, relenting, I added quickly, "Well, until I saw the Rabbits, of course! Then, I thought only of them! But that's understandable, given the circumstances."

He narrowed one eye.

"Honestly!" I insisted, "I'm neither horrified nor disgusted by you! I'm not afraid of you in the least!"

One tentacle wrapped around my body and pulled me closer, and the eyes stared deeply into mine, trying to root out any deception there. From his skin I felt—oh, how to describe it?—disbelief and hesitation, suspicion and trepidation. He did not believe me, but oh, how he yearned to!

So I laid my hands on either side of his pulpous head and pressed a passionate kiss directly between his eyes, just below the white line of the little scar. I had always been a passive observer in the secrets of another's sensibilities, but this time, I pressed my own fervor upon him, imparting through his skin the fullness of affection, fascination, and elation I felt at the smallest thought of him. My ardor was boundless; I wanted Nate to know my heart, all of it.

But maybe I was too intense. It seemed that, of late, my Quirk had grown in strength, and I had not yet learned to temper it. When we parted, he wobbled on his legs and looked a little stunned.

"I don't care in the least what body you wear, Nate," I whispered in (possibly) the general direction of his ear, "I think you are an astonishing person, and I only wish to know you better."

A tidal wave of exhilaration flowed through him, but there was no time to savor it: he wrapped me up in a mass of churning tentacles and slurping suction cups, and we flew up the stairs soundlessly, through corridors and staircases and halls, at the same rapid pace as a galloping horse. It wasn't until we burst through a large door into a circular room of tall, arched windows that I realized he'd carried me to the top of the highest tower.

The room had a diameter of twenty paces, and boasted a ring of tall arched windows that provided an unobstructed view to the north and east. A few eccentric contraptions built of brass and iron were scattered around the space; at first glance I mistook them to be weird sextants and absurd telescopes, the likes of which would send Emma into a joyous frenzy, but before I could examine them further, my attention was snagged by the stacks of books that littered the floor. Volumes of a mammoth size, some as big as a man's chest, towered in the corners. Still others were pamphlets as tiny as a baby's palm, as delicate as gingko leaves. A velvet couch with a floral pattern sat against an interior wall, but it had been rendered useless by the sheer number of books balanced upon it. In the center of the room stretched a long wooden table, spread with rolls of parchment papers; Thorne stood beside it, wearing his outrageous six-lensed spectacles on the end of his nose. As the door burst open and we exploded in, he turned and grabbed his chest as if he were about to suffer a coronary. "By Mithras' whip!" he yelped, then saw me, and gaped. "Miss Lovecraft, what is the meaning of this?!"

"The Rabbits are dead," I said as Nate gently set my feet upon the ground. I attempted to pull myself together with as much humility as possible. My dress was askew, my hair was unpinned, and somewhere along the way, I'd lost my shawl, my hat, and one of my shoes, but I stood up straight and tall, and folded my hands before me. "Both the baker and his wife were hung, or hung themselves, from the top of the canyon walls outside the entrance to the caverns. I do not know if it is suicide, or murder, but I thought I must inform you immediately."

If he was surprised, he hid it well. Thorne removed his spectacles and set them on the table, then he strode to the window, thinking furiously, his hands clasped at the base of his spine.

"What does it mean?" I pressed.

"Were there birds?"

Startled, it took a moment for me to answer. "Yes, hundreds of them. Thousands, perhaps. How did you know?"

Thorne stared in contemplation out the window in the direction of the woods. I crossed the round tower room to stand beside him, and was instantly struck by the stunning view. One could see as far as the Barnacle Mountains, with their jagged square peaks and glittering snow caps shrouded in clouds.

He turned to Nate.

"Psychopomps?"

Have you ever seen an octopus shrug? It's a most remarkable thing. The expression ripples through tissue and muscle, and colors shift from dull matte to shimmering iridescent.

"We must capture one, then, and put the screws to it," Thorne replied. "If it is a psychopomp, then perhaps it will know the identity of our quarry." He strode back to the table, leaving me at the window. "You must catch one, Nate, if you can, and we'll look for evidence of its purpose. Neither Harry nor I have the dexterity or speed for the task, and I'm afraid we'll be of no use to you."

Nate hesitated, then surged back down the tower stairs and disappeared.

Thorne returned to his books, in particular a large leather-bound tome that appeared to have been written by a medieval scribe in a monastery long since set ablaze by Vikings. He gave every indication that he'd forgotten completely I was here.

"I'm sorry," I began, "But what, pray tell, is a psychopomp?"

He finished reading his passage before addressing me.

"What do you believe happens to us after we die, Miss Lovecraft?"

"I don't profess to know," I said.

He grimaced. "Oh, such modesty." He glanced down at his book and said, "Do you believe in a loving God?"

I considered his question. "No," I said at last, "I do not."

This surprised him. "I thought an upstanding lady like yourself would be a regular fixture in the pews of St. Dismas on Sunday."

I shook my head. "My mother is a Bierce, Mr. Thorne, and they have long been known as agnostics. She does not profess to know the truth, and distrusts anyone who makes such a claim." I glanced once more out the window, with its breathtaking vista and blue skies. "Against her better judgment, I've nurtured a friendship with Father Noonan, but it's rooted in philosophical conversations rather than sermons, and so she lets me continue."

"Interesting," he said. "Tell me Harry, why does God not love us, His creation?"

I circled the table. "Because a God who loves us would not give us Free Will, then punish us when we use it," I replied. "If there is a God, it's despondent, at best. We've been given Free Will to do as we please, and we will reap the rewards or suffer the consequences of our actions; God has decided to let us choose our own destiny, and stepped out of the room."

"How progressive of you," Thorne replied, "Utterly wrong, of course."

I blinked. "You can not know," I said with a wry grin, "No mortal can."

"That's true, a complete knowledge of the universe is beyond our frail physical capabilities. In that, your mother is correct," he replied, "But you would be mistaken if you think the Gods have no interest in the trials of man. They delight in it. We are here for their sport, Miss Lovecraft, and when they tire of us, they destroy us." He gestured to the open book on the table. "You've already seen the caliber of book in Posey's library; he wasn't the kind of man to be satisfied with a general reading list. He knew, as you may suspect, that the world is not exactly what we believe it to be. Humanity exists on a tiny ship that bobs helplessly on the surface of a vast ocean, full of secrets. We know the shape and contents of our boat, but we can not see over the side, and we remain blissfully unaware of what lurks all around and under us, exerting constant influence over us, and plotting our demise."

"Hardly comforting," I said.

"Through Posey's collection, we can catch the faintest glimpse of what exists beyond our boat, Miss Lovecraft. See? Other travellers before us have recorded their own journeys, so that we may stand on their shoulders to look a little farther."

He flipped open a page of the book. It was blank.

"I see nothing, sir."

"Of course not," he replied with exasperation, "Haven't you heard a word I said, Harry? Just because you lack the ability to see, that does not mean that nothing's there."

Thorne took the spectacles from the table and hooked them over my ears, and flipped the shimmering blue lenses down.

Instantly, they revealed a dreadful scene painted in faded inks. I saw horrible lithographs of awful creatures: some were shaped like men, and some like snakes, and yet others like amorphous blobs with rows of oversized ivory teeth. Tiny birds flew in the corners, as if frantic to escape the riotous cacophony of demonic figures. I gasped.

"How can this be?"

"The hermetiscope allows us to see through our reality and into other versions of our place and time," he explained, "In another reality, lying atop ours like a palimpsest, a blessed scholar has written in his book, whereas in our reality, the scholar never bothered, or was never able. You are looking at the same book, but another version. Do you understand?"

"Not exactly," I said, still drinking in the myriad of figures.

"A tragedy," he replied. "Neither pretty nor intelligent. At least you can bake a decent sponge cake, if your mother is to be believed."

Thorne stepped back to let me gaze upon the bestiary, one form after another, until I noticed a figure in the corner that looked horribly familiar.

"There!" I said, pointing to it, "That's the one on the heath!"

And truly, the artist had drawn it perfectly. The rag-bound body, the emaciated limbs, the bone-white face. On this image, though, the eyes were missing—no, not just missing, but scratched out—as if the artist could not bear to leave intact the full force of that hypnotic gaze.

He took the spectacles and followed my finger to the figure. "You came upon this and lived?" he said, astounded, "And with all your wits intact? Well, Miss Lovecraft, perhaps there's more to you than meets the eye." His lips curled up in scheming and he said, "I should marry you myself, just to keep you in my collection. A girl of your abilities could be handy to have in a situation."

I flashed him a look of disdain as he handed me the glasses, but I decided to ignore the proposal.

"Tell me now what you see," he said as I hooked them over my ears, and he reached over to flip the green lenses down over the blue.

Instantly the page was alive with motion. Lines appeared and disappeared, shimmering and snaking over the vellum. "All of it, moving," I said, "And here, words appearing …"

"And next to the heath monster? What does it say?"

"I think it must be Greek," I said, "I can't read … wait! It moves. It is being written, even as I watch!" I looked over the rim of the glasses at Thorne in wonder, "How can this even be possible?"

"All things are possible, given enough time," he replied. "But for you and I, time may be in short supply. Go on, Harry, what does it say?"

"I think … Eidolon? Does that mean anything to you?"

But he removed the glasses from my face and turned away. The page emptied; it appeared as pristine as if it had never been used.

"What do the starlings have to do with all of this?" I pressed.

"The ancients assured us that a psychopomp carries the soul to heaven." He looked again to the blank book. "If there are thousands, then deaths are coming to Dunham, Miss Lovecraft, and in great numbers. That black and sinister tide under our little boat is rising, and the leaks in the shipboards are starting to appear, and if we are not very careful, this little county is poised on the edge of utter destruction." He paused, his eyes narrowed and focused on some distant dramatic point, then he looked at me and said, "While we wait for Nate's return, can I interest you in tea?"

# FIFTEEN

He made a pot of Earl Grey and a plate of toast with marmalade, and we sat in the large, empty kitchens wrapped in an awkward and uncomfortable silence, waiting for our mutual friend to return. On our travels from the tower to the main floor, I'd found my shawl and my shoe, but my hat was still missing somewhere in Northwich Hall's maze of corridors.

As befitting a grand house, the kitchens were spacious enough for a full staff of cooks and helpers, with three iron stoves and a massive pantry, but Thorne had no staff to attend to him. While a kitchen in any other home is the heart and hub of all activity, the kitchens of Northwich Hall were drab and dreary, garlanded with dusty cobwebs, and held the aura of abandonment. The main table was a huge slab of oak-wood, slashed and marred from generations of use as a cutting surface, and three mismatch chairs surrounded it. I saw no meats or cheeses in the larder, nor pots and pans, nor even a wooden spoon for stirring, but there were a score of empty cups by the sink, and a tower of crumb-covered plates on the sideboard. It seemed the only meal made in Northwich Hall was toast and tea.

At last, I could bear it no longer. My curiosity had grown too great to suppress. I set down my tea cup and said, "How did Nate come to be cursed?"

Thorne looked disappointed. "Really? Must I explain it again to you?" When I continued to stare pointedly at him, he said, "He read the wrong book, Miss Lovecraft."

I balked. "So you claimed, but surely one can not be transformed by a book—"

"For the love of all things hidden, woman!" Thorne said, exasperated, "We sit amongst the greatest library in all the world, full of miracles that you can barely comprehend, and you think to argue with me about the nature of my half-brother's transformation? Some of the volumes on these shelves have caused the collapse of kingdoms, some have breathed sentience into stars ... turning a man into a monster is child's play!" He hunched his shoulders and gave a bitter sigh. "You know that Nate and I grew up together, in our father's house; the portrait in the ballroom is of him, George Spencer Blackwood, the Chief Factor for the most prosperous fort of the Northwest Company, and a restless scholar at heart. When he retired from his post, he took his amassed fortune and began the collection of a library for the benefit of the University of Ravensrodd. You've heard of it?"

I shook my head.

"A pity. As a center for learning and the free exchange of ideas, it is unparalleled in all of Cascadia." Thorne took a nibble of toast. "The elder Mr. Blackwood was fascinated by tales of sunken countries and lost islands; he used to regale us for hours with astonishing tales, plucked from his time exploring the Arctic wastes, and we were hungry for as many uncanny stories as he could tell us.

"He traveled widely, corresponded with scholars and explorers, and purchased crates of books—his greatest dream was to build a grand library of the occult for the University of Ravensrodd. Believe me, he was careful to keep his books locked away from our prying eyes. We grew up surrounded by a labyrinth of tomes that we were forbidden to touch—do you know how much that eats away at a curious boy's resolve? Soon after joining the Chief Factor's household, I became obsessed with a desire for knowledge. Little did I know then, Miss Lovecraft, that the books were exerting their powers over us, shaping us and fortifying us, influencing our development in such slow paces that no one noticed. What could I have been, if I were not living in such close quarters to their foul ether?" He looked at me with pity. "What could you have been, if you were not raised in Northwich's shadow? Perhaps you'd be happier, too."

"I'm quite happy," I insisted.

"But why?" he pressed. "You have nothing to be happy about! You are without family or prospects, a forgotten spinster in charge of a piteous moth-eaten collection of children's books, destined for no greater purpose than to care for her aging parents! And now, to make matters worse, you've fallen in love with a disgusting monstrosity that ought to be locked away, for his own safety as much as anyone else's."

"How can you say such a thing about your brother?"

Thorne snorted. "Because the sight of him drives the weak and infirm mad, Miss Lovecraft. Because he inspires terror, and terrified people lash out in unpredictable ways, and he will be hounded to the ends of the Earth should he ever be discovered."

"And yet you accompany him on his travels, even after his transformation?"

Thorne shook his head sadly. "We were fools, both Nate and I: we snuck into our father's library to read that which was not meant for mortal eyes. He found a volume entitled The Dowry of the Copper Maker, and reading only a few paragraphs resulted in his metamorphosis. To see his body stretch and distort, mangled by cosmic forces into the parody of an aquatic demon—I pray you never see such a thing, Miss Lovecraft! Any human not so protected by a life lived in the books' sphere would have surely gone insane, trapped inside such a hideous form." He waved his hand dismissively. "You think I am cruel to him, but in truth, I've brought him here at great expense and peril in the faint hope of finding a cure for his situation."

"I can clearly see that you're a saint."

"You mock me, but you don't know what I've sacrificed to help him." Thorne snarled. "I have scoured the Earth for a way to restore him, but I'm beginning to suspect there's no cure to be found, and in my fool's quest to save my brother, I've somehow made all worse, and released yet another monstrosity on the world in the form of your leprous fiend, your Eidolon."

"What happened to the book, The Dowry of the Copper Maker?"

For a heartbeat, Thorne looked remorseful. "Our father was a learned man, but he was not a brave one. In his horror, the elder Mr. Blackwood destroyed the book with fire and dumped the ashes in the sea, but he never recovered from the shock of losing his beloved heir, and he died only a year later, having never regained his wits. He left behind a miserable widow and a generous endowment of books to the University." Thorne's expression became one of dark satisfaction. "George Spencer Blackwood went to join his mistress in whatever doldrums the afterlife affords us; I hope she abandons him to a miserable eternity with as little thought as she abandoned me." His grin grew malicious, all teeth and gums. "The old man never updated his will, so all his fortune fell to Nate, and with my half-brother's permission—yes, he gave his blessing!—I adopted his persona and inherited his wealth. You must admit, Nate is in no position to spend his own money. I'd hoped that miserly fool John Posey might've hidden a copy of The Dowry of the Copper Maker away on his shelves, and that we might find within it the cure for Nate's disfigurement, but so far, my search has been fruitless." He gave a helpless shrug. "The library is large, I've had no time to go through all, and to be honest, the current situation demands my immediate attention. Nate will have to wait to be returned to human form; the end of God's creation will not be postponed."

"You're in need of a librarian to save the world."

Thorne snorted. "You want the job? It's yours." Then his eyes affixed on a point behind and above me, and he said, "Ah, you've returned. Triumphant, I hope?"

As quiet as a spider, Nate crawled down from the ceiling, over the floor, and slunk under the table. One pale green tentacle snaked up and slapped a dead starling next to the teapot.

I jumped back but Thorne was energized. "Excellent!" he exclaimed as he took up the starling and examined it closely, peering into each eye and down the beak into the throat, making growls and groans of scientific interest. The brown feathers shimmered in the lamplight as if made of oil. "The starling's plumage is deceptively dull from a distance, don't you think, Miss Lovecraft?" he said, "It looks like nothing more than a simple brown bird, utterly unremarkable, but upon closer inspection?" He stretched out one dead wing, and the drab plumage proved vibrant and iridescent under the glow. "It's not pigment that causes such pretty colors, but the structure of the feathers; the starling's framework is beautiful, yet it garbs itself in brown, and so it goes about its day, unassuming and unnoticed." He smirked and crooked one eyebrow. "It reminds me of someone I know."

From under the table, a tentacle slipped around my bare calf, pressing urgent emotions into my skin like nettles.

Dread. Disquietude. An unease that I had seen too much.

"You don't need to worry for me," I assured, "I can make my own decisions, and I am not looking for a knight to save me."

"I wouldn't," said Thorne, and then one thin eyebrow arched. "Oh, you're not speaking with me, are you, Miss Lovecraft."

"No," I replied, and I looked under the table to catch Nate's eye. "Please, don't try to keep information from me. That would only leave me naive in the face of certain danger."

Satisfaction, with a hint of adoration, and a measure of guilt.

"It's not your fault, do not censure yourself further," I assured. "If anyone is to blame, it's that craven Mr. Posey. He willfully assembled a dangerous collection and then left it unsecured."

"Ah-ha!" said Thorne, and he pushed the sparrow forward. "Touch it," he demanded.

But it was dead and dusty, and spattered with gore.

"No, thank you. I'd rather not."

"I'm not asking, Miss Lovecraft, I'm ordering," he said. "Put your Quirk to good use. Touch it and tell me what you feel."

I reached out one finger and stroked the dry feathers.

A flash of red, like a slash of blood across a plaster wall. The sensation was sharp and bright, and it filled me with the feeling of a door falling off its hinges, or a box smashed with a mallet, or a pane of glass broken across concrete. The filaments of my consciousness began to unravel with the bright agony of a needle to the eye. I yelped and recoiled as if stung.

Arms were all around me. They pulled me away from the table, they held me in a tight yet comforting embrace.

"What did you see?" said Thorne with an eagerness that bordered on maniacal.

Tears threatened. I trembled ferociously, and Nate's multitude of tentacles pushed sensations of warmth and comfort into me, fortifying me, giving me strength, piecing together the weft of my thoughts.

"I saw it before," I said, "In Mrs. Rabbit's mind, the morning after Earl disappeared. I saw—I don't know precisely what I saw. Blood and chalk? Broken glass, but not of a physical kind? I don't know. Words fail me." The end of one tentacle caressed my cheek and left a line of kisses. "Thank you, I'm alright. Just startled by the intensity of it, that's all."

Thorne bristled at this show of affection. He returned his attention to the dead bird in his hands.

"The tongue is gone," he said, "And the body is quickly turning to ash. See?"

Even now, the wings were fragile. The tips crumbled under the lightest touch.

"One more time, Miss Lovecraft, before it's completely dissolved."

No no no.

But though every loving tentacle around me protested, I reached out my hand again and seized the psychopomp in my grip.

God, it burned like a coal in my palm! I felt the unbearable heat course up my arm as my mind filled with images of red and white, of bloodless meat and beating hearts. I saw the pale curve of horns, the sharp bony tips plucking the eyes from hapless victims, solid wood melting like tallow and bodies stashed away where they'd never be found, greedy tongues slurping nourishment from gelatinous flesh. There was fog, and rain, and confusion, and a melody on the still air that felt like boiling water poured down my ear canals. In a meadow, lines of flowers bloomed, but their petals were made of flayed skin and their stamens were strings of human teeth.

Muted, as if through water, I heard Thorne say, "What do you see?"

"Orchids and snapdragons," I whispered, straining to listen to the lyrics, "Biting at my legs, eating me alive."

Then the sensations swelled over my head like a wine-dark sea and I drowned in my own animalistic fear. The East Bridge, covered in pulsating pink flesh. Piles of balanced river stones. Faerie pillars on Dreadmoor. Murky water tumbling over and over and stained scarlet with blood. I saw Earl fracturing into a broken mirror, and Mrs. Rabbit in the doorway, catching the barest glimpse of the hypnotic molten eyes that bore into her chest, the skeletal hands that stole her son. Some images made no sense, some I could not set into language, and some were too horrible to dwell upon. I closed my eyes and heard a terrible, frantic screaming, and I felt pity for the poor tortured beast that made such a hopeless sound.

    I only realized, as darkness claimed me, that the screaming was my own.

# SIXTEEN

My eyes flashed open to gloom and grey, punctuated by a disc of white. At first, I mistook it to be a mask of bone under a pair of ivory-colored antlers, surrounded by a black bristly mane. I startled backwards, taking a sharp breath. But then, the disc swam clearly into view: a full, round, silver dollar moon stared down through the window. I collapsed into my own bed as a sheen of cold sweat covered my skin. Where I'd clutched the psychopomp, my swollen hand throbbed and ached, as if my fingers had been wrenched backwards in their sockets.

Emma sat in the chair at my bedside. Her red hair was tangled and uncombed, her eyes were tumescent from weeping. When she saw me jerk awake, she caught her breath in her throat, and threw her arms around me before beginning to cry anew.

"Oh, Harry!" she gasped.

"What's happened?"

"Mr. Blackwood brought you home. He said you'd had a fit, and fell to the kitchen floor and struck your head," she said, and she lay her right hand upon my neck, and her skin felt warm and dry. "But he's lying, isn't he. I don't sense any hint of a seizure about you. Seizures feel all bubbly and sparky, but you feel cool and dark, like the underside of a stone." She peered into my eyes, seeking clarity. "When he brought you home, you were on the cusp of death, your spirit was so diminished and hiding deep in your core!"

"What else do you sense?"

"Confusion," she said, and her eyes grew wide and fearful, "I don't know. I've helped with sprains and broken bones and bruises, but I've never come across this. You are burned? Or, no, not burned …" Her voice dropped to a hush. "You are burned, but not physically?"

"An apt description," I said, struggling to sit, holding my palm to my pounding head.

"Why did he lie to Mama and Papa?" she said, "Harry, here, let me help you up ... why would he not tell the truth?"

"Because the truth is too strange to digest all in one sitting," I answered. "There is something ancient and malevolent stalking the people of Dunham, Emma, and it is fierce, and frightful, and wholly without mercy. It's like a disease, infecting everyone it touches. We must proceed with caution; it feeds on the minds of those who cross its path, and it hungers for chaos and disarray."

She looked stunned, then in a haste, she took up my injured hand. The warmth of her healing touch spread like summer sunlight over my skin.

"We must warn the regiment," she said.

"I agree," I said, "But we must be careful, too. The monster wears the face of someone we know. It could be anyone."

"Mr. Marsh will not have been so cursed," she said firmly, "He is worthy of our trust, and he will believe me if I tell him."

I nodded. "I like him very much, Emma. He has a good heart."

She bent her head to the task of healing, but said with self-depreciation, "I was very jealous when I saw him riding up to the cottage with you, sitting before him on his horse."

"I have no designs upon him, I assure you," I replied. "He's not my type."

"In the morning, straight away, you and I will go into town," she began, "And we shall head directly to Mr. Marsh, and he will be our support when we tell Captain Crankshaw that—" Her comment died on her lips. Her eyes widened, starting at the window. She shunted back, and I managed to clamp my hand over her mouth to muffle her blood-curdling scream.

The moon in the window was gone. In fact, all the view was gone, disappeared behind a shifting curtain of purple tentacles and pale suckers, slurping at the glass.

"Don't be afraid," I said to Emma, removing my hand from her mouth. I unlatched the window and let a few of the more persistent tendrils in, and they wrapped around my injured hand with such grace and gallantry that even Emma could see their intent was honorable.

"I'm alright," I said, "I'm much improved."

Nate was a swirling mix of relief, and fear, and anger. There was culpability, too, and that particularly intimate form of bitter hatred reserved for relations who betray you.

"He was only doing what he thought best," I said, but Nate would not accept that. Almost as if he spoke words, I felt his intentions: Thorne does not consider the human cost of his goal, and one must be careful around him, for he can be lost in his ambitions and not weigh the outcome. For

Thorne, the end always justified the means.

Emma was breathing in small, shallow gulps.

"How rude of me!" I said, "Nate, this is my youngest sister." And turning to my sister, I said, "Emma, this is my friend, Nate."

"Oh," she said, very quickly and very quietly. "It has a name!"

One tentacle snaked forward, wrapped around Emma's hand, and gave it a firm shake.

I returned my attention to Nate. "In the morning, Emma and I will inform the regiment; I fear that anyone who looks upon the beast, who has not grown up under the influence of the books, will unravel under the strain. I saw it in Mrs. Rabbit: her mind was disintegrating. I'd never felt the onslaught of madness before, and did not recognize the sensations or the signs."

There was a question upon his skin. I closed my eyes, concentrating.

"I don't understand, Nate," I said, "Slow down. You're all muddled."

The tentacles whipped around my arms, my neck, my hands, increasing the contact area of our skin. His complexion flushed from orange to purple, then to a magical iridescent silver-white that almost glowed in the candlelight. I felt suction cups pulling at my cheek, and tendrils winding through my hair. The sensations were urgent, compelling, troubled, and over all of these impulses arched an umbrella of dissatisfaction.

I took a stab at translating his heart. "If you're worried for me, please, you must set that aside. It will do neither of us any good for you to be distracted by concern."

Such frustration! His silver-white skin darkened into mottled red.

"I can not understand—" Then, quite suddenly, he sorted his thoughts into clear focus and the message pealed clear and loud in my mind.

My eyes flashed open. "Oh! I'm your only link to the world! I'm the only one who understands you! If I am lost, you are again trapped in a world without conversation, and you would rather die than spend another day in solitary, wordless hopelessness." I flushed with warmth and I caressed my fingers over his skin. "You can't bear to be without me!"

Such relief flooded through him, I almost collapsed at the strength of it.

I pressed a kiss to one tentacle. "Silly octopus," I teased, "I won't be lost, nor will you be silenced, and I shall not leave you. We'll find a copy of that wretched copper book and bring you back to your former self, I promise."

One particularly large suction cup smacked a huge sloppy kiss on my cheek, so impassioned that I continued to feel the sensation of it after all the tentacles withdrew from the window, and the motion of an invisible body slinking through the garden had stilled. I reclined against the window and watched him go, my heart in my throat.

When I glanced back at Emma, she was smiling broadly.

"He has your affections!" she gasped.

"Did I not assure you? Mr. Marsh is not my type."

"I suppose not," she replied, "He hasn't enough limbs!"

I gazed out the window once more, in the direction of dark and dreary Northwich Hall. "My feelings will not be repressed. How ardently I admire and adore him! He's the most clever, most thoughtful, most handsome gentleman I've ever had the pleasure of meeting," I sighed.

"Handsome? Not in the least!" Emma replied as she dissolved into laughter. "But my goodness, he certainly does make an impression!"

---

When my sisters and I hurried straight to the camp after our breakfast, we were informed by the bugle boy that Captain Crankshaw had ridden out to Dreadmoor with a cohort of men at dawn. They intended to search the cliffs above the canyon for evidence that might explain the circumstances behind the Rabbits' death, and if we were so inclined to walk the breadth of the wild heath, we'd find the captain there.

It was a long hike in damp conditions, and the harsh wind gnawed at our hands and tugged at our skirts, but we arrived at the boundary between heath and canyon within the hour, having been spurred to a fast pace by the general misery of the weather. Men in red jackets had scattered themselves across the rolling landscape with heads down, looking for any tracks or scraps of clothing, for signs of struggle or spatters of blood, but from their drawn faces and stoic concentration, it was clear that the search had, thus far, been unsuccessful.

Mr. Marsh spotted us first, four women in pale dresses striding over the blackened land, and he galloped his horse out to greet us.

"As pleased as I am to see the Lovecraft sisters, this is no place for young ladies," he called out as he drew rein, "You must head back to the village!"

"Has there been any news, sir?"

"None," he said to me, "I'm afraid there are no clues to follow. The captain has us looking for wolf prints, but the men are restless, and many suspect that we are following a ghost."

"You're in peril, Richard," Emma said, "You won't find the culprit out here, and if you do find him, the mere sight of him will drive you mad, just as it did the poor Rabbit family."

Mr. Marsh dismounted so that we might speak on equal terms.

"Are you saying," he asked slowly, looking pointedly at Emma, "That the mother and father did themselves self-harm?" He looked to me. "Impossible! It was no suicide!"

"How can you know for sure?"

"They were woven too tightly with brambles, Miss Harriet," he said to me, and he dropped his voice to a rasp. He could no longer hide his fear or confusion. I saw a sheen of perspiration appear on his brow, an involuntary reaction to his superstitious horror, only barely contained. "The vines had grown straight down their gullets. The thorns had torn their innards to shreds! From the evidence of a struggle, and the agony they must have suffered …" His throat hitched, and he shook his head, unable to describe further.

Jane stepped forward. "The circumstances of their deaths may not have been suicide, but they were driven to lunacy by an outside force, just as the Posey family was cursed, so long ago. It's Harry's theory that whomever catches sight of the culprit will find himself rendered useless, and perhaps even dangerous, to his companions."

"Then you certainly must leave," Mr. Marsh insisted. "Young women should not roam about the countryside unaided—"

As he spoke, Jane laid a hand upon his wrist. Instantly he froze.

"This gets us nowhere," she said to us, as if Mr. Marsh had ceased to be in our party. It's true, he looked as though he was no longer in attendance; his eyes were dull and stared at a distant point on the horizon, his mouth was parted mid-sentence. Jane kept her hand on his arm, and said, "The men will never listen to us. We can beg and plead all day long, and the captain will insist this is the work of a non-existent wolf, and we'll be no farther ahead in our task."

"Please don't do that to him, Jane," Emma pleaded. "Oh, poor man! Can he still hear us?"

Mary spoke to Jane and me, ignoring our youngest sister's distress. "We must make them listen," said Mary, "If they're really here to protect the village, then we must give them all the tools they need to do their job and fulfill their responsibility."

The horse nuzzled up against me, befuddled by the stone-like stillness of its rider. "Jane may be right," I said, and with a certain snide brassiness, added, "They'll cast aside our good advice because we lack the proper genitalia to have a worthy opinion."

"Harry!" Emma scolded.

"It's true," Jane agreed.

"Can you bewitch them?" Mary asked, but Jane scoffed at the suggestion.

"A whole army? I doubt it!" She tapped her hand against Mr. Marsh's unflinching arm. "One man, maybe, but not a hundred."

"Then for their own safety, we must send them on a goose chase and keep them far from the path of our quarry," I continued. "But I dare not send them too far afield, because we'll need them to apprehend our culprit, too, once he's been unmasked. Ah! I know. Jane, please restore Mr. Marsh to his former awareness."

She looked up to him, removed her hand, and he blinked a few times as if waking.

"I forgot what I was saying …." he muttered.

I stepped forward. "Mr. Marsh, please inform the captain that there have been sightings of a frightful beast around the fairy stones, and it may have constructed a den there. He might even wish for the soldiers to dig up a stone or two, just to make sure there's no tunnels under them—as you no doubt have heard, the badgers in this country can reach an astronomical size, and we may yet find that Earl's disappearance was due to a particularly ornery one."

Still befuddled, he accepted my explanation with the ease and pliability of one in a dream. "Of course, thank you, Miss Lovecraft," he said with a rush of breath. "I've never heard of extraordinary badgers in Upper Whatley."

"Then count your town fortunate. They give us a great deal of trouble, here in Dunham."

"Huge things," Mary replied. "Much bigger than average."

He took her comment as truth, for she was a better example than any of us.

"I'll go at once," he said, and offered us a pert nod before unsteadily mounting the horse and galloping off, calling out for the captain as he left.

Emma folded her arms, looking cross. "'Tis bad enough to bend one's intentions, Jane! Now you've started removing a gentleman's free will completely!"

"A very nifty trick," Mary complimented.

Jane looked very pleased with herself, but said, "My apologies, Emma."

We watched the soldiers collect themselves into tidy lines, sling their shovels over their shoulders, and march towards the distant rise in the land, south of us, where the pillars of the fairy stones jutted upwards to a steel-grey sky. The red jackets looked like bright garnets cast over a dark carpet, or spots of blood against a wiry black hide. We turned towards the east and began rambling back in the direction of the village, and Mary looked down at me.

"How can the Rabbits have died with brambles growing through their gullets?" she said, "It's just as strange as Earl's death, trapped in a tree."

Jane said, "And didn't the old tree have fresh leaves growing upon it? That's what caught Teddy Crumpsall's attention, and led him to see Earl's foot."

I held my shawl more tightly to my throat. "Nature herself is rising up against us."

We walked a little farther in silence, and when Emma slipped her hand over the crook of my arm, I felt the brittle sheen of dread on her skin.

"Do you think the fact that Teddy found Earl might link them together?"

"Perhaps," I replied to her. "But what about George? What connection does he have to Teddy or Earl?"

"None that I can see," Mary said as she stomped over a rise in the land, and plucked a sprig of heather from the ground. Little purple flowers bloomed between her strong fingers. "The heather blooms very early."

Jane took the sprig from her. "The brambles, the tree, the heather … amid so much death, new life springs?"

But I was unsettled by it, rather than comforted. "The world is unbalanced," I said, musing to myself. "Can you feel it? Everything seems crooked, somehow, like the tower of St. Dismas. It's all just tilted enough for us to doubt our senses." I looked back the way we'd come. "Something's not right."

"Well, I think it was a good idea, Harry, sending the soldiers to the fairy stones," said Mary, "I don't much like the idea of the men digging them up, but it'll keep the regiment occupied for days."

"If only our problem was as simple as an oversized badger," said Emma.

We walked on a little further. My hand began to ache.

"Sore?" said Emma when she saw me favoring it.

"Yes."

"And your ankle?"

"As good as new," I replied, "And my hand will be fine, in a day or two."

"Can I tell Jane and Mary about your friend?" she said, her eyes twinkling. When Jane turned with a puzzled look, Emma said, "He came to visit Harry last night, and inquired after her health."

"Friend?" said Mary. "Harry has no friends."

"It can't be Mr. Blackwood," said Jane as we reached the wider track, and turned towards the Darling house and the vale. "He was in a tizzy when he brought you home, and knew full well the state of your mind. He thought he'd killed you for sure."

"We all thought you were good as dead," said Emma. "It's no wonder your friend would venture out to see you. He must have been worried sick!"

Mary nodded. "And when the life started to come back to you, you ranted about all manner of things, like a child with a high fever."

I stopped.

"Like what?"

Mary and Jane looked at each other. "I don't remember," said Jane, "I think, teeth? Yes, you were frightened of teeth."

"And the East Bridge," said Mary, "You muttered about the Waters under the East Bridge."

"Did I mention the fairy stones?"

"I don't know," said Emma. "Why?"

Why, indeed. I'd given it no thought. The suggestion to Mr. Marsh had sprung as easily to my lips as if the stones had been forefront in my mind.

"You look stricken, Harry," said Jane. "What's wrong?"

My gut clenched. I'd suggested they visit the fairy stones in a fit of inspiration, but the place had come to my lips because it had been brought there through the song of the psychopomp. I'd seen Mrs. Rabbit's madness, I'd felt her thoughts fraying, I'd seen the smashed glass of Earl's psyche. I'd seen things I couldn't describe, things I wouldn't describe—but I had also caught a glimpse of the fairy stones.

Had I not crossed paths with the monster here, on Dreadmoor Heath?

"I've sent them to the mouth of the devil," I gasped. I clutched Mary's hand, felt her confusion and concern. "The stones—they were a melody in the song of the psychopomp!"

Her confusion increased ten-fold.

"Oh, d-—it! Trust me, I've put them in danger!"

We turned back upon our path and ran to catch up with the regiment. For every pace, I felt my fear increase, and when we crested the highest point in the heath land, I was sure that a horror awaited us. I braced myself for the sight of blood and gore, of agony and writhing terror.

But instead, we discovered a scene of clockwork perfection.

Captain Crankshaw portioned out the work from horseback, and the men were pulling shovels and axes, preparing to topple the pillars. The grey mizzle had broken, the fog had evaporated, and shafts of golden sunlight pierced the thinning clouds, striking the uneven landscape and warming the soil. There was even a blush of purple on the high ground, where more of the tiny heather flowers had bloomed early under these fine and clement conditions. I hurried straight through the lines of men pulling up the turf and crested the embankment until I stood before the captain.

"Sir, I am mistaken, this is not the place," I replied, stammering in my haste. "I am sorry, I've made an error!"

The man regarded me with gruff disdain. He looked down his nose and ran one finger thoughtfully over the scar on his chin. "I should think this is as good a place to check as any," he said, "The earth is dewy, the place quite wild. Go on, Mr. Frame, Mr. Keel. Bring down the north stone, and let us search for tunnels underneath. If there are any predators here, we shall root them out."

"No, I think you might wish to concentrate your efforts closer to town," I said as my sisters raced up the mound behind me.

The captain gave a dismissive grunt. "My dear lady, who ever heard of a feral wolf living in town? No, no, if we hope to capture the beast, then this is a good place to begin."

"But it's a mistake," I said. I was huffing and puffing from the exertion, and I laid my injured hand upon the central rock. "You ought to—"

Such a powerful blast rocketed up through my fingers that I recoiled with a cry. Emma reached out to me, Mary seized me before I collapsed to the ground.

"Are you quite alright?" said the captain.

My hand throbbed. A spasm of pain shot through the tips of my fingers like electricity, and there was a smell of ozone in the air. As the vibrations subsided, I reached out again, much more cautiously this time, and dragged one finger across the lichen-speckled stone.

This was no passing creature. Stones do not hold such powerful emotion. I could barely contain myself, and in a harsh whisper, I said, "Captain, you must smash this down. And do not tarry, for there is something alive entombed within."

# SEVENTEEN

My request was odd, but Captain Crankshaw was a military man and accustomed to action without questions; spurred by the tone of my voice, he proved to be very accommodating.

Using iron bars and sledge hammers, the soldiers pried apart the weathered stone to reveal a cavity, and like a chick tucked inside an egg, we found George Darling's body entombed, whole and unharmed but cold and malnourished. His mind was clearly broken after days alone in a solitary, lightless, and inescapable cell. His gooey eyes blinked at the bright light, his gaping mouth took huge gasps of fresh air, and when the soldiers tried to help him stand, George flinched and screamed at their touch. His fingers were worn to bloodied nubs from days of scratching at the rock; all the flesh was gone and the tips reduced to pink-grey bones.

In an awed tone, Mr. Marsh asked how I came to discover George, but Emma assured him that it was no more than an unfortunate coincidence. He seemed to be eager to believe any answer she gave him, and for her quick-witted intervention, I was very grateful. I didn't want any suspicions to be placed upon me, nor did I wish to explain my Quirk.

But I carefully watched the villagers as they came, one by one, across the bleak scrubland to see the removal of George's trembling body from the stone. He was gaunt, green-pale, and trembling violently, his night garments turned to filthy rags. Sores had opened along his legs and he smelled strongly of urine. Whenever anyone approached him, he cowered, and if they dared to lay a hand upon him, he'd cringe as if he'd been struck. The poor man seemed not to recognize anyone. Mr. Winterbottom and Father Noonan soon arrived on the scene, followed quickly after by Marvin Runkle and Mr. Cripplegate, who sent the boy off with urgings for great haste in the direction of the Darling property. Once summoned, Mr. Darling came running over the heath and, with the assistance of three soldiers and an old hay cart, he ferried George home. They headed east across the wagon track towards his residence, and I was quite certain that Mrs. Darling would be overcome with relief at the gladsome news. Frederick would be pleased at their reunion, but I suspected he would be solemn and grave, too, upon seeing the fragile state of George's mind.

I stood at the side of the fairy stones and watched, hands clasped at my back, as George was freed and the hay cart led away. Eventually I grew aware of a figure standing behind me, and I glanced over my shoulder to see the imposter Mr. Blackwood watching the affair from lower on the plain, resting against his expensive walking stick. He nodded his head to me, and I nodded in reply, then left my sisters to join him.

"I've heard from Mrs. Runkle that you were the one to find him," he said as I approached.

"I was."

"Is this another of your tricks? To locate the missing?"

"No," I replied, standing beside him.

"How did you come to the conclusion that he would be entombed?"

"In the psychopomp's vision, I saw the stones," I said, "But I thought little about it. There were so many images, piled one atop the other. Only after I suggested it to the army to send them hither on a fool's quest did I realize, my inspiration was misplaced."

"Isn't that Mr. Darling's good fortune!" Mr. Blackwood said. He seemed angry, not that such a travesty occurred, but that he had not thought of the idea first. "And what about Mr. Crumpsall the younger?"

"As I said, there were many images, piled on atop the other. They're fading like a dream," I admitted. "But I saw the East Bridge, I recall that."

"Well, he's most likely dead, and therefore not going anywhere, no matter where he's been stuck," Blackwood replied. "Best leave your theories to yourself, or else you'll come under suspicion."

I was horrified at the thought. "If he is still alive as George is …?"

Blackwood tipped his chin towards the empty cavity in the stone. "What sort of quality of life would that be, I wonder? But no, I suppose you're right, we mustn't leave Teddy stuck in a rock. As always, Miss Lovecraft, your compassion does you credit." He hailed one of the soldiers loitering on the opposite verge of the wagon track.

The young man seemed stunned by the events of the day. He blinked slowly in our direction, scratching absently at the rear of his trousers.

"Sir," Blackwood continued, "Do you think the last lost gentleman could be both under a bridge AND entombed in stone? What about the East Bridge, which is made of good solid granite, and offers enough space to stash a Crumpsall, if it pleases you?"

The soldier gapped at the thought, pulled at his uniform, shifted his weight from foot to foot. "I ... I don't know, sir ..."

"Good lord, trust me to engage the laziest imbecile in all the King's army," said Mr. Blackwood to me, then he returned his attention to the young man, and spoke in slow, enunciated words, "Take a moment's pause from scratching your pimpled buttocks and please convey my assumption to your captain, you tallow-headed, slack-jawed, soporific, pigeon-livered louse."

The soldier stared at the gentleman, aghast.

"Hurry now," I urged, "There may be a life hanging in the balance!"

This broke him from his stunned pause. He scampered away, calling out for Captain Crankshaw, who stood surveying the land with hands on hip, high up on the far slope.

The imposter Blackwood tapped the silver head of the black cane with one hand into his opposite palm. "What a rare treat this must be for him, to be given the prospect of heroism."

"You were very unkind, sir," I scolded, "The poor man is probably a farmer's son, and has never seen battle, never mind such oddness as this."

"They do all look dumbfounded, don't they," he said, surveying the groups of men. "As long as one of those dolts take the accolades, you're secure from suspicion. Have they found any further information regarding the Rabbit hangings?"

I shook my head. "No."

"Pity. We're short on clues, Harry, and who knows which poor villager is next."

I folded my arms and watched as the soldiers began to fill in the holes dug around the ancient temple, mixing mortar and organizing the broken stones. "To be trapped for days on end, with no hope of rescue ... Do you think George will recover?"

"I doubt it," came the bored reply.

"Pity," I replied, "I thought George had great potential."

Mr. Blackwood's lip kinked into a smirk.

"You seem unaffected by this."

"I cried a great deal after they retrieved Earl, but I hardly knew George. To be honest, I'm more upset for Mrs. Darling—she'll be at her wit's end."

The imposter Mr. Blackwood and I began to stroll down the wagon track towards the village. He'd clasped his hands and cane at the small of his back, and his face was downcast. "They'll all be at wit's end, quite literally, if we don't find the fellow responsible." Then he glanced at me and said, "I suspect you have looked upon the face of an Eidolon of the Old Gods—a possessor-spirit, a daemon, a mania—and come away unscathed. That, in itself, is remarkable."

"An Eidolon? The Greek word from your book in the tower? What a frightful title. I assure you, I've not forgotten the vibrancy of its eyes," I replied, suppressing a shiver. "I don't think I ever will."

Even now, bathed in warm spring sunlight, I felt the coldness of the giant's inhuman gaze piercing the depths of my body, and my fingers trembled. They'd been ghastly, those eyes, set deeply in a bone-white mask and surrounded by a mane so black, it let no light escape. The strong, unyielding body wreathed in grey rags moved with stealth, sliding over the uneven ground as though untouched by gravity. Such a phantasm I had never before seen, nor wished to see again!

Mr. Blackwood shook his head. "Most of humanity would be driven mad by such an encounter; I wager our good gentleman George Darling laid sight upon that same face, and has come away with a broken mind, as did the Rabbits." He took a deep breath. "And, perhaps, the Posey's, too."

"Did one of the Posey boys become this ... this Eidolon demon?"

"That is my assumption," he replied. "And when his family looked upon his sinister visage, they were shattered in mind and spirit."

I frowned at this. "Then why am I unaffected?" I looked to him as we strolled together. "Is it the same inoculation that you mentioned before? That I have grown up so closely to the books, that they have given me a measure of protection?"

"I believe so. I've spent long hours, pondering that very question, poring through Posey's old notes. I believe you and your sisters wear an armor that none can see."

The mention of research sparked a question.

"And your books," I said. "Are they safe? Have you accounted for all of them?"

He paused, weighing his answer.

"Mostly."

I gave a haughty snort. "That's not good enough! You sit on an arsenal of knowledge, Mr. Thorne! It ought to be secure!"

He looked scandalized that I'd dare to use his real name, his bastard name, and he cast his eyes about to ensure no one had heard me. "Your attention to my arsenal is appreciated, Miss Lovecraft, but I can assure you, it is quite secure."

"You know the precise placement of every volume?" I pressed, "And three in particular: The Final Confessions of Bai Xi, Songs of the Scented Gardens, and The Widow's Rites?"

His skin turned sallow. His huge eyes rolled towards me, and they were full of accusation and abhorrence. "Be quiet, you foolish quim!" He stammered, faltered, ground his teeth. "Those titles have been lost to priests and scholars for centuries! How do you know to speak them?"

His fear was consummate. I dared not give him more information than necessary, so I replied, "How I know of them does not matter. That I know you have them in your possession is more important, for if I know, perhaps others do, too. Please, Mr. Thorne, tell me you have secured them completely in your fortress."

From the way he chewed his lip to the manner in which his fingers twitched, I'd planted a seed of doubt in his despicable heart.

"You don't understand the predicament in which I find myself, Harry. Mr. Posey's library is extensive," he said. "Thousands of volumes. I've done my best to catalogue them, but the scope of the project is vast. Nate is highly motivated, of course, but I'm just one man."

"I don't care about thousands of titles," I replied. "I only care about three."

"Fine," he spat, "Come with me to Northwich Hall, and I will show you myself that they're secure." He would not touch my hand to guide me, but he beckoned for me to follow, and we went through the vale to the Church Bridge, and began walking at a brisk pace towards the crossroads, where Mill Road meets the Green Track.

---

Down we went into the cellar of Northwich, into the dank and the musty gloom, with only a single lantern to light our way. For every step I descended, I felt my heart grow lighter and lighter. We reached the slate floor and the endless arched corridor of stunted doors, and Mr. Thorne called out into the echoing dark, "Nate? Are you here?"

There was no reply.

"Does he go out often?"

"He prefers to avoid broad daylight," Thorne replied as he scuttled down the hall, holding the lamp aloft, "When he's feeling moody, he'll spend hours sitting in the middle of the river, completely submerged."

"Must he be under water?"

Thorne shook his head. "No, but he prefers places that are dismal and damp. It isn't uncommon for him to seek solitude in the forest, where the air is moist and there are very few people to catch a glimpse of him. He fears that anyone who gazes upon him will become insane, and so he prefers to wander about like a lost poet, all moon-eyed and melancholy, feeling badly for himself."

"You have so little empathy for his situation!"

"I've been his companion for almost five years in this damnable state," Thorne replied, "All his moping and complaining? Frankly, it's boring, Miss Lovecraft. At some point, he ought to embrace the situation and get on with living, and enjoy the fruits of which his curious predicament can provide him." He glanced over his shoulder at me, his expression infused with a wicked imagination. "Can you imagine it? Exploring the depth of the oceans, unfettered by technology, going where no man has gone before? We can scarcely comprehend the wonders he could discover! Instead, he prefers wallowing in melancholy, the cretin. 'Oh, I'm so lonely! No one understands me! I have no bones!' Utter balderdash! Ah, here we are."

We'd come to the oak door banded with iron. From the inside pocket of his coat, Mr. Thorne produced an ornate brass key with which he opened the lock. The hinges gave a theatrical squeak that shivered up my spine and made my toes curl.

Inside was a dark, empty room with a dirt floor and a low, cramped ceiling. In the center lay an immense flat slab of undressed stone.

Thorne entered without hesitation. I'd begun to follow when a gentle weight slithered over my shoulder; the tentacle wrapped itself around my shoulders, and yanked me back into the corridor. I managed a small, strangled squeak of surprise before Thorne turned, and his brows drew down, thunderous.

"Oh, she requested to come here," he said in his own defense. "It wasn't my idea."

Two more tentacles snaked around my torso, and I found myself boldly pressed to Nate's body. A touch of my hand revealed this to be, not an attack, but an act of salvation.

"You don't wish for me to go in, but I must see if the books are there," I replied.

No! No no no! A million times, no!

"Mr. Blackwood," I said, addressing the monster by his family name, and instantly I felt a fusillade of affection sparkle over his blue mottled skin, "I am in no danger. I will not read any of the words, I promise. I only wish to ensure that the books are secure."

His reluctance was as heavy and suffocating as a wet blanket.

"If you wouldn't mind releasing me …?" I urged, for the tentacles had grown as unyielding as a boa constrictor. Muscles relaxed and tendrils slackened. "Thank you." I stepped out of his embrace and, not wishing to slight him, I leaned forward and pressed a kiss to the space between his eyes. "I do appreciate your concern."

If Thorne was unimpressed at this show of affection, he said nothing. He was too busy trying to push the heavy slate tile to one side to reveal a hole underneath.

"There," he said at last, clapping the dirt from his hands. "At the bottom of the well."

Perhaps four feet wide in diameter, the hole created a round spot of stygian blackness in the middle of the chamber floor. The well had been constructed of good, interlocking bricks, and I knelt at the side, leaning over to peer into it; perhaps I looked precariously balanced, for one chivalrous tentacle slipped around my waist to keep me from falling in. I squinted down into the darkness as my eyes adjusted, but the well was much too deep for me to see the bottom, even with the lamp.

"The books are down there?"

"The three worst," he replied. "You've already named them. I will not."

"I can't see."

"Then let Nate drop the light down, and you'll spot them," he suggested.

We clustered around the hole, and Nate took the lantern in one tentacle and lowered it slowly into the darkness, revealing patterns of brickwork and spirals of moss. At one point, quite close to the bottom, I saw scratches on the walls: a series of long grooves left behind by claws and teeth.

"Those are marks made by Posey's sons, trying to escape?" I said.

"So I believe," Thorne replied.

Down went the lamp, casting its circle of quivering light, until at last, the bare dirt floor was revealed. In the center of the hole were three books. They were too distant for me to read the words embossed upon their covers, but I saw that one had been bound in a ghostly white leather, and I remembered what my father had said, and how he'd described Songs of the Scented Garden.

"You see?" Thorne said. "They're still as I left them." All three of us leaned back from the edge and sat on the floor as Nate lifted the lantern back to our level. "No one has come or gone from this cellar, Miss Lovecraft, and I've made every effort to ensure no one lays eyes on these pages."

I was both relieved to see them and profoundly disappointed. "Are there other volumes that could have resulted in such a transformation?" I asked. "Surely these three can't be the only ones; wasn't it a different title that led to Nate's unfortunate predicament?"

He looked to the cephalopod, and those amber eyes looked back with hesitation, blinking twice. "Should I tell her of the other titles, Nate? I think I must. She's far too clever to leave unarmed and uninformed, don't you think?"

One tentacle remained wrapped protectively around my waist, and a second tentacle snaked around my wrist and slipped into my grasp.

171

Through my palm, I felt his dread. It was a creeping anxiety, a rise in heart rate and a burst of adrenaline.

"So, there are more, but you're afraid that I'll seek them out if I know their identities?" I said, and I wound the tentacle through and around my fingers. "Nate, I would rather know and be able to help you, than remain ignorant and set safely to one side. To keep me from further education does me no good! How can I be of service if I'm not given the opportunity to understand?" To Thorne, I said, "You must tell me of the others."

Thorne pulled himself up from the floor and dusted off his trousers. "Some books are mere blips of light in the firmament. Others are collapsing stars and capable of destroying worlds. I'm afraid there is no comprehensive reading list, Miss Lovecraft, but in this place—in this reality—I'm certain that these three are worst."

"But in other realities, they are not?"

He tipped his head to acknowledge the truth of the statement. "The books are linked together across the multitude of universes, but I have not yet ascertained how. I suspect that the knowledge they contain are the pillars that bear the weight of construction." He moved into the corridor and slapped his hand against one stone column. "They give structure to the whole of Creation."

Nate helped me to my feet, and when we had exited the chamber, one tentacle fumbled as it shut the oak door and threw the latch closed. Thorne was already half-way up the stairs to the main floor; we hurried to catch him.

"We do not own these books, Miss Lovecraft. They own us," he said as we joined him. "You recall, of course, that great tome with the paintings of demons which I showed you? The Rubrication Codex? The writing in the book was made by a man named Father Humbolt; you saw his words as he added his notes into the margins. He and I are following parallel paths, it seems, and the Rubrication Codex has chosen to chain us together."

"Where is the Mr. Thorne of Humbolt's reality?"

He shrugged. "I don't know. Dead, probably." He led us past the library and into the main foyer. "Life is full of endless perils. In any given universe on any given day, you have a better chance of dying than of living." His grin was serpentine, his mirth carried a certain sinister quality. "How lucky we are, to all be here at the same time, at the same place, together. The odds against it are astronomical."

We climbed up the main staircase, then turned along the uppermost corridor towards the tower.

"So anything is possible?"

"You're standing next to a giant octopus, Miss Lovecraft," Thorne replied,

"You tell me."

Nate's skin blushed a bright coral shade, and I held his tentacle a little tighter.

With every floor we climbed, the corridors grew more and more narrow, the rooms crowding together, and the furnishings of an older style. Dust lay thick upon the carpets. Cobwebs festooned the fixtures. There were no windows, and the only light came from Thorne's lantern, which made the shadows sway and lurch as he passed.

He said nothing more until we reached the tower room. When he entered, the light from the circle of windows blinded me momentarily, and when I blinked away the tears, I saw Thorne striding through the piles of books on the floor.

He set his lamp upon the table. "Under normal circumstances, I would be reluctant to tell anyone my research, but I don't think it'll have much effect on you, Miss Lovecraft," he said, "Your reality is already one in flux, and you seem to be able to reconcile all strangeness that casts itself before you. I have never met someone who could remain so calm in the face of such horrors. It's almost as if you refuse to recognize the abhorrent as something to be feared."

"You think me unable to identify the eldritch and strange!" I said.

"Are you?" Thorne asked over his shoulder. "Even now, you and Nate are holding hands, as if it is perfectly normal for a young lady of your standing to be in such close proximity to a disgusting, depraved, revolting monster." He turned and looked straight into the amber eyes. "Yes, I said it. Monster! Don't be so sensitive, Nate."

"He's hardly a monster," I replied.

"Don't defend him, Harry, it only makes you as deplorable as he is," Thorne replied, returning to the shelves. "Ah, here we are." He picked up the large volume, the Rubrication Codex, and set it on the table again. He pulled the spectacles from the inside pocket of his coat, then he beckoned for me to join him. "I've already told you that the boat you call Reality is beginning to sink. Life in Dunham has always been sleepy and sedate, but I dare say it teeters on the edge of a grand transformation, Miss Lovecraft. The Gates of Madness are opening. Ah!" said Thorne, with the glasses perched on his nose. "This is the one, was it not?"

He ran his finger over the blank page, and when he stopped, he transferred the glasses to me with one hand while pointing with the other. The image swam into view, and the vision captured there was all too familiar.

"Yes, that's the titan on the heath," I whispered. "The very same. The Eidolon."

But Nate could not bear to look upon it, and had flattened himself against the ground, under the velvet sofa, and covered himself in a matching floral pattern.

Thorne took the glasses back from me, flipped the red lenses down, and ran his finger along the bottom of the picture. If there was a script there, it was invisible to me in this reality, but he seemed well-versed and hesitated only a little as he translated it. "After your unfortunate hysteria under the influence of the psychopomp, I spent all night seeking information; in your frenzy, you cried out that you saw flowers blooming, Miss Lovecraft—flowers with teeth, no less!—and that proclamation sent me in a few profitable directions. One version of Father Humbolt fought against the Eidolon last year—last year in another reality, of course. It seems that, in our reality, Father Humbolt perished of scarlet fever while still a child."

"How tragic!"

Thorne waved away my comment as insignificant. "I've spent hours slogging through his work, Harry. The man was verbose and dull. He grew up to become a terrible writer—one of those wretched curs who does not recognize the worth of a well-placed comma—and our reality has been spared his excessive volumes of drivel. For that, we can be grateful."

"And yet you've uncovered something significant in all his drivel?"

"I have, yes!" Thorne said with a burst of inspiration, "Based on his writing, I believe the Eidolon is shaping itself a new empire, beginning in Dunham County. For some reason, we've fallen behind other realms. An event in our past disrupted the universes, and consequently our time has become stunted, and moves slightly slower than the rest."

"And this gives us an advantage."

"Precisely," he said, flipping all the lenses up.

I felt Nate's presence at my elbow, and I glanced at him, then back to Thorne. "How, precisely?"

The man looked terribly disappointed in me. "We know the reason why this devil does what it does, Harry! We can put a title and a purpose to the face of our evil! As Humbolt tells us, it is the Eidolon."

"How can that help? I've never heard of such a thing!"

"No? Not up on our Ancient Greek mythology, are we? What a pity. An Eidolon is a powerful spirit, sometimes of the dead, but sometimes of the living. Perhaps you're more familiar with the German term, doppelganger? Or the Irish term, fetch?"

I shook my head.

He clucked with disapproval. "You've spent too much time with children's books, Miss Lovecraft." Thorne replied. "That romantic Mr. Humbolt, for some unknown reason, thought the title of Eidolon was apt. Certainly, his identification makes it clear to me that this spirit has possessed a villager's body to give it corporeal strength, to root it in this place and time."

"But why?"

"Ah!" he said, "That is most interesting! Based on Humbolt's theories, the Eidolon possesses a singular function: to prepare his kingdom for the return of the Old Gods. He strews the path with mad followers in much the same way as a flower girl strews petals and prepares the path for a bride. He wishes to have the whole place tidied and re-arranged before the Ancient Ones arrive."

I startled at this revelation. I dared not imagine such a thing: were we not having difficulty with one supernatural entity? I wouldn't wish to fight off a whole pantheon!

"So the Old Gods are returning?"

To my relief, Thorne rolled his eyes dismissively.

"By the whip of Mithras, Miss Lovecraft, how should I know?" he snapped, "The Old Gods abandoned this realm eons ago, when men were nothing better than grunting, naked beasts, cowering in caves at the crash of thunder. Mankind possessed no language to share ideas from one mind to another, nor did they have the art of writing to share those same ideas across centuries." One hand drifted over the book, caressing the page. "And even if brutish man could have, somehow, transmitted his opinions forward through the many generations to our eager ears, I doubt the exalted Ancient Ones would've told their intentions to a bunch of smelly, flea-infested monkeys! No, Miss Lovecraft, I doubt the Old Gods are returning—if they were, we wouldn't have a chance of salvation, and all of this conversation would be wasted breath."

"But Humbolt said—"

"Think of the Eidolon as a kind of automaton: it has a singular purpose, regardless of the outcome, and that is its threat. The reader who opens themselves to the Eidolon's influence can still wreak havoc over the landscape, trying to fulfill its purpose. Any mere mortal who lays their eyes upon this devil while he wears his face of bone will have their mind torn to threads, and as the Eidolon's power grows, the laws of nature to which we eagerly cling will begin to fray, as we've already seen with Earl and George."

"So our culprit will destroy Dunham, given a chance, and his presence has tempted an army of psychopomps, for they sense that there will soon be many souls to harvest and deliver."

Thorne looked impressed. "So you aren't a turnip-headed ninny, after all! My apologies, Miss Lovecraft. I leapt to conclusions."

I scowled at him, but said, "Then our course is clear and unchanged, sir. We must stop the Eidolon immediately, and destroy any of these books which might be keys to the destruction of our framework of reality. We must burn this collection to the ground!"

Thorne gave a horrified cry. Even Nate rippled and flushed a bright turquoise with surprise.

"We'll find the Eidolon, I have no quarrel with that, but I will not destroy these books!" he said, scandalized. He thumped the volume closed and set it back upon a tower on the floor. "How could you suggest such a crude thing, Harry? You're a librarian. You know that all books have value." He swept his hand wide. "These very tomes have protected you, yet you'd betray them and set them on fire?"

I did feel queasy, having suggested setting thousands of rare books ablaze. It would be the sacking of the Library of Alexandria, all over again.

"Beside," Thorne continued, and now his voice contained a measure of amusement, and his lips had turned up in a sneer, "One of these books may have the cure for poor Nate's predicament. How could you deny him the chance to return to his original form? I'm sure he'd love to be a man again, wouldn't you, Nate?" He slapped his hand over Nate's head. "Walk on two legs again, have a voice, have a family. You could show Harry how you feel about her, not with slimy tentacles and suction cups, but fingers and hands and throbbing—"

"Enough," I said, "There's no call for vulgarities, Mr. Thorne, no matter how much joy you derive from your brother's embarrassment." I looked to Nate and smiled. "If there's a cure, we'll find it. And until then," I held my chin up. "We'll simply have to be creative with our relationship."

Nate flushed that pretty yellow-gold of happiness, but Thorne laughed raucously. "Well, I won't stand in your nasty, perverted way, you adorable reprobates." He leaned his hip against the shelf and crossed his arms. "But for now, we must find the human face of our Eidolon of the Old Gods, and I have no idea how. The ball was a failure, and I'm not about to open my home again to every roustabout and cowherd in the county. It took days to get rid of the manure smell."

"Never fear, Mr. Thorne: there is a way that doesn't require you to further feign kindness," I said.

"How?" Thorne pressed.

"One person has laid eyes upon our culprit and still draws breath." I smiled. "It may be difficult, it may be dangerous, but I shall attempt a conversation with George."

# EIGHTEEN

It was my decision to go alone. Nate protested but Mr. Thorne gave no argument; chivalry was not his strong suit. However, he did offer me a gift before I left.

He dropped the spectacles in a grey velvet bag and, hailing me as I exited the main doors of Northwich Hall, he set it in my hands. "Take the hermetiscope," he said, "And when you meet with George, use them to examine him. I want to know what you see." He waggled one finger at me. "And don't break them! Do you have any idea how long it took me to craft them? The cost? You couldn't hope to replace them, not in a million years."

"How do I even use these?" I replied. They felt much heavier than expected.

He curled his lip in disgust. "You hook them over your ears, Harry, and then you look through them. Haven't you used glasses before? They don't come with instructions." Then he shut the front door with a bang.

I met my sisters on the road coming home from the village. When I told them my plan, Mary insisted that she accompany me. She seemed shaken by the events of the morning, more than any of the others.

"I can't reconcile what's happening," she admitted to me once Jane and Emma were gone, continuing home to tell our parents of George's return. "I've wracked my brain for the circumstances that would've left young Mr. Darling entombed in stone, and Earl bound up in wood, and I can't see how it's possible."

"I know you won't be happy with this suggestion," I replied. "But what if it's magic?"

She looked down at me with such stern eyes, I had to laugh, even in the midst of our reality falling to pieces.

"Hear me out: what if this is science, but a realm of science that's much bigger and broader than our fragile human minds can comprehend?" I continued. "How would ancient man have interpreted our taming of fire?

Or the printing of words on a page? Or Emma's impressions of light upon silver? Or any number of technological marvels that we take for granted? They would have said it was magic, and even though we know differently, they would've lacked the vocabulary or comprehension for us to explain."

"But doesn't that feel like, I don't know …" she began, casting about for an explanation, "Giving up? We can't understand, therefore we shouldn't try?"

We walked in silence for half a mile until we reached the church, and Father Noonan waved at us from the doorway of St. Dismas. Mary waved back and said to me, "If we give up, then we're no better than Father Noonan, relying on blind faith to guide us. I don't know if I could do that and be content."

I felt the heavy swing of the glasses in my pocket, and at the apex of Church Bridge, I withdrew them from their velvet bag and showed them to Mary. "What sort of technology is this, then?"

She took them with care, and flipped the lenses back and forth.

"I've never seen anything like them," she replied.

I took them back and hooked them over my ears, and she laughed at how ridiculously they sat on my nose.

"I've been told that different lenses show you different things," I said, flipping down the blue lenses, "And different combinations, too. Like this," I flipped down the red lenses, "Now everything has a purple hue."

"What are they good for, other than changing the color of the world?"

"I'm not sure," I said, and I looked at her as I flipped the red lenses up.

And everything around us changed.

The bridge was suddenly crammed with people, ghostly shades of all shapes and sizes. Towers of glass rose up on either side of the river, and in the sky, I saw birds with iron wings soaring from east to west. Mary still stood before me, the same height and broadness, but any softness to her appearance disappeared. Her features were blocky and bold, and a thick miasma of light tangerine swirled around her shoulders like a cloak. Half of her face had been terribly burned in a fire; the skin was puckered and white. The most arresting feature, though, was a walnut-sized eye in the middle of her forehead, bright as an emerald, which stared down at me unblinking. Mary stepped towards me and held out one hand, and as she towered over me, that eye never waivered from my own. It stared at me like an open challenge.

"Harry?" she said, "Are you alright?"

I ripped the glasses off and stumbled back from her.

"Dear God!"

"What?" she said, full of concern, "What is it?"

I put the glasses in her hand. "Look at me. Look! What do you see when you look at me?"

She put the glasses on her nose. They were comically tiny on her face. When she glanced in my direction, she jerked back.

"Goodness, Harry!"

"What do I look like?"

Mary reached out with a shaking hand to run her fingers over my neck. "There's a mist around you—"

"Yes, same with you!" I interrupted.

"—and your eye!"

"In the middle of my forehead?"

She shook her head, stunned. "No, your left eye is gone! Just a socket—what happened to you? You look hard, and spiteful, and—" She peered closer, fascinated. "You're covered in bruises, Harry, and wearing a tattered green dress, and you look like you've been through a war."

She lowered the glasses down her nose and looked relieved to see me, whole and unblemished.

"What does it mean?"

"There's another reality where you and I are living very different lives."

Mary went back and forth, peering at me through the glasses and then without, comparing the two visions. "That's for certain. You look like you could chew coins and spit nails." She grinned. "Goodness, I don't think I'd trust you to turn my back on you!"

"Mr. Tho—Blackwood ... Mr. Blackwood," I began, "He says there are many realities that sit one-atop-the-other, and the hermetiscope allows us to glimpse between them." Mary put them back on her nose, and flipped between lenses, and peered around at the world giving little grunts of interest and surprise. "But knowing that there are different realities does little to help us interpret them. You had a great emerald eye in the middle of your brow. What could that mean?" I said.

But she was too busy cycling through combinations of lenses. "Ah," she said, "In this one, there are hardly any people about, and the bridge is a ruin. You look closer to how you are, Harry—two eyes, much friendlier—but this dress is blue instead of green, and your hair is quite short." She peeked over the rip of the hermetiscope. "It's a good style for you."

I glanced at her wide forehead, and knew that beyond my limited vision and in some mysterious realm, there was a great eye staring out at the world. "Perhaps you see how the world is, the truth of it all, and that's given you remarkable strength, both physically and intellectually. The books in Mr. Posey's library have influenced how we grew, and they've made you as close to omniscient as a human can be."

I caught sight of Father Noonan in the churchyard, strolling between the gravestones with his hands clenched at the small of his back.

"What about the Father?" I said, "Does he look strange, too?"

She turned and stared at the priest through the hermetiscope, flipping through the lenses. He walked slowly between the gravestones with his head bowed in thought.

"No," she said. "He looks perfectly normal in all realities." She stopped flipping and peered closer, squinting with the distance, "But he has a little black terrier with him, trotting at his heels."

·· —o‑o‑o— ··

When we reached the Darling residence, the elder Mr. Darling opened the door.

Never had I seen the man in such a state of disarray. An accountant is typically prim and neat, composed and measured, but Mr. Darling exhibited none of these qualities. His hair was a tameless swirl of knots and mats; his face carried a layer of grime that appeared to be a mix of smoke, grit, mustard and grease. Only a few hours had passed since we'd seen him escort George home, but he'd changed from his canvas hunting clothes to a grey velvet dressing gown, and he wore neither socks nor slippers on his gangly, warty feet. He refused to look directly at Mary or me. When he saw us, his face dropped to the floor and contorted violently, as if he tried to wear all expressions at once.

"It is not a good time for company," he said.

"May I speak only a few words with George?" I implored. "We'll take but a moment of his time."

"No," he said firmly, staring at the floor.

"What about Frederick?" Mary asked. "Is he home?"

Again, Mr. Darling shook his head. "No. He is no longer with us."

"Where has he gone?" she said.

"I don't know," he whispered, then repeated, "It is not a good time for company."

Word-for-word, the intonation was identical.

A screech erupted from within.

Mary glanced at me. "Have they acquired a parrot?" she whispered.

Before I had a chance to answer, Mrs. Darling stepped into view from the parlor, and caused us both quite a shock.

Cassilda Darling had always prided herself on being a woman of fine costume and precise habits, but this creature was her in face alone. She wore not a stitch of clothing. She had dark, distended nipples and brown moles speckled over her pasty skin; wattles of fat hung off her arms and drooped from her hips. Her knobby, sagging body wobbled with every step as she pranced on tip-toes through the unlit corridors of the house, and her hands contorted above her head with her fingers making weird formations. Her grey hair had been tied up in a tangle of ribbons and feathers and bits of grass. When she saw us at the threshold, she held out her hands in an exaggerated motion and screeched to the heavens, "Oh, 'tis the Lovecraft girls!"

We heard wild, cackling laughter from deep within the house.

"Is that George?" Mary asked with concern.

"Mrs. Darling!" I stammered, trying to make sense of the scene before us, "We did not mean to intrude—"

"This is no intrusion, dear girls! How happy we are to welcome you in, aren't we, Reginald! Come in!" She stumbled into the light of the front door, revealing the fullness of her nudity, and grabbed Mary's wrist. "We are about to have tea! There are scones and sandwiches and sweets—can you smell that, girls? A thousand forgotten fragrances to enhance your appetite!" She tugged on my sister's arm. "Fish paste of ancient Pompeii, and a roasted joint of auroch, and oh! Oh! The baked bread of the Middle Kingdom, fit for a pharaoh's table! You shall not be turned away hungry! Come! Come!"

Mr. Darling stepped aside and held his face away, crossing his hands over his heart. Once again, in the same intonation, he droned, "It is not a good time for company."

But Mrs. Darling, releasing Mary's wrist, grabbed my neck in strong fingers and dragged me inside.

And, in that singular flash of her touch, I witnessed a crescent of blood and the full, erotic rhythm of a pulsing heart, exposed to the elements from between cracked ribs, and I felt the pleasure of hot liquid splattering over naked skin. The vision had the taint of Mrs. Rabbit's despair about it, the very same erratic pattern of harsh light and grating sound. This emotion was more than I could bear: it was savage, primal, inhuman, springing from the most primordial depths of my brain. I struggled back but her fingernails crooked into the soft meat of my neck.

From inside, the wild cackling turned into words, and George said, "Bring her here, Auntie!"

Half-dragged, dazed by weird desires, I found myself ushered into the parlor, and the stench hit me first: bile and blood, pig manure and fermentation. I coughed and choked as I found myself pushed into the middle of the room.

The tidy parlor had been transformed into an abattoir. The piano, the table, the rugs, all turned crimson and sopping, and in the center of the room, George reclined upon a single chair with the relaxed confidence of a king, his head bound up in a crown of brambles and one leg hooked over the armrest. Ropes of intestines garnished his chair and lay coiled about the legs. He, too, was naked, and every inch of his skin was covered in red lines, as if he'd been flayed by wires. His eyes were wild and luminous pinwheels; I recognized in them the same unnatural light as the Eidolon.

"I've come to ask what you saw, George," I began, trembling under the weight of his maniacal gaze, "But I fear the answer."

"I saw a new civilization, Miss Harriet," he crooned. "A new order to things, rising from the fertile soil of Dunham County! I saw the way the world ought to be, not this vile parody of what it is."

His body rippled and bubbled. The motion was unnatural; my first thought was of a muscle contraction, but the spasms continued with growing strength, as if mice wriggled under his skin. The whip marks merged and melted into scarlet words, and one seemed brighter than the others: did it read, 'unmask'?

I blinked twice, and his flesh was restored. Had I dreamt the motion? He scratched at the gaping slashes across his chest.

"Where is Frederick?" Mary asked.

"He is all around us, here in this house," George said, sweeping his hand across the room.

Oh, God! So much blood! My breath caught in my throat.

"He thought to be the victor, but I have won, and I shall claim my kingdom," George continued. "Welcome to my Arcadia, Harriet Lovecraft! See how my blossom grows!"

I fumbled at the hermetiscope and put them on my nose, and I tried to squash down the growing terror of what I would see.

The floor was a jungle of deep purple succulents, their serrated leaves sprouting through the boards and cutting bloodied gashes into George's naked legs. The walls were alive with shadowy lizards, terrible black forms of faceless nothings, that reached out to caress George's head and body. They moved and stretched, they gnawed on his flesh, they drew sustenance from his vitality. He seemed to find pleasure in their devouring of him, and in this vision of reality, his laughing eyes were replaced by diamonds that flashed and whirled like twin suns setting over a black lake. Ghoulish shades swirled around Mr. and Mrs. Darling, too, and licked their bodies all over with slender, flickering tongues, leaving gossamer trails of saliva.

But when they advanced on Mary, her essence repelled their assault, and they shied back as if burnt.

"Go to the king of the rockery path, my dove," whispered Mrs. Darling into my ear, pushing me forward as George fumbled with his manhood and presented it across his upper thigh like a gift. "Put aside your disguise, kiss him on the tulip, and give him your allegiance, and then we shall feast, and you will eat meats the likes of which you have not enjoyed before."

She reached to the sideboard to grab something, then she turned to me, and held out in her hand a liver, black-red, that quivered like jelly.

Most would have recoiled from the bloody flesh, but I recoiled from her touch. The sensations that flowed across her skin were utterly alien; I'd never perceived such unbridled madness, like a puckered scar transecting her spirit. Mrs. Darling had lived too far away on the opposite side of the valley to be influenced by Posey's books, and in her delicate state, she'd been shattered into a thousand pieces, bound together by the finest threads of spittle and ghosts.

"We must go," I said, struggling to retain my composure, putting the hermetiscope back into my pocket. "Mama will be most upset if I soil my dress."

"Posh, she will come to understand the nature of sacrifice," said Mrs. Darling in a sing-song voice. "Come along, Harriet dear."

From the hall, Mr. Darling droned, "It is not a good time for company."

"No, it is not, sir," Mary agreed, and she grabbed my hand. "Our apologies for intruding. Come, Harry."

Mrs. Darling opened her mouth impossibly wide and fell into mad keening. She tossed the liver aside and flew at me, but before she could grab me, Mary set one hand on the woman's heaving breasts and shoved her, hard. She stumbled back into the blood-spattered room, sprawling over the carpet at her nephew's feet. George leapt up and rushed us, and Mary threw a punch that landed with a satisfying crunch on his nose. He clasped his hands over his face, braying like a spooked horse, and the marks on his skin wriggled again as they melted into letters, and I tried to decipher them, but they moved too quickly for me to fasten upon one or another. Before I could read a word, Mary seized me around the waist and hauled me effortlessly after her, out into the yard. Together we managed to slam the door after us.

Throughout the entire event, the elder Mr. Darling had moved not an inch.

"Oh, God!" I said, stumbling back from the entrance, feeling my stomach lurch at the sight of gore staining my boots and the hem of my skirt, "Do you think ... do you think Frederick ...?"

"I don't wish to think it," said Mary, staring at the house as a cacophony of squawks and squeals rose from inside. "What's happened to them?" I said.

"They've been unhinged!" I said.

"Did you see the marks on George?"

I nodded, staring at the door, waiting for them to follow, and the Darlings made horrible howls, but they didn't try to escape. The voices faded as they retreated into the center of the house, and the howls were quickly replaced by the light girlish voice of Mrs. Darling, singing a hymn about roses and bones.

We heard a polite cough from the direction of the woods.

Both Mary and I reeled around, fists raised, ready to defend ourselves.

In the afternoon shade of the trees stood Frederick. His suit coat was torn, his boots were muddy, but otherwise, he looked unscathed. He held a hatchet in one hand. "Good afternoon, ladies," he greeted.

Mary fumbled at my pocket to snatch up the hermetiscope, and she put them on and flipped through the retinue of lenses.

"Well?" I asked.

"He looks normal in all instances," she said. "Not dead in the least."

Great relief flooded through me. "Thank goodness for that! We thought you'd been killed, Mr. Darling!"

"I would have been, if George had his way," Frederick said, his eyes flitting to the house, "But they seem to forget that which is no longer in their presence, and George reverted to his singing and feasting as soon as I fled. Still, I don't dare stay here any longer than I must, ladies. Will you do me the honor of accompanying me?"

Frederick began to hike along the road, and down into the vale we followed him, and I marveled at his composure.

"We came to speak with George, but instead found utter chaos!" said Mary as she caught up to him. "I'm happy to see you well. Both Harry and I thought the worst!"

"I appreciate your concern," he said warmly, "I'm not sure I yet understand what's happened, it's all too fresh in my mind." He shivered and gripped his ax a little tighter. "As soon as my uncle returned from the heath with George, they butchered all the pigs in the parlor and ate them raw. I've never seen anything so brutal! I might expect it of a Lower Whatley chap, but it's quite unbefitting a gentleman of my uncle's standing!" He led us through a break in the grove to a small bower, where a nest of branches and a half-circle of logs provided a spot for resting. "Please, have a seat. I've set up camp here, and dare not stay any closer to my uncle's home."

"We should continue into the town, and tell the regiment—"

Frederick shook his head. "I don't trust any of the men from the heath, now, Miss Mary, and I warn you to take care, too. They've all been touched in the head."

I took a seat on the log. "What happened?"

"When Uncle brought George back to the house, my brother was ranting," Frederick explained, "At first, we thought he was spouting gibberish, and Auntie wanted to call the doctor to sedate him. But Uncle would not let her—he said a good thrashing was all that was needed to bring George back to himself. Uncle went up to the room with a willow switch and stripped the bed of sheets, so that George lay upon it naked, and he bid George to turn on his stomach, so that he might thrash his back. I felt such a treatment was old-fashioned and barbaric, but Auntie said we must let Uncle administer a few good whacks, just to see if it would have any effect." He furrowed his brow. "There were lines upon George's back, red and raw. Burned into his skin, I think; I caught only a glimpse. But Uncle brought Auntie into the room to examine the injuries, and next I knew?" He held out his hand in the direction of the house. "She was stripping off her garments and sharpening the knives, and he was herding the pigs into the parlor! I'm sure I would've been next to fall afoul of her blade if I'd remained!"

"The lines upon his skin," I said, "Are they words?"

"Possibly," said Frederick. "I confess, I did not get a clear look."

To his good fortune, I thought.

"But I don't know how many men have seen the marks upon George's skin, and I can't tell how many are hiding their broken nature. Uncle looked hale enough until he threatened to do George violence. That did seem out of character."

I said, "This is ill-luck. I must warn Blackwood."

Frederick sat on the log next to Mary. "Do you know what's happened to them?"

"Only fragments and pieces," I admitted, "I suppose the best way to explain is that our dear Dunham County has been infected with a virus, and it must not be allowed to spread."

"This is no virus!" said Mary.

"Not in the strictest sense of the word, no. Perhaps not quite a virus, but an idea," I said. I struggled to explain. "You and I have been raised in the sphere of influence emitted by the book which held it, and we will be immune from its power; we will see it for the lie that it is. But the others? They won't be so fortunate. They won't know to question it, and they'll be influenced by it, and descend into fanatical madness."

"Books?" said Frederick, "Ideas? What the devil are you talking about?"

Mary looked down to him. "Dunham is normally a very boring place, sir, yet of late, we've found ourselves living in the midst of strange times."

"Indeed!" he said, "My uncle and aunt have become the epitome of strangeness!"

"I hold the greatest hope that they will be restored," she assured him, then to me, said, "What must we do, Harry, to stop the spread of this virus?"

I gestured to the gentleman sitting at her side. "Keep him away from the Darling house, Mary. Of all of us, Frederick will be most in peril, for he's only been in Dunham County a short while, and he'll be highly susceptible to their influence."

"We must inform the regiment, too," Mary said again, but Frederick took her large hand in both of his.

"No!" he implored, "They are even more green here than me! Can you imagine, an entire body of soldiers, raving like my aunt and uncle? It would be mayhem!" He turned back to me, and I was very impressed by his steady manner and logical mind. He had a great fortitude about him that I hadn't noticed before, and what I'd previously interpreted as pomposity and ambition, I now recognized as determination and confidence; turmoil had galvanized his negative traits and annoyances into the qualities of a valuable ally. "Miss Harriet, if my uncle was the only one infected when they brought George home, then we mustn't let my family spread it further." He brandished his ax. "My uncle, aunt and brother must not be allowed to venture out, especially to town."

"The placement of the house is quite secure," Mary noted, "There are only two routes: up to the heath, where they'll find no population to infect, or down through the single track into the village."

Frederick gave her a hopeful smile. "Then I'll stay here and do what I must to keep them contained," he said. "I'll have a good view of the track, and I'll be certain to avoid looking at any words upon their bodies."

"I'll stay with you and even the odds," Mary offered. "There may be three of them, but I'm worth two in a fight."

"Don't read anything they give you," I warned as I stood.

That made Mary laugh. "I'd never have thought I'd hear you say that, Harry," she teased, reaching over to pinch my cheek. "This surely must be the end of the world!"

# NINETEEN

I returned at once to Northwich by way of the footbridge, hopping over the splintered remains and averting my eyes from the timber, for I was quite sure there were still splatters of blood against the golden wood to match the smattering across my hem. As I plucked my way along the river bank and through the copse of alders, I heard the twitter of song birds; once, that sound would have brought joy to my heart—a hallmark of summer's return—but today, it rose gooseflesh to my skin, and I hurried with my head hunched down, terrified to feel them peck at the nape of my neck.

I rounded the pond and found the kitchen door unlocked, and hurried inside, listening for sounds of life, but the place was too sprawling for me to hear any noise. Thorne could be in the cellar or the tower, and I'd never know in which direction to find him. As I hurried into the ballroom from the main hall, I called out his name.

"Thorne! Where are you?"

"He's gone to town."

The voice from the far corridor was deep, dulcet, and soft, almost too quiet for me to hear over the echoes of my own calls. I startled and raised my fists, for I was already full of adrenaline from my run and my encounters with the Darlings, and fear prowled close to the surface of my heart.

The giant figure stood in the corridor, half-obscured by shadows, in that same place where I'd first laid eyes upon him. His body was a parody of human form, green-white and spattered with black mud, as if a child had taken an lump of clay and squished it into the rough shape of a man. I marveled that the features were not unlike the gentleman in the portrait, except that the elements didn't fit together correctly. The amber eyes were lopsided, the jaw uneven.

"Nate?"

He recoiled and held his distorted face down. "I apologize ... I ...

headache ..."

I hurried across the ballroom but, for every step I advanced, he backed deeper into the darkness.

"No ..." he said, holding out his hands, "Hideous."

"I don't give a d-—what you look like, Nathaniel Blackwood," I said, striding down the corridor until I stood before him. I took one hand in mine. He had a large frame, strong legs and a straight spine, and while he was completely naked and hairless, he possessed nothing untoward to hide from my female eyes.

"I am afraid ..." he began, bashful, "That I ... lack equipment for ... husbandly duties."

"And why should I care?" I said quietly, for the volume of my voice seemed to give him discomfort, "You've proven yourself very deft with what you have. Besides, I have little use for such equipment, as I'm an old spinster, and therefore rendered unsuitable for marriage or children." I smiled and caressed his cheek. "I don't care what form you wear, because I adore that you are so very clever, and ... and ...." Through my fingertips, I impressed upon him the fullness of my emotions, and said, "I am thrilled beyond my wildest dreams that I can simply talk to you, even if we must hide in the shadows."

Did he blush? The skin went from greenish-white to a mottled boysenberry pink.

"I admit," he began, "My own biology ... confounds me." He squeezed my hand. "Most ... of the time, the arms have ... minds of their own."

I felt the division across his palm; this limb was constructed of two tentacles wound together, with only two fingers and a stubby thumb. The discovery of this approximation made me smile.

"I have ached ... to converse ... with you ... but I can not ... for long." He winced.

"This is painful for you?"

His laugh was very reserved. "This ... takes concentration."

"Then let us be quick," I said to that unbalanced face, hardly handsome but endlessly fascinating, "I think I know which book was read, if that helps us narrow down the culprit. I've seen words written upon the flesh of the accursed—" His jaw fell open in surprise, and I said, "I am quite fine, it was only a fragment of a sentence. But the wicked words are out in the world now, and we must be quick before their influence spreads."

"What .... book?"

"Cassilda spoke of rockery paths and tulips," I said, "So I surmise it must be Songs of the Scented Garden."

He glanced to the floor. The nose, which was crooked, shifted to one side with the motion. "How can ... that be?" he said as he nudged it into place with one finger, which I noticed lacked a nail.

"I don't know," I said, "That particular book is safely stowed in the well, is it not? I saw it there myself."

He grabbed my hands with both of his, and I felt the apprehension flood through his skin as he leaned down towards me. "Harry," he began, "Run away! Leave! ... I can not ... bear to have you ... hurt through our ... mistakes."

"You silly octopus," I replied, and I grasped his head and pressed my lips against his. Until now, he'd had no mouth to kiss; I couldn't let such an opportunity slip past. A frisson of surprise and pleasure radiated from him, and when I let him go, I said, "We have no choice but to see this completed, for good or for ill."

He kissed me again, then said, "The book ... is still in ... cellar."

"Then how did our quarry find it? And how did its words appear on George's skin?" I pulled at his hand. "Let us go and make sure."

By the time we reached the base of the stairs, he'd abandoned his mimicry and returned to his ordinary state; he moved with more grace and speed as a cephalopod than as a man, and I could see in his eyes that the pain was much diminished. He was no longer distracted by the constant agony of intense concentration. As we passed through the corridor, one tentacle plucked up a lantern and held it aloft, and when we reached the oak door, another tentacle opened it.

"Was it not locked?" I said, but Nate slipped one tendril around my wrist, and I felt the unmistakable, smug self-appreciation of a rule successfully broken.

He set my hand to the door handle and I looked closer: a tiny polished stone had been wedged inside the strike plate, so that the bolt could not slide out fully into the doorframe.

"Did you do this, last time we were here, and you closed the door? Oh, love, Thorne would be most upset," I warned, but he was already in the center of the room, shunting aside the undressed slate slab with very little effort.

I peered over the edge and into the stygian black.

"I need light, Nate."

He took the lantern and lowered it slowly down, until the three volumes at the bottom of the well were illuminated in shifting, quavering beams.

"All three are there." I sat up, frustrated. "It is the only copy?"

One tentacle snaked around my ankle. I felt his affirmation.

"Are you certain?"

Absolutely.

I chewed on my lip in consideration, then said, "Can you lower me down?"

The sensation of refusal on my ankle was like a sharp stab of a pin to bone.

"You must," I insisted, "We can't read the title from here, and we're assuming too much. I need to have proof, Nate, that the books are safe." I stood, and straightened my skirt. "Lower me down and I'll check."

He recoiled from the suggestion.

"Am I not inoculated? I'll be fine!"

That one tentacle returned, and this time it wrapped around my leg while another wrapped around my neck. The sensation on his skin came heavy as an autumn fog, and I was filled with regret and despair. I saw as he had seen, felt as he had felt: tempted with a burning curiosity to read that which was forbidden. As my gaze followed the jumbled, blurred ink on the page, I felt the irritation start in the eyes, then move into the brain like a fever. I sensed my body losing its conformation, its integrity; my bones were melting, my skull liquefied, I spread into a pool of skin and muscle. How do I even move? How can I reconcile these new limbs, each one with its own will and impulses? My mind was overwhelmed. My helplessness spiraled towards delirium as I fought to keep my fractured spirit together, even as my flesh mutated into a horrific mockery of God's creation and, all around me, my environment lost sense or meaning. I rallied against misery, I gave up all hope of every returning to myself, I sank into brackish water and hid myself from the terrible revulsion exhibited by those I loved, and I surrendered to—

"Stop it, Nate!" I gasped, struggling out from under his touch. "I understand! You also thought yourself safe, yet you were not safe enough. I ought not to trust Thorne when he says I am protected, yes? I can repel the sight of the Eidolon's gaze, but I may not be able to repel the source."

Relief.

"Then I shan't read it, I promise," I said. "No matter how great the temptation."

He swirled around and enveloped me fully as he sent two tentacles plunging into the dark.

"No, no, no, you must not bring the volume up from the well!" I said, guessing at his motive. "It must stay buried. Better to put me down there; if I should I be affected, I'll be trapped and unable to hurt anyone." Then I seized up his head—or, at least, that which I interpreted as a head—I seized up his head in both hands and pressed a kiss to the spot between his eyes. "I'm a librarian. Books are my dearest friends. There is no one else in all of Dunham better suited to this task than me."

Reluctantly, one tentacle wrapped itself around my boot, and as I stood and wrapped one arm around the tendril, he began lowering me down into the pit. The air grew very close and moist; I couldn't help but silently scold Mr. Posey, for this was no fit condition to keep precious volumes. The walls were mossy, and the light glinted off water droplets that had formed on the tiny green stalks. I held the lantern in one hand, and as I descended, the ether that surrounded me increased in weight, as though gravity was pressing more strongly upon me. Every foot that I dropped closer to the three volumes on the floor added to the miasma.

The bottom of the well was five feet across; spacious enough for a woman of my frame, but made claustrophobic by the high walls that towered up twenty feet on either side. I stepped off the tentacle. The dirt was compacted but not damp. I released Nate's arm and bent down, setting the lantern on the ground.

The books hummed with life.

All three were leather-bound; one was red, one green, and the last white. The red book was such a rich and luxurious hue that I felt my fingers reaching out to stroke it, just as one might caress the secret regions of a lover's body, drawn like a magnet to its perfection and beauty. This must be *The Confessions of Bai Xi*, and oh! How I burned to open the cover. This was the volume that had destroyed the long and venerable line of emperors of Carcossa, who had by Divine Right been set upon the throne, but who had grown so inbred and rapacious that the Gods themselves destroyed them and wiped all mention of their names from human history. It whispered its story to me in the captivating voice of a beauteous and righteous woman: a temptress crafted from sea foam and the cries of lustful jaguars, destined to be the instrument of mortal destruction. How I wanted to sip at its secrets like a cool sorbet on an August afternoon! How I desired to taste its beauty on my tongue, to lick at the sweet nectar that gathered between its thighs, to feel such perfect ecstasy—

A sharp pain on the back of my head roused me from my stupor. I gave a little yelp as the tentacle flicked my head again.

"Yes, right, I'm okay," I assured him, yanking back my hand.

The second book, *The Widow's Rites*, was not so seductive. It, too, thrummed with depraved power, but it carried a measure of corruption and villainy that made it easier to avoid. I imagined the pages were made of nettles and broken glass. It possessed a voice that was caustic and flinty, but it was haughty, too, and openly snubbed me. Perhaps it had been designed to tempt those wishing to dominate, like a battle-thirsty king or a greedy warlord, and I showed no such ambitions. I was only a quiet village librarian, powerless and forgettable, whose only fate was to turn to dust. Obviously, I did not meet its requirements; it found me lacking in class and quality.

The third book lay asleep. I recognized the white leather, the gilt letters, the ponderous spine: Songs of the Scented Garden, the most wicked and dangerous book known to mankind. I circled it, holding up the lantern, wondering if it was waiting to strike.

I heard a sound from above: a distant rhythm advancing, tap tap tap, like the drip of water.

"What's going on?" I said, looking up.

In the gloom, I saw Nate peep over the edge as he quickly withdrew his tentacle. Then, with rising horror, the stone slab moved across the circle of the wellhead like an eclipse. The thump as it fell into place reverberated down the walls and caused a rain of dewdrops off the moss.

I was trapped.

Panic and confusion sparked in my chest. I've never been fond of close spaces, and this sudden confinement made my gasp stick in my dry throat; the atmosphere pressed in upon me. I was about to yell for clarification when I heard, muffled by stone, the progression of footsteps and a familiar voice, turned shrill with anger.

"What are you doing in here?" shouted Thorne. "Get out, you stupid oaf! How did you even get in?" I heard the dull sound of a punch on flesh. "Can I not leave you alone for a single afternoon?" Another thump. "By all the heavens, Nate … you, of all people, know how dangerous this place is! Has your brain turned to mush, too? Close the door after you, you sack of porridge, and come upstairs. I need you to move one of the book shelves—"

I heard the door thump closed, and the click of the latch. All fell silent.

My breath became thunder in the silence. I found myself trembling, trying to keep from crying out, and my eyes were drawn again and again to the marks on the walls: scratches made by the fingernails of trapped children. I noticed smudges of black soot between the stones, and a peppering of tiny white fragments of bone amongst the grains of sand. I was alone, deep in the ground, in a grave: this was not a well, but the crematorium of John Posey's sons. I crouched against the cobbled side and I whimpered as the lantern gutted. For a heart-stopping second, the light dipped into dusk, and I cried out as the fire threatened to die.

Then it flared again, but not as high as before. The levels of oxygen in this dreadful sepulcher were finite, it seemed.

Stay calm, I ordered myself. Breathe slowly.

For almost an hour I sat in solitude, and but in steady paces, I began to hear the faint whisper of a woman's voice. I struggled to ignore it, but The Confessions of Bai Xi would not be easily rejected. I knew I must not look, but it was so tempting. It promised me many things: to be more beautiful than a summer's twilight, to possess the hearts of all men, to be the envy of every woman I met. It dredged up the sensations of Nate's touch upon my flesh, and I resisted that swell of pleasure; I knew I mustn't let it overwhelm me, but oh! Resisting was agony! My traitorous hands drifted to my thighs, my fingers slipped under my skirts and petticoats, and for a moment I felt myself tempted by Bai Xi's seductions.

Then, defiant, I squeezed my eyes closed and sat on my hands. Biting my lip, I tried to distract myself by counting Fibonacci numbers.

0, 1, 1, 2, 3, 5, 8, 13, 21 …

The Widow's Rites pulsed in the darkness, too, and like a bored child finding amusement in some paltry trinket, it toyed with me. In its husky whisper, it promised the world would be mine for the taking. Open the cover and I would rule empires. I continued to sit on my hands in the dirt, counting to myself with my eyes shut, but as red Bai Xi sulked, the temptation to see within the green leather cover grew in steady paces. I felt pulled like taffy between the two of them. I'd counted to 6765 by the time I dared open my eyes again, to see that the lantern's flame was merely a nub of orange.

I glanced fearfully at Songs of the Scented Garden.

The ghostly white-bound book lay in the dirt, saying nothing. It seemed to exude no force at all. Imagine, if you will, the difference between a living man and a corpse: such was the comparison between the two temptations and the third. Songs of the Scented Garden remained curiously mute. It was dull in comparison.

That is its trick, I warned myself. It's dangerous because it seems harmless.

I stared at it, daring it to make a move, but its patience was enormous. The white book simply sat, inert. I studied the swirls of white-on-white across its cover, and noticed a faint peach fuzz of hair on the leather. The words had been rendered in shimmering gold. Under the title was a small gilt ornament of a blooming lotus. All of these elements seemed quiet, contemplative, almost soulless.

Do not touch it, I thought. Nate will be back. Do not fall to temptation.

And yet, the longer I looked at it, the more certain I became that the book was harmless. It said nothing. It made no motion towards me. My consuming interest in the white cover drowned away the voices of the other two books, and I had the fleeting thought that Songs of the Scented Garden was the most powerful of the three, and they had backed away in submission to their more-potent cousin. Certainly, The Confessions of Bai Xi and The Widow's Rites were no longer pulling at me with the same hungry fervor. My attention had been drawn elsewhere.

But this was no benevolent withdrawal. I was certain that together, they were letting me walk into a trap.

Do not touch it, I thought again.

But my hand drifted towards it.

The stillness was assuring. Maybe it was waiting to spring? Or maybe, just maybe, it was dead—but could a book die?

My fingers paused, a fraction of an inch above the white leather.

If I touch it, I will be consumed by it, I thought, and one half of my mind screamed a frantic warning to retreat while the other leaned into temptation. I waited to see if it would do anything: emit a sound, an emotion, a burst of lightning.

But no. It did nothing. It lay as still and silent as a leopard waiting to pounce.

I took a deep breath, and opened the cover.

# TWENTY

The white cover flipped open to reveal the title page. I flinched back, expecting a flood of pleasure or pain, or maybe both in equal measure.

Instead, I read the words, "Mrs. Beaton's Book of Household Management".

My gaze raced over the title page, stunned.

It was painted in fine hues of pinks, greens and yellows, faded from the many years at the bottom of the well, but still perfectly legible. The title had been rendered in a cartouche surrounded by olive leaves and ivy vines, with the printers name scribed with pride below. The artistry was pretty but not beautiful. Compared to the gilded cover, the contents were mundane.

I leafed through a few pages and found recipes for cookies, a treatise on cleaning windows, and hints for hiring servants. Confusion washed through me. Nothing in this book spoke to magic or madness; there was no myths of long-vanished kingdoms, or seductive ideas to drown my rational thought. I was underwhelmed, even a little disappointed.

By the time the stone cap shifted and a dusting of sand rained down upon my head, I'd read the first chapter of Mrs. Beeton's book. I'd also noticed the flyleaf was mismatched, marbled in a mash of colors, and poorly pasted in place.

One tentacle unfurled to the ground. I clenched the white volume to my chest as I let Nate pull me up.

His touch was full of apology, and when I stepped from the well, I was covered in kisses from a thousand dexterous suckers. Thorne's ornate key dangled from one tentacle, pilfered from its owner at great peril.

"Oh, stop, stop with the kissing," I laughed with relief. "I'm fine."

Gratitude percolated through him.

"But," I continued, "Look at this! Someone has replaced the pages of

Songs of the Scented Garden with another book! All this time, its cover lay in the bottom of the well, and Mr. Posey thought he'd left the world safe and secure from its terrible ideas!"

I set the book down on the floor. Nate held up the lantern with one tentacle as he flipped through the pages with another, and a third wrapped itself around my wrist to retain our contact and communication. He was full of wonder. A fourth tentacle, perhaps acting of its own volition, stroked the back of my neck and continued to set chaste kisses there.

"I think Mr. Posey threw the book down there years ago," I said, "See? There's mildew on the pages, and foxing as well. That sort of damage comes from years in the pit, not just a few weeks."

Nate stroked his scar thoughtfully with the tip of a fifth tentacle.

"If Mr. Posey didn't know, then he mustn't have been the one to make the swap," I said. "So who do you think might have done such a thing?"

He'd flipped it to a page upon which was scrawled a woman's writing, making notes to alter a recipe for chicken-and-oyster pie.

"You think, because it's Mrs. Posey's book, she must've been the one to swap it?" I clarified. "Perhaps. But why?"

Nate shrugged which, as I've said before, is a remarkable gesture.

I examined the flyleaf as a theory rose to my mind. "Mama said the boys were given to pranks, and mostly illiterate," I began, "What if they swapped it? They couldn't read it, but they thought to make her life difficult by replacing one book with another. Unwittingly, Mrs. Posey read, and was ensnared?"

Agreement.

"I suppose, whether it was Mrs. Posey or the boys, it doesn't matter," I said as I flipped the book closed. "A more important question remains: what did Thorne do with the other copy? The one that looks like Mrs. Beeton's Book of Household Management, but contains Songs of the Scented Garden?"

··—o-o-o—··

Thorne had sequestered himself in the tower. When he saw me in the doorway, holding the white-bound volume to my chest, his complexion turned as cadaverous as the poor individual who'd provided the book's leather.

"Wh-wh-what ...?"

"Calm yourself," I said, slamming the book down upon the table. "This is not Songs of the Scented Garden. Like you, it's an imposter." I flipped open the cover to reveal Mrs. Beeton's watercolor title page. "The guts of the book have been switched."

He gapped and gasped like a dying fish. His alarm was most satisfying. "How ... how did you fetch it ... ?"

"I've been down the well and up again," I replied, and handed him back his ornate key.

His eyes boggled. "Impossible!" But he could not tear his gaze from the white book. "To resist their temptation and be unchanged—it can't be!"

"They called out to me, but I've had a lifetime of exposure to Posey's library. It took a great force of will, but I'm none the worse for it, thank you for asking." I crossed my arms. "So what's become of the book with Mrs. Beeton's cover? Is it somewhere in the house?"

He traced his fingers over the white leather, stunned.

"Thorne!" I snapped, "Where is it?"

"I ... I ..."

One tentacle whipped across the room and slapped him across the forehead.

That knocked the sense back into him. "God d———!" he shouted, clapping one hand over his brow as he looked to me, "I sent it away!"

"You did what?!?"

His long face crinkled in a mask of concern. "I sent it away, Miss Lovecraft! I'm still in correspondence with the elder Mrs. Blackwood in Cascadia, and I thought she might find it to be a quaint souvenir of the Old Country." Those goggled eyes flashed between the book and me, and they were bright with horror as he made a dreadful realization. "Mercy, I have sent Minerva a terrible gift!"

"One which she has obviously not received," I replied evenly, "Good sense tells us that the package must have been intercepted before leaving Dunham County."

He slumped against the wall. "Thank God for that!"

"Now we know how the book escaped your watch," I replied, "But we still don't know who's read it."

"It was one of the first books I sent," he replied, "I hadn't even been here a week. I saw no one, I'd made no acquaintances. I don't think anyone even knew I was here!"

"The village council must have known you were coming," I urged, "You'd purchased the property, you'd expressed an interest—"

He cast about for an explanation. "The mayor, perhaps? No, Mr. Chowder and I conducted all business by letter, and I had not yet met him. I was sure to be coy in giving the council a firm date for my arrival. I wanted to come in the cover of night and with no fanfare, Miss Lovecraft, as the shipping crate containing our mutual friend would doubtlessly have caused a great deal of speculation."

I turned to Nate. "You came in a box?'

"How else is he supposed to travel? First class?" Thorne snapped, "I couldn't exactly mail him!"

And such a bolt hit me between the eyes, I half-thought Nate had snapped me with one of his tendrils.

"Marvin Runkle knew you were here."

"The blond brat behind the postal counter?" Thorne sneered.

I felt my pulse increase. "And he was friends with Earl Rabbit, but they'd had a quarrel, and there was strife between them."

Thorne cast about, thinking furiously, pacing to the windows of the tower.

"Mrs. Runkle knows all the gossip of the town," I began, "If she'd heard of anyone acting strangely, she would know, but she might have missed the same eccentricities in her own grandson. Marvin comes and goes as he pleases. He has no need to be anywhere in particular, no job or school, nor anyone to miss him. His only family is Mrs. Runkle, and she's too befuddled to follow his schedule. Marvin could easily spend days wandering Dreadmoor Heath, or sneaking out in the middle of the night to steal Earl Rabbit from his bed, and neither George nor Teddy would have had reason to fear him." I'd seen the boy only rarely since these events began, always keeping to himself. "Yes, Mr. Thorne, I believe he may be the Eidolon of the Old Gods, our mysterious murderer, who has destroyed Earl in body and George in mind. And as for Teddy—"

"Teddy," said Thorne, staring out the window, eyes wide.

"We do not yet know what's happened to Teddy," I said, "He could be deposited in any feature of the landscape! Bridge, or stone, or even deep in the soil—"

But he turned to me and shook his head.

"No, you fool," he hissed, teeth bared as he pointed northward, "Teddy!"

I followed his finger to see a naked figure stumbling out of the wilderness, smeared with mud and sand.

Thorne and I raced down the tower and across the lawn, and it was only when we drew close to Teddy that I realized our peril. His hair was wild and frizzled, his gait was stiff and unbalanced. A fringe of mushrooms grew from his shoulders and down his arms, as if he were already a rotten corpse, sprouting mold and giving nourishment back to the earth. But most arresting of all were the eyes—oh the eyes! Red and gold, flashing with an ungodly fire, and pointing in adjunct directions.

Teddy had always been bandy-legged and rangy in height with a round barrel of a belly, and this gave him a great amount of flesh upon which to impress those dangerous words. He had a full paragraph branded upon him. I'd almost read a sentence before Mr. Thorne clapped his hand over my face and yanked me away. I felt the emotions on Thorne's clammy skin: disdain, fear, a steely resolve to root out the source of Dunham's peril. His confidence was intoxicating.

"Don't look, Harry!" he commanded.

I heard a moan as unformed and shapeless as a bolus of cud, and I peeped out of one eye, taking great care to avoid Teddy's chest and belly. The man's mouth and chin were a sticky smear of crimson. In his hand, he brandished his tongue, ripped out by the root.

"Teddy," I began, levering myself from Thorne's grip and taking his suit jacket. I crept towards the boy with face averted, much like Perseus advancing on Medusa, "Teddy, I need you to put on Mr. Blackwood's coat."

How unsettling it is, to witness a beast make a human sound, but equally unsettling is it to hear a human make the sound of a beast! The howl Teddy let forth was the most brutish, most uncultivated ululation that could be created by an anthropoid's throat, and it sent shivers down my nerves to the tips of my toes. He bellowed like a bull, sniveled like a weasel. His eyes did not move together or blink in unison, but one pupil followed after the other, a half-second later. Every element of his person was unnatural, and he moved in halting paces, as if his limbs were attached to wires cruelly jerked by an invisible puppeteer.

"We can't let you walk to town, Teddy," I said, though I doubted he understood me. "Anyone who sets their sights upon you—"

A series of rushing vibrations came from above, circling the tower, as a cloud passed over us and cut off the light of the spring sun. I looked over my shoulder at Thorne. He'd fallen behind, his gaze trained skyward. "Miss Lovecraft," he said in a reverent hush, "You may wish to retreat."

I turned and looked up.

The sky was overcast with brown wings, all in motion. Thousands upon thousands of starlings gathered in a silent murmuration directly above our heads, swirling in a great tornado of feathers and beaks, their glittering beady eyes like a million whirling stars. For almost a minute, they simply eddied around us in a vortex, then suddenly, spurred by some trigger which my feeble human senses could not detect, the flock plunged to Earth in a whorl, and slammed into Teddy's nude form with the mercy and moderation of a runaway steam train. The man's bullish lowing became a screech of agony. Thorne grabbed my arms and dragged me to safety as the swarm of ravenous birds, whipped into a squawking tidal wave, crashed over Teddy and tore the man to a million tiny shreds.

We fled to the house and Nate slammed the doors behind us while, outside, a cacophony of squawks and chirping erupted from all directions. We three stared out the windows of the ballroom as thousands of birds turned the view into an impenetrable current of feathers, claws, beaks and motion.

Precisely half-an-hour later, the starlings suddenly dispersed. The screeching ceased. All that remained was sunshine and silence, and a drift of mangled scarlet pulp on the lawn.

"Well," said Thorne in awe, "It seems I've misjudged the psychopomps. They may be on our side after all."

# TWENTY-ONE

Thorne, armed with the knowledge of the Eidolon's identity, hurried into town as swiftly as the flight of beautiful Buraq, and paused for no one, as if the hounds of Hades nipped at his heels. He refused to let Nate accompany him, preferring instead that the cephalopod guard the library. "We do not know what other terrors will try to infiltrate Northwich Hall," Thorne said to his half-brother as he departed, and I heard a hint of sentimentality in his words—pride, perhaps, and a smattering of fraternal affection. "There's no one else I'd trust to watch over the volumes, even if you can be a soppy nitwit from time to time."

Though every muscle in my body cried out for rest, I scurried to catch Thorne. We went directly to the post office, but the hour was growing late and we found the doors locked.

The village was very quiet, preternaturally so. I hoped that most people had simply retired home for supper, but Frederick's warning rang clearly in my ears, and I suspected the virus was spreading, and this lull was the work of some malevolent force: a hush before a storm. As Thorne prowled between the narrow stone buildings, I wondered if this was not some aberrant somnambulant trance that had been cast across the town—even for sleepy Dunham, the lanes and byways were more desolate than usual, and the air held a oppressive, soupy thickness. The military camp, traditionally a beehive of activity, had fallen into a queer sort of stupor, too, and I dearly hoped the soldiers were patrolling the fields, looking for Teddy, and far from the influence of these wicked doldrums.

Yes, that must be where they are, I decided. They were following the logic that, if George was alive, then the Crumpsall fellow may be, too. If I was of a stronger constitution, I'd have marched into the midst of the camp to inform Captain Crankshaw of Teddy's weird and abrupt destruction, but the vision of that body pecked into pieces was too fresh in my mind, and I wanted only to ignore the memory, and lock it away to deal with later. If I shared my knowledge with the soldiers, there would be too many questions inspired, and I doubted that either Thorne or Nate would wish to have a cohort of mounted soldiers patrolling the grounds of Northwich Hall.

Outside the post office, Thorne peered through the little window and sneered in frustration. "Where does this Runkle boy live?" he growled to me.

"There are lodgings at the back of the post building." I led him to an alleyway that smelled of cat urine and wood smoke. "Down this way. Here, the last door on the left."

Flower pots overflowing with blue monkshood and lacy red poppies flanked the skinny brown door. Mrs. Runkle had lived here with her grandson since the death of her husband, almost three years ago, and she enjoyed a quiet and contented existence, with her main connection to the wide world being her beloved hours behind the postal counter.

Without regard for the serenity and sanctity of the dinner hour, Thorne pounded hard upon the door. "Good evening, madam!" he said loudly, "Are you there?"

Utter stillness.

"She may not be home," I said, looking at the windows. All seemed deserted. "Sometimes, she and Marvin dine with the Poole family. Mrs. Poole was a cousin to her husband, you see, and they have long been—"

"Good Lord, Harry, I don't give a bull-scutter about Dunham's family connections," Thorne said. He set his shoulder to the door frame and gave a sharp shove, and the old lock popped. Thorne entered.

"You can't go in!" I said.

"How curious, that today you would suffer such a moral quandary!" he replied over his shoulder, "Did you not enter my home in just this same manner?"

I hurried after and closed the door, hoping no neighbors had heard us. "That was different," I replied, "I wanted to make sure your house was safe from vermin."

"There wasn't the smallest hint of curiosity in your motives? Not even a bit? You're a true philanthropist, Harry," he mocked, "Well, aim your boundless charity in this direction, you pious saint, and find my d—— book." Thorne cast around the small, cramped and cluttered apartment. "The boy has hidden it somewhere, and I mean to have it back!"

But the apartment was merely a kitchen and two small bedchambers, and it took no time at all for our eyes to range over every surface, nook, and cranny. I hurried into one chamber as Thorne disappeared into the other, but when I peered under Martin's bed, I found only a chamber pot.

"Nothing," I said as I returned to the kitchen.

"It seems the boy has evaded us," he said. "Do you still have my glasses in your possession?"

I pulled them out of my pocket and set them in his waiting hand.

With a deft snap of the wrist, he put them on and began cycling through the lenses, leaning close to examine different items as he took a turn around the home.

My patience flagged. "Well?"

"Not a single hint of the book or the Eidolon, or indeed, anything supernatural," he said. He removed them and put them in his breast pocket. "Either the boy has not been here since his transformation, or he's learned how to evade the hermetiscope."

"You were wearing those when I first met you," I said.

Thorne cocked one eyebrow at me. "And that makes you uncomfortable, obviously." He circled around the room until he stood before me, drawing himself up to become very tall and imposing, and peering down at me along the length of his nose. "Miss Lovecraft, I knew you were monstrous from the very beginning," he said, "You were lousy with magic." His probing gaze made my skin crawl.

I stood my ground. "If I was to look at you through your glasses, Mr. Thorne, what would I see?"

But he clucked in dismissal and shook his head. "It's never a good idea to use the hermetiscope for party tricks, Harry. Once witnessed, some things can never be forgotten." He pointed to a door on the opposite side of the apartment. "Does that lead through to the post office? Maybe we'll have more luck there."

He elbowed the lock open and barged through this door, too, and we stumbled into the dim post office to diverge in opposite directions: Thorne went to the counter, and I went to the post boxes. He rummaged about in the shelves, and I poked through every cavity, but the town of Dunham has very little need for shipping. The only items we found were two envelopes to distant relatives, one from the Chowder household and another from Mrs. Cripplegate, both set aside in a bin marked 'Outgoing'. Under the counter were bins for sorting, but they contained a few balls of yarn and an old cheese sandwich, fuzzy with mold.

"Empty," I said.

Thorne looked around in disgust, hands on waist. "Would the boy have anyone else in the vicinity to whom he'd entrust a cherished book?"

I shook my head. "To be honest, no one in Dunham reads much at all. I have serious doubts about their literacy."

"That may be to our benefit," he replied.

I toyed with the little key around my neck. "There were whole days when I'd be the only human creature to visit the library," I continued. "It's a lonely place. I can not impress upon you how happy I was when I found Northwich had been sold, and I thought at last, the possibility of a neighbor who enjoyed the simple pleasure of reading!"

"I'm sorry to disappoint you," he said. "I do not read for pleasure, only for self-improvement."

"Well, at least you're more aware of the power of books than any of the other fools in this village," I replied.

His thin lips crinkled into a smile. "Harry! Is that a smidgen of cynicism I hear from you?" He chuckled. "Is this Christmas? Is there hope for you yet? Oh joy!"

I grumped. "I've long nurtured a disappointment in Dunham's treatment of its library. Your arrival has simply made it clear to me that the village has no need—"

Then I stopped mid-sentence.

Thorne studied my face. "What?"

"I've had a thought," I replied, slowly, for I wasn't yet sure of my abilities of deduction. "An inspiration. Where is the best place to hide a book, Mr. Thorne?"

"I would've said a well in Northwich's cellar, but I think that may be the incorrect answer."

"In a library," I replied. "Surrounded by other books. And, better yet, a library that's dreadfully underused to the point of abandonment." I smiled and pulled the key from my necklace. "Even the librarian has been there but rarely in all these troubled days. It would be perfectly safe."

Thorne grinned. "Oh, Harry, your cynicism does you credit. We must nurture it further."

We mounted the stairs. My key resisted fitting into the lock—perhaps it didn't wish me to enter—but at last my trembling fingers were able to manipulate the door, and it creaked open on reluctant hinges. I felt a pang of regret that I'd been such a poor guardian, and had left my beloved collection alone for so long.

The room smelled stale. Dust motes floated upon the air. The library contained very little furnishing: to the left of the door and in front of the windows, a couch offered patrons a place to sit, but the hand-me-down sofa was made of a murky yellow velvet that contained some questionable stains, and it clashed spectacularly against the pink-and-green floor-length curtains behind it. To the right of the door was a wooden table and chair where I could write. The majority of the room was taken up with a series of six tall shelves; these carried the entirety of the collection and, by their height, created five narrow corridors. A needlepoint screen hid a far nook on the other side of the room, behind which sat a chamber pot.

"Is anything out of the ordinary?" asked Thorne.

No singular item stood out as different, but something was wrong. I felt it in my bones.

"Someone had passed over this threshold, not long ago," I said.

Thorne looked at me askance. "You can sense this with your Quirk?"

"No," I replied, and tipped my head to the ground. "I can see this with my eyes, Mr. Thorne."

The wooden floorboards had not been swept in almost a week, certainly not since I was last here, and a light velvet of dust covered the floor. We'd only opened the door half way in its semi-circle, but the marks in the dust carried on to the wall.

Without a word passed between us, we prowled between the shelves, and as he moved to the farthest corridor, I let my eyes rove over the titles, but nothing appeared out of place. The books were as I'd left them, neatly faced and squared. My desk was tidy, the piles of paper not too large, and the curtains across the windows had not been opened in some time.

"There's nothing amiss," I said, brow furrowed. "Everything is in perfect order."

"This is your perfection?" he said from the far side of the room, hidden by the high shelves. "Such insipid titles, Miss Lovecraft! Your library is appalling." He held up one book and waved it over his head, and then brought it down to read the cover. "A Treatise on the Care and Breeding of Bait Worms. And someone has taken this out? To actually read?" I heard him shove it back on the shelf with contempt. "Fit only for the lining of bird cages, I swear. Does the village council know you tend such a woeful collection?"

"No one visits, so no one complains," I replied as moved towards the couch, and stepped behind it to spread wide the curtains.

And found myself directly staring into a plaster white face and a pair of glittering hypnotic eyes.

There was no time to scream. I saw only the hint of a tiny human form as it swelled into a behemoth, as soundless as a gust of air. It seemed to sprout from the space behind the curtains, materializing like a swirl of leaves in a whirlwind and, as I watched, the antlers grew and spread like tree branches above us, crackling as they unfurled. The spindle fingers wrapped around my throat and squeezed. I felt the eyes boring into me, as if wishing to suck out my soul. Its touch, as unyielding and cold as oblivion, burned tracks into my skin as its sinewy grey slug of a tongue slithered from between its lips and left a trail of saliva across my cheek.

I bared my teeth. I struggled. I pressed my palms to its chest to push it away, and the cold texture of the rotted rags seared my skin.

Oh, God, it was terrifying to behold! The eyes were twin flames, dancing tall and bright. They beckoned to me, they burned themselves into my mind. The devil's pallid mask branded itself on the screen of my imagination, and I knew in that moment that its gaze would haunt my dreams for the rest of my life.

I strained for breath. Stars popped across my vision. The edges of the room grew fuzzy.

Then it pressed the bony tip of its right index finger to my sternum. It slowly, patiently wriggled its jaundiced nail into my flesh, burrowing towards my naked heart. Pain flared through my core. My cotton dress tore. My flesh crisped and curled.

The diabolical smile grew as wide as a gaping wound.

I tried to back away but its left hand held me fast around the throat, and as I struggled, I pressed my palm to its cheek, and did the only thing I could.

I let myself feel.

As one can detect one flavor amongst many, one perfume amid a funk of hundreds, so I felt one emotion through its carnival of sensations, and I recognized it as the blood fury of Mrs. Rabbit, and the blood ecstasy of Mrs. Darling. This creature had tainted the thoughts of both women. They had looked directly upon these horrible eyes and been forever altered.

"Honestly, Harry," said Thorne from behind the shelves, "Dreck and trash, all of it. No wonder you're so eager to get your hands on my books."

I kicked out, struggling for breath, straining to cry for help. That cracked, grey tongue appeared again, emitting the charnel stench of rotten flesh as it grazed along my cheek. The Eidolon was hungry for emotion, for competition, for lust. It probed my heart for any strong feelings upon which it might feast, and the taste of dread on my skin caused a shiver of excitement to travel down its shoulders.

But I have always been stubborn, and I ground my teeth together, and with both my hands, I grasped its right fingers. I struggled, I resisted. I did not fall to its allures as easily as its other victims. My eyes narrowed, and with the last of my air, I hissed through a clenched jaw, "You can not have me, Marvin."

The fiend faltered. Perhaps it expected an easy conquest. I saw its confidence flicker and felt its frustration rise.

"What's that, Harry?" said Thorne from behind the shelves.

I would not let it take me, I would not surrender or succumb. I set my hands upon either side of the Eidolon's face and squirmed my psyche into its brackish soul.

As I burrowed into its heart, it suddenly recognized the peril in which it had placed itself. I was no innocent country girl, frail and helpless. I embraced the Eidolon, I stared fully at the hypnotic eyes without blinking and with purpose. I peeled back the layers of sensation, alternating delight and discovery, hunger and crushing desire, giddy power and helpless compulsion. Most surprising of all, every stratum of his personality was stained with a yearning for liberty: Marvin was merely a tool of the book that held him in its thrall. It ate at his flesh like a cancer, it suckled the life-force from the marrow of his bones. The Eidolon whipped back and tried to hide its true face, for the tables were turned; now it fought to escape my clutches. For a moment, I thought I might have glimpsed its human soul, but then the feeling was gone, and the spider hands released me, tossing me backwards across the wooden floor. I hit the table, books crashed to the ground, and the monster gave a horrible, unearthly howl as it shrank against the door.

Thorne looked up from the shelves and gave a shout of alarm. He stumbled and tripped towards us, fumbling to put the hermetiscope over his nose, but by the time he reached me, it was too late. The antlers scratched ruts from the ceiling, and the rags swirled like water, and the nightmare flowed like a rushing river out the open door and down the stairs as though its feet were wings.

A suffocating stillness fell over the library as I collapsed on the floor.

"Oh, God, are you alright?" Thorne asked, hauling me to my feet. His hands touched mine, and his emotions were a muddle of surprise, horror, and uncharacteristic concern. He was worried for me; I had stared down the demented eyes of the Eidolon, and that was a state from which none returned unscathed.

Certainly, my mind felt bruised, but I still had my wits.

"The book is here," I rasped, invigorated, "It wouldn't have attacked me, if we weren't so near its hiding place." I hurried to lock and bolt the door, then I ran to the window to see if it had rushed from the building, but the streets of Dunham showed nothing out of the ordinary. The landscape was an still and empty as a painting.

The Eidolon had returned to its human form and vanished completely.

But the book! The book was here, somewhere within our grasp!

··—o-o-o—··

All night we searched by candlelight, through every title, looking for the beastly text. We used logic, we used persistence, we used the hermetiscope, but our efforts failed. In the gloaming of dawn, voices and lights from the streets broke my concentration, and when I looked out, I saw soldiers with lanterns roaming the streets, calling my name.

But I was afraid to leave the library. Any of those faces could hide demons. I waited until I saw Emma and Jane, then I waved to them from the window and called out to them.

"Goodness, Harry! We thought you'd disappeared," Emma said in anger. "You sent no word of your predicament!"

"And Mary, is she with you?" said Jane.

"She's with Frederick in the woods, where they've taken shelter from the Darlings, who have all been affected," I said, "And I was attacked again by the devil from Dreadmoor."

Emma gave a little squeak. They hurried up the stairs and I let them in the library, and bolted the door after them. Hundreds of books in piles on the floor, empty shelves, and ruts torn from the ceiling: both of my sisters stared slack-jawed at the mess. They may have had a million questions, but when they saw Thorne in the corner, leafing through books, they both were struck dumb with shock.

"Greetings, ladies," he replied. "I hope the morning finds you well."

"Mr. Blackwood!" Jane said, "What a surprise!"

Emma turned to me. "Mama is in a state, I can tell you! And Papa is on the cusp of worry, too, and he never worries about anything!" She clasped my hands in her own to show me the full extent of her concern for me. "And now, to find that you were boldly attacked by this dreadful creature? Harry, you must come home!" The warmth of her intentions flowed across my skin like syrup, and as a flush rose to my cheeks, I realized she was trying to heal whatever injury had marked me.

"I'm not hurt, Emma," I said, "And I can't come home, not yet. The book is here somewhere, I'm sure of it. I can think of no other reason why it would attack me with such determination if we weren't close to discovering its treasure. It will return, given half a chance, so we must stay until we've found Songs of the Scented Garden."

"I beg of you, at the very least, let me ask Mr. Marsh to hurry home and inform Mama and Papa that you are safe," said Emma, opening the window. "Mama is terribly worried, and her nervous disposition is sure to drive Papa into fits. We must put them at ease!" She called down to the street, and like a mystical djinn, Mr. Marsh appeared.

Jane looked to me and, under her breath, said, "Wherever Emma goes, he's never far away."

"They seem to be gravitationally bound," I replied with a smirk.

She nodded. "He came by the house yesterday to speak with Papa, and then spent an hour in the garden with Emma. His intentions have not been put into words, but Mama has already picked out the date, the dress, and the name of the first grandchild."

"Mercy, that woman will have you three wedded off if it kills her," Thorne replied.

"She's determined to secure a happy life for us, Mr. Blackwood," Jane replied, chin held high, "It's her singular duty as our mother, and one she takes very seriously. Mama may have failed Harriet, but this has only enhanced her commitment to find a suitable match for Emma, Mary and me."

He dismissed this comment with a flap of one long hand. "You'll have no difficulty, Jane Lovecraft," he replied. "I'm sure you could secure the affections of any ham-headed yokel from here to Lower Whatley with the snap of your fingers." My sister's eyes widened, thinking he was referring to her Quirk, when he added, "There's no more lovelier face than yours for a hundred miles. You're the closest thing to Helen that Dunham will ever see, and you might not launch a thousand ships, but you could probably send off four or five."

"You think me beautiful?" she said, incredulous.

"As a specimen of femininity, you're pleasing enough, although you smile far too much," he said bluntly. "Any of these bumpkins will be lucky to have you on his arm." Thorne quickly glanced to me with an air of appraisal, then added, "Certainly, you aren't as bland as your older sister. Simply stand next to Harry, and your position as a beauty is assured."

"As always, you are very kind," I sneered.

"Oh, come now, Harry," he said, "You know it as well as I. With that beak of yours? And well past your prime? As mediocre as a bowl of oatmeal? The only thing you'll attract is an eerie, tentacle-limbed gargoyle that spends its days sulking in an underground lair." And he cast me a smirk that was remarkably friendly, and full of comradery, and instead of feeling insulted like anyone of normal constitution would feel, a warm blush cross my cheeks.

Emma returned from the window. "I'm frightened for Mary. I'll go and find her. If this monster is roaming the countryside, she'll be in horrible danger."

"No, you stay and help your sister," said Thorne. "If all the Lovecraft girls are as similarly affected as Harry, you'll be able to repel the book's siren song, more so than me. I'll go and locate Mr. Darling and the amazon. They shouldn't be difficult to find."

"You ought not to go alone," I said.

"I'll go with him," Jane volunteered. "Together, we'll be able to fight off any demon that crosses our path."

And so it was settled. "Once Emma and I find the book, we'll join you at Northwich Hall." I said. Then I locked the door after them, and turned back to the library, and said, "We must find that book, Emma, or we are all lost."

# TWENTY-TWO

It was my youngest sister who discovered the tantalizing, insidious, utterly-beguiling Songs of the Scented Garden. The volume had been wrapped in a leather satchel and tucked under a loose floorboard by the window sill. When I heard her soft, inoffensive coo of discovery, I glanced across the room to see the floorboard set to one side and my sister unwrapping the satchel, and I sprinted as fast as my skirts would allow me, vaulting over a barricade of books.

"Oh, here is one!" she began in all innocence, withdrawing it from the bag, "Mrs. Beeton? Is this what you're looking—"

I slammed the green linen cover closed before she had time to read the interior. The touch of my hand to the page felt like shards of ice. I heard the distant, delicate, and bewitching sound of a blackbird's song.

"Yes! That's it! Don't read it!" I said.

"Do you hear music?" she said, eyes glittering.

"Emma!" I shouted, pulling her back to herself, "Listen to me! It must be read by no one! Do you understand?" I pulled her away from the book, lying askew on the floor. "The words themselves are poison, and we must not read it at all! Not even a little peek! For the love of all things sacred, don't read!"

She stared anxiously at me. "Don't read? That doesn't sound like you at all!"

I plucked the book from the floor and held it at arms length, tucked it back in its leather satchel, and tied it up tightly. The whole thing quivered in my grasp as if alive. "Look, here," I said, pointing out the stitching along the bottom edge of the flap, where a name had been embroidered. "This is Marvin's school bag."

"You think the monster is the Runkle boy?"

"He has read, and been transformed," I replied. "We must get this back to Northwich Hall as fast as we can!"

We hurried out to the street, and she hailed Mr. Marsh, who sat astride his black horse on the opposite side of the Waters and had been patiently waiting for her to appear. "I told your parents that you've been detained at the library, and assured them that all is well," he said to me as he crossed the bridge and drew rein. "Have I told them the truth or a lie?"

"A lie, I'm afraid," I said, "All has not yet been made right. Can I borrow your horse?" I held up the satchel as if it were something fetid. "I need to get this back to the manor's library as quickly as possible."

"I can take it," he began helpfully, only to be shouted down by both Emma and I.

"No!" I said, "You mustn't go anywhere near it!"

"Please don't touch it, Richard," Emma continued, "Give Harriet the horse, and she'll take very good care of the animal, and bring it back to you when all is done. Or, better yet," she said with a flirtatious grin, "You and I will walk the distance to Northwich Hall, and fetch the horse ourselves. It's only a few miles; the weather is fair and the walk will do us both good."

The prospect of time in the company of a pretty girl was too enticing to refuse. He dismounted and handed the reins to me. "Do you ride?"

"A little," I said.

"Please, if you would be so kind, Miss Lovecraft, could you say nothing about this to the captain?"

"Not a word," I agreed, climbing into the saddle and settling my skirts around me. The horse sidestepped and tossed its head, and I wondered how much the book's weird emanations upset it. I set heels to flank and we were off at a quick canter, down the West Road and past the steeple of St. Dismas, following the river upstream.

As I rode, I felt as though angels were singing me forward. It was half a mile before I realized the refrains of pleasure and joy were coming from the parcel in my lap; they filled me with all facets of happiness. I thought of strawberry tarts and friendly puppies and crisp icicles glittering under a December sun, I thought of the smell of baking bread, the sound of babies laughing, the touch of a feather against my cheek. I thought how warm and comforting the book must feel in my fingers, and I found myself wriggling the satchel open, bit by bit, loosening the ties ...

"No!" I yelled to myself.

The horse, thinking itself scolded, flattened its ears and galloped faster.

With some difficulty, I tucked the book in its satchel under the front of my dress, and that helped keep my treacherous hands away from the ties, but it did nothing to quell the growing sensations of allurement that wafted from the pages like the fragrance of tea roses. Songs of the Scented

Garden rubbed itself against my belly like a kitten begging for attention—foul, beastly thing! I reached the yard of Northwich Hall in a struggle, and I hurried passed the trout pond and through the front doors without paying much attention to the horse I'd abandoned in the garden. I must get to the cellar, to the well, before I drowned in these infernal, alluring pages!

Down the corridor I stumbled. The weight of the book increased in steady paces until I crawled on hands and knees passed the library doors. They lay open and tempting, showing shafts of welcoming sunlight gleaming on a thousand gilded spines. As if calling out to its siblings, the charismatic songs which radiated from the book in my arms grew more intoxicating—the delicate, airy melodies floated like a siren song, enticing me to leave all the world behind and willingly dash myself to pieces. I barely noticed that I'd altered my trajectory: I'd left the corridor and dragged myself across the library floor, towards the heavenly chair under three arched windows, where the afternoon light begged me to read in its embrace. How perfect! The harmonies increased in volume and refinement, and by the time I reached the chair, my vision was swimming and my mind was wrapped in a stupor. Oh, how I fought it! I wanted nothing more than to open the drab olive-green cover and read the poems contained within, lap them up like a cat with a saucer of silky cream. Songs of the Scented Garden assured me that we had been made for one another, a perfect match—was I not drab on the outside, too? Knowing the caliber of my passions, it urged me to imagine all the glorious dreams contained inside its pages, a carousel of light and music to drown away all sorrows! I would welcome them into the very cellular fiber of my body, integrate their ideas with my own, and lose myself to their timeless stories.

I was going to fail. I knew it in my heart and bones. I dragged myself into the chair, and the songs had grown too alluring for me to withstand. I realized that I'd forgotten why I wasn't supposed to read it, and I could even feel myself forgetting that I'd forgotten. I ought to read this book, no? Wasn't that why I had carried it so far? There could be no other reason for me to be sitting in a library, holding a book. I tore the satchel off, held the worn cover in my hands. A shiver of anticipation trembled through Songs of the Scented Garden and skittered into my fingertips.

It hungered to possess me completely.

Oh God, how I longed to be possessed.

And then, as I began to open the book, a heavy weight slipped over my upper arm, burrowing under my sleeve and between my breasts, nestling up the length of my neck, and curling around to the soft, sensitive space behind my ear.

A single sucker placed one delicate kiss there.

Emotions, real and solid and living, flooded through me: strength, resolve, and resistance.

Like a drowning swimmer breaking the surface of the water, I gasped for breath as Nate took the satchel in one tentacle, the book in another, and held me close to his body with a third. Emboldened with a sense of purpose, he shoved the book into the bag and tossed the satchel with a flick of his tentacle across the library where, after a long arc, it thumped unceremoniously on the upper balcony.

Sense and reason returned to me in a rush. "Burn it," I croaked, "Burn them all, just to be sure."

But he refused. Instead, cradling me tightly, he retreated from the library, slammed the doors shut and carried me to the corridor.

"You have saved me," I whispered to him.

Oh, such euphoria he felt, a heady mix of pride and satisfaction and gladness, along with a dash of swashbuckling amusement at being a hero! It made me swoon.

As I roused from my stupor, I felt a sickening disappointment rise in my throat. "Songs of the Scented Garden is back, but its devil still roams free," I replied, "Its concepts remain unleashed. I don't know how we can contain it. How does one stop an idea once it runs rampant?"

Nate was not so hopeless as me; he had within him a font of positivity that I'd never before sensed in another human being, and I tried to glean faith from it. Those amber eyes sparkled. His skin flushed from glass green to silver with streaks of burgundy.

"Honestly, I don't know what you're trying to say," I said in frustration.

He shook his head until his eyes wobbled, and suddenly there were three or four tentacles wrapping themselves around my bare legs, and another two snaking through my sleeves to snuggle against my bare skin. At first, I thought this to be highly inappropriate behavior, but then I realized his motives were completely practical: Nate was doing his best to place the most contact between our skin in the hopes of communicating more fully. He pressed me against him, and I laid my cheek against his, and closed my eyes as my feet were lifted off the ground.

*It will not leave Dunham.*

"No?" I whispered. "Why not?"

*The Eidolon will want its book. The Songs will not let its devoted servant go.*

I peeled back my face an inch, shaking my head as I tried to comprehend his certainty. "But you were not made a servant of the book that ensnared you."

I heard him give a breathy sigh, and the tip of one tentacle gently brought my head close again.

Fire. Horrible, dreadful, cleansing, liberating fire, that simultaneously broke his enslavement to the book and consigned him to this terrible form for as long as he lives. His opinions on the matter were terribly complex: in one swoop, he was thankful to be free of the book's influence, grateful to have retained his mind, but heartbroken to be trapped in its curse and forever severed from all of human society. And if his ability to keep his wits and will were any indication, his particular book had been far less powerful than the two which were currently trapped in the basement, or the third abandoned in the library. Songs of the Scented Garden had existed for centuries, handed down from one tragedy to another—if it could be easily destroyed, it would have been, generations ago.

He felt remorse for all he'd brought to Dunham County.

"John Posey brought the books to Dunham," I reminded him, "And your half-brother lost one. I don't hold you responsible in the slightest."

He didn't agree that he was entirely blameless, but was content to let the matter rest.

I still felt weak about the knees, so he carried me to the front room and set me down upon the marble floor, and I leaned against him, entangled in a multitude of slithering limbs. As the squares of sunlight progressed across the windows, we simply lay together in mutual comfort, sharing our hushed thoughts back and forth across the contact of our skin. I was adamant that there must be some method of destroying these esoteric grimoires that plagued us, and he was equally convinced that no such method existed, but our mute discussion was not a heated conversation, but an enjoyable one, for we both wanted the same outcome: a secure future. He tried to express a complex thought, and eventually, I fell back to the use of fallible words, and whispered, "I think I understand what you mean. Destroying the book will not destroy the idea, only take away the context from which it was born." I pressed my cheek against his. "No matter how hard we try, nothing will ever be the same again."

I heard voices on the step.

Jane and Mary found me still wrapped in tendrils and tentacles, for to be honest, each one seemed to have its own intentions and they were no easy thing to escape. Mary, who had spent a full night in the proximity of lunacy, was eager to vent her frustrations on the first monster she saw. When she glimpsed me, she rushed inside with arm raised, yowling in rage, and only came to a skidding stop when I held up both hands.

"Wait, Mary!" I cried.

She stood with fists clenched, looking at me with incredulity as the very large cephalopod attempted to hide itself behind me, adopting the same hue and texture as the white marble floor.

"This," I began, slowly and calmly, "This is Nate, he is my friend, and he has saved me many times over." Then, to the pair of amber eyes that bugged out in fear and surprise, "This is my sister Mary. And there, hiding at the doorjamb, that is my other sister Jane. They will do you no harm, I promise."

One tentacle popped up from the floor to give a cautious wave.

Frederick and Thorne appeared on the steps, for they had been conversing while the girls walked ahead down Northwich's wide driveway. Frederick's face blanched. Thorne, of course, remained unfazed.

"Good God, get your grubby paws off her, you miserable squid," he said, striding into the hall. "Have some decency!" And to me, he said, "You were able to get the book back in the well, Harry?"

"Not yet; it's still free in your library. But I would've failed, if Nate hadn't been there to save me."

"He is endlessly helpful." Thorne rolled his eyes.

"Where's Emma?" said Jane.

"She walking here by way of the Mill Road, I believe. She's in the company of Mr. Marsh, who lent me the use of his horse." I went to the door and saw the animal standing in the garden, contentedly munching, and I was relieved to see it hadn't run away. Across the parkland towards our house, a little chalk line of smoke rose from our chimney, and the tiny figure of Papa moved about the garden, tending to the bees. The tableau was the epitome of domestic comfort, and it lent me strength.

"One of us will have to move the book," said Thorne, "It can't stay where it is."

"Well, we certainly can't let anyone read it," Mary replied as she and Frederick sat on the staircase. "The Darlings are in a state beyond anything I've ever witnessed, and they read only a sentence or two."

"I'm so sorry, Frederick," said Jane to the stunned and silent gentleman, who was obviously still processing the scene before him, "Perhaps Emma can help. She's very talented when it comes to healing, although I don't know how far her Quirk will extend."

Thorne narrowed his eyes and peered at me. "She is not an empath like yourself?"

Jane shook her head. "No, only Harriet can do that trick."

"Did you lie to me, Harry?" he accused.

"I'm afraid so, Mr. Thorne," I replied, "Please understand, I would do anything to protect my sisters, and I didn't know you then."

"But you know me now?"

"Hardly," I replied, "But I trust you." Then I returned my gaze outside, and added, "I may even have started to like you, somewhat."

A movement to the south-east caught my eyes, and I smiled.

"Ah, yes, here comes Emma and Mr. Marsh now," I said, pointing to the two figures just clearing the hedges.

And, almost immediately, I saw a wizened figure between them, hunched and grey-haired, and leaning heavily on Mr. Marsh's arm.

Jane joined me at the door, and shielding her eyes from the sun, she said, "Is that ... is that Mrs. Runkle?"

# TWENTY-THREE

The old woman wailed at the top of her lungs, her tear-stained face contorted with grief. Her knobby legs were unable to move quickly over the bumpy grass, and Mr. Marsh had slowed his gait to give her support. Emma, seeing us in the doorway, waved over her head. "Help!"

I hurried across the park land with Jane, Mary, and Frederick behind me. "What's happened?" he yelled ahead.

"We found her by the river in distress!" said Emma.

"The woman says her grandson has gone missing," Mr. Marsh yelled back, "Another young man abducted!"

Mrs. Runkle hugged her shawl around her shoulders. "He did not come home yesterday. I've been out walking for hours," she wept. Her whole body trembled with exhaustion. The lacy hem of her dress was torn in shreds, and burrs covered her shawl. "I can find no trace of him!" By this time, our party had reached them, and she looked from face to face, pleading. "Oh, I do not know what's come of him! What if ... what if—"

"Bring her back to Northwich," I said, "Come, Mrs. Runkle, tell me when you saw him last."

"I don't know," she faltered, limping, one arm still crooked over Mr. Marsh's elbow. "I suppose it was the day before last? He has been so strange since Earl's death! He leaves early and does not come home until late."

"We must inform the mayor and the regiment," said Emma, "They can send out hunting parties—"

Goodness, that was the last thing I wished to see! A hundred unprotected men, marching into a battle they could not win, engaging an enemy that would turn their minds inside out and fashion them into weapons against each other? Why not rip a hole in our reality and let the Old Gods return to devour us? For the residents of Dunham, the results would be the same: utter devastation.

"Mrs. Runkle," I said, "Do you know a place where Marvin and Earl liked to go?"

"Oh, I'm not sure," she panted, casting about for an answer, "He's always loved the heath. Perhaps he's there now? When he heard the regiment were tearing up the fairy stones, he was very upset! Perhaps … perhaps …" Her voice wavered, and she stared towards Northwich Hall as her face blanched. "I must sit down, Harriet dear. I feel faint."

We'd almost reached the steps to the front hall when the sound of erratic, shuffling footsteps caught my ear. I turned to look straight down the driveway, passed the trout pond and between the twin rows of trees.

In the middle of the roadway stood Marvin, looking small, skinny, starved. He dragged one foot behind him. His blond hair was plastered with mud, he was naked and covered in sand, and his eyes were unnaturally bright, as if he suffered a fever. When he saw that he'd caught my eye, he sang a wordless melody, loud and clear.

I was not the only one to notice his approach.

"Take ease, madam! Here's the scamp!" said Mr. Marsh with good cheer.

"Oh, Marvin!" she cried out, reaching towards her grandson with tears in her eyes. "Do you know how you make me worry!"

But I stepped between them. "Take her inside," I told Mr. Marsh, and then turned my back on them to stride toward Marvin.

He moved with an erratic purpose that was, by its conflicted nature, very bizarre. He jerked and stumbled as if under the influence of too much sherry, then shambled to the side of the road before lurching back to the center. I heard the others retreating up the steps, and from my peripheral vision I saw the kitchen door open and a familiar shape ooze down the steps, tumble over the lawns, and slip under the far surface of the pond. As Nate was swimming closer, I felt a presence to my left.

"I shall not let you face this devil alone again," said Emma, laying her light fingers upon my shoulder.

I was much heartened. The center of my chest still ached from its claws, and I wasn't sure I could survive its touch a second time.

"Marvin," I began as we drew closer, "Marvin, can you hear me?"

The boy stopped singing and cocked his head to one side like a bird. The unblinking eyes stared at me, and I stared back, bracing for the sensation of my reasonable mind straining under his magic.

Emma called out, "Marvin, we're here to help you."

"You can't heal him," I said to my sister quietly, "He's beyond our help."

She stared hard at him, and said, "No one is beyond help, Harry."

Marvin gave a sharp, bird-like squawk.

I stopped.

Something is not right.

We were only a few paces away. The pond lay to my right, and I heard the gentle swish of waves as Nate crawled onto the near shore, his body black and slippery.

"That noise," I said, "Mrs. Darling made the same."

The naked youth stood in the middle of the roadway, and how I wished for the hermetiscope, to see through the veils of our limited perception to the truth of him. He shuddered all over. I braced myself for his transformation, but instead, he threw out his arms and flung back his head, and then grabbed the sides of his mouth with each hand. He pulled, pulled, pulled, arms straining. I heard the moist tearing of flesh.

"Oh, God!" Emma gasped as we realized his intent. She ran forward to grab Marvin around the shoulders and toppled him to the ground, struggling to pull his hands from his mouth.

The cheeks were torn asunder, the lips ripped into a bloodied maw, molars fully exposed. The flaps of his flesh flopped back like the petals of a garish tropical flower. Blood gushed from his mauled face, and Marvin gurgled and slurred as we tried to stop him, but he fought us with the vitality and determination of one possessed. His heels dug ruts in the driveway, his hips jerked and bucked, and the gravel rubbed his elbows raw. I saw the first hint of a creeping purple vine, twisting and sprouting from the egress of his ear.

Emma set her hands on that mutilated face, and Nate had wrapped tentacles around the boy's wrists to keep him from ripping the rest of his jaw off. I stumbled back, appalled, but Emma was not so delicate as me: she wrapped her shawl tightly around the boy's head, keeping all the pieces together, ignoring the fluids that gushed over her hands. Blood pulsed and pooled in the roadway. Where it hit the dirt, I saw the ground shimmer like oil on water.

I reached out one hand to touch the colors, drawn to them. They were cold and sticky, tingling like pins and needles, and where the blood had hit the soil, small shoots of plants burst up through the dirt. Each was a delicate pink like baby fingers.

"What—"

The plants unfurled into blossoms. I gasped, for they were the flowers of the psychopomp's vision, which I suddenly realized had not been a threat, but a warning. The petals were soft translucent flesh, the stamens were ivory teeth. The purple vines growing out of his brain began to wend around his convulsing body, sweeping over his frame like a blanket, burying their roots into his flesh and eating him alive.

His emotions leaked through the blood, flowing raw and ragged through my hands. The sinister vines fed upon his frustrations, his desires, his lust, and they grew strong and supple on the twisted, curdled entitlements of a boy in his youth: Marvin's vitality and unfocused resentments provided the perfect fertile soil for the Eidolon's seeds. His spirit was as scarred and contorted as Mrs. Darling and Mrs. Rabbit, and I realized that he had stared deeply into the Eidolon's eyes—just as they had—and been destroyed from the inside out.

But, if Marvin had been able to look upon the Eidolon's face ...

I recoiled as I recognized my error.

"Oh God!" I said to Emma, "It's not him!"

A shriek erupted from the house. With the shimmering oil clinging to my hands, I bolted for Northwich Hall, leaving Emma and Nate to deal with Marvin.

Inside, the ballroom was embroiled in chaos. I tried to take all in, from the gentleman in the portrait above it all to the waves of motions coming from every corner. Frederick stood at the far side of the room, and Mary stood beside him, her arms encircling him; she stood so that her body blocked the visions of madness from his gaze, but her eyes remained transfixed upon the center of the room, and never had I seen such panic in her features. Jane, cowering against the wall by to the servant's corridor, was screaming in terror, and at her feet, Mr. Thorne lay sprawled across the ground, a gash across the back of his skull, with the cracked hermetiscope clenched in his hand.

But the spectacle in the middle of the ballroom pushed all these elements aside. Mrs. Runkle had her right fingers wrapped tightly around Mr. Marsh's throat. Her fingers were skeletal and skinny, and her eyes were dark stars. Jane screamed again as the old woman plunged her left hand upwards with incredible force, tearing through the soldier's body, driving her arm up between his hips into his intestines. He gave a sickening gasp.

Then, as if rending a piece of cloth, she jerked open her arms, and Mr. Marsh was torn in two.

The halves of his body, still twitching, fell to either side of the foyer. Confusion crossed his face as the life drained away, and his guts sloshed across the wooden parquet floor as if dumped from a barrel. The polished boots jerked, the convulsing hands flexed, then each portion slumped, empty and extinguished fully.

I stared in mute horror.

Mrs. Runkle turned to me and removed her bonnet with her blood-soaked hands, staring unblinking with those tiny, sinister eyes. The old woman shook and trembled like a dog dislodging fleas, then she peeled off her dress to expose a swelling boil of a body. The antlers sprouted like saplings, branching outwards until they struck the gold chandelier like the chimes of tiny bells. The titanic Eidolon, servant of the Scented Garden, towered over me in the center of the dance floor. The bone-white face grinned and exposed hundreds of glistening needle-teeth, and licked its lips with its grey tongue.

Emma cried out from the entrance foyer. Blinded by grief to the demonic force in the middle of the room, she ran passed me to the nearest portion of Mr. Marsh and collapsed over him, cradling his head in her arms, sobbing.

The Eidolon looked directly at me, and whispered in a sing-song voice, "It is time to unmask thyself, Har-ree-et. Prepare the garden and water the roots. Be my Hyades and nourish the soil."

It stretched out its fingers to tangle the ends in Emma's red hair.

I wanted to deny it, I wanted to fight it, but the eyes burrowed into my bones. I could feel the heat of their gaze on the inner curve of my skull. My core was on fire, a spontaneous combustion spreading through my innards, invisible to the outside world.

The Eidolon clenched its fingers and Emma squealed in agony, dragged backwards from Mr. Marsh's corpse. The glowing eyes never faltered. A manic, unrestrained joy crossed its face as it began to slowly twist Emma's head from her body.

What could I do? Mr. Marsh was lost to us, and Emma would soon be, too. I can't lie: the horror I felt at staring into those tiny brilliant eyes was unparalleled. It did not blink. It did not flinch. The wicked smile inched wider and wider.

A thump rattled the windows of the ballroom. Once, then twice, then a patter of bumps, as tiny bodies struck the glass.

Birds flew into the windows, and only then did the Eidolon break its gaze and pause, and look with anger towards the psychopomps, flinging their tiny feathered bodies as they sought a weakness in the house. It dropped Emma from its grip, took a deep breath, and began to sing.

The mix of song and birds grew deafening. The cacophony rose in scope and size as thousands of black starlings pummeled the glass, but the break of the Eidolon's hypnotic gaze freed me, and I looked towards Jane. She was trying to help Mr. Thorne to his feet, but her eyes were frantic. He stumbled, dazed and injured, but I feared he was the more whole of either of them.

Mary had fled from the room in terror. Frederick was stunned into uselessness by the sounds of the scene before him, and had curled into a ball, his arms thrown over his head.

Emma, free of the Eidolon's grasp, put out her hands to Mr. Marsh, and was drawing his halves together like a child trying to fix a broken doll. My heart wept for her. Her face was a mask of horror and grief at the loss of a life unlived, at a happy future she would never see. She gathered up his two halves and clenched them to her breast, his blood pouring across her white dress until it matched the hue of his soldier's jacket.

Seeing that the birds could not enter, the Eidolon returned its attention me and shook its antlers, rattling the chandelier, stepping forward. It crooned soft words that stabbed into my ear drums like knives of black obsidian. I felt my body eaten alive by its words, as if every note was a little nibble, greedily taking more and more. Carnivorous plants chewed me, their roots burrowed into my muscles. Slimy fungi liquefied my body into nourishment. The scented garden was growing. It would feed upon the corpses of Dunham and spread like a blight over the countryside.

And then, something quite unexpected happened.

A second voice began to sing.

I turned my head, feeling the skin of my neck crack with the effort, and saw Mary standing in the doorway between ballroom and entrance, holding Songs of the Scented Garden open in her arms. Of all the unspeakable parts of this eldritch scene, this was by far the strangest. She glowed with an phantasmagorical light. She grew taller, and her powerful voice reached down into the depths of the Earth until its molten heart trembled. I'd heard her sing many times before with the village choir, but I had never heard her sing like this. Mary's voice grew otherworldly as it ascended, note by note, into a clear pure melody; it made the glass panes shiver, the walls shudder, and coaxed gooseflesh to my arms. The air stirred around us, reminiscent of the shimmering oil from Marvin's blood: it became a warp of light and vision, but also of sound and sense. How best to describe it? Our reality flowed. It frayed. It dripped down the walls and pooled on the floor.

I saw, through the sticky oil on my fingertips and the drips on the walls, another universe. I witnessed men and women in other places, but I didn't recognize their clothes or surroundings, I couldn't process what they were doing or what they were saying, for it was so strange to my mind and foreign to my experience, I had not the vocabulary to describe it. My brain ached as I tried to comprehend the visions contained within the liquid reality, melting around me.

I heard a gasp and looked to my left.

Nate stood beside me, only he was no longer an octopus. He was no longer a man, either. He was shifting in and out of multiple realities, and in some he had read a cursed book, and in some he had resisted temptation. Here, in this liminal space, he was neither one nor the other, but only a set of eyes fighting to comprehend what was happening around us. Time took material form until our temporal journey lay thickly upon us like the layers of a cake, each moment visible and heavy, our multiple actions linked together with a net of intention. How does one describe the indescribable? My mind struggled to understand—tried to take in the entirety of Nate's form and function—but it was beyond my feeble, mortal comprehension. His eyes examined me with confusion, too; what must I look like to Nate? I was not as I had been, nor was I what I could be: I was all that had come before and was coming ahead, future and past, a multi-headed hydra of possibility.

Looking around the hall, the others had lost definition, too. They were shades seen through gauzy curtains, dissolving and parting, sharing space without restriction. Only the Eidolon and Mary stood alone. She stitched multiple realities together as she sang words from a long-dead language, and in the center of her brow, the emerald eye blazed like a beacon.

I stumbled across the room and snatched up the broken remains of the hermetiscope from the floor. Putting the spectacles on my nose, I cycled through the lenses over my right eye until suddenly the ballroom was transformed. The hermetiscope gave form and definition to the layers, and through half of my vision, I could latch on to solid forms between the shifting veils of perception: long gashes in our reality were bursting open, fracturing to reveal distant landscapes of other worlds. I saw black plants with flowers made of fingers prying apart the floorboards, and vines of glossy pubic hair and glistening labia wrapping themselves tightly around the furniture. I saw arms, legs, ears, eyes, tongues, set like jewels along winding paths, where flocks of butterflies sipped at ocular fluid and puddles of rancid sweat. I saw hungry plants drawing life-force from the scattered remains of Dunham's delirious victims. The ballroom was gone, replaced by a garden of living human atrocities, rooted into the bloody soil. Their tortured breath fed the fertile barrows. Through the rips, there were jungles, deserts, cities of stone and brass, creatures bound mercilessly tight in ropes made of still-living flesh. Every rent in the fabric of our perception showed a different version of Hell.

The shipboards are bursting. The sea is rushing in.

The Eidolon crept towards Mary, showing every indication of unrestrained joy at the destruction of our reality. It rode the warping world with a sense of glee.

The flickering shade of Emma still clung to the wispy remains of Mr. Marsh, and Jane lay collapsed over Mr. Thorne. I looked towards Mary, afraid of what I might see, but the emerald eye rolled towards me and in it, I saw determination and a strength unmatched. She had not fallen to temptation, she had not resisted until she was too weak to fight—Mary had chosen to read, and by embracing her fate without fighting, she had claimed the song for her own. Mary had always been powerful and serious, and provided a stunning presence in any situation, but we had never fully recognized her Quirk; I saw now that Posey's library had, over time, intensified her resolution and boundless fortitude into an angelic virtue. Her voice set her apart, and her courage in the face of the unknown was unrivaled. She was a scientist, after all—she ran boldly towards the unknown and took joy in challenging the boundaries of knowledge. The emerald eye beheld the world as it is, not as we wish it to be; Mary was incorruptible because she sought the truths of the universe and accepted the results without judgment or dismay.

That eye, that fiery green sun, stared pointedly at me. Time was running short. The realities were laying one upon the other, and all versions of ourselves were compounding into single creatures, monstrosities of a million variations.

The pillars are cracking. The building can not hold.

With every muscle straining, I picked up Thorne's cane and its silver head, and I thought of my father's words, and of Mr. Posey's confession.

And with the hermetiscope on my nose, and one eye able to see in this world, and the other gazing upon the next, I knew what I must do.

At the Eidolon's feet, a weak spot warbled in the wall under the portrait. Mary's song was pushing our reality too hard, and it had grown thin and frail. The spot undulated and pulsed, as glossy as a blister on the verge of splitting. The Eidolon had not noticed, for it was enraptured by her voice, and it paid no attention to anyone but her.

The eye, staring at me, narrowed.

Be ready, it implored.

I gave it a nod in reply.

Defiant and steadfast, the Mary-that-was-many-Marys lifted the book. She opened it wide and took each half in a hand, and still singing, my sister effortlessly tore it in half.

When the Eidolon screeched in horror, I lowered my head and ran.

My shoulder caught the Eidolon in the gut. I wrapped both arms around its wispy body and together we burst through the blister, into another form of place, where the air smelled of dust and the wind blew hot and dry. We crashed down into a drift of gritty, rust-colored sand.

Quiet.

Still.

The Eidolon thrashed under me, taking in our sudden change of surroundings with a blood-chilling screech.

The desert sun was setting in a riot of magentas and oranges, and in the fading light, I saw that the Eidolon and I lay in the center of a shallow box canyon made of red stone. The sandy floor of the canyon was barren and shadowy, but through the distant entrance, in the direction of Dunham, I saw lights twinkling and a phalanx of tall glass towers circled by iron birds. The buildings were festooned in garish lights as though a field of stars had fallen from the sky. In the gorge behind us, at the base of the cliffs, was a little hut made of ebony sticks, and around it were the unmistakable humps of a hundred shallow graves. Plants covered with needles pierced the palm of my hands as I tried to stand. Tiny lizards skittered over my legs. The wind smelled of vinegar and brimstone. I knew that I lay in the bowels of Hell.

The Eidolon stumbled to its feet, casting about left and right, winded and disoriented by the sudden silence.

The hermetiscope had shattered into a multitude of brass fragments and glass shards, rendering the lenses useless. I held them to my face to discover that I was blind to any reality beyond the limits of my body's evolution; there was no way to see our path back. We were together in Hell, the Eidolon and me, and there would be no escape.

Before it could rise, I reeled back with the walking cane in both hands and swung hard, and brought the silver head down on the back of the Eidolon's skull. A moist crack erupted. The devil howled and thrashed, and the Eidolon's skeleton fingers scratched long lines in the sand, but I gave it no quarter to rally. Again and again, I brought down the silver head, smashing at the bones and the antlers until they fractured into brittle pieces, screaming in my fury. Blood spattered over my dress. My arms ached, my legs cramped.

At last, the fiend lay still, face down in the dirt, its mask split open and its skull crushed like an egg. The rag-wrapped body slowly deflating into the form of an old woman, moaning in pain.

I dropped the cane. I hiccoughed, held my hands to my mouth in horror.

Mrs. Runkle looked up at me with confusion. Her expression was pleading through eyes swelling into purple orbs. She tried to speak, but her jaw had been broken in multiple places and her teeth were smashed. I recoiled, horrified at what I'd done.

"Oh, God, Mrs. Runkle—" I said, shaking. "I'm sorry! I'm so sorry!" Tears streamed down my cheeks.

A figure walked across the canyon floor from the direction of the hut, dressed in the tatters of a green dress and heavy leather boots. She looked as familiar to me as the face in a mirror, except that she was covered in bruises and missing her left eye.

"Kill it," she commanded.

I shook my head. "I can't! It's ... it's Mrs. Runkle! She was ... she was a friend ..."

My other reality picked up the ebony cane and bounced the blood-spattered silver head in the palm of her calloused hand.

"Harriet," she said, "You can't hesitate, not here."

She lifted the cane in two hands and brought it down hard to deliver the killing blow.

I squeaked and covered my face, and turned away to shield myself from the sight, but I couldn't hide from the wet sounds of bones cracked and brains mashed.

When it was done, my other self lowered the cane. "The Mrs. Runkle you knew vanished when she read the book," she assured me, "Every story changes us, Harry. We're never the same person at the end of a book as we were at the beginning."

Oh, how hollow and cold my words sounded, out in this barren wasteland. I dragged my fingers over the hermetiscope's shattered remains. A million fragments of glass glittered in the sand, rose and azure and lime. The desert wind skittered over them, and in the final shaft of sunlight, they sparkled like gems as the finest particles stuck to the blood on my hands.

My other self, looking content, stared down at the remains of Mrs. Runkle.

"How did you know I'd be here?" I said, grit catching in the back of my throat.

"I killed Mrs. Runkle on this spot, a few months ago," she said. "I've been waiting for the rest of me to arrive, one by one, as the realities line up." She rolled over the corpse with her foot, looked at it with disgust. "Didn't Humbolt tell you? Our timelines are misaligned."

I couldn't answer; I was still too winded and weak.

"This isn't your place, Harry," she said, "And there's no way back."

I saw her raise the silver cane again.

"You know what that means."

I nodded.

Yes.

I knew what she was about to do.

But I didn't resist. I didn't blame her, because I would have come to the same conclusion. Both of us understood that I didn't belong here, an outlier and a liability, an anomaly that put all versions of our universe in jeopardy, and the longer I remained, the more unstable this place became. This brutal country was her reality, not mine.

"I've done this before, Harry," she said, and her ruthless voice took the smallest measure of warmth, growing a fraction more kindly, "Every time the Runkle woman comes through, you do, too. I've grown quick with all the practice."

I fell to my knees and bowed my head, and tears tumbled down my cheeks until they dripped to the russet dirt and made little pockets of mud. I wept openly, but I didn't cry from remorse or horror or fear. These tears weren't from the grief I felt of never seeing Jane, Emma, or Mary again. No, they were tears of relief and joy. We'd saved the world, we'd saved our reality, and I would happily perish by my own hands in Hell, knowing my sisters were safe.

It didn't matter that I was going to die, because they were going to live.

"Are you ready?" she said.

I nodded.

"Go," I whispered.

She took a deep, centering breath and wound back, stepping into the swing.

Something tickled at my ankle.

And then, as the silver cane fell, the tentacle wrapped once, twice, thrice around my calf as quick as a lightning strike, and yanked me backwards across the red sand, through the punctured blister covered over with molten air, between the Gates of Madness, from this accursed reality back into my own.

# TWENTY-FOUR

I skidded across the parquet dancing floor and thudded to a stop at Nate's side.

My head spun. I'd been slung into Northwich Hall with the force of a trebuchet, and I collapsed on the ground, hands outstretched, terrified to look up. I had no idea what sort of reality I was in, but the world gelled and coagulated as the shapes around me grew defined. A knot of seething tendrils wrapped themselves around me in all directions. One squeezed my hand in desperation, probing for life, and I squeezed it back to show that I was still present, if breathless. My heart nearly burst, feeling both my happiness and his, compounded.

"Harry?" said Emma. I glimpsed between the slithering tendrils, and my youngest sister stood before me, spattered in gore. Her face glowed. She looked like a woman who has walked a long way out-of-doors, fresh faced and breathless but happy with the zest of exercise. Emma held my hands as she guided me to my feet, and her fingers thrummed with power. Instantly I felt revived, as if I'd woken from a good, long sleep.

"Are you alright?" she asked.

"I think so," I wheezed.

But I wasn't, not really. My knees wobbled and I crumpled back into Nate's embrace. This must be what it feels like, to be dragged backwards through a keyhole.

The ballroom was in ruins. Broken glass glittered across the floor, peppered with the bashed remains and broken feathers of hundreds of starlings. The chandelier hung askew from its chain, the piano in the corner had collapsed. The portrait of elder Mr. Blackwood had sustained a gash across its side, though the man looked down upon us with the same poetic restlessness as before, and seemed wholly unconcerned with his superficial injury. Mary stood to one side of the piano, holding her head as if stunned, and Mr. Darling stood beside her, inquiring after her health. Her hands were red and burned, and her black hair had turned as white as a cloud. The two halves of the drab green book lay at her feet, and they whimpered when she kicked them aside.

Afraid, I looked around Emma to the remains of Mr. Marsh. She had dragged his halves together, set them alongside one another, and they lay in a pool of carnage, surrounded by the torn shreds of his uniform.

But as I watched, the battered corpse twitched, then moved, then gave a gut-wrenching groan. The legs were bending, the arms were flexing. He tested each limb's worth as he drew himself slowly, painfully, to his knees. Of course, his torn garments sloughed away as he rose, and to be honest, I saw more of his arbor vitae than good manners should allow, but I was too engrossed by the thick, ropy scar that orbited his naked body—from shoulder to hip, across chest and back—to notice the exposed privy features of his nether regions.

Emma bent to him and caressed his face. The flush of good health traversed his pallid complexion from his neck to his toes until he, too, looked restored.

"You've made me whole," he whispered in awe, his fingers playing across the scar bisecting his chest.

"I have," she replied, equally awed.

Mr. Thorne's voice rang out from the corridor, and when I looked over, he was leaning heavily on Jane, holding the back of his head.

"It was that wretched, meddlesome imbecile from the post office!" he barked, "That senile old hag! She jumped me!"

"Mary read from the book—" Jane said, and Thorne turned hard to Mary. "Well?" he demanded, "Are you whole?"

She shook her head, her words coming out as a rasp. She touched her fingers to the center of her brow. "I don't know. I hope so. I only sang a song or two." She looked at me. "Harry was the one who tackled the frightful thing."

"And from the looks of your dress," said Frederick, noting the blood, "You pounded it into jelly!"

"What else could I do?" I said as guilt welled up, and Nate held me close in support, with the warmth of affection rippling between us. "Mrs. Runkle was dismantling our existence! I had to bludgeon her!"

Thorne hobbled close, holding onto Jane's arm. "I can't tell you how many times I was tempted to do so myself, waiting an eternity for my change at the postal counter!"

Mary limped towards us, leaning on Frederick. "How did you know what to do?"

"I saw the cane," I said, "Papa told me that Mr. Posey, all those years ago, defeated the demon with a silver mace; when Mrs. Posey read the book and was possessed, he bashed in her skull. It was the only thing I could think to do."

Jane reached out to me. "What did you see on the other side?"

But I only shook my head. It was a long time before I was able to confide in them, and tell them about the dry chemical smells or the fiery red rocks, the lizards or the ferocious plants, or worst of all, a version of myself that had grown hard-hearted, scarred, and sadistic, efficient at killing herself over and over for all eternity. I hoped never to look at myself in that way again.

---

Nate took one half of the book, and I took the other, and together we tossed Songs of the Scented Garden down into the well where it belonged. He covered the well head over once more with the stone, then he locked the door and gave me the key to hang on my necklace for safe keeping.

By the time we finished, the others had retired outside to avoid the wreckage of the ballroom. We joined them on the front steps of Northwich Hall, sitting together and watching the birds swarm in the air, swooping and diving as if they no longer cared for souls or devils or foul beastly creatures. Where Marvin had fallen, there was only a mound of queer flowers, but they had withered and blackened, having fed of his corpse and then died with the book that had seeded them. I stared for long minutes at that ugly patch of alien blossoms, and when Nate held my hand, I laid my head against him, and we shared a silent conversation of relief, and astonishment, and wordless wonder. No one seemed to pay any attention to Nate or his strange form; I suppose, for Mr. Marsh and Mr. Darling, a gigantic benevolent terrestrial octopus was the least terrifying of all our experiences since breakfast.

An hour of silence and sunshine restored us. At last, in a soft rush of astonishment, Jane said, "Well, never have I seen anything so dramatic in all my life!"

"You'll get used to it," Thorne replied as he sat next to her, taking off his jacket and placing it on the top step.

"I sincerely hope not," I said, reeling on him in anger. "You've been lax in your care of a dangerous cargo, Mr. Thorne, and I will not have you place us all in such peril again!"

He cocked one eyebrow in my direction. "Do you think I'd be so irresponsible as to let any of those three books out of my sight?"

"You already did," I pointed out. "And who can say, what other horrible volumes you have on your shelves! History proves you to be a poor guardian for them."

"You're over-reacting, Harry," he dismissed, and he waved his hand in my general direction. "Your concern is completely unfounded. I don't need a musty old spinster to tell me my business."

I was about to protest when I saw Jane move a little closer to Mr. Thorne. She looked at me, unimpressed, then slipped her hand into his.

"You have a bitter heart, sir," she said, "You've spent too long feeling grief and guilt, and it has soured you."

Thorne's eyebrows arched, then I saw a flash of fear in those goggled eyes as he realized the danger of Jane's touch. He tried to withdraw his hand but she would not let him.

"I don't see into men's hearts as Harriet does," she replied. "But I can see enough to know that you're not happy, and you take out your ill-ease on those around you. Yes, mistakes have been made, but I don't think you wish to put Dunham in danger again, do you."

"Of course not," he said mildly.

"And I think you and I should have a little chat about the value of community, and how we might better serve our little town, and keep all within it safe from harm. Don't you agree?"

"Oh, I do," he replied, showing all the self-determination of a puppet.

Honestly, watching their conversation almost disturbed me to an equal degree as any other scene this morning.

"Come, then, sir. Let us enjoy a walk together, you and I." She smiled sweetly. "Your library is of too great a value to leave in the hands of just one man, alone, don't you think? I will endeavor to make you a more joyful person, more in keeping with the responsibility you must bear, and more pleasing to your neighbors both in countenance and respectability." She set a light kiss upon his cheek. "And, if all can be made right within your damaged psyche, I suspect that a gentleman in possession of such an important wealth of books and knowledge may well be in need of a wife."

Together, they rambled away, with Jane's hand on his forearm and Aloysius' head in the clouds.

Nate helped Mr. Marsh to his feet with three tentacles, and with another two, he grabbed his half-brother's jacket and offered it with all politeness to the naked soldier. Mr. Marsh took it with thanks, and once suitably covered, the recently deceased man found himself fairly tackled by an enthusiastic Emma. She gave a girlish squeal before peppering him with kisses.

"Good Lord," I said to Mary, sitting beside me. "What a strange turn of events." We watched as Emma and Mr. Marsh pressed their foreheads together, drunk on their affection for one another, gazing into each others' eyes and ignoring the rest of us. "Well, Mary?" I said, "Should we head home and see how Mama and Papa weathered the weirdness?"

Mary glanced at Frederick, and when she stood up, she gave me a coy smile. "I think I shall accompany Mr. Darling to assess the state of his household, and I shall take Emma with me, to see if we might restore the rest of his family back to good health." She turned to our youngest sister, and said, "Would you and Mr. Marsh care to join us?"

"By all means," she replied, full of smiles, "I'm too happy to refuse anyone anything! I'll do whatever I can to lend a hand."

Leaving Nate and I alone on the steps of Northwich Hall, the four of them began to stroll down the driveway in the direction of town, the sun and the trees conspiring to cast stripes across them. It was only then that I noticed, as they passed out of sight, that Mary and Frederick were holding hands.

# TWENTY-FIVE

Late spring is such a enchanting season for a wedding, especially one held on the lawns of Northwich Hall, and the Lovecraft family was thrice-blessed to celebrate the unions of their youngest daughters to fine, upstanding men. The delightfully inventive Miss Emma had been matched to a brave and distinguished young soldier, Richard Marsh, who was the pride of the highly-regarded Marsh lineage of Upper Whatley. The imposing, handsome figure of Miss Mary—her stark white hair braided and garnished with tiny blue forget-me-nots—balanced well with the fine trim and dashing manners of Mr. Frederick Darling, who had taken command of his uncle's firm after the sad incarceration of his brother, aunt, and uncle at Broadmoor Asylum. Lastly, Miss Jane had secured the affections of the man known to all as Mr. Aloysius Blackwood, who had been previously thought to be peevish and sour, but had since remedied that poor reputation by showing himself as helpful, convivial, and pleasant to even the most humble farmer or smallest child. In point of fact, it was Mr. Blackwood who suggested they invite the entire population of Dunham County to the wedding, and certainly, no one had refused this generous offer, for the grounds were filled with people, food, drink, music and much rejoicing.

None could be happier than Mrs. Lovecraft, who sat in pride of place in the front row, awaiting the arrival of Father Noonan with as much patience as a child needing a chamber pot. Her pink batiste gown and gloriously feathered bonnet lent her the appearance of a fine, high-born lady, but her squirming undermined all attempts at decorum. To her left sat Mr. Lovecraft, dressed in his cleanest jacket, and he appeared unmoved by any romantic motions; in fact, he wore the countenance and bearing of a man heading forth to a relaxing vacation, where all worries and cares would soon lose their sting, and he could retire in peace to read his books and write his memoir and tend his precious bees. That Father Noonan had not yet arrived did not vex him, for the day was too clement and merry to wish away.

A sweeping glance over the crowd showed the entire village to be in attendance, save for two. Mrs. Runkle and her grandson Marvin had not been seen since early spring. Some said she had gone to London to live with a sister after Marvin had lost his dear friend, and others claimed that they had ventured south to take residence with a cousin in Tasmania. The most imaginative children said that Mrs. Runkle had been transformed into a grim and whisked away to Hell on a raft of bird wings, but no one paid much attention to their beastly fairy tales.

"Oh, Harriet," said Mama, bending her head to the right to speak, her eyes still locked on the enchanting scene of my three sisters, decked in finery and flowers, "This is such a joyous day, do you not think? To see your sister Jane installed as the Lady of Northwich Hall! And Mary so suitably matched to a man of business! And even Emma, bursting with love at the sight of her exquisite soldier! Oh! My heart could not be lighter! I have done my duty very well, don't you think? Very well, indeed!"

The three couples waited patiently at the lectern, which had been employed to play the part of an altar and placed at the garden's edge, with the trout pond providing a very pleasing background. Emma, Mary and Jane were garbed in matching whites, while Mr. Darling wore a deep blue suit, the imposter Mr. Blackwood in grey, and Mr. Marsh in his red coat. As a set, they did look splendid.

"It's all perfect," I agreed.

"And I'm sure you will be quite well taken care of, if not a little lonely, once your father dies and leaves us penniless," my mother continued. Papa, sitting on her other side, raised one hoary eyebrow but said nothing. Mama continued, "Jane will find a little corner of her great mansion in which you might wile away your final years in the company of books. Would that not make you happy? You have always appreciated your solitude."

"It would make me happy enough," I replied.

"We must accept that there is no match for you, my dear," my mother continued, her voice now adopting the timbre of a lament, "You are destined to be alone, I'm afraid, and I only wish I had tried harder to keep you from being so plain and dull." She pinched my cheek. "If only we'd marketed your dullness as predictability, and your plainness as constancy, some man might have fancied you."

"It was never my intention to marry just any fellow who would take me," I replied with a laugh, but she wasn't listening.

"I should have recognized that your interests in literacy and philosophical contemplations might make a gentleman uneasy, and I should have spoken of your tedium and solitary ways as inoffensive. Perhaps if your father had not taught you to read at such an early age, you would not have frightened off so many potential suitors with the strength of your opinions, and then …"

Her words trailed off as a well-dressed gentleman sat down beside me.

I did not, at first, recognize him. His features were balanced and measured, and quite stable, without a single wobble or change of color. He had no hair, but he wore an expensive beaver hat to cover his bare head, as well as a modest frock coat in a subdued charcoal grey over his athletic frame. He'd adopted the face from the portrait in the ballroom, but he'd added a dash of comeliness about the bland features and wore a dimple on his chin, and his eyes remained the rich, warm amber that I'd grown to love.

"Hello, Harry," he said in a voice that was, all at once, deep and beguiling, quiet and restrained.

I gave a little gasp of delight and surprise.

He grinned. "It's a fine day for a wedding, isn't it."

"How is this possible?!"

"With a lot of practice and a great deal of difficulty," he replied, "I admit, I really don't know how long I can stay."

I traced my fingers across his hand and felt the tide of magnificent joy flooding over his skin.

"And who is this?" said Mama, peering around my shoulder. The heat of her interest seared the back of my neck.

He bowed his head. "I am Nathaniel Blackwood, madam, the elder brother to the man who will be marrying your Jane," he said.

Mama fluttered her hands in rapid excitement. "Oh, sir! Oh! Then we are to be family! What a delight it is to make your acquaintance! This is my eldest daughter, Harriet."

"Yes, I know," he said, "We've met many times."

"Have you?" my mother said, turning on me as if I were a traitor, "Harry, you have never spoken to me of this! What do you do, sir? Have you come to visit your brother, and rejoice in his union?"

"No," said Nate, then looking to me, added, "I've come to ask Harry if she will consent to take me as her husband."

It's a rare occurrence for my mother to be rendered speechless, but she was struck perfectly, beautifully mute in that moment, as was I.

"Well?" Nate pressed. He gave a bashful smile and said "I've been practicing, but this takes a lot of concentration. The headaches are coming; there isn't much time." He stood, pulled me to my feet, and lowered himself to one knee. "Harriet Lovecraft, will you marry me?"

I gapped and stammered. "But how will we live?"

"In Northwich Hall," he said. "Technically, it's my house—I bought it. And there's plenty of room. If we stay to the cellar and the library and the pond, I doubt anyone will even notice we're there."

I bent to him, so that our voices were only for each other.

"And if your feelings change? I'll know it instantly if they do."

His eyes sparkled. He entwined his fingers in mine, and amongst his many happy emotions, I found confidence there, matched with a steady and constant affection. "Maybe they will change, but what if they change for the better, and grow only deeper with the years? I'd be remiss to let such a chance for incandescent happiness slip away." He squeezed my fingers, and I felt the bifurcation of two tentacles across his palm. "But consider this, Harry: I can never lie to you. Our relationship will always be rooted in honesty, and there's no stronger foundation for marriage than that."

I furrowed my brow and frowned.

"There may never be children," I warned him.

"Of course there won't. We've already established that I lack the equipment," he said, and his serious expression dissolved into mischief. "But I promise you, our attempts at intimacy will never be boring." And desire raced over his skin with such passion and ardor that I felt a blush rise to my cheeks.

"Then, yes," I said, "Yes, I'll marry you, Nathaniel Blackwood, and accept whatever adventure comes from it."

And so it was that, when the priest arrived not fifteen minutes later, there were four Lovecraft girls at the altar, and four men to attend them, and such a celebration was had that the people of Dunham County spoke on it for generations to come.

While it was gossiped that my husband was a recluse in all respects of the word, rarely seen by the Lovecraft family and never by the villagers, the children at the library claimed I had been spotted on rare occasions walking across the foggy Dreadmoor Heath in the company of a gigantic kraken. None of the adults believed them, of course. We're much too far from the sea for such exotic creatures! But the children also said, by all accounts, I was holding the monster's tentacle in my hand and, in its terrifying company, looked to be the happiest of all the Lovecraft girls.

Who am I to quarrel with that? I do believe I am.

# ACKNOWLEDGMENTS

First of all, I am grateful to the people who, when I explained the premise of 'Love and Lovecraft', were curious and/or crazy enough to think it might just have merit. Thank you to Shawn Pigott, Jennye Holm, and Jeff Holm for reading the earlier drafts and providing invaluable feedback and guidance. A mighty heaping of gratitude to Claire Guiot for her impeccable cover design and beautiful layout; one can not help but judge a book by its cover, and she has created a marvelous body to contain this story's soul.

Thank you to Damien Seaman for his support and Lovecraftian conversation, and to Adele Wearing of Fox Spirit Press for connecting us, and to Matt Williams for our discussions on multiverse theories. Thanks to Mary at Tarbell's Deli and the staff of Wandering Moose for all the coffee. Thanks to Zoe Pigott for listening to my ideas, and to Linus Pigott for keeping me grounded.

Lastly, a huge thank you to you, who have read this book and (hopefully) enjoyed it. I appreciate the time we've shared, and I am grateful to my readers for all their support. Your online reviews, book club recommendations, bookstore patronage, letters and conversations have provided joy and hope in the midst of chaos. Please continue to support your local artists and storytellers, and read as many strange and wonderful things as possible.

Kim

# Love and Lovecraft